HIDDEN AMONG YOURSELVES

by Bill Hiatt

with cover art by Michael Federman

Dedication

This novel is dedicated to the Indie YA Wolves, a spirited group of young adult fiction writers who have provided invaluable support and advice to me in recent years.

What Has Gone Before

Hidden among Yourselves is the third book in the Spell Weaver series. If you are interested in reading the preceding books first, you can find links to them in "The Adventure Isn't Over!" However, if you can't wait to read this book, I have tried to include in the text enough information about earlier events in the Spell Weaver series to make it possible for someone new to the series to understand and enjoy the adventures in this book without having read the earlier ones.

CONTENTS

Chapter 1: Comedy or Tragedy?

Have you ever thought about what your life would be like as a movie, particularly what genre it would be? When I was younger, my life seemed to be almost a fairy tale, one that was going to include a scene with me and my girlfriend riding off into the sunset, with a feeling of "happily ever after" hanging in the air.

Yeah, happily ever after. Well, might as well forget the fairy tale. I'd settle for a sit-com. Hell, I'd have sold my soul…uh, scratch that. The way my life had been going, I might just have the opportunity to sell my soul—literally. Better not to tempt fate. Let's just say I would have given a great deal if my life could be a sit-com, even one in which the hero doesn't get the girl. I'd even have settled for a pretty dark comedy. On most days, though, I could feel tragedy lurking nearby, a sourceless shadow on a seemingly sunny day—incongruous but mockingly real, nonetheless.

Today, however, I had some hope for comedy when I woke up. Perhaps it was the angel sitting on the edge of my bed, wearing a face oddly like mine but otherwise looking as if he had stepped out of a Renaissance painting. Yeah, he had a blindingly white robe and wings to match. I might have been shocked if I hadn't seen the same thing so often before.

"Taliesin, today is the day that you forgive Dan Stevens," the angel announced solemnly, his voice sounding a lot like mine.

They'll be giving ski reports from hell before that happens, I thought, though not loudly enough for him to hear me.

"Jimmie, quit screwing around!" I tried to sound angry, but I didn't really feel angry. It wasn't Jimmie's fault that he wanted me to resume my friendship with his brother, Dan. Jimmie's habit of taking the form of an angel and pretending to be my conscience was starting to get on my nerves, however.

"Taliesin!"

"Knock it off!" I ordered, as loudly as I could. My parents might still be in bed, and if so, I didn't want to wake them, though it was pretty likely Mom was already up.

Jimmie hesitated for a moment, but evidently I had succeeded in sounding just angry enough to convince him that this was not the time. There was a momentary ripple; he seemed undecided about which form to switch to. Then he took on his nine-year-old form. He really preferred the sixteen-year-old one these days, but he probably figured I couldn't stay mad at his nine-year-old self. He was right. After all, nine was how old he had been when he died. I had never told him how much it hurt me to see him as a nine-year-old. On the other hand, the sixteen-year-old form looked a lot like Dan, and having a constant reminder of Dan around wasn't exactly a nonstop thrill ride either.

"I'm sorry, Tal," he said, his eyes focused on the carpet. "It's just...well, you know I can't move on until this fight between you gets settled."

How could I forget? You bring it up about once every half hour!

"I know, Jimmie. I told you, I'm working on it."

He nodded but still didn't meet my eyes. Maybe he was too afraid he would able to see what I was really thinking if he looked into those eyes.

Yeah, I know—I'm a bastard for not forgiving Dan. I was single-handedly keeping Jimmie from being at peace, a fact that someone managed to point out virtually every day. I would have forgiven Dan already...if he hadn't so completely ruined my life.

I know how melodramatic that sounds, but I promise you, I'm not really a drama king. You be the judge. When Jimmie died, I had been nine and Dan ten, the three of us inseparable. Dan and I had gotten through the loss of Jimmie together, become even more like brothers. Then, after I turned twelve, everybody thought I lost my mind. What really happened was that the witch Ceridwen cast a spell on me that caused me to remember all my previous lives, and it took me some time to pull myself together after that. While I was in the hospital, Dan had convinced my girlfriend, Eva, that I was far worse than I really was, that I would be better off without her, and that her being with me would actually hinder what little chance for recovery I had left. Then, as you might guess, Dan, playing the sympathetic friend, managed to end up with Eva as *his* girl-friend.

At the time, I had no idea why Dan didn't visit me in the hospital, or why he cut me off so completely even after I got out. Nor could I figure out why Eva stopped coming and became evasive. I thought she couldn't handle what had happened to me. What she really couldn't handle was Dan's version of what happened, the idea that she might make my situation worse. I was too insecure to push, and so I watched her slip away from me and into Dan's arms.

A few weeks ago, I found out the truth—and I made sure Eva knew it also. In case you haven't figured this out yet, Eva was supposed to be my happy-ending girl, the one I ultimately had the fairy tale life with. She broke up with Dan, but she didn't get back together with me. I couldn't blame her, really. I knew she couldn't just flick her emotions on and off like a light switch. But I did blame her a little, despite myself, for writing off her earlier feelings for me as just "puppy love."

I didn't know about her, but I was no dog. I knew what I had felt then, and I knew what I felt now—not that anyone else much gave a damn, one way or the other.

Not wanting to rehash the recent past anymore, I convinced Jimmie to go take a walk while I took my morning shower. I bet you expected him to just disappear or something like that. Unfortunately, Jimmie was with me more or less 24-7. Something about me since the awakening of my past lives brought out any latent magic in ordinary people and kept supernaturals like Jimmie operating at full power all the time, so he could maintain his haunting without ever needing to rest. Even more eerie, although he could change shape or become immaterial when he wanted to be, he was solid most of the time and could pass for human without difficulty. I'm sure all the neighborhood ghosts, if there were any, must have envied him.

I guess I should have mentioned earlier who I was. Aside from being the universe's punching bag lately, I had lived many lives before, hundreds of them. That's why my awakening had been so traumatic; the human brain was never meant to process that much information, and mine had at first reacted by making each set of memories into its own personality, giving me something like the ultimate case of dissociative personality disorder. I had managed to reintegrate these past-self personalities into my own, but the experience left me radically different in at least one way: with a little effort, I could make use of the memories, and even the skills, of my previous lives.

The most memorable of those lives was Taliesin, my namesake and King Arthur's bard. Taliesin had helped me rebuild my mind, as well as leaving me his music and his magic, among other things. If I wanted to, I probably could become one of the best musicians in the world. If I wanted to, I could also become a sorcerer powerful enough to rival even Merlin.

My, or rather the original Taliesin's, peculiar origin, particularly his trans-forming taste from the cauldron of knowledge and his rebirth through the womb of Ceridwen, had left me with an ability to learn unfamiliar magic and even to create completely new magic much faster than anyone could normally do. Taliesin himself had never had the need to use those abilities to the full, but I had been under almost constant attack for the better part of a year, and I had learned how to get maximum mileage out of those talents, mostly because I had no choice.

Are you thinking, "What's he crying about? Having magic sounds pretty cool." You know what? I had felt that way myself at times. But let me be clear about one thing: I would give it all up in a second if going back to the original me meant that I could have Eva. I really would!

I got out of the shower feeling marginally better—until I heard a floorboard creak in my bedroom.

Jimmie had promised not to come back until I was ready to go to school. Anyway, he usually didn't make that board creak, even when he was solid. Mom and Dad didn't come in without knocking, and if they didn't get an answer, came in, and discovered I was in the shower, they would have just gone downstairs, at least until I was out of the shower and dressed. Nobody else should have been in the house. No one. And if Mom or Dad had an early morning visitor, that person certainly wouldn't have been in my bedroom.

The floor board creaked again.

Ever since Morgan le Fay had been captured and turned over to the appropriate authorities in Annwn, the Welsh name for the Celtic Other-world, I had gotten sloppy with my security arrangements. While Morgan was still at large, I had the house extremely well protected. An powerful enough spell caster might have been able to break in, but not without my knowing. Spells like that need to be renewed often, though, and I hadn't been bothering lately.

Now an intruder was in my room, and I was about as poorly set up to defend myself as I could have imagined.

Of course my sword, White Hilt, as well as anything else that could have been useful, was in my bedroom. Not only that, but since the bath-room was my own and was entered through my bedroom, not through a hallway, I hadn't bothered to take clothes in with me. It wasn't as if I had a suit of armor in my bedroom, but somehow in a fight for my life, having to worry about keeping a towel around me seemed inconvenient, to say the least. Well, there was no use worrying about that now. I wrapped the towel around myself as securely as I could and reached out with my mind to see if I could tell who was on the other side of the door.

What I felt was so intense that I trembled and nearly fell to my knees. Rage red as blood and hot as an inferno burned through my brain. No, not just rage, but rage focused with a laser-like, deadly intensity—rage desiring only to kill and kill and kill, a truly unquenchable fury. I had never read a serial killer, but I could imagine such a mind being like that. No, not even a serial killer could be quite like this. Surely nothing human could be. Whatever it was wanted to tear the door between us to splinters with its…claws, but instead it was waiting, waiting for me to open the door so it could take me by surprise. Well, maybe I could give it a little surprise, but I needed to take care of a couple of things first.

"Mom! Get yourself and Dad out of the house—right now!" I thought to her as urgently as I could. Fortunately, Mom knew about my…special nature. I couldn't really keep it from her once I inadvertently stimulated her latent psychic ability. I didn't know how she could get Dad out of the house without a lot of questions, but I knew she would find a way. She had to, because, though the…thing in my bedroom apparently wanted me, there was nothing preventing it from charging downstairs and killing both of them if I somehow managed to hold it at bay.

"OK," replied Mom. I sensed her question, but I ignored it. I had to move fast now.

"Nurse Florence!" I broadcast much more strongly this time, as our resident Lady of the Lake was on the other side of Santa Brígida. *"I'm up against some kind of supernatural intrusion at home. Get the guys here—yesterday!"*

My adventures over the past few months had had the side effect of sucking in some of the guys at school. They were combat trained and armed with a variety of supernatural weapons now. Even so, I didn't want to bring them into such a dangerous situation with so many unknown variables. Unfortunately, I had little choice. This wasn't just about saving my neck. If I couldn't contain this…whatever it was, it might not stop with killing me. If the intensity of its rage was any reflection of its power level, it could probably slaughter everyone in town before breakfast, then head on to Santa Barbara and be done there before lunch.

At that point the rage in the next room hit me like a sledgehammer, and I missed Nurse Florence's reply, if there was one. Whatever it was, it had figured out I knew it was there. So much for surprising it.

At almost exactly that moment, the bathroom door exploded in a shower of splinters, and I realized just how right I had been: what came charging into the bathroom was definitely not human.

It was tall enough to have to crouch on its way in, I suppose to save the split second it would have used tearing out the doorjamb. Its exact form was hard to make out, as if its uncontainable rage kept it in a constant state of flux. It was midnight black, black as the altar on which Ceridwen had once tried to sacrifice me. In that blackness, though, were swirls of red, as if the thing had already slaughtered someone and was drenched in its victim's blood. There was a projection on top of its body that roughly corresponded to a head, but no discernible facial features except for eyes, blazing red like blood on fire. There were flickering arms and something like hands, even fingers, and from each finger projected a dagger-like claw, also glistening red as if already bloody.

You know the old expression about your life flashing before you right before you die? Well, mine was flashing at this point. I barely had time to realize just how hopeless my situation was. The bathroom was small, with no room to maneuver. The thing was charging at me too fast for me to be able to do much with magic, and I was unarmed, so unless its menacing appearance was all illusion, I wouldn't stand a chance in a fight.

I crouched and thought about trying to dodge around it, but again, the bathroom was just too small, and the creature was clearly too fast.

I had faced death before, but somehow those other times had not made me any more accepting of it.

I could see one of the claws sweeping down toward me, ready to rip off my face—and I was completely out of options. I tried to duck, but I was already so low to the ground that there was really not much chance of getting below that swing.

And then Jimmie, now in his sixteen-year-old form, slammed into the thing from behind. Even though Jimmie's older shape was athletically built, I doubted he could do much to that swirling mass of hatred. However, the impact jolted the thing just enough that its claw missed me by about the width of a three-by-five card. Distracted by the unexpected interference, the undulating mass spun around, and its claws ripped through Jimmie's throat in one smooth motion.

I gasped, forgetting for a fraction of a second that Jimmie was already dead. Even after I remembered, the sight of that nightmare creature ripping him to shreds was almost more than I could stand. For once, I was glad I had been in so much combat recently, since I was able to start functioning on autopilot. Though Jimmie's body appeared to be mortally wounded, if not already dead, he was still fighting the creature, and it could have been confused by the obvious discrepancy. While it was preoccupied, I scrambled past it—a risky move, but there weren't a whole lot of options—and Jimmie's pseudo-body continued to baffle the attacker. Miraculously, it didn't try to gut me as I ran behind it, and I was in my bedroom in seconds. Once there, it was an easy matter to grab White Hilt and shoot intense flame in a surgically precise blast right at the creature.

As I had suspected from its appearance, the shadowy being, though solid enough to smash doors and rend flesh, was not solid in the same way that I was. Still, it was physical enough for that volcanically hot burst to affect it. Its substance shuddered, writhing in the heat, though it did not actually catch fire. Dropping the fragments of Jimmie, the thing charged at me, but I had a steady stream of flame going now, getting increasingly hotter, and the creature backed away, gray smoke rising from it. It was hard to gauge its intelligence, but because of the sheer magnitude of its emotions, I doubted it had much room for very sophisticated thought. It did, however, have enough thought, or at least instinct, to realize that it could not retain solid form for very long without burning in flame that potent, and so it let go of its physical shape, flickering back into an immaterial state—and then tried to pour itself into me, to possess me, to destroy me from within.

I should have been safe, because most supernatural forces can't possess someone with a strong enough will, and, at the risk of sounding cocky, mine was pretty strong. However, there was now a chink in my armor. A few weeks ago, I had toyed with dark magic. I did it for a good purpose, but no intent can redeem dark magic, and I had accidentally created a tainted reflection of myself: Dark Me, I called him. I had managed to reintegrate him into my mind in the same way I had earlier integrated my past selves, but now I could feel him inside me, ready to burst forth, like an old wound ripping open. I could beat this intruder...but could I beat it and him at the same time?

Again, Jimmie came to the rescue. Instead of reassembling his mangled physical form, he, too, had become immaterial and jumped straight into my brain. I could feel his support, his reassuring warmth, and the light he radiated that somehow could keep Dark Me at bay. However, Jimmie was not all that restrained him. Even Dark Me could tell that this new darkness trying to twist into my soul like serrated knives was different from him. Dark Me was like deceptive shadow, tricky, dangerous to anyone who stood in his way, but still somewhere close to light; the intruder was more like the absolute blackness of a planet whose sun had died a millennium ago. Dark Me wanted to rule the world, more or less, but this gibbering whirlwind wanted only to destroy—and if it managed to kill me, Dark Me would never get what he wanted. Under those circumstances, there was no way Dark Me would risk siding with the invader. I could feel the old wound close, even feel Dark Me's support as he faded back into whatever gloomy recess of my mind from which he had come.

Even so, the raging, homicidal hurricane within me was not easy to subdue. Its sheer intensity made even Dark Me's sulking, twisted energy pale by comparison. Though it was an outsider in my mind and therefore inherently vulnerable, its strength seemed ancient and deeply rooted. It was not something to be easily dismissed.

Finally, I felt its hold give way, and it shrieked out of my mind and out of the house, frightened perhaps by the ancientness of my previous lives but more likely by Jimmie's light. I would have liked to trap it, perhaps even to destroy it, but the way my body was shaking told me getting rid of it was probably the best outcome I could have hoped for.

In a moment Jimmie popped out, still in his teenage form but looking more pale than usual. "Tal, what was that thing?"

"I only wish I knew," I replied, walking somewhat unsteadily into my bedroom and sitting on the bed. "Even the original Taliesin never encountered anything like it, as far as I can remember."

Jimmie shuddered. "If I hadn't already been dead, it would have scared me to death."

I smiled at him. "If you hadn't already been dead, I might have been. I'm not sure if I could have handled that thing without you."

Jimmie snorted derisively. "You know you could have. I just helped you win a little faster."

Even a little faster could be important at this point. I could hear the front door slam, followed by the sound of my parents arguing. Evidently, whatever hasty pretext Mom had used to get Dad out of the house had caused some kind of friction between them.

I glanced over at the gaping hole where the bathroom door had once been and at the scattered wood fragments and splinters. I had no time to fix the damage now, but leaving this mess for someone to stumble upon was too big a risk. It took only a few moments to weave a convincing illusion that would make any normal person believe the door was still intact, and everything was as it should be.

How exactly I was going to fix it later, I wasn't sure—the original Taliesin's repertoire did not include carpentry spells, and I hadn't had any reason until now to develop magic like that. Well, there wasn't much use in worrying about the problem right now. I needed to get dressed and downstairs as fast as possible to figure out what was happening with my parents. Humming a little and accelerating myself to faerie speed, I was ready in half a minute and bounding down the stairs with an invisible Jimmie drifting along behind me.

Mom and Dad were still arguing when I reached them, though they stopped as soon as they saw me. We all made awkward small talk, and I peeked into Dad's mind, just enough to tell what was going on: Mom had gotten him outside on the pretext that she had heard someone calling for help, and then she had insisted they do a thorough search, even when it was obvious to him that there was no real emergency. With just a couple of little tweaks, I quieted his irritation, not that hard a job considering how much he loved Mom, we got through breakfast, and Dad was off to the office in a considerable hurry. I would have followed him out the door, but Mom put a gentle hand on my shoulder, and I knew she wanted to talk.

"Tal," she said nervously as I turned in her direction, "I don't like it when you do that."

"Do what?" I asked. There were so many things she could have been referring to at this point.

She looked momentarily annoyed herself. "You know perfectly well what I mean: mess around in your father's head like that." Her psychic senses were getting stronger all the time. Just a few days ago, she only got general impressions of what I was doing with magic. Now she could apparently see exactly what was going on.

"I only do what I have to do," I replied patiently. "You know I don't intrude in someone's mind unless I have to."

"Did you really have to, this time? Your father and I could have handled that disagreement on our own."

"In this case it was my fault. My mess, my responsibility to fix it."

Mom looked distant for a moment, as if she was not quite sure how to respond. Finally she said, "I'm proud of you for taking responsibility, but what happened wasn't your fault, was it?"

"I guess not," I conceded. "Still, that doesn't keep me from feeling responsible."

"Did you do that with me very often, before I could sense what was going on?" she asked worriedly.

"I told you when I first convinced you that you weren't going insane. Sometimes I had to manipulate you or Dad or both to keep you from finding out what was really going on, to keep you safe."

She laughed, but the sound was more hollow than her normal laugh, almost fake. "I wish sometimes that you were still doing that and that I had never learned the truth." Then, almost immediately, she realized how her statement sounded. "Oh Tal, I didn't mean it like that. I love you, even though you're different now. And I want to love you for who you really are. It's just that it was easier the other way. Now I know when you've been in great danger…just like today, right?"

I nodded. There would have been no point lying about it. She would have known the truth, regardless of what I said.

"What was it?" she asked, clearly dreading the answer but needing to know.

"I don't know, but I'll tell you when I find out. I promise."

She nodded, still clearly dissatisfied. "A word popped into my head even before you sent your message: 'phonos.' Do you know what that means?"

This time it was my turn to shudder. I did know, but I had not thought about a phonos since my last life in ancient Greece, when I had been a close companion of Alexander the Great. "The phonoi are personifications of murder. But I've never encountered one, not even in much more primitive times. I need to find out how it got into our world."

"Not if it means putting yourself in further danger," she cautioned, sounding like her maternal instincts were leading her toward laying down the law.

"It might be more dangerous not to find out—and not just for me. This…intrusion is unusual."

My mother raised an eyebrow at that. "Son, earlier this morning you sent me a psychic message to get out of the house and take your father, apparently because the…spirit of murder was invading our home. Now…that ghost is standing almost right behind you. Oh, and then there is that invisible magic sword you're wearing. Define 'unusual' for me." Well, she had me there, and now apparently she could see Jimmie when he was invisible. I told her about Jimmie when I first told her the truth, but she had never before mentioned being able to see him.

"Yeah, our lives are unusual right now. I get that. But everything is a question of degree. This is more unusual. These days even the Welsh faeries, for all their earlier ties to humanity, hardly ever venture into our world. Ancient Greek…beings? A lot less often. Even when I was an ancient Greek, I can't ever remember seeing one."

Let alone having one crawling around in my head.

"You'll talk to Viv…to Nurse Florence about it, then?"

"Yeah, she's pretty much my go-to person for information. After all, the Order of Ladies of the Lake has been doing research on all things supernatural for centuries."

Mom, who was evidently now on a first-name basis with Nurse Florence, seemed reassured. "Well, then, probably she'll have an answer." Once Mom had found out the truth, Nurse Florence had been working with her to help Mom get control of those rapidly growing new abilities. They worked together well, and Mom trusted her implicitly.

"There is one more thing," said Mom abruptly, just when I thought the conversation was over.

"OK, but I do need to get to school pretty soon."

Mom sighed. "I'll make it quick. We need to tell your father the truth." The words hit me like bullets.

"You know we can't," I snapped, more harshly than I intended. Then, more calmly, I continued. "I explained why we can't already. The powers that be in Annwn are already nervous about the number of people who know about me, and by extension, them. Nurse Florence sold them on the need to tell you because you were going to find out anyway. They would never accept telling Dad just because we wanted to."

"Don't you know how hard it is not to tell him?" Mom asked, almost desperately, her voice trembling slightly. "He's my husband, your father, and every day we have to lie to him, usually repeatedly. Every day." The words hit the ground like the first stones of an avalanche. "I don't know…how much longer I can keep doing this."

"Mom!" I said urgently. "I want to tell him, too. I wanted to tell both of you from the very beginning. But it might not be safe for any of us if he knows."

Mom knew I was right, but that didn't mean she liked the situation any better. I could almost see her crumbling inwardly, and she brushed aside a tear. Then she shooed me away when I tried to give her a hug.

"I know," she said wearily. "I know it all." Again I tried to hug her, but she dodged me. "I'm all right, Tal. I just need...a little time. You need to get to school, and I think I need to lie down for a few minutes anyway."

"Do I at least get a good-bye kiss?" I asked. She leaned slightly in my direction and let me kiss her on the cheek. I could feel her quivering just a little.

Damn! Her knowing was supposed to make it easier on her, not harder.

Reluctantly I walked out the front door, with Jimmie, as always, in tow.

"Jimmie, could you stay with her for a while this morning?"

Jimmie chuckled a little. "Tal, you know I would, but she really doesn't like having me around. I think I give her the creeps."

"You knew she could see you?" I asked.

"I figured she would, sooner or later. She's been able to sense me around for at least a few days."

Then a different thought struck me. "Jimmie, you felt the phonos! Do you think you can figure out where it went?"

Jimmie shook his head. "Maybe if I were psychic, like your mom. Just because I'm...different doesn't mean I can track other...beings." Jimmie knew he was a ghost, of course, but he still thought of himself as human, so saying "other supernatural beings" was still hard for him.

"All right, then," I said, sighing inwardly. As much as Jimmie was like a brother to me, the constant haunting was beginning to give *me* the creeps. You don't know how much you need some alone time...until you don't have any. I couldn't be mad at Jimmie, though. It wasn't his fault I couldn't bring myself to forgive Dan yet. One moment of genuine forgiveness, and Jimmie could be at peace. Perhaps so could I. However, we weren't going to find that out any time soon. I was still a long way from forgiving Dan.

"Don't worry, Tal," said Jimmie, patting me on the arm. "Didn't you tell me once that something like that phonos can't stay in our world for long because..." And then Jimmie stopped, realizing how completely he had just jammed his foot in his mouth.

Our world was not particularly friendly to supernatural intruders. In the first place, though magic did work, of which I was living proof, it was harder for most people to cast spells here than it would be in a place like Annwn, and someone using magic would normally lose power over time unless that spell caster recharged in a supernatural realm every so often. Creatures like the phonos would have an even harder time. Manifesting here at all took an enormous effort, so typically if a phonos or other intruder could get to our world at all, it would soon have to return to its own plane of existence or destroy itself trying to remain.

So Jimmie was right...except anywhere near me. He should have remembered that, considering how much proximity to me increased his own ability to manifest himself to unheard-of levels. I didn't doubt for a minute that being close to me could do the same for the phonos if it hung around enough. Primitive as its intellect seemed to be, if it somehow figured out that hanging out with me would make it stronger, then I might be haunted by more than just Jimmie.

And if the phonos managed to kill someone else, it would be partly my fault.

The day was sunny and warm, almost springlike, but a chill settled around me.

"Oh, I just made it worse!" Jimmie exclaimed unhappily.

"It's all right, Jimmie," I said in a reassuring tone I didn't feel. I think he could sense my true emotions, and he started to say something more but then stopped.

"Anyway, you've been around me for the whole time since I was awakened, and it took four years for you to become...more than just an ordinary ghost. It also took four years for my mom to become psychic. One close brush with me isn't going to supercharge the phonos, and I certainly don't feel it around right now. My guess is that it has already returned to its native plane."

Jimmie nodded, though he didn't look like he was entirely convinced. Hell, I couldn't blame him, since I wasn't entirely convinced myself. What I was saying made sense...yet I could not help feeling a little uncertain, no doubt a side effect of having been taken by surprise so many times since August.

"Come on, Jimmie. Stan will be wondering what happened to us by now," I said, trying to getting his mind off our problems. It's too bad

I couldn't get mine off them as easily.

Jimmie and I walked down my excessively gardened street, nature tamed and molded to human will, but we didn't have to go far; Stan's house was only three doors down. I was right, too—Stan looked like the living incarnation of tension by the time we spotted him.

Despite Stan's obvious concern, I couldn't help smiling a little when I saw him. Dan had betrayed me, but Stan? Never! We had been friends as long as I could remember, so long that even ordinary, non-psychic people occasionally asked if we were brothers. Physically, the question was ridiculous. Some of the differences between us a few months ago had lessened as Stan got taller and as his training built his muscles, but we still didn't look like brothers. I was at least a little tan; Stan was pale. I was brown eyed; he, blue eyed. I had straight brown hair; his was curly black. Nor were our facial features even remotely similar, though the consensus among the girls seemed to be that we were both good looking. I'd been told that I was classically good looking, with that symmetry that is supposed to make a guy handsome. I wouldn't know. The most I would say with certainty was that my eyes, nose, and mouth were all approximately in the right place. Though I had been a lot more social this year, I was still apparently putting out that secretive loner vibe that some girls took as a challenge. As for Stan, Carla once told me girls looked at him as "the nerd with possibilities," the could-be-cute-with-a-little-help kid who is so often a character in romantic comedies and always emerges by the end as the truer man than the macho idiots who serve as his foils. The fact that Stan was getting taller and buffer at a very fast rate didn't hurt, either; he had been upgraded from could-be-cute-with-a-little-help to already-there. Still, to think that we were really brothers, someone would almost have to be psychically aware of the closeness of the bond between us.

There was another bond between us, one that very few people knew about: Stan, like me, had been hit by one of Ceridwen's spells and had past-life memories of his own. In my case, I could remember not only the original Taliesin but a multitude of others, though remembering those further back than Taliesin took more effort. Stan, on the other hand, could only consciously remember one, but that one was more than enough: King David of Israel. Despite having only one past life to deal with, Stan had had more than his share of problems with it; David did not reintegrate with Stan as easily as I had reintegrated the hundreds of past-life personas within me. In fact, David remained a separate consciousness even now, but I thought we were past the point at which there was much risk that David would accidentally end up in control of their body, with Stan submerged forever. Still, I would have liked to complete their fusion—if only I could figure out how to take that final step.

"I was worried about you!" said Stan quickly, as soon as I was close enough for him to be able to speak quietly.

"I had a little…problem this morning. Evidently my message to Nurse Florence didn't get through if you didn't hear anything about it." In case of emergency, Nurse Florence could relay any psychic message to Stan and the other guys who were, for lack of any better way of putting it, my warriors. Perhaps the phonos had been emitting some kind of static that blocked my distress call. Fortunately, the short walk from Stan's house to school was long enough for me to fill him in, with Jimmie adding a detail here and there. By now, Stan was as used to having Jimmie around as I was. Normally I would have insisted Jimmie remain invisible and inaudible on the walk to school, but since Stan wasn't psychic, Jimmie could only communicate with him by making himself visible or audible. Today, since Jimmie had once again saved my life, I figured he had earned the right to have a little casual conversation with Stan without my scolding him about it. Still, Jimmie would be too hard to explain if anybody outside our little group saw him, whether in his nine-year-old or sixteen-year-old form, so I carefully wove a spell around us that would make us, not invisible exactly, but unnoticeable. We walked along as if in a bubble, and we would have had a pleasant chat if the subject matter had not been so threatening.

"Could this…thing possibly have shown up by coincidence?" asked Stan when he had heard all the information we had.

"Yeah…about as coincidental as King David popping up in November." Stan chuckled a little at that.

"Speaking of, David says he'll pray for this evil spirit to be banished." Yeah, Stan and David were still separate enough that he and David had a running conversation going on in Stan's head most of the time, but Stan seemed used to that unsettling dialogue by now.

"That's good," I replied. "Something tells me we need all the help we can get right now."

We were now close enough to the school that there were a lot of people around, and continuing to maintain my spell would be difficult.

"Jimmie, you need to get invisible now," I cautioned. With a wink he vanished, and I let the spell around us dissolve. A few people nearby jumped as they suddenly noticed Stan and me—we really had gotten too close to the school before I let go of the magic—but otherwise we arrived without incident, with Jimmie floating along invisibly somewhere behind us.

I got through the early part of the day, but as often happened these days, I was having difficulty concentrating. Stan's question about coincidence kept rattling around in my head. Yeah, the phonos could have slid into our reality through some random crack in the barrier between worlds; that kind of accident was not unheard of. Yet everything that had happened to me in the last four years, however coincidental it had seemed at the time, had turned out to be part of someone's agenda. Even the awakening of my past-life memories, which had seemed at first like some freak accident, had turned out to be part of the witch Ceridwen's plan. So had my first trip to Annwn in this life. After we had defeated Ceridwen, Morgan le Fay had started orchestrating seemingly random events; her agenda was far different from that of Ceridwen, but the way her plans kept interfering with my life was annoyingly similar.

The authorities in Annwn currently had Morgan in custody, so the question of the day was, who was messing with me now? The only obvious answer was someone who wanted me dead. What's that old saying, often described as a curse? Oh yeah, "May you live in interesting times." How I longed for boredom!

Finally it was time for nutrition, which gave me a few minutes to rush over to the nurse's office and see Nurse Florence. Needless to say, she was as alarmed as I was. As always, I couldn't help noticing she was still the best-looking adult woman I knew, with her blond hair and model-perfect face, despite the lines of worry creasing her forehead. In my heart I still thought of Eva as being even more beautiful—for all the good thinking about Eva did me.

"Have you tried looking for the phonos? Could it still be around?" By looking, she meant scanning for it telepathically.

"I have, and I don't feel that homicidal rage anywhere nearby, but that doesn't mean the phonos isn't still somewhere in town. You know how finicky my ability to read people and...things...is where distance is concerned. To be sure, I'd have to let my mind flow outward and do a detailed search of each part of Santa Brígida—and even that wouldn't necessarily be enough to spot the thing if it were moving around."

Nurse Florence sighed. "Well, it isn't likely it could have stayed in physical form for very long, right?"

"True, but with a phonos, that isn't our biggest worry," I pointed out. "I have been trying to recall as much as I could from my ancient Greek lives. I can't think of a single time such a spirit attacked somebody physically. I can remember people being possessed by one. Well, not exactly possessed, but phonoi were always attracted to someone with murder in his heart." I looked over, expecting some word of wisdom from Nurse Florence.

"I'll check with the Order later today, but I doubt they have anything on phonoi," she said apologetically. "Is there anything else you can remember about them?"

"Not much, but judging from this morning's encounter, I'd say this one could pretty effectively stun a normal person it entered, maybe even push that person into a coma."

"Or make them into a homicidal maniac?" asked Nurse Florence, trying to sound matter-of-fact about the situation but not quite succeeding; I could hear a hint of fear in her voice.

"I've never heard of anything like that," I said slowly, trying to search those ancient memories for any other clues, "but then this phonos was not behaving normally. I'm pretty sure I'm not nursing the impulse to kill anyone, but it entered me anyway and tried to force those feelings upon me. I could resist, but the average person might not be able to. If I had to guess, though, I'd say the phonos would try to seek out an easier target, someone who might be tipped over the edge with less effort than the average person would require. I think it was nearing exhaustion when it fled from me and Jimmie. If it wanted to stay on this plane, it would have had to possess someone pretty quickly, and probably the less struggle the person could put up, the better."

"And once in someone, it would be even harder to find, right?"

I didn't have to think long about that answer. "I'm sure I could read it inside someone, but if it were smart enough to be subtle about its occupation, I might have to probe deep to be sure it was there, and I can't...won't do that to everyone in town, unless there is no other choice. Right now we don't even know it's still around."

Nurse Florence seemed less than convinced—and I was pretty sure myself that the phonos was lurking around somewhere. However, the pro-spect of having to probe everyone in town to find it was too daunting to embrace easily. Besides, whatever other virtues the creature had, subtlety did not seem to be one of them. If it still happened to be around, I was willing to bet that it would reveal itself long before I could find it.

Unfortunately, I was proved right all too soon.

Chapter 2: A War God Intervenes

I found myself figuratively looking over my shoulder for the rest of the day—hardly an enviable situation, but one I was used to. Luckily, things at good old Santa Brígida High School seemed calm. Jimmie was still hanging around invisibly, waiting for another opportunity to nag me about forgiving Dan, but I could hardly blame him for that, and he tended to stay quiet during class and soccer practice.

I usually enjoyed soccer practice, but recently it had become kind of an ordeal for me. As it happens, the team captain was none other than…wait for it…Dan Stevens. That's right—the backstabbing bastard who had stolen Eva from me four years ago, the brother whom Jimmie wanted so desperately for me to forgive. I could—and did—pretend to be on good terms with him, both on and off the soccer field, because doing otherwise generated too much high-school gossip. High schools tend to be just like small towns, with everyone in everyone else's business. People knew about Dan's breakup with Eva; that couldn't be helped. But adding a public end to our friendship to that mix would have led to unhealthy rumors, some of them too close to the truth, and Eva's situation would have become even more uncomfortable. No, I couldn't allow that to happen.

I also had to pretend for Jimmie's sake that I was trying to forgive Dan, though to be honest, most days I wondered if I would ever be ready to do that. Most days, swimming with piranhas or wearing barbed-wire underwear seemed better.

Today was one of those, but partly because Coach Morton was droning on again about the upcoming CIF playoffs, and I just wasn't in the mood to hear it anymore. Aside from Dan, I was the best player on the team, and I still tried to be dedicated, but the sport was so closely associated with Dan in my mind that I just couldn't keep up the level of enthusiasm I once had. Still, Dan wasn't the only guy on the team, and I didn't want to let the others down, so I kept trying to maintain my playing as best I could.

Finally, practice ended, but when everyone else headed to the locker room, I found an excuse to talk to the coach for a few minutes, long enough for Dan to shower, change, and get out. I was sure he would take the hint and do just that. Unfortunately, Jimmie, reasoning more like the sixteen-year-old he appeared to be than the nine-year-old he had been when he died, figured out what I was doing and whispered to me the whole time I was trying to talk to Morton. I think the coach was convinced I wasn't really paying attention and gave me another lecture about focus before letting me go. Well, that just made it all the more likely that Dan would be out of the way by the time I got to the locker room.

When I finally arrived, sure enough, Dan was already gone—and so was everyone else, for that matter. My nerves were pretty well shredded by now, anyway, so I was glad of the chance to avoid small talk while I showered and changed. Unfortunately, I did still have Jimmie to contend with.

"You did that on purpose!" he said accusingly. "You talked to the coach so you wouldn't have to talk to Dan."

I sat down to take off my shoes and sighed. "Jimmie, I am trying; I really am! Right now, though, I just need a little time to myself. I need to think. I need to figure out this phonos thing before someone gets hurt."

"Dan could help with that!" offered Jimmie, his tone suddenly less scolding and more hopeful.

"Dan has many talents," I replied, "but extensive knowledge of ancient Greek supernatural beings isn't one of them. However, I'm sure I can use his help if the phonos gets into somebody else. Why don't you go tell him what's been happening?"

"You're trying to get rid of me!" said Jimmie, now sounding sulky and much more like a nine-year-old.

I looked him in the eyes and said, "Jimmie, you know you're like a brother to me, and you probably saved my life today…again. But right now I really need to figure out what's going on, and I do my best thinking when I'm alone."

For a moment Jimmie looked so sad that I almost took back what I had just said and asked him to stay. Before I could relent, however, he had vanished, much more abruptly and quietly than usual. I guessed he was finally beginning to take my hints. Either that or he needed time to think himself.

As much as I had wanted to be alone, showering and changing in the completely empty locker room was oddly unsettling. I felt like the next victim in a horror movie. Considering that the phonos had tried to kill me when I showered this morning, I supposed what I was feeling was natural. I let my mind wander—literally—while I was standing in the warm spray. I could sense no lurking presence anywhere nearby, but I was still nervous. I dressed quickly and headed for the parking lot. By the time I got there, I had slowed my pace deliberately. I was just being silly. If I let myself get spooked this easily, I might not be able to concentrate well in a real emergency.

As I started to walk across the parking lot, I thought I heard something behind me, a footstep perhaps, and turned, but no one was there. I scanned the path back to the gym. No, nobody was around at all, and my mind didn't catch any hint of phonos.

Wow, my nerves must really be shot!

Then I jumped a little when I realized someone was standing almost right next to my Prius. I had been so focused on what was going on—or rather, not going on—behind me that I hadn't noticed him at first.

He looked like a student...but why was he hovering near my car? Was I just being paranoid, or was his solitary presence in a parking lot a little odd?

Odd or not, aside from the fact that he was just hanging out in the parking lot, he didn't appear menacing at all. He seemed to be daydreaming, so maybe his being so close to my car was just coincidence.

He looked like someone I should know, but I couldn't quite remember his name. I studied him more closely as I walked in his direction, but the name would not come to me. He appeared to be about my age, so he could be a junior like me, perhaps even in one of my classes. Horror movie analogies came to mind again. This guy's appearance reminded me of the picked-on nerd who ends up either being an early victim or the one who sells his soul to the devil to get revenge. There was something about the way he was standing—slouching, really—that somehow suggested victim. His brown hair, about the same shade as mine, was not especially well-combed, and he wore his clothes in a careless way, as if he had slept in them or left them on the floor and crawled back into them in the morning. Some guys could pull off that look, usually buff guys who made girls want to offer advice or perhaps offer to rebutton the shirt that was one button off. This guy, however, was scrawny. I wasn't thinking that in a judgmental way—Stan used to be the same, after all, and he was my best friend. There was no denying, though, that the guy was not in any kind of shape, and the look didn't work for him. He also had just a touch of acne and appeared otherwise very pale, making me think he spent most of his time indoors.

I knew I should recognize him. Why couldn't I remember his name?

It was his turn to jump when I was almost on top of him. He really must have been focused on that daydream.

"Hey, Tal," he said with a wave, trying to cover the fact that he had just jumped at the sight of me but also making it obvious he did know me.

"Hey…" I said, waving back as I walked toward him. "Hey…" Damn! This would have been a good time for me to remember his name, but I was still drawing a blank, and something in his eyes suggested he had realized I didn't recognize him. For a moment I even thought his face twisted with anger. Then he looked as if he were listening to someone, though there was nobody around, and he wasn't wearing an earpiece.

I was almost in normal conversation range, trying to frame an apology for not remembering his name, when I saw the sword in his hand. It had not been there a second ago, but it was there now, radiating some kind of off-the-charts power and flickering, as if its substance was not metal but some otherworldly material. Even with all my experience with faerie weapons, I had never seen anything like it. Apparently my earlier uneasy feelings had not been entirely groundless after all.

Taking just another second to check to make sure no one else was around and watching, I drew White Hilt and let it flame in my hand.

"Whoever you are, drop the sword now!" I yelled at him in my most commanding tone, letting the flames, which fortunately I had learned to control, flare ominously in his direction. "I don't want to hurt you." I didn't particularly want to blow up my car's gas tank either, so I kept very tight control over the fire, though I hoped it still looked threatening enough to get my point across. Luckily, there were no other cars nearby to worry about.

"Tal, you…you know me!" he stammered. "I came here to warn you!" I could see the fire—and his own fear—reflected in his eyes. If he had come after me, he did not at first glance seem to be a very well-prepared assailant; anyone who had done his homework would certainly have known about White Hilt. Still, I knew I couldn't afford to take chances.

"With a sword in your hand?" I asked, somewhat more quietly. I couldn't think of a good reason. Then again, I carried a sword, and so did the rest of my merry band. Maybe he had an equally good reason for carrying one—though that didn't explain why he had drawn it on me.

"Tal, I'm in your U.S. history class…"

"Drop the sword!" I demanded, keeping the fire between him and me. He sounded ordinary enough, and I could almost place his face now…but what was an ordinary teenager doing with an obviously powerful magic sword?

"Tal, please! I can't let go of the sword. This is all a trick!" He looked so panicked at that point that I was almost inclined to believe him. But if I was being tricked, whose trick was it? And could this guy still be dangerous, even if he was wielding the sword unwillingly?

Well, I couldn't answer all those questions, but if I could probe his mind, I could at least test the truth of his words. Unfortunately, just as I started to reach out, a swirling, throbbing, absolute blackness hurled itself in his direction. I had only seen it once before, but I knew it was the phonos. Before I had time to plan a decent strategy, it encircled the strange sword and soaked into the metal with lightning speed. I knew a phonos could possess a human, but I had never heard of one possessing a weapon before.

The sword, powerful enough to begin with, now pulsated with the phonos's incoherent rage.

"I'm not doing this!" the guy yelled, his voice cracking. He almost seemed to be cringing away from the blade he was holding, and again I wanted to believe him, but if I were being tricked, could he be the trickster, just feigning reluctance?

At that moment he started to charge awkwardly in my direction, and I used White Hilt to create a wall of flame between us. The phonos-possessed sword might be powerful beyond measure, but its wielder was clearly afraid of fire, so I doubted he would just charge through a fiery barrier.

However, the firewall gave me only a moment's respite; after a few seconds, the sword tore through it. No, that wasn't quite right. As the sword sliced through, the fire randomly turned into a variety of other things: water, earth, flashes of light, crackles of electricity, and even something that looked like living tissue. Each of these seemed to explode away from the others and then disappear, leaving a gap in my flaming barrier, through which he plunged. I managed to raise a new one a couple more times, but each time the sword ripped through, chaos ensued, and my defenses collapsed.

As a last resort, I tried shooting fire right at the guy, not hoping to burn him but hoping to make him dodge reflexively away, perhaps stumbling in the process. His run, though fast, looked stiff and awkward, so getting him to trip seemed like a good way to buy time. Yet, awkward as he seemed, he parried my shot with little outward effort, and the moment the fiery blast touched the sword, it too exploded into anarchy.

The assailant was almost upon me now, so I did the only thing I could do under the circumstances—I ran like hell! There was other magic I could try but none that I could cast in the few seconds before he would reach me. My only chance was that he was as weak physically as he looked, in which case I could certainly outrun him.

I allowed myself a glance back. He seemed to be in pain, as if his muscles were being pushed harder than they could really take, but he was keeping up with me, maybe even gaining on me a bit.

Singing to myself a little, I pushed my speed up to faerie levels. Momentarily, I gained some ground, but then he started accelerating, too. I couldn't afford to watch him too much, but it looked as if the sword was pushing him to go faster. However, he seemed to be getting shaky, his leg movements became more erratic, and his breath was coming in short, ragged gasps. Clearly, he could not sustain this pace as long as I could, so at least I had one thing going for me.

Thinking there might still be a few guys near the gym, I veered north abruptly, toward the landscaped "woods" north of campus. The last thing I needed right now was innocent bystanders getting in the way of that sword—I shuddered at what its touch might do to human flesh. Also, though it had taken work, I had gotten the trees to be somewhat responsive to my will without my having to use too much magic on them. They didn't make the best allies, but at this point, I would take whatever help I could get. I could have sent out a mental SOS to the guys and to Nurse Florence, but without knowing the extent of this sword's power, I wasn't about to risk my friends' lives.

I turned to face my foe once I was safely within the woods. He looked as if he was almost ready to drop, but his body surged forward. Fear showed on his face even more clearly than fatigue.

He tripped over a root, which then took the opportunity to grab both his feet. He swung the sword, and the root dissolved in a jumble of different kinds of nonliving matter. I could see and feel other roots and branches stretching toward him, but I knew he would not be slowed very much by their efforts. Fortunately, I had at least one other strategy worth trying.

I sang with as much magic force as I could summon up and then threw myself into the air. Flying was not what I was best at, but there was at least a chance that my opponent couldn't follow me.

Sure enough, he stared after me in surprise but didn't try to pursue me into the air.

"Taliesin!" shouted the guy below in a bone-chilling tone unlike the one he had used before. "Surrender now, or I will kill everyone I can find. You may be able to fly away, but you can't take everyone with you!"

Still thinking in horror movie terms, I visualized the campus, hell, the entire town, drenched in blood and littered with corpses. Physical hindrances like trees might slow him but would not stop the carnage.

Then I realized that Jimmie had appeared right behind the guy—whose name I still couldn't remember. I had no idea what effect the sword might have on Jimmie and didn't want to find out.

"Jimmie, no!" I yelled as forcefully as I could.

"Dead already, remember?" replied Jimmie with a shrug. With surprising speed the unknown swordsman turned and sliced right through him. For a second my heart stopped beating. Jimmie actually staggered backward a little, but at least he didn't dissolve into chaos. He did, however, disappear as the second sword stroke came down on him. I hoped his disappearance was strategy rather than some delayed aftereffect of the first stroke.

After a few seconds, Jimmie reappeared behind his assailant. "Tal, I could feel that blade even though I wasn't physical!" he shouted. The swordsman spun around and sliced again, but again Jimmie vanished before the sword could actually hit.

Jimmie wasn't visible, but I knew he was still listening. "Stay away from it!" I yelled back. "I've never seen anything like it. You could be hurt by it."

Abruptly, Jimmie materialized right next to me in the air, comfortably out of reach of that unpredictable weapon.

"Why haven't you called the other guys?" he asked.

"Because I don't know what we're dealing with, and none of the other guys can fly away if the battle turns against them."

"Come down, both of you. Come down now, or everyone else I can reach dies!" the inhuman voice shrieked from below us. If the phonos, or the sword, or whoever was using that guy as a mouthpiece actually started to follow through, I would have to call everyone else, but I wished there was a different way to contain the threat.

"Leave this to me," said Jimmie, and then he dove straight at the mystery student before I could say anything—not that he would have listened anyway. He was moving so fast that the swordsman swung at him but failed to connect. Then Jimmie collided with his body and flowed into it almost as effortlessly as the phonos had done with the sword earlier.

The swordsman shuddered at what must have been an intense internal struggle, but then Jimmie shot out of him like a cannonball. He began to get control again just as he was passing me.

"Tal, he's possessed. It's the phonos that attacked you earlier!" yelled Jimmie as he drifted past, still not able to come to a complete stop.

"He's not a killer then?" I asked quickly, already knowing the answer. What was happening to this guy did look an awful lot like possession, even from a distance.

"No," said Jimmie, finally managing to halt himself. "I just got a quick look, but I would say he'd like to fight the phonos. He just doesn't know how. If I could get back in there…"

"Too dangerous!" I snapped, but Jimmie was already bracing himself for another attempt.

"Come down now!" demanded the phonos, speaking through the stranger's mouth again. "If you do not obey immediately, your friends will pay for your resistance."

Again Jimmie plunged at the body the phonos was occupying, again it shuddered, harder this time, right after he entered, and for just a moment, I got a glimpse of the poor guy trapped within.

"Tal," he whispered, as if an almost inaudible sound was the most he could force himself to make. His whole body was shaking convulsively as Jimmie fought the phonos. I started magicking my hearing to more sensitive levels, but then he managed to speak in a normal tone.

"Tal! Ares wants you dead. I didn't agree to help, but he shoved this sword of chaos into my hand and…" At that point I could almost feel the phonos clamp down on him again. I could see him struggle to get out the rest of what he was trying to say, but after a few seconds, it was clear he was going to fail. It only took a few more seconds for the phonos to expel Jimmie, this time with such explosive force that he shot far past me before getting control again.

"Enough of this!" screamed the phonos, every syllable filled to overflowing with the creature's hatred. "Because you would not surrender, others will die." With that, the body below us turned away and started to move in the opposite direction, no doubt expecting us to follow.

Well, I had to do something, but what? Not for the first time, I found myself in a situation that nothing, not even all my earlier lives, had prepared me for. Yeah, when I had been a friend of Alexander the Great, I had worshiped gods like Ares, but even all those centuries ago, I hadn't seen that much evidence of their active intervention, any more than I had seen a genuine case of phonos possession. When I was the original Taliesin, I had seen faeries—many of them—but never even once anything remotely resembling a Greek god. If Ares really existed, and if he really had created this situation, I was utterly clueless what to do about it.

"Tal!" said Jimmie urgently. "He's getting away!"

I looked down, and sure enough, the phonos was dragging its victim away, dicing any obstructing tree limbs into atomic disarray as it went. Sword of chaos, indeed!

"What's his name?" I whispered, figuring that Jimmie would probably have picked it up while in the guy's mind.

"Alexandros Stratos. He's in your history class," said Jimmie, in a tone that suggested I really should have remembered him.

"Alex!" I thought as loudly as I could. Maybe his movement slowed a little, but the change might just have been my imagination.

"Alex!" I tried again, even more insistently. Could he even hear me over the uproar the phonos was doubtless creating in his head?

"Tal, can you hear me?" he thought back so faintly that for a second, I wasn't sure whether I was hearing him or just imagining his thoughts.

"Yeah, but stay focused. You can't project, so I have to read you, and the phonos creates all kinds of static. If I lose the connection, I may not be able to reestablish it."

"I'll try," he replied weakly. *"What can I do? I don't want to hurt anybody!"*

"The phonos controls your body by the power of murderous hatred. You might be able to counter that hatred if you can generate enough love. Think about someone you love. Think hard! Think fast! When you have a focus, Jimmie and I will both try to lend you strength. But you have to make a move soon."

The phonos was dragging his body closer and closer to campus. I wasn't sure how many people would be there this late in the afternoon, but almost certainly someone would be.

"*Tal!*" I jumped a little at the shrillness of his mental tone. "*I can't focus well enough. Help me!*"

I could see why Alex might have difficulty concentrating, but that probably meant we were not going to be able to break the phonos's control. He was nearing the north entrance to the school, so I had to come up with a plan B—and damn fast!

Just in time I realized what I had to do. I chanted up as much power as I could as quickly as I could and opened a portal right in the phonos's path—actually blocking the north entrance. The phonos wasn't much of a thinker, and not realizing what it was up against, it raised the sword to strike. While it was focused on the portal, I shot down with faerie speed and hit Alex with all the force I could muster. Alex, who was not exactly built to resist that kind of impact, stumbled right through the portal and straight into another world. I sped through myself an instant later. Jimmie tried to follow, but I signaled him to stay put. He was too far away from me; waiting for him to reach the portal before I started closing it was far too great a risk. Now, if the phonos couldn't open portals itself, I had at least bought myself some time.

Naturally, as soon as the creature got Alex's body back on its feet, it spun poor Alex around and took a swing at me with that angrily pulsating sword, but I was too quick and had already soared into the air, once again out of reach. Then the phonos turned toward the rapidly shrinking portal and swung at it with the sword, probably trying to rip it back open. For a split second, I had an apocalyptic vision of the phonos succeeding but permanently ripping a hole in the wall between the universes, with God only knew what doomsday consequences. The sword, however, was not quite that powerful, and all hitting the portal accomplished was collapsing what was left of that possible exit. The phonos was trapped.

It threw back Alex's head and howled in frustration, but since I was safely out of range of the sword, I just ignored it. Alex was my biggest concern now.

"*You all right in there?*" I thought to him. Projecting my thoughts through the seething anger of the phonos wasn't easy, but Alex could still hear me.

"*Yeah,*" Alex said faintly, trying not to sound shaky and not quite succeeding. "*What did you do? Where are we?*"

"In an...otherworld. This was once the island of Alcina, a great sorceress. I have been here before, so I was able to open the portal that brought us here."

"Taliesin!" demanded the phonos in a tone that was hatred made audible. "Take me back to where I was, or I will kill whoever lives here."

I probably shouldn't have been flip, but after all the phonos had put me through today, I wanted it to be the one feeling helpless for a while.

"As it happens, no one lives here anymore. I'm afraid you're out of luck."

Despite being pretty far away from the phonos, I could feel its anger reach even higher levels. I could feel emotion spewing at me like lava from the biggest volcanic eruption imaginable.

"If you want to get out of here," I said slowly, "you will need to release that body. Do that, and I will open a portal to send you back."

"Never!" rasped the phonos finally. "Never! If I cannot kill anyone else, I can at least hold this body. If you want it free, you will have to meet my demand."

"And what exactly is that demand?" I asked, though I already knew.

"I have come for your life. Give that to me, and I will leave the body. Even more, I will leave your world."

"What's so special about my life? I've never heard of a phonos caring who it killed."

"I have been sent. He who sent me would have you dead."

"And who is that?" Yeah, Alex had already told me Ares was responsible, but I wanted to see how the phonos would respond, and I needed to gather energy for another portal opening.

"What matters who sent me?" shouted the phonos. "I will have your life, or I will keep this body forever."

"Suit yourself," I said flatly.

"I'll be back, Alex!" I thought to him, but I didn't believe he heard me that time. Well, that couldn't be helped. Unlike the faeries, I wasn't a natural flier; I had to expend magic constantly to stay airborne, just as I did to accelerate to faerie speed. Opening portals was even more energy intensive, and that very fast opening I had just pulled off at the school was far more draining than normal. I didn't want to leave Alex hanging, but I needed to get back home and gather reinforcements before I got too worn out to do it—or worse, dropped out of the air and got impaled on the phonos's sword point. I conjured a portal, this time in midair, so the phonos couldn't reach it, and I threw myself through it as fast as I could, with the creature's screams echoing in my ears.

Normally, I would have connected the portal to my bedroom at home to minimize the risk of either the portal or my reappearance being seen, but I didn't have the luxury of doing that this time. Instead, I popped back into our world in Nurse Florence's office.

"Tal, what you are doing?" she practically hissed. "I know it's late, but there are still some people on campus who—"

Cutting her off abruptly, I said, "Emergency! Listen now; scold later." Immediately, Nurse Florence switched modes and let me outline the situation.

"That poor boy!" she said when I was done. "He must be so frightened."

"He's hanging in," I replied, somewhat impatiently. "The bigger problem is what to do with the phonos—oh, and the sword that apparently can disintegrate anything it touches."

Nurse Florence frowned, looking far less like the confident woman I could always count on than usual. "I studied magic artifacts pretty extensively during my training with the Order, and I don't remember any reference to a sword of chaos. It seems a contradiction. How could anyone, even someone as gifted as Hephaestus, get the force of chaos into a definable shape like a sword?"

"I take it that the Greek gods actually exist, then?" I said, already knowing the answer.

"Beings the Greeks worshiped as gods, anyway. The specialists in the Order typically refer to them as Olympians. Yes, they exist, though the Order has no record of any recent contact between them and any mortals. I can tell you more later, but as you said, this is an emergency, so we'd better work out a plan to deal with it."

Yeah, deal with a sword of chaos flung into our world by the Greek god of war. Just another typical day in the life of Taliesin Weaver!

"Any suggestions?" I asked finally.

"Trying to physically contain the sword is out, obviously. Based on what you told me about the portal collapsing, I would guess the sword can't be contained magically either."

"Right, the best we can do there is stay out of its way until we get it away from Alex, uh, from the phonos. I'm more worried about how to get the phonos out of Alex."

"You said Jimmie had some luck with putting Alex back in control of his own body."

"Yeah, but only for a few seconds. The phonos is strong enough to take on both Alex and Jimmie at the same time."

"Maybe, but perhaps the phonos is not strong enough to take all of us on."

I shook my head quickly. "I can't bring the guys into this. They can't just fly away if something goes wrong."

"Neither can I," said Nurse Florence, raising an eyebrow. "Were you contemplating using me as a human sacrifice?" she asked with a mischievous smile.

"I can hold one other person up in the air. Stan and I have practiced it, so I know. I've never tried levitating a large group, though. Jimmie *can* fly, so he's in no danger, but the other guys would be vulnerable. Well, Khalid could probably jump high enough and far enough to stay away from the phonos, but Khalid's too impulsive. The three of us will have to be enough."

"I'm pretty sure Carla can fly now," said Nurse Florence gently. "She has less training than you do, at least in this life, but her power level is quite high." She hesitated for a moment and then added, "Tal, I wouldn't bring her up, but we may need her."

I guess it was too much to get through a whole day, even in the middle of a crisis, without some reference to my fake-but-wants-to-be-more-than-fake girlfriend.

OK, so Carla's situation wasn't her fault. She didn't even know magic existed when she accidentally cast a love spell on me. And it certainly wasn't her fault when she became an aware reincarnate like Stan and me. It especially wasn't her fault that the past personality that took over when she first awakened was the evil sorceress, Alcina, or that the only way to suppress Alcina was the very use of dark magic that nearly cost me my soul and everyone else their lives.

Yeah, none of it was her fault. But, damn it, it wasn't mine either! That didn't make me any less stuck with the consequences. Carla's parents and her little brother Gianni still thought we were boyfriend and girl-friend, at least until we could figure out a way to let them down gently, especially Gianni, who looked at me as a big brother. Going through that

masquerade shouldn't have been painful—Carla was drop-dead gor-
geous—except that Carla wanted us to end up together and made no effort to conceal her desire. I was stuck constantly reminding her about my
feelings for Eva, feelings about which Carla was in total denial. Our "relationship" was like a sword with no hilt; it cut no matter how I tried to
hold it. Every time I was nice to Carla, I felt as if I was just leading her
on, but every time I was blunt with her, I felt guilty. The worst part was
that I could almost see Carla's point: Eva had made it clear that she wasn't
interested in me romantically. Carla and I *were* friends, and even when
not under a spell, we had undeniable sexual chemistry, so why not give a
real relationship a try?

"Tal..." prompted Nurse Florence. She was being as gentle as she
could, and she was right. Like it or not, it didn't make sense to leave a
sorceress as powerful as Carla out of a mission when we had no idea how
much power we needed.

"Of course she can come," I said, a little proud of myself for not
sounding too grudging. "Why don't you summon her here, and I'll find
Jimmie..."

"No need—I found you," said Jimmie, giggling as he materialized. "Tal," he continued in a more serious tone. "I was worried. Why
didn't you take me with you?"

"Sorry, buddy, I had to move fast. You're coming with us now,
though. I'll fill you in."

While I was explaining the plan to Jimmie, Nurse Florence sent
out a psychic message to Carla, who said she'd be over immediately. Unfortunately, that meant by car. Like me, Carla could travel across great
distances by using a portal to go to Alcina's island and then creating a
second portal connected to a different spot in our world. However, going
to Alcina's island by herself was too dangerous with the phonos there, so
we waited nervously until she finally arrived.

As soon as she stepped into the nurse's office, I regretted saying
she could come. I knew she was wearing that overly tight black dress for
my benefit. I was probably the only guy on campus who would have ob-
jected to seeing her in it. Would it kill her to wear something a little looser
once in a while?

I knew she couldn't read minds the way I could, but I buried my
feelings as deeply as possible just in case and briefed her. She hung on my
every word and then assured me she would do everything she could. I

knew she would, too, yet another complication—she was a genuinely nice person who deserved better than I was ever going to be able to give her.

Once we were all ready, I sang us all into the most highly magically energized state we could attain, floated Nurse Florence and me, opened a portal connected to the air above the phonos's last known location, and shepherded everyone through.

The phonos had not moved. It was staring at us through Alex's eyes. If looks could kill, we would all have died instantly. Fortunately, the phonos was not that powerful. The sword, still flickering and radiating a kind of negative light, was another matter.

Wasting no time, I connected the four of us psychically for the attack to come and then attempted to link all of us to Alex. Unluckily for him, I succeeded immediately.

Unluckily, because he was visualizing Carla at that particular moment and picturing her naked, picturing her so emphatically that the image carried across the link to all of us.

Awkward!

"Uh, I thought I said focus on someone you love, not someone you lust after," I thought to him, trying to use as light a tone as possible. He blushed, his red cheeks looking out of place on a face twisted by the phonos's hatred.

"Sorry, I didn't mean…"

"It happens to all of us, dude."

"Actually, I'll take it as a compliment," Carla thought to him before I realized she was going to. She was trying to be nice, but I knew he would be even more embarrassed to realize that she had also seen what he was thinking. Sure enough, his cheeks got even redder.

"If we're done with the introductions, we need to act quickly," thought the usually more sensitive Nurse Florence. Alex's cheeks had gone totally crimson. It was going to take him a long time to get over this embarrassment.

"Yes, right away," I thought to all of them, knowing Alex would be the most willing of any of us to change the subject. *"Alex, since I take it you haven't been able to focus on someone you love, we'll have to move to plan B. I have Jimmie and me psychically linked to Carla and Nurse Florence. We'll each focus on the people we love, pour the resulting energy into you, and through you it will hit the phonos. With any luck, that heavy a jolt will stun*

it and let us remove it; if we're really lucky, we might even force it out com-
pletely."

"*OK,*" Alex thought. "*What do I need to do?*"

"*Just concentrate on staying connected to me. The phonos may try to
break the link.*" I could tell he didn't know what I meant, but he had been
able to stay with me before, and the phonos was bound to act if we waited
much longer, so I had to start and hope that Alex would take care of his
part of the plan.

My focus was Eva. I thought about the future I wanted with her
and might never have, and my aching love for her poured into the link. I
knew Carla would know and would be hurt, but it wasn't as if I hadn't
been honest with her.

In fact, Carla, far from being distracted, poured her love for me
into the link, wave after wave of overwhelming passion, naked feelings
that longed to find expression in naked bodies and never would.

I felt an urgent warning from Nurse Florence and knew that we
were getting off focus, that unrequited love might generate sorrow the
phonos could feed on. I forcibly suppressed my thoughts of Eva and focused instead on my parents, who had always been there for me, even
during the insanity of the last four years. Carla took the hint and, though
I could still feel echoes of her feelings for me, she was now using her parents and Gianni as a focus. Jimmie had already focused on Dan, me, and
his parents. Nurse Florence focused on us and on the other members of
our strange band, particularly the uncanny, almost familial closeness
among us, a closeness the other three of us quickly echoed. As our feelings
flowed back and forth, they harmonized, becoming a virtual symphony
both to family and to friendship.

Once we were all properly focused, it took us only seconds to
achieve the energy we needed. Then I let the energy flow—no, flood—
through the link and into Alex. The phonos, as long as it stayed within
him, would be hit by the same emotions Alex was feeling. To him they
were soothing. To the phonos…not so much.

It screamed, but not at me this time. It just screamed, so loudly I
began to fear damage to Alex's vocal chords, but we had to keep going,
keep feeding it positive energy it had no way to process, no way to ignore,
no way to survive.

I was just beginning to wonder how long we could keep this attack up if the phonos kept resisting, when the creature exploded out of

the sword and out of Alex, who fell to the ground, momentarily stunned but otherwise OK physically, at least as far as I could tell.

The writhing phonos could now have flown at us and launched a magical attack. Instead it was struggling back into physical form, perhaps intending to take out its anger on the defenseless Alex.

We were still focusing our love into magical energy, so I had the team visualize the phonos captured, held by golden cords of our affection, and incapacitated. That tactic produced mixed results. We got a grip on the creature very quickly, but it was thrashing so much the grip was not solid, and the thing was still too close to Alex for me to be happy about the situation. We were tiring, and one slip would let the creature fling itself on Alex, who was not exactly combat ready.

"Tal, how can I help?" Alex yelled, sounding shaky but now at least fully conscious. I glanced in his direction and saw that he had managed to get back on his feet.

"Alex, just stay out of the way!" I yelled back. I knew why he wanted to help, and I probably should have explained why he couldn't, but I didn't dare lessen my focus on the murderous spirit, still struggling, still waiting for any minor slip it could exploit.

"*Tal!*" Nurse Florence's warning made me glance back at Alex, who was awkwardly raising the sword of chaos to strike at the phonos. I could see he was no swordsman, and if he hit the psychic energy we were using to hold the phonos, he might just set it free.

"Don't!" I yelled, but Alex had already raised the sword to strike, and given the beating his scrawny arm muscles must have taken while the phonos was controlling him, the blade came down despite my warning. By some miracle it missed hitting our ropes of energy and actually struck the creature, who abandoned his effort to be physical as the sword began to tear him apart. When the phonos dematerialized, Alex lost his grip on the sword, which plunged point first into the soil.

I would have liked to keep track of the phonos, still dangerous as a spirit that might try to repossess Alex, but now we had a new problem: the sword apparently didn't need a wielder to send out its chaotic energies. It rent the ground into which it had plunged, digging ever deeper and sending jumbled elements spraying out in all directions. Fortunately, Alex managed to stumble out of the way of the potentially flesh ripping spray. It took me a few seconds to realize how dangerous the situations was. Alcina's island, its substance created by magic in the first place and not renewed magically in hundreds of years, seemed more vulnerable to the sword's power than ordinary matter. That was the only explanation I could think of for the sword's rapid rending of the ground and for the way the destruction spread over a much larger area than I would have thought a sword moving straight down into the soil could possibly have generated.

I shot downward, attempting to grab the hilt while it was still in reach, simultaneously singing a defensive spell to ward off the spray.

"Don't touch it!" thought Carla urgently. *"It's unstable. You could end up being controlled the way Alex was."*

"I'm not Alex," I said, realizing too late Alex might pick up that thought and take it as a put-down. Well, time to worry about his feelings in a minute, once I had retrieved the sword.

I was about to grab the hilt when Nurse Florence shouted mentally, *"Tal, Carla's right. We have to think through this."*

"While the sword destroys the whole island?" I asked, hovering above the spreading cataclysm the sword was creating in what had once been solid ground. I just wanted to grab that sword hilt and stop the destruction. I wanted to feel that metal in my hand with all my heart and soul—but Nurse Florence had spooked me just enough that I held back. *"Anyway, it was the phonos, not the sword itself, that was controlling Alex."*

"And it could be back any time," Carla reminded us. *"It got away, remember? And from what you said, it can't leave this plane of existence."*

"Some of that vapor is poisonous," insisted Nurse Florence, *"and some of it may even be explosive. One good spark from the chaos, and the whole thing will blow. Back off now."*

I reluctantly flew back up to where Carla, Jimmie, and Nurse Florence floated. Then I remembered Alex, whose connection to us had been replaced by a throbbing emptiness. I looked back down and saw him near the fountaining chaos, seemingly oblivious to it. "Alex, you're standing too close," I yelled to him. "The whole mess could explode! Run!"

He started walking away from the ever-expanding disaster, then abruptly looked at me and tried to shout back. It sounded as if he was trying to tell me he knew how to stop the sword, but I couldn't really be sure over the growing sound of anarchy claiming the island. More important, he seemed dazed and didn't appear to realize how close the waves of destruction were to him. After getting Carla to hold Nurse Florence, I reached out with my mind and grabbed Alex. Tired as I was fast becoming, I knew he needed to be off the ground, and I pulled him up to where we were.

"What you got, Alex?" I asked as soon as he was close enough for me to hear him. At first I thought his sudden flight might have been the last straw and caused him to shut down on us, but then he pulled himself together.

"That sword is just one small piece of chaos. Chaos was as vast as the universe in the beginning, at least according to the Greeks. It was still overcome, though. It was overcome by Eros…by love incarnate, who extracted order from the chaos."

Why hadn't I thought of that? "Alex, that's brilliant! Guys, can we use that idea to neutralize the sword?"

"Imagining love surrounding it, forcing the chaos within the sword to stay confined inside it might do the trick," replied Nurse Florence. "You've never tried that, but no one I know can improvise better than you can with magic."

"Well, it's either try or let the whole place disintegrate," said Carla. "And it is such a convenient place!"

How true! I was still banned from opening portals into Annwn as Nurse Florence could, so using the island was the only way I could travel quickly. It was also a great place to practice magic with no chance of being seen. Aside from that, if the island were completely destroyed, such a catastrophe might have repercussions in other worlds. Anyway, we might as well try Alex's suggestion; in the absence of a better plan, we had nothing to lose.

"Everyone else is still wired for collaboration. Alex, take my hand!" Now alert, he grabbed my hand immediately. His felt cold and clammy in mine, but after what he had been through, I was surprised it wasn't shaking.

At that point we were rocked by the explosion Nurse Florence had predicted, but we managed to ascend fast enough to avoid the blast of dirt, rocks, and fire. We needed to work even faster if we wanted to have any real chance of implementing Alex's idea.

The biggest problem was Alex himself. I didn't mean to pry into his private thoughts, but in the process of linking to him, it became painfully apparent to me that his problem wasn't focus. He just didn't know whether he loved anyone—and on some level, he wasn't sure anyone, not even his parents, loved him. That put him in an emotional place that made it impossible for him to help implement his own idea, except as a source of raw energy. I could, and did, draw on him, borrowing his strength to help fuel the rest of us, but the emotions we used did not come from him at all.

The four of us visualized our love as a gigantic hand that reached down into the elemental maelstrom, grasping at the sword. It fought back, somehow evading the hand, but we persisted, and eventually we caught it. However, that was just the beginning. As if the sword had a mind of its own, it kept trying to squirm away, its chaos softening the hand of our love, weakening its grip, and compelling us to constantly reinforce that grip.

Finally we managed a firm grasp and held tightly onto the sword. Then we extracted the sword from the confusion that quickly subsided without the power of chaos to fuel it. Even then the sword kept up the struggle, every bit as persistent as the phonos that had inhabited it, but we were equally tenacious, and in the end we won. Maintaining an adamantine grip, we shrunk the hand smaller and smaller but kept it just as strong. Finally the hand became a thin but unbreakable coating around the sword, neutralizing this small piece of chaos as the Greeks had once believed Love brought order from a chaotic universe.

Well, Alex might not have had love to contribute, but we could have failed without the energy he lent. As it was, we were all exhausted. Carla and I got everyone safely to the ground and then nearly lay down on the debris field right next to an enormous crater created by the explosion. As it was, Carla leaned on me for support. I couldn't really complain this time—I was leaning on her, too. It did beat falling on my face. Jimmie was standing but looked much more transparent than usual, as if he were too tired to manifest completely. Nurse Florence found a semi-comfortable spot in the rubble and sat down, looking as worn out as I had ever seen her.

After a while I looked over at Alex, who appeared barely conscious and even paler than usual. "You all right?" I asked him. "We're a little more…used to this kind of thing than you are."

"I'm OK," he replied, trying to sound casual, as if this kind of thing happened to him every day. Carla and I slowly walked over in his direction, still holding on to each other. Despite the beating Alex had taken, first from possession by the phonos and then from our magic working, he looked as if he was smiling a little.

Since Alex seemed to be in a decent mood, I figured now might be as good a time as any to try to get a better understanding of what had happened. "Tell me more about how Ares approached you," I said as Carla and I sat down next to him. Jimmie, already looking a bit more solid, hovered nearby. With some effort, Nurse Florence also moved closer to us, even though her movements were very slow and stiff, making her seem much older than she actually was. Alex seemed pleased by our attention. Given what I'd seen in his mind, that didn't surprise me.

The tale he told would have been unbelievable to most people, but to someone like me, it seemed pretty much like everything else that had happened to me over the last four years. Apparently, Ares communicated with Alex by appearing in Alex's copy of the *Iliad*.

As Alex talked, I began to form a theory about why the Olympians had not had much contact with humans for so many centuries. Alex described Ares as being drained by even a short conversation and mentioned other times at which he now believed Ares had tried to communicate with him and failed. Not only that, but Ares, without actually admitting any weakness, made it clear that he thought I posed some great threat to his destiny and offered to give Alex a special sword if Alex would use it to kill me. As if all of that wasn't enough, Ares warned Alex that the only help the war god could give would be the sword; once Ares had sent that into our world, he would not be able to manifest his power here for many days.

If Alex's account was accurate, the reason the Olympians did not intervene in human affairs much was clear: they lacked the strength to do so. Why that was the case, however, still remained a mystery.

I was too exhausted to read Alex's mind at this point, even if I had wanted to, but his description of events gave away more, not only about Ares but about himself, than I thought he intended. For instance, Alex didn't seem to have anyone to socialize with and clearly spent most of his free time in the library. No wonder Ares spoke to him through a book!

Alex's story also made me realize he resented me for something. Ares didn't pick him at random, and though Alex said he went down to the parking lot to warn me, that was the one part of his story I doubted.

On some level, he wanted to hurt me, not help me—of that I was reasonably sure. I was also sure he felt sorry now, but that didn't change the fact that he had entertained the possibility, even if only slightly. I did believe him, though, when he said the sword had suddenly appeared in his hand and that he couldn't get rid of it once he had it.

Was Alex a murderer? No...but he did seem like someone who could be easily manipulated.

"Well, that explains how the phonos got into our world; Ares must have let it in," said Nurse Florence quietly after Alex finished his story.

"It doesn't explain why Ares is so hostile to me," I pointed out. "As the original Taliesin, I never even came close to interacting with him." I strained a little to access my ancient Greek knowledge. The lives before Taliesin were always harder to remember. Finally, though, those memories became distinct. "I didn't have any contact with him when I was with Alexander either, though there were times when Ares was nearby. By that time the Olympians were already not interacting much with mortals."

Alex looked completely confused.

"I don't mean you, Alex. I was talking about Alexander the Great."

"You don't want to tell him too much!" interrupted Nurse Florence sharply.

"It won't matter," I replied quickly, already knowing what we would have to do at the end of the conversation. Even the briefest mental contact with Nurse Florence was painful, but I managed to confirm she agreed with me without having to ask the question in front of Alex. Then I turned my attention back to him.

"I...I guess you could say I'm living proof that reincarnation exists. I was with Alexander the Great in a previous life. I was also with King Arthur as his bard, Taliesin. That's where I get my magic and a few other things. When I was twelve, I first started remembering those past lives and many, many others."

"That's when you were in the hospital?" Alex asked.

"Did you know me then?" I asked, trying not to sound as puzzled as I felt.

"I've known you since kindergarten," Alex said, attempting to sound indifferent but not succeeding in covering his disappointment. I nodded, though it was a little hard to believe he had really known me all that time.

"Anyway, Alex," I continued, "you're right. At first I had trouble coping with all those memories. My parents and the doctors all thought I was going nuts. Fortunately, I learned how to control, how to use, that flow of information."

"Tal isn't the only one with an...interesting past history," added Carla. "I was once the sorceress Alcina, half-sister to King Arthur. That's why I can also use magic."

Alex gawked for a moment and then looked at Nurse Florence inquisitively. "Who were you...in your earlier lives?"

"I don't know," she said. Alex might not have noticed, but I was pretty sure the terse answer was Nurse Florence being overly cautious about how much she shared, really a pointless worry under the circumstances.

"Nurse Florence is a member of the Order of the Ladies of the Lake," I explained. "She may have been someone with power in one of her past lives, but there is no easy way to tell that. People like Carla and me are...accidents."

"If you can call someone using dark magic on you an accident," said Carla.

"Well," began Jimmie, sounding a little irritated that Alex hadn't asked about him. "I'm Dan Stevens's brother, and I wasn't anyone special in a previous life, at least not that I know of. I'm just dead, waiting for—"

"That's enough, Jimmie," snapped Carla. Alex must have been puzzled that Carla, who had just shared so much, didn't want Jimmie sharing anything. Then I felt a pang of guilt when I realized what she was doing was protecting me. She didn't want Alex to know I was the one whose stubbornness was keeping Jimmie from moving on.

"Thanks for everything you did, Alex," I said, standing up abruptly...and just a bit shakily. Alex looked a little alarmed, as if he didn't want the conversation to come to an end.

"Wait!" Alex insisted. "What about me? I know what makes each of you special, but why did Ares approach me?"

Nurse Florence cleared her throat in a preemptive way.

"We may as well tell him. He won't remember anyway," I said. A second later, I realized I'd said too much. Trying to cover my fatigue slip, I just kept talking, doing my best to ignore the fact that Alex's eyes had narrowed in suspicion.

"Alex, we don't know. This kind of intervention by one of the Olympians is very, very unusual. Actually, your story gives us a possible explanation for the rarity of their visits; if what Ares told you is true, the Olympians now seem to have difficulty manifesting their power in our world. We can't be sure yet, but that would certainly explain why they've hardly interacted with any human in the last two thousand years, as far as we know."

"I get that what happened is not very common," said Alex quickly, "but that doesn't explain why it happened to *me*."

I was so tired by that point that I felt like just telling him I didn't have a clue. That seemed mean, though, especially after all he had been through, so I took a stab at an explanation.

"Alex, I've sometimes wondered the same thing about events in my life. In my experience, when something like this happens, no matter how random it appears to be at first, there is always a reason.

"Ares clearly has some motive for wanting me dead, but that's part of a puzzle we can't even begin to put together right now. As for your role in all this, well, that might be a littler simpler to figure out. From what you've told us, you're interested in Greek mythology and have been for years. That might make you more receptive to Ares, and the fact that you go to my school would have made it logical to approach you.

"That isn't enough by itself; at least I don't think it is. If I'm right, and the Olympians have a hard time making their will felt on earth these days, Ares would have needed something unusual to help him make a link with our world; it's pretty hard to imagine that just your taste in reading would be enough. There are two possible ways, though, in which you might be a stronger candidate for connection with Ares than just your interest in mythology. You could be the reincarnation of someone close to Ares in the past. I've had enough experience to know how much a past life could draw the attention of supernatural forces. Alternatively, you could be a descendant of Ares. You're Greek, after all, and you know how the Greek gods are portrayed as having sex with mortals on a fairly regular basis..."

I don't think I had ever seen anything quite like Alex's facial expression at that moment. There was elation, as if I had just told him he had been selected as a member of a very exclusive club. At the same time, there was still that hint of suspicion in his eyes.

"Tal, what did you mean when you said I wouldn't remember anyway?" Well, there it was—the one question I didn't want to answer.

"Alex, we appreciate everything you did. If you hadn't resisted the phonos so well—"

"Answer me!" he interrupted rudely, though I couldn't really blame him for that.

"I am answering you," I replied, drawing on the more authoritative tone of the original Taliesin so that I might get the whole explanation out. That would be hard enough even without interruptions.

"If you hadn't resisted the phonos so well," I continued, "innocent people might have died. And if you hadn't figured out so quickly how to neutralize the sword of chaos, it might have destroyed the whole island, maybe even us with it. It isn't that we don't appreciate all that you've done, but..."

"But you're going to make me forget the whole thing?" he blurted out angrily. How could I possibly make him understand?

"There are...rules in this kind of situation. The rulers of Annwn, the Celtic Otherworld, are very picky about ordinary mortals not finding out too much about them...or me, now. They don't want to risk people in general finding out that they really exist."

"But didn't you just say I might not be an ordinary mortal?" Alex asked, sounding more than a little desperate, like someone who had just gotten an acceptance letter from Harvard, then the next day another one telling him the first letter had been a mistake.

"He has a point," said Jimmie.

"The average person would probably lose consciousness completely under the attack of a phonos," I conceded. Maybe Alex was unusual...but he was definitely unusually troubled, and we did have more than our share of problems to solve already.

"We can't take the chance, Tal!" cut in Nurse Florence very abruptly. "I had to maneuver quite a bit to sell the idea that you should be able to tell your own mother. There is no way I can sell revealing everything to a complete stranger..."

"I am not a stranger!" Alex yelled. "I've known Tal for years!" I wanted to respond but had no idea what to say. Nurse Florence, however, was not so tongue-tied.

"How well have you known him?" she snapped. "His own father can't be told who Tal really is. We only won the argument about his mother because she's now psychic and would have found out anyway."

Alex started to protest, but Nurse Florence cut him off. "I only know because I'm a Lady of the Lake. Carla knows because she, like Tal, is the reincarnation of someone who already knew about Annwn. Jimmie doesn't count as a mortal, obviously, and there is no way to erase his memories. Every single person who knows the truth about Tal either would have figured it out anyway or has a reason to know. You have no reason!" I couldn't remember ever hearing Nurse Florence take such a harsh tone with anyone, except perhaps Morgan le Fay.

Alex opened his mouth but then closed it again. After the ordeal he had been through, I was half expecting him to just faint or something.

"Perhaps there is a way..." I began gently. Immediately, I regretted those words. I was trying to find a way to let Alex down easily, but it was clear from Alex's expression that what I had done was give him false hope, doubtless because I was thinking and paused long enough at that point that he thought that was the end of a sentence. I had been going to finish with something like, "to help Alex understand the situation better, so he can accept it," but I never got the chance to finish.

"How can you possibly even consider..." started Nurse Florence.

"Hear me out!" I said in my best original Taliesin tone, and Nurse Florence desisted, at least for the moment. At that point I could have finished my original sentence, perhaps given Alex a vision of the future if we let him keep his memories or maybe even convinced him that forgetting what he knew was for the best. If I had done that, the rest of the conversation would have gone very differently. Unfortunately, I looked at Alex before I continued, and he was looking at me with so much hope, so much...desperation, that saying what I had originally intended seemed like kicking a puppy. I had enough of that feeling already with Carla and Jimmie. I couldn't give them what they wanted. Maybe I could find a way to give Alex what he wanted. Yeah, he was a little creepy, and I wasn't sure he would be trustworthy, but he had fought the phonos pretty hard. Maybe becoming part of our group would help him overcome his problems.

"If Alex is a descendant of Ares, perhaps the rulers of Annwn will see him as an exceptional case. And if he becomes one of my...warriors, they certainly will."

"There are those in Annwn who already think you have recruited too many ordinary humans into your group," cautioned Nurse Florence.

"I think there may be a limit to how many times that card can be played. Besides, you know Gwynn warned us not to add anyone else after you refused to erase the memories of the student 'civilians' who were with us on Samhain."

"They stood by us and risked their lives," I replied firmly. "After that they have a right to those memories. Gwynn accepted that idea. Come to think of it, Alex fits in the same category."

"He didn't have much choice," pointed out Nurse Florence, "not with the phonos inside him."

"He could have given in to it, though, and he didn't. I think Gwynn would appreciate the strength of character he showed. By the way," I said, turning to Alex, "that's Gwynn ap Nudd, king of the Welsh faeries and one of the rulers of Annwn. Anyway," I said, turning back to Nurse Florence, "it can't hurt to ask."

"It's not Gwynn I'm worried about. Gwynn knows you and likes you. It's the other rulers whose reactions should concern us. But let's say, just for the sake of argument, that we take the time to run this by Gwynn. What are you going to do with Alex in the meantime? We can't very well leave him here, and if we take him back home, he might tell someone else about us."

"That's simple enough. I can bury his memories of this time rather than erasing them outright. If we get permission to include him, I can dig them up again. If not, I can erase them then."

"Can't what I know just be a secret among us?" asked Alex, his desperation becoming more obvious. For whatever reason, he had an enormous emotional investment in becoming one of us. That made me feel I was right to want to include him, but it also troubled me. Was he stable enough to endure what we endured on a daily basis?

"Why do you have to tell this Gwynn—or anyone else?" Alex demanded.

I looked at Alex, wishing very hard that he would just shut the hell up. Clearly, I could advocate for him better than he could for himself.

"Gwynn has done a lot for us," I said. "I won't be dishonest with him."

"What if I don't allow you to meddle with my memories?" Alex asked, his tone shifting ominously from desperate to belligerent. "Aren't there...rules about that?"

I hesitated but only for a moment. "Dude, I don't like this any better than you do, but don't live by any code that prevents me from protecting me and my friends from discovery—and from the wrath of Annwn. I promise I will do what I can to let you keep these memories, but I cannot promise I'll succeed."

I could see something die in Alex's eyes in that moment. Hope, perhaps. I didn't know. What I did find out very quickly was that this conversation should have waited until we were all better rested. If I had been able to sense what was going on as well as I normally could, I would have realized that when Alex jumped up awkwardly and tried to run, he was not just running away; he was in fact trying to get to the sword.

As it was, none of us realized what he was up to until he had actually grabbed the sword from where it lay on the ground and started waving it at us. He grimaced in pain; probably his muscles had been pushed to the breaking point already by the phonos, and it was a wonder he could even hold the blade—but hold it he did and with a fairly good imitation of menace.

"You will not touch my memories!" he yelled, so shrilly that it was really more like a whine.

"*He's obviously unstable. We can't even consider leaving him his memories now…*" thought Nurse Florence. I was used to dealing with people who acted impulsively, myself included. Khalid and Jimmie both came to mind…but they impulsively put themselves in harm's way; they didn't threaten people they wanted to claim as friends. No, definitely Alex was too big a risk to add to the group.

"Alex," I said with affected calm, "put down the sword. You don't really want to do this." Carla, Nurse Florence, and Jimmie all moved in different directions, knowing that Alex might need to be restrained. Unfortunately, Alex also realized what they were doing, and with what was probably his last strength, he thrust the sword into the ground.

I cringed, knowing we no longer had the strength to keep the sword from destroying the island, but of course absolutely nothing happened. Alex had forgotten his own plan to neutralize the sword, and he had no way to break the coating of love that now enveloped the weapon. At first the truth didn't register on him. When it did, he fell down sobbing.

I didn't think Alex posed a threat at this point, but just in case, Carla and I sung him to sleep. It was a good thing he was so weak, because the two of us together could barely manage such a simple working.

We had no choice but to give ourselves a few hours to rest. Nurse Florence didn't have a date with Coach Miller that night, so no one would notice she wasn't around. My mom knew to cover with my dad if I mysteriously didn't show up. Carla's family would assume she was with me and smile indulgently. You would have thought a strict Italian family would have had more concerns about their daughter "carrying on" with a guy they didn't know very well, but they thought of me as a perfect gentleman. They were right to think I was no threat to their daughter's virtue, though they had the reason wrong.

That just left Alex. We carried him up to Alcina's palace, which we had reprovisioned for just such an emergency, and after we had eaten and rested a little, I probed Alex just enough to pick up some details we could use. As it turned out, Alex was pretty hostile to his parents because of their belief he needed therapy. He almost certainly did need therapy, though I could understand his resistance to it. His way of showing his unhappiness was to sometimes come home late…very late. They weren't happy, but as long as he came home in one piece, they didn't ask too many questions. He had taken to climbing into his bedroom window in an effort to avoid having to talk when he got home. That, too, they tolerated…for the moment. I couldn't believe that could go on for very long before his parents got fed up. However, the fact that it was currently happening would make it easy for us to slip him into the house, still asleep, without anyone being the wiser.

Wiping out his memories and getting back to our plane of existence were both more challenging. The first required considerable skill. We needed to erase exactly the right parts and substitute plausible fake memories, neither of which was easy in a state not far removed from total exhaustion. The second required considerable skill *and* a high power level. Even with several hours rest, I didn't feel as if I had either the skill or the power level. Anyone who might have helped was in a different plane, and making contact would have required a fair amount of energy, too. We should have had a good night's sleep, but from what I could glean from Alex's mind, his parents would freak out if he was not home by midnight. My dad would probably freak out, too, and the Rinaldis might begin to doubt my gentlemanliness.

Carla saved the day. Once she had gotten enough rest to clear her head, she reminded us of Alcina's uncanny command of sea creatures. Like me, Carla could draw on the powers of her magical ancestor, and so summoning sea life was something Carla could do with comparatively little effort. We walked down to the seashore, and she drew to us a vast group of dolphins, creatures with enough intellect to have the kind of energy we needed to recharge. We could draw on them as we had often drawn on each other. Unlike the way Alcina would have handled such a situation, Carla gave them a choice, and they chose to help. We took just enough energy to make Alex's mental adjustments and then to get ourselves back to our world, and we left the dolphins sleeping peacefully.

By the time we reappeared in Nurse Florence's office, it was nearly midnight, and we still had the sleeping Alex to return home. It would have been nice to open a portal straight into his bedroom, but none of us had been there, so we had to settle for more mundane methods: Nurse Florence drove us to his house, and Jimmie, Carla, and I did the rest. It took some doing to drag Alex, still asleep, through his window and get him into bed without having his parents walk in on us, especially since we hardly had the juice left for even one decent spell among the three of us. Nonetheless, we had a rare moment of luck and pulled off the "insertion." We even made our escape undetected.

Back in Nurse Florence's old Chevrolet, I just wanted to sleep, but there was one more conversation we needed to have. "We need to keep an eye on Alex," I said quietly. "He's in a bad way."

"What was your first clue?" asked Carla lightly. "Was it his threatening us with the sword of chaos, or are you just jealous that we caught him picturing me naked?"

"No, every guy in the school pictures you naked," I replied.

"Well, every guy but one," she responded. The words matched our earlier banter, but the tone had a touch of sadness in it. I was too tired to deal with any more drama, so I just pushed on.

"Seriously, we need to help him somehow. I think there's a decent guy in him, but that guy's suffocating in loneliness."

"I'll keep an eye on him," said Nurse Florence, "but we have a more pressing problem."

"Don't we always?" said Jimmie sulkily.

"Carla," Nurse Florence continued, "Alex's image of you seemed rather…vivid. I don't mean to be indelicate, but is there any possibility he's actually seen you naked?"

Carla didn't answer for a few seconds. "Unless he has the technological know-how to install a hidden camera in the girls' locker room, I don't really see how he could have."

"Was the image...accurate?" asked Nurse Florence.

"Well, now that you mention it, I didn't think about it at the time, but, yeah, for someone who has presumably never seen me, the image was...creepily accurate."

"Are you saying Alex is some kind of psychic peeping tom?" I asked. "I didn't sense any particular psychic ability, and I doubt he'd know enough to hide it from me."

It took Nurse Florence a while to reply—never a good sign. Finally, she said, "I don't want to worry you unnecessarily, but it's not Alex I'm thinking about. It's Ares. Alex told us Ares tried to bribe him into agreeing to kill you. What's a better bribe for a teenage boy than...sex?"

"Ares was trying to bribe Alex with me?" asked Carla, suddenly pale.

"Think about it. Ares has a conversation with Alex, which Alex told us was intended to convince him to kill Tal. Shortly after, Alex knows exactly what you look like naked. He didn't make the connection for us, but I think it has to have been there."

"Which means Ares has been watching for some time," I said wearily. It would occasionally be nice to solve one problem without having three more sprout up in its place.

"I'm afraid so. Alex was no random choice. Ares picked up on the same thing you did, Tal. Alex is a troubled young man, someone Ares could realistically think might kill you. That means Ares was watching him. And Ares's fixation with you and the threat you allegedly pose suggests he has been watching you as well, maybe watching all of us.

"What makes this particular situation troubling is how atypical it is. The Olympians seem to have a much harder time reaching our world than the faeries do, just as Tal suggested. Yet Ares seems to have established a much stronger connection with Alex than he should have been able to. Tal, your theory about that is promising, but we need to find out for sure why Ares was able to manifest so strongly, and if he has found a new pathway into this world, we need to block it. Otherwise, you will continue to be in danger."

"Am I ever out of danger?" I asked jokingly.

"I'm serious!" said Nurse Florence firmly. "Our top priority needs to be solving this mystery. I wish I had put two and two together earlier, before we erased Alex's memories; we might have found some useful details there."

At that point Nurse Florence pulled up in front of Carla's house, yet another Spanish Colonial Revival structure that looked suspiciously like my house. Actually, anyone looking around good old Santa Brígida would discover that all the houses were built on the same basic plan.

"My mom's watching," said Carla quickly. "Get out and walk me to the door."

Wearily, I dragged myself out of the car and put my arm around Carla, and together we shuffled toward her front porch, trying not to look drunk, which in our current fatigued condition would be an easy mistake for her parents to make.

When we reached the front steps, Carla turned to me and gave me a fervent good-bye kiss that I knew she wasn't faking.

"Carla," I whispered into her ear, "it's time to think about how best to ease your family out of the idea that we're boyfriend and girlfriend."

Yeah, I should have waited until a time when we both weren't exhausted. Carla jerked back as if I had slapped her across the face.

"Tal, I can't even think about that right now! Anyway, you can't leave me at a time like this. I have to cope with the idea that a supernatural being is spying on me. You wouldn't leave me to face that alone, would you?"

At least I had the sense not to call her on her obvious guilt manipulation. Instead, I settled for the more diplomatic, "Carla, we will always be friends, and I'll always be there when you need me."

"Isn't it ironic?" she said with unconcealed bitterness. "You are doing to me exactly what Eva did to you." She stepped away, sarcastically blew me a kiss, and turned her back on me to unlock the door. I waited until she was inside and then dragged myself back to Nurse Florence's car. To get my mind off Carla, I asked Nurse Florence what our next move would be.

"I think we need to bring your mother into this." Well, I didn't see that one coming.

"Yes," she said, reacting to my surprised expression, "and sooner rather than later. Tal, she's not just a psychic; she's a genuine seer. You and I would have to do a slow, methodical search to find whatever doorway Ares is using to connect with this world. Seers are more...random in the way they obtain information. Your mom might just be able to point to it. Maybe she's already dreamed where it is but doesn't realize what she's seen."

"There are many seers in Annwn," I pointed out.

"Yes, and many spies—and, as you keep making me remind you, at least a few potential enemies. If I go looking for a seer, someone could find out. Do you really want a potential enemy to know you are having another problem? On the other hand, we can approach your mom without anyone in Annwn ever finding out."

"Well," I said grudgingly, "I don't like that she's involved in these things at all, but since she is, I guess we might as well consult her."

"Good. Sometime tomorrow afternoon, before your father comes home from the office, then. Right after soccer practice?"

"Works for me," I said.

"And me," Jimmie put in, not that he needed to be there, but since he had taken on following me around as his full-time job, he would inevitably be there anyway.

Santa Brígida was a relatively small town, but it seemed to take us an eternity to drive from Carla's house to mine. Finally, we pulled up in front of my place. I thanked Nurse Florence for everything and more or less staggered to the door, Jimmie as always floating behind me.

Much to my surprise, my mom was still up. She was sitting in her favorite chair, drinking tea, and reading Robertson Davies's *Lyre of Orpheus*.

"I didn't think you were a Robertson Davies fan," I said as I walked over to hug her.

"It's actually one of your dad's books," she replied, giving me a peck on the cheek. Then, at a much lower volume, she asked, "What happened this time?"

"I'll tell you tomorrow, if you don't mind. I'm beat."

"All right," she said with obvious reluctance. "Everyone is all right, though?"

Well, one of my basket-case fellow students is channeling the god of war and brought a sword into our plane of existence that could destroy anything in its path. Oh, and FYI, the god of war wants me dead.

"Yeah, everyone's all right." I knew she didn't really buy that, but she could also see how tired I was, so she let the matter drop for the time being.

Jimmie, who recovered from being completely drained faster than a human could, practically had to drag me up the stairs, but I did finally make it to my room.

I had meant what I said about keeping an eye on Alex and trying to help him, but with so much else for me to think about, his problems got crowded over to the back burner. Forgetting about them was, as it turned out, a big mistake.

Chapter 3: An Unexpected Visit

The next afternoon Nurse Florence and I had planned to see my mom, but for a short time, I thought the meeting might not happen. Nurse Florence, who was never late, arrived in front of my house almost forty-five minutes after she was supposed to. She arrived on foot, out of breath, flustered, and unfocused. Something had to be wrong.

"Are you all right?" I asked. "I was beginning to worry."

Nurse Florence smiled, brushed her bangs out of her eyes, and took a couple of slow, deep breaths. "I didn't mean to worry you. I got a relatively urgent phone call from the Order just as I was stepping out of the office. I have news, by the way, but it will wait until after we talk to your mother. Anyway, when I got out to the parking lot, my car wouldn't start. I jogged most of the way here. I didn't want to be any later than necessary, that's all. No big crisis this time."

"My, what a refreshing change!" I said jokingly. "Shall we?" Nurse Florence nodded and walked ahead of me up to the front door. Much to my surprise, when I opened it and ushered Nurse Florence in, I heard "The Lyre of Orpheus" by Nick Cave and the Bad Seeds playing loudly in the living room.

"Mom, we need to talk to you!" I yelled over the music. She walked in quickly, nodded to us, and turned off the stereo.

"Since when have you liked alternative rock?" I asked. It seemed a simple enough question, but my mom stood for a moment, looking very confused.

"I haven't. I was listening to the radio, and it just came on."

"And you had the radio volume all the way up because—" I said expectantly.

"We have more pressing concerns," interrupted Nurse Florence. "Sophia, I'm sorry to bother you, but as I explained on the phone, we need a seer's help…need it urgently." My mom nodded, looked directly at Nurse Florence—and froze.

"Viviane, you aren't here! When I look at you, I see nothing. You…you're over at Carrie Winn's place."

Reflexively, my hand went to White Hilt.

"Oh, Sophia, I'm so sorry! I should have explained the moment I came in. Vanora and I are testing some new spells. I'm using one that would make anyone looking for me psychically think I'm somewhere else.

Evidently, it works."

My mom looked dissatisfied with the explanation. I glanced at Nurse Florence, who chuckled a little.

"Tal, you can read my thoughts. Am I who I appear to be?"

"At first glance, anyway. I don't like to go deeper…unless I have to."

"Go as deep as you need to. I'm sorry, Sophia, Tal. This was a bad time for this test. The last thing I wanted was to cause either of you any more anxiety."

"Well, you shouldn't have been able to get into the house if you were someone intent on doing evil," I said, quickly checking the new wards, which were still very much intact. I had renewed them that morning. "I can't imagine someone impersonating Nurse Florence for the purpose of doing good." I could see my mom relax a little.

"Well," said Mom, "I don't really sense evil either, and I probably would if you weren't the real Viviane Florence. Tal, remember how I reacted when I first met Morgan le Fay?"

"Too well," I said with mock sternness. "You almost got yourself killed, as I recall."

"If you are both convinced I am who I say I am, it might be wise for us to get down to business."

"Of course," said Mom, motioning both of us to be seated. "Viviane, you know I'll do what I can, but I can't seem to just ask a question and get a straight answer."

"The universe is like that," replied Nurse Florence with a smile. "I know you get bits and pieces rather than the whole picture, but bits and pieces are more than we have now."

Nurse Florence and I filled my mom in on what had happened yesterday. I had been worried about my mom's reaction, but she took the whole thing surprisingly calmly.

"Yes," she said, nodding thoughtfully. "I dreamed something very like that before Tal came home. I also remember something else, something about thin walls."

"Thin walls?" I asked.

My mom hesitated. "Speaking of bits and pieces, I know that sounds pretty random. Even when I'm awake, I keep thinking about how hard it is to live in an apartment and hear everything going on next door through the walls. But I don't think the walls in my dream are necessarily physical."

Nurse Florence looked as if she were having a light-bulb moment. "You mean like walls between the different planes of existence?"

"I hadn't thought of that," said Mom, toying absentmindedly with one of her earrings. "In my dream, they were very tall walls, hard like…stone, I guess, and Tal was hammering on them, breaking them down."

Suddenly, I felt nauseated. I knew where this was going.

"I'm certainly not trying to tear down the barriers between the worlds," I protested weakly.

"I think you're being too literal," said Nurse Florence. "We know that your presence is enough to amplify magic. That's why Carla was developing magic even before her past lives were awakened. It's why your mom is a seer. It's why Jimmie can manifest so easily."

"We know all that, but so what?" I said, even though I knew exactly what.

Nurse Florence looked at me sympathetically. "Tal, this isn't your fault, but isn't it obvious that your continuous residence in Santa Brígida is thinning the barriers here between this world and others?"

My mom's eyes widened in shock. "Viviane, does that mean we have to move? I don't think I can explain that to Tal's father."

"Don't worry, Sophia. Now that we know we aren't looking for one hole but for general thinning, we should be able to reinforce those barriers without Tal having to get out of Santa Brígida. Anyway, at the moment all that's happened is that one very powerful being made contact with one person, whom we have since ensured will cause no further trouble. It isn't exactly as if the walls are collapsing, and supernatural beings are flocking into town."

"Yet, anyway," I said unhappily. Both women looked at me with concern.

"Tal, if something that dramatic were coming, I'm pretty sure I would have some inkling," said Mom in her most reassuring tone.

"We'd all feel that," added Nurse Florence.

"We didn't know a half-djinn was in town until he tried to steal Shar's sword," I pointed out.

"Khalid has a physical body and not very much magic," said Nurse Florence. "And there is only one of him, not the army you seem to be visualizing. Honestly, Tal, if you could find a way to make yourself responsible for global warming, you'd do it!"

"You mean I'm not?" I asked jokingly. That line got a laugh even from Mom.

"Sophia, one more thing. Do you have any idea why Ares used Alex as a vessel?"

"Based on my dreams, I'd say one of Tal's guesses is right. Alex is definitely descended from Ares. I just know," she added defensively in response to my incredulous stare. "I know he doesn't look the part, but he is. I don't always have the answer, but when I'm sure, I'm sure."

"Is anyone else on campus or in town related to an Olympian?" I asked quickly. "It might help to know if there is another person Ares could try to contact."

My mom shook her head apologetically. "That question I can't answer, but I'll think about it. I'm sure something will come to me eventually."

Hopefully before some other descendant of Ares shoots me through the heart or something.

"Yes, hopefully," replied my mom with an enigmatic smile.

"You can read minds now?" I asked.

"Intermittently. I just get bits and pieces, like everything else."

"Tal, maybe we can design a way to test people for Olympian or other supernatural ancestry," suggested Nurse Florence.

Now that was an interesting idea! "Do you really think we could?"

"Considering all the other innovative magic you've come up with in the last few weeks, yes I do. In fact you could probably go a step further and test people for past lives connected to ancient Greece as well. I imagine that kind of bond could also be used by Ares."

I could hardly believe what I was hearing. "You know how dangerous that could be? That's exactly what Morgan wanted me to do when she was searching for the spirit of Lancelot."

"Morgan is in custody, and even if she somehow gets out, we can make sure to keep that particular spell confidential."

"I don't—"

"Tal, it may be the only way to keep everyone safe. You saw what happened when Ares got through to Alex. Ares wants you dead and clearly isn't picky about how many people he has to kill to get to you. Using a phonos to do his dirty work is totally reckless, suggesting Ares will stop at nothing. Our best shot at preventing a similar attack is by finding anyone Ares could conceivably use and blocking his access to them."

Mom, feeling the rising tension, went off to get cookies so that Nurse Florence and I could talk privately. Actually, we could talk really privately for once; Jimmie seemed to have taken the afternoon off, probably to visit Dan.

"Actually, as I think about it, I believe you could design an appropriate spell easily. Hear me out!" she added preemptively as I started to protest. "We have enough people around with supernatural ancestry for you to look for patterns that differentiate them from others, sort of like otherworldly genetics. Once you know what makes them different from ordinary human beings, you can cast a spell that looks for those markers."

"When I developed ways to make magic work on technology, I used Stan's knowledge of the physical sciences so that I could visualize what I was doing properly for spell casting. Stan isn't as knowledgeable about life science."

"No, but I am," pointed out Nurse Florence. "Use my knowledge to help you understand what you need to, at least assuming it's genetic or related in some other way to human biology."

"Well, that could work for supernatural ancestry," I admitted. "But that kind of approach won't work with past lives. I'd be very surprised if who people were in the past left any physical signs in their current bodies."

"I've been thinking about that. You're right—we need a different approach. I believe it would be possible to create a very much weaker version of the awakening spell, one that would detect past lives without causing them to emerge."

"But that spell is dark magic!" I protested. "You're the one who warned me about its use before. I ignored you and nearly destroyed my own soul. How can you even suggest this?"

Nurse Florence looked at me with irritation—not the reaction I was expecting. "Of course you're right, but what makes magic dark is its intended effect. Moderate the spell so that it doesn't actually awaken past lives, and it is no longer dark."

"But how could we be sure of the effect without testing it on someone? And if we hadn't moderated it enough, we could awaken that person's past lives, change his or her current life forever, or maybe even destroy it. On top of that, Dark Me would emerge again, and who knows what catastrophes he would bring if he managed to retain control?"

Nurse Florence was looking at me, not with the understanding I expected, and certainly not apologetically, which I also expected. Instead, she looked more and more annoyed.

OK, so I guess I should have probed more deeply after all.

I drew White Hilt and brandished its flaming blade at the intruder, singing a song of binding as I did so.

"Wait!" yelled the intruder in an all-too-familiar voice. I watched her features melt, shift, and become those of Vanora—well, actually of Carrie Winn, the identity created by the witch Ceridwen, an identity Vanora assumed after we had defeated the witch.

"Well," said my mom, walking back into the room with the cookies, "I guess I was right." I noticed a knife under the plate.

"What were you planning on doing with that?" I asked with studied casualness. Mom looked at me as if I were an idiot.

"Why, stab the impostor and give you a chance to attack, of course!" said my mom, so seriously that I almost wanted to laugh.

"Mom, you wouldn't hurt a fly!"

"Maybe you don't know me as well as you think," she said solemnly. I choked down another laugh and turned to Vanora.

"You're lucky I'm not a shoot-first-and-ask-questions-later kind of guy. I could just as easily have kicked myself up to faerie speed and taken off your head before you had a chance to say anything."

"Taliesin," she said without even a hint of apology or explanation, "please release me from your binding spell."

"Not until you explain what the hell you're doing."

"Release me now!" she demanded. "Then we will talk." With a gesture, I let her go. Maybe I should have let her break loose on her own. It was a hasty spell; I'm sure she could have broken it. But then she wouldn't have had the satisfaction of ordering me around.

"I was…experimenting. I wanted to see if I could counterfeit Nurse Florence well enough to fool you."

"Why?" I asked suspiciously.

"Because I won't be Carrie Winn forever. It's been my longest role and my most successful, but sooner or later I'll need to assume some other guise, and I didn't want to get too out of practice."

"That's not even a good lie," I said contemptuously, torn between anger and amazement.

Vanora sighed, and for just a moment she seemed a little less sure of herself. Then the moment passed. "You are right," she said dismissively, as if my being right was a small matter in the great scheme of things. "The truth is that I wanted to have a chance to talk to you without Viviane standing by to contradict everything I said."

That explanation didn't sound right, either. "You could have just invited me over. I'm Carrie Winn's intern, after all. I can come and go at Awen without even attracting anyone's notice."

"You would inevitably say something to Viviane, even if I told you not to. The only way I could be sure you didn't do that would be to make you think you were meeting with Viviane, not with me. She's at Awen right now, on a long-distance call with some of our associates in Cardiff. I told her I would let you know what was happening. And so I did…eventually."

"OK, so what's the big message that Nurse Florence would have disagreed with? Oh, it's that you want me to create a spell that detects who people were in past lives? Even assuming it wasn't dangerous, what do you need that kind of spell for?"

"It isn't I who will need it, but you. Your mother is not the only seer in the universe, you know. I consulted one in Annwn just a few days ago. She revealed that you would soon be in a situation in which you needed to find Alexander the Great."

"That's farfetched," I said, though it was odd a seer had predicted I would need Alexander just before the phonos and Ares started attacking.

"We have had this conversation before, I think. Taliesin, you are destined for great things. Remember the prophecy in the *Book of Taliesin*; you were with God at the beginning of the world and will be with Him at its end. Somewhere in between you will have a key role to play in the destiny of the whole human race. The day you will play that role is fast approaching."

"Do you have any idea how much you sound like a religious nut?" I asked as harshly as I could.

Vanora was not even slowed down by my obvious skepticism. "King David is mentioned in the same poem, and suddenly King David pops up among your friends and plays a pivotal role in saving you. That can't be coincidence. I believe Alexander is among your friends as well and that at some point you will need his help, just as you needed David's."

"Really? The poem also mentions Moses, Elijah, Mary Magdalene, Jesus, and about a dozen figures in Welsh mythology. Are they all among my friends as well?"

"Tal, I don't have all the answers," said Vanora, about the closest she had ever come so far to admitting she didn't know everything. "You did find Alcina, though, among your friends, who also include a half-djinn and a ghost—and Merlin, however briefly. It strains credibility to assume that all of these developments are coincidences."

"You're right—we've had this discussion before, and I don't intend to have it again. That 'prophecy' in the *Book of Taliesin* is nonsense, and you are not to mention it to me again!"

"Who do you think you are to give me orders?" asked Vanora, glaring at me.

"According to you, I'm the one who was with God at the beginning and will be with Him at the end."

"Taliesin, the day will come when you will beg me to help you with that spell..."

"Yeah, right around the twelfth of never." I didn't know whether Vanora was a Johnny Mathis fan or not, but I figured the message was clear enough either way.

"I want you to leave my home...now!" said my mom with surprising force.

Vanora glared at her also but said nothing; instead, she rose from the couch, turned without a word, and left.

"I don't like that woman anymore!" Mom said, still emphatic and not at all like her usual self.

"I guess I'll have to change the wards on the house to keep out misguided people as well as evil ones," I said half-jokingly. "Mom, how did you know?"

"I'm a seer, remember? I didn't really think that story about new security precautions sounded right. I began to wonder if perhaps Viviane really was at Awen, and the woman we had here was an intruder with some kind of...oh, I don't know, cloaking spell preventing me from seeing who she really was. By the time I went to the kitchen, I knew she was someone other than Viviane. How about you?" Listening to Mom talk about magic in the same matter-of-fact way she discussed the weather made me want to laugh again, but once more I stifled the impulse.

"She's good," I admitted. "I wasn't seeing her as blank; that part of the spell must have been aimed at seers specifically. From what I could see, the top layers of her mind were Nurse Florence's. That isn't at all easy to do; shifting into someone else's form only covers the physical part. Vanora obviously has great skill to imitate Nurse Florence's mind that way. She slipped up right at the start, though. She walked over here, claiming her car broke down. Nurse Florence would have remembered the fountain in the backyard through which she could have traveled, but Vanora has never seen our backyard, so she doesn't know about the fountain. For that matter, Nurse Florence could have gotten inside the house by portal, but Vanora, who has never been in the house, couldn't do that.

"I didn't think of any of that until later, though. What tipped me off was the idea that I should start messing with dark magic. That was much more like Vanora's kind of argument. Nurse Florence would never have assumed something like that was safe. Never. At the same time, I knew whoever it was had gotten past the wards, so the impostor had to be someone who wasn't consciously evil. Vanora was the logical candidate."

"Has she always been trying to turn you into Jesus?" I couldn't help but snicker a little.

"She sees me in a role somewhat different from that of Jesus…but somewhere along the way, I'm afraid the whole idea has unhinged her a little. I think I'll ask Nurse Florence to talk to the head of the Order about getting her replaced. There must be some other shifter who could do a plausible Carrie Winn."

My mom's eyes narrowed a little. "Something tells me we haven't seen the last of her."

Mom was a seer, after all, so I shouldn't have been surprised later when she proved right.

Chapter 4: An Unusual Challenge

The very first thing I did after Vanora left was get in psychic touch with the real Nurse Florence and ask her to come to my house right away. She had learned to respect my judgment of what constituted an emergency; in about a minute and a half, a portal shimmered into being in the living room, and Nurse Florence stepped through it, poised to defend herself if needed.

"We're not actually under attack," I said. "I would have warned you more explicitly if we were facing some deadly foe."

Nurse Florence relaxed but only a little. "There was something about the feeling I got from your message that made me think the worst."

I glanced at my mom.

"Yes, it's definitely Viviane this time," Mom said in answer to my unspoken question. "Would you care for some tea, Viviane?" asked my mom. "Tal can fill you in while I'm getting it."

"Thank you, yes," said Nurse Florence, much more at ease now, though clearly puzzled. "Tal, I take it we're having shifter problems."

"You could say that. Vanora was here pretending to be you."

"What?" Nurse Florence was clearly as shocked as I had been. "Why would she have done such a thing?"

"Oh, she just wanted to talk me into using dark magic."

Nurse Florence looked as if she had just been slapped across the face—hard. "Tell me everything," she said, leaning forward expectantly.

It didn't take long for me to give her all the juicy details. Interestingly, though, the more I talked, the less surprised she looked. I had expected the opposite response.

"This explains why Vanora wanted to get me to Awen so badly, even though I now know she already had all the information the Order's Greek specialist gave me. Getting me tied up on that long-distance call to Cardiff was the perfect excuse to keep me out of the way so she could take my place."

"Don't all you Ladies of the Lake communicate psychically?" asked my mom as she came in with the tea tray.

Nurse Florence smiled. "Getting a stable connection over the distance between here and Wales requires enormous amounts of energy. Much as I hate to admit it, modern technology has its uses."

"So what did you learn from your Greek specialist?" I asked.

"Pretty much what you already guessed while you were talking to Alex. What little evidence is in the Order's archives supports the idea that the Olympians can only communicate with descendants or reincarnations of descendants, and even that rare contact seems to require the descendant to be trying to communicate with them first."

"Odd that the faeries can communicate so much more easily. Are the Olympians that much less powerful?"

"In this world, anyway. The Order speculates that the barriers between our world and the Olympian realm are much stronger, though clearly they couldn't have been so powerful in ancient times. Why the situation changed, no one knows."

"I don't give two hoots in a hailstorm *why* it changed," cut in Mom, still clearly keyed up. "I just thank God it did. Otherwise Ares might have showed up in person."

"I don't think we have to worry about that, Sophia," said Nurse Florence with her most reassuring smile. "From what Alex told us, it was hard for Ares to get through to him, and bringing the sword through to our world seems to have exhausted Ares for quite some time."

"Even so, it would be nice to know what his motive was," I said, trying to figure out how we could possibly find out now.

"I don't agree with Vanora's methods or her suggestion about the awakening spell, but she is right about one thing," said Nurse Florence grudgingly. "It would be nice to know who else in town might be used as a way for Ares to strike at you again."

"She actually had a good suggestion about finding people with supernatural ancestry," I admitted, equally grudgingly. "But I don't have the first clue how to find supernatural connections in people's past lives. Should we try to find some non-dark magic way to do that?"

"If we can, but Tal, strange as it may sound, that's not our most urgent problem." I should have been used to announcements of impending doom by now, but I still shuddered a little.

"Do tell," I said, trying to keep a light mood and failing utterly.

"Just a short time ago, I got word from Gwynn that Morgan's trial is set to begin." At the mention of Morgan, my mom shuddered as well.

"That's good news, right?" I said. "We want her to be convicted."

"You are thinking too much in terms of the modern American legal system. The faeries still use a more...medieval model, at least for cases involving members of a faerie royal family."

"Is Oberon still buying that...BS," I asked, remembering at the last minute that my mom was in the room, "about Morgan being a reincarnation of his mother?"

"Yes, and the *Tribiwnlys* has accepted his motion to have her treated as royal. Oh, *Tribiwnlys* means 'tribunal,'" she clarified for my mom. Then Nurse Florence paused uncomfortably.

"OK, out with it," I said impatiently. "What is it you don't want to tell us?"

"Treating Morgan as royal gives her the right to demand trial by combat, and she wasted no time doing exactly that. As she was presented to the *Tribiwnlys* as your prisoner, you would need to be the one to fight her."

"She could go free...after all she's done?"

"Some of the faerie rulers agree with you, at least from what I've heard, but they remember too well the old days when faerie tribes used to fight each other constantly. None of them are willing to risk anarchy by denying Morgan the traditional right of a royal prisoner. They know that Oberon would raise hell—literally—and war would follow."

"I guess I'll just have to beat her, then," I said resignedly.

"Isn't it...unchivalrous or something to fight a woman?" asked Mom. I noticed her teacup shaking a little in her hand and knew what was coming.

"Actually, Sophia, faerie law is surprisingly gender neutral. Faeries tend to be matriarchal, if anything. Tal can fight Morgan. Unfortunately, this isn't going to be a physical fight, but a magical one, doubtless because Morgan feels more confident of victory."

"She will win?" asked Mom, her voice sounding just a little shrill.

"She thinks so," said Nurse Florence, trying to sound comforting. "I'm not so sure. In terms of raw power, Morgan can probably beat Tal, but he has shown himself far more inventive than she is." Not exactly a ringing endorsement, but I'd take it.

Mom, however, was not reassured. "I don't like this one bit. But this tribunal can't make Tal fight, can it?"

"Tal is not exactly subject to faerie law, so he could probably refuse," replied Nurse Florence, a little rattled by the question. "However, in that case Morgan wins by default and goes free. Within three days she'd be back in Santa Brígida, threatening everybody's lives to get whatever it is she wants from Tal."

Mom looked ready to make me the first magic user in…probably forever, to be grounded by his mother to keep him out of a magic duel. However, Nurse Florence was not done yet.

"Sophia, I'm usually the one counseling Tal against doing something risky, but in this case, I don't think we have a choice. Morgan loose threatens Tal more than Morgan in a trial by combat situation. At least this way, Morgan can't bring in allies and has to abide by some other rules.

"Tal has another protection in this situation," Nurse Florence continued quickly, before Mom could interrupt. "We know Morgan wants Tal alive. Even if she wins, she won't kill him."

"You mean…this fight could be to the death?" asked Mom, her voice dropping almost to a whisper.

"Again, Morgan has an interest in keeping him alive, and nothing in the rules says she has to kill him. The *barnwyr*, the judges, can rule that the fight is over as soon as either combatant concedes. The victor can demand the life of the vanquished but doesn't have to."

"I forbid it!" snapped Mom. "He may be the reincarnation of Taliesin, and he may be able to do magic, but he is still my *sixteen-year-old* son, and he is not going to Annwn to fight Morgan le Fay!"

"Do you know the outcome?" asked Nurse Florence, suddenly alarmed by the possibility that Mom might have had a vision of me losing.

"Nothing yet, but I will not take the chance. I often dream about Tal's situation only as it is happening…and in this case, that would be too late."

I got up, walked over, and hugged Mom. Despite the strength of her tone, she was trembling.

"I thought you were getting used to this," I said, patting her on the back. "A few minutes ago, you were ready to have a knife fight with an unknown intruder."

"To protect you, which is what I'm doing now," she replied in her best my-word-is-final tone.

"And don't either one of you think you can manipulate me the way Tal used to!" she said in an almost accusing tone, looking suspiciously at both of us. "I don't think either one of you could do that kind of magic on me now that I'm a seer." She could have been right…or her being a seer might just have made the process harder. I really didn't want to find out.

"Mom, you have to let me do this! Morgan's the same woman who put a knife to Gianni Rinaldi's throat to get what she wanted. She's the same woman who still wants to turn Carla back into Alcina. She's the same woman who sent a dragon after me, Mom—a dragon! She's every bit as dangerous as Ares…and I have the power to stop her, once and for all."

Mom looked at both of us, struggled a little to say something, and then started crying. I hugged her again. Now she was really shaking, her small body racked by one sob after another. Like many guys, I didn't really know what to do in this situation except hug her even harder.

"I know…I know she's a terrible person. I sensed it…when I met her at the soccer game. But why does it always have to be you? Why can't someone else accept Morgan's challenge?"

"Gwynn ap Nudd already tried that, Sophia, by trying to claim Morgan as his prisoner, but the *barnwyr* ruled against him. Based on what Morgan has done, he could have asserted his own royal interest in her punishment, except that he can't prove Morgan sent invaders like the dragon to his kingdom. Tal has the right to appoint a champion to fight in his place, but who would that be? Gwynn is the logical choice, but after denying him the right to fight Morgan in his own name, the *barnwyr* have given him another role in the trial, so he cannot serve as your champion. Stan? He doesn't have magic. Shar? Without the anti-magical power of his sword, even he wouldn't last three minutes with Morgan, and he wouldn't be able to bring that kind of weapon into the arena. Carla is the only one of Tal's friends that does have magic, but it isn't safe for her in Annwn right now. Morgan could renew her claim that we are unlawfully keeping her sister from her. The way the *barnwyr* have been ruling, I can't guarantee they won't agree with Morgan, and Carla will end up a prisoner, with a huge number of faerie sorcerers trying to put Alcina back in control of her."

"That poor girl!" said my mom, no longer sobbing but still crying a little. "Of course I don't want that to happen." She wiped her eyes and stared at us. "You're sure there is no other way?"

"I have to ask that about my life at least three times a week, Mom. Yeah, it has to be me. And I should start preparing myself now if the trial by combat is tomorrow."

Mom sighed like a condemned convict approaching the gallows. "I guess I can't say no. But I'm coming with you."

My jaw and Nurse Florence's both dropped in unison.

"I want to help," Mom continued, clearly oblivious to our horror. "I might notice something that could be helpful."

Great, now I get to make history as the first participant of a trial by combat who has to bring his mommy with him!

"I understand why you want to do that," said Nurse Florence patiently, "but having our own seer is a valuable asset, particularly if no one else knows about you. I'm afraid if you come, someone will discern your true nature."

By this point, my mom looked defeated. "Then you have to promise this is the last time, Tal!"

"I can't make that promise…and you know it," I said gently. "I can promise I will do everything I can to keep myself safe. Mom, I've beaten tougher opponents than Morgan."

I was emotionally exhausted by the time the conversation finally ended. Mom kept finding other objections and trying to impose conditions. In the end she didn't so much give permission as give up. She turned without another word and left the room. I could hear her footsteps on the stairs, and I think I could hear her crying again.

"Just a short while ago, I would have sworn she was OK with the way my life was."

"No mother is ever going to be OK with her son going into danger," Nurse Florence replied, looking almost as bad as I felt. "Remember, she's only known the truth for a few days, and she not only has to digest that but her own new role as a seer. I'd be worried about her if she had managed to swallow all that this quickly. Then she had to deal with an impostor invading her own home. I can't blame her for being a little unhinged. She will come around in time."

"I hope so," I said doubtfully. "Well, I guess we had better get going before she changes her mind and tries to keep me from leaving again. Can you find me a good place to prepare?"

"Before that, there is one more thing you need to know. I don't want you to be taken by surprise."

This can't be good.

"Well…" I said in mock expectancy.

"The *barnwyr* are selected by lot from among the faerie royal families; Oberon is excluded, since Morgan is allegedly related to him. Three others have been chosen: Queen Mab, whom you met when you were at

Gwynn's castle; the Amadan Dubh—"

"The Fairy Fool?" I asked incredulously.

"Let's not call him that while we're in Annwn, shall we? He's a lot more dangerous than his name makes him sound. Apparently, he is related to one of the Irish faerie royal families. Anyway, the third *barnwr* is…Arawn, Gwynn's predecessor as king of the Welsh faeries."

"What?" I asked, my voice cracking for the first time in at least three years. "The same Arawn?"

"Yes, the very one Arthur and the original Taliesin stole White Hilt from fifteen hundred years ago. That little escapade undermined the confidence of his subjects and is one of the reasons he lost his throne to Gwynn. The only person he hates more than Gwynn is you, and he'd like nothing better than to see Morgan kill you."

"Can't he be forced to recuse himself?"

"Gwynn did object to his presence on the *Tribiwnlys*, but faerie law favors respecting the choice of the lots, and Gwynn couldn't prove any manipulation."

"Thank God my mom doesn't know about this…although I guess she will soon enough."

"Yes, it will figure in her nightmares. However, the *barnwyr* don't determine the winner in trial by combat. They announce it, but if their announcement is contrary to the outcome witnessed by the audience, well, the audience could acclaim the true victor. That's too much a part of faerie law to leave Arawn any room for interpretation. Make no mistake: Arawn sees this trial as an opportunity to hurt you, but the outcome can still go against him.

"And that's not all. Queen Mab has consistently voted against Arawn's position. The Amadan Dubh has provided Arawn with his majority, and Dubh is, let's just say, erratic. At any time he could switch sides for no apparent reason."

"It's always good to know my fate might rest in the hands of the village idiot."

"Careful!" cautioned Nurse Florence. "You don't really know him except by reputation. Remember he is also known as the bringer of madness and oblivion and used to be widely feared by mortals in the area where he lived. I know his reputation isn't good, and he is not particularly…stable, but he isn't really a fool in the modern sense. In fact, I think part of his public behavior is an act of some kind, though what his agenda is, I can't pretend to know. Everyone expected him to turn down the appointment when he was chosen, but he didn't."

"Well, as you said, the outcome of the combat still rests on me. Let's go somewhere…quiet…and talk strategy."

"Tal, you need to check on your mother first."

"I know I do," I said and sighed. "But right now I'd rather face a dragon."

"I heard that!" said Mom. I hadn't noticed her coming down the stairs, but suddenly there she was.

"Mom," I started, but she cut me off.

"I know, I know," she said, hugging me so hard I expected a rib to crack. "I'm just being foolish. I know you have to do this, and I should have more confidence in you." Her mood was so different from what it had been just a few minutes ago that for a moment I wondered if a shifter had taken her place.

"Sophia, you've had a vision, haven't you?" asked Nurse Florence.

"Maybe a little one," Mom admitted. "I saw a way I could help, and it made me feel better. I'll be back in a minute." With that, she almost ran up the stairs. After a couple of minutes, I heard her climbing the ladder into the attic.

"What could we possibly have in the attic that could be useful?" I wondered out loud.

"Attics can be very uncanny places," observed Nurse Florence mysteriously.

After a few minutes, Mom returned, brushing cobwebs out of her hair. I don't think anyone had been in the attic since my parents first stored things there when they moved in. In her hands she held small, dusty reed pipes—the oldest musical instrument I had ever seen…in this life.

"These have been in the family for years," Mom practically gushed. "My grandmother told me they were ancient. I know your magic works better with music. You certainly can't take your harp, and your acoustical guitar is pretty heavy for this kind of situation. Will these do? I've never seen you play a wind instrument, but I believe you can play pretty much anything, right?"

"I can indeed! Mom, these are perfect!" I gave her a kiss. "Does this mean I have your blessing?"

"If you promise to be careful, yes, it does." I could still hear a note of reluctance in her voice, but her mood was so completely different from before, I had to think the vision she had seen was very strong. It was almost enough to make me feel more confident in the face of Arawn's sabotage.

As soon as we were out the front door, Nurse Florence chuckled. "I wonder if your mother realizes the significance of that gift?"

"What do you mean? What is the significance?"

"Those reed pipes look identical to the ones I have seen the Amadan Dubh playing. I can't think that's coincidence."

"Then she must have known!"

"It's hard to be sure. Sometimes the information she gets as a seer is pretty disjointed, and even she doesn't realize its significance. Either way, I would hang onto those. If she gave them to you with such confidence, some use for them is bound to present itself."

"Speaking of holding onto things, is it safe to take White Hilt with Arawn around?"

Nurse Florence pondered for a moment. "I imagine he'll find some way to demand it back, but I think he'll do that whether it is physically present or not, so you might as well take it. You won't be able to use it in the battle with Morgan, but something else might come up while we're there."

I had to laugh at that. "Something usually does, doesn't it? OK, what about the guys? Should I bring them?"

"They won't have a formal role to play in the process, but yes. This isn't going to be the last time you have business in Annwn, and most faeries will take you more seriously if you look more like a ruler with your own men. The fact that you are the one Morgan is meeting in combat gives you a certain status, but there is no harm in reinforcing it visually. In fact, I wish we had time to get you appropriate outfits, but I think your group will look impressive enough without that."

We went back to school and summoned the guys to join us. As they assembled, I realized how right Nurse Florence was. Even Stan, who had looked like a stereotypical nerd just a few months ago, now carried himself with an air of authority. His combat experience, to say nothing of having King David inside of him, made quite a difference, and when he wielded David's sword, he looked like the cover illustration for a fantasy novel.

As for the others, Shar was pure, well-trained muscle, and even without Shamshir-e Zomorrodnegār (Zom), his emerald sword, flashing in his hand, no one was likely to mess with him. With Shar was the nine-year-old Khalid, a half-djinn who had been living on the streets until Shar and his family took him in. We had tried so often to get him to stay safely at home, but he always became invisible and sneaked along anyway, so eventually we just gave up trying. Aside from being able to disappear, Khalid was faerie fast and agile, as well as being able to jump over walls, so at least he could stay out of harm's way—if he felt like it, anyway. He carried a faerie dagger that had been a gift from Gwynn ap Nudd himself; alone among all of us, Khalid had gone through no trial to earn his weapon. Maybe Gwynn had a soft spot for him.

Dan, much as I hated to admit it, was almost as impressive look-ing as Shar, sort of a football captain from Central Casting. He carried a custom-made sword from Govannon, the Welsh faerie smith, a blade that kept him from bleeding in combat. Jimmie accompanied him, looking younger but taller—a basketball build rather than a football one. I often wondered whether Jimmie would have been on the school team had he lived. So he wouldn't feel left out, I let him carry Black Hilt, the sinister, icy twin of White Hilt that Morgan le Fay had gotten from somewhere. We hadn't really trained him much in sword fighting, but, being already dead, he wasn't at very much risk.

Really, it was Dan and I who were at risk, though I never said that to Jimmie. The longer he was around, the more we became used to his presence, but sooner or later he would have to move on, and then we would have to go through losing him again. That realization was almost enough to make me want to never forgive Dan just to keep Jimmie here, but I knew staying on our plane was once getting extremely painful for him and might again. Ghosts were not supposed to linger as long as Jim-mie had for what the universe might have considered a relatively trivial reason.

Gordy was as tall as Jimmie—well, at least the form Jimmie nor-mally assumed—and as muscular as Dan, so clearly no one was likely to mess with him either. His sword, also made for him, would strike fear into any mortal enemy. Unfortunately, most of his enemies were not mortal, but he still managed to make good use of the sword. Carlos, the last to arrive, was shorter and tanner than Gordy. Carlos was an accomplished aquatic athlete but had picked up swordsmanship quickly and carried yet another custom sword, one that could drown an opponent from just a scratch unless the wound was healed.

Yes, definitely an impressive group. The faeries might look down their noses at their jeans-and-T-shirt kind of outfits, but they would stop and take notice of their unique weaponry. Collectively, we had more faerie weapons than any group since Camelot had fallen. (Even David's sword had been modified by Govannon—and the faeries would probably not need to be reminded that the only other person who wielded a sword of David's had been Sir Galahad, the grail knight!)

So much for appearances. Nurse Florence, as always, took care of the logistics. Since tomorrow was Saturday, we could all be gone awhile without arousing our parents' suspicions, so no elaborate cover story was required. Transportation was also pretty easy—with the help of a little magic. By way of Annwn, Nurse Florence took us via portal to Glastonbury Tor, which had a fixed portal hidden in St. Michael's Tower. This portal took us directly to Gwynn's castle.

Talk about the royal treatment! Gwynn himself awaited us in the massive courtyard, and from there led us to the great hall, glowing with unearthly light, and there we shamelessly feasted on pretty much anything we wanted while faerie musicians played in the background. I had yet to figure out how Gwynn's kitchen could so rapidly create whatever we wished for, but there is a time to stop asking questions, and this was it. For a little while, I enjoyed myself, trying to avoid that condemned-man-ate-a-hearty-meal feeling.

"Are you ready for the trial by combat?" asked Gwynn, who I suddenly realized was right behind me.

I turned and started to rise, but he motioned me to stay seated. Gwynn was exceptionally large for a faerie and certainly towered over me. He was smiling now, but his dark face, also uncharacteristic for a faerie, could equally well have looked menacing. I was glad to have him as a friend, especially considering the number of enemies I had.

"Yes, Your Majesty. I've spent most of the afternoon planning strategy."

"I won't ask for details," said Gwynn, indicating with a quick glance the possibility of spies in the room. "I have faith you will make Morgan pay for her crimes. I don't know what game Oberon is playing, but he isn't going to win."

"Thank you for your hospitality. Someday I must find an appropriate way to thank you for all you done for me…for us."

"Beating that witch will be thanks enough," replied Gwynn with another smile. "Whenever you are ready, I have chambers prepared for you, your men, and Viviane. After last time, I understand that you will not be wanting a faerie maiden to…warm your bed." It had come as something of a surprise last time when Gwyn had tried to provide all of us with sex partners for the night; I was glad he had figured out that particular cultural difference. My love life was complicated enough as it was without adding random sexual encounters with strangers to the mix.

It was not long before we did retire to our rooms. Gwyn had omitted the female companionship but certainly not the security. Outside my door were four faerie archers, with two more at each end of the hallway. Gwyn had definitely not guarded me that way on my last visit. Evidently, he didn't trust Morgan any more than I did.

I slept well but was up at daybreak, reviewing the battle plan Nurse Florence and I had worked out.

The rules allowed me no weapons or magic objects, which was just as well, because through Oberon, Morgan might have had access to many potent mystic articles, but she couldn't use any of them. Yeah, I was feeling a little lost knowing I would be without White Hilt, but I shouldn't be totally dependent on that sword, anyway.

Morgan was an aggressive fighter and had tended to summon up electrical storms in the past. I would counter with the old Lady-of-the-Lake spell Nurse Florence taught me that would deflect the lightning from me, at least long enough for me to close the distance between me and Morgan.

Strangely, even though the duel was supposed to be magic against magic, unarmed physical combat was not prohibited. Morgan probably wouldn't be expecting such a move, and it could change the nature of the contest in my favor. Morgan might be a better spell caster, but she was going to have a hard time using that advantage while I was punching her into unconsciousness with my fists, particularly since she couldn't carry any of those poisoned daggers she was so partial to.

I had expected the trial by combat to take place in Gwyn's courtyard, but he told me that, as he was the *eiriolwr* (advocate) against Morgan, his castle was not a neutral enough territory. Fortunately, the rules also excluded any location controlled by Oberon, whom I was not surprised to learn was the *eiriolwr* for Morgan. Instead, the trial would occur on the Annwn side of one of the old *raths*, or faerie forts, in Ireland. Two of the *barnwyr* were Irish, so that made sense, though the site was actually well away from either of their homes, at Ardnamagh, near Moynalty in County Meath. The side on our world was an ancient ring fort pretty well overgrown with lush green vegetation. On the Annwn side, the Irish faeries had long ago built a large arena, still surrounded by greenery but providing seating enough for a very large group of faeries, as well as a raised platform from which the *barnwyr* could hold court and a very large central field in which Morgan and I would fight.

"Are they really going to need that much seating?" I asked.

"There will be, as you say in your world, 'standing room only,'" replied Gwynn with just a hint of grimness. "Quite aside from Morgan's infamy and Oberon's senseless defense of her, many of the faeries have never seen you."

I chuckled at that. "Can I really be that exciting to look at, particularly for faeries who behold wonders every day?"

"Not one quite like you. Has not Viviane told you of the political situation?"

"I know some faeries are concerned that too many mortals know about me and that we must be careful."

Gwynn frowned. "I don't want to distract you before the battle, but it is best you know that many faeries fear you, perhaps some more than Morgan."

Now it was my turn to frown. "Your Majesty, I'm just trying to mind my own business. Beings from the Otherworld keep coming after me."

"I know that," said Gwynn, "and you know I see you as a trusted ally, not an object of fear. But there are some who worry about how powerful you have become. You, and you alone, at least as far as we know, have used magic to influence your technology. The fear is that you will find a way to make that same technology work in Annwn..."

"Yes, I think Nurse Florence did mention that at some point, but it's not as if I'm trying to do something like that, and even if I knew how to make technology work here, it's not as if I plan to lead a party armed with machine guns here to gun down the faeries. Perhaps I should be bound by a *tynged* to put these fears to rest."

"I have upset you. I can tell from your voice. I should never have brought this up now." Gwynn looked even more worried than before.

"Majesty, it's good that you reminded me of this problem. Now I won't be thrown at the last minute if someone reacts oddly to me at

Ardnamagh."

"That's good to hear," said Gwynn. "Because those fears can be dispelled…but if Morgan triumphs, we will have a much bigger problem."

"Not to sound arrogant, Majesty, but there isn't a chance she will do that."

Gwynn was smiling now. "That's the spirit," he said, slapping me on the back in an oddly human way. Then he quickly bid me good-bye and hurried off to arrange our travel to Ardnamagh.

Luckily, there was a fixed portal nearby that connected to Ardnamagh, so we were there almost before we knew it. Gwynn was certainly right about the crowd. Even though we were there an hour before the trial by combat was scheduled to start, most seats were already taken, but there was a section reserved for Gwynn's men, and Sir Arian, who had guarded us when we were last in Annwn, made sure that the guys and Nurse Florence had seats.

Shortly after, a couple of Queen Mab's men escorted me into the arena and onto the field. I had already given White Hilt to Shar for safekeeping and had no other weapons nor any magic objects. One of them hesitated over the reed pipes, though.

"My magic is stronger when I have music," I explained, "but the pipes themselves are not magical." The two conferred, decided they could sense no magic, and handed them back to me.

"May I ask a quick question before you go?"

"You may," said one of the guards.

"This is a very large space. What if a combatant needs to communicate with the judges, uh, *barnwyr*, or they with us?" I was worried about needing to draw their attention to some breach of the rules by Morgan.

"The arena has magic…in your world you say 'acoustics,'" replied the guard. "Anything the *barnwyr* or *eiriolwyr* say in a normal voice can be heard by you or by the audience. You need to shout if you want to communicate with them, but your voice will carry well enough, even if you are on the far end of the field." I must have looked a little skeptical, since the guard continued, "We have been using this arena since before the time of the first Taliesin."

"I didn't doubt your word," I said. "I have just never been in this part of Annwn before, and much is strange to me."

The guard nodded but clearly had no desire to continue the conversation. "If there is nothing else…"

"No, thank you, I have everything I need."

With that, both faeries nodded again and departed quickly.

Once in the arena, I was the sole focus of audience attention, since Morgan and the *barnwyr* had not yet arrived. I had been a musician and an athlete for as long as I could remember (in this life and in others), so I was used to being scrutinized. Nonetheless, I found this attention particularly uncomfortable. Perhaps I was letting what Gwynn had said get to me too much. I magicked up my hearing a little to pick up some of the crowd conversation and immediately regretted doing that.

"The best outcome would be if they killed each other…," said someone, one of the Irish faeries, since the language was clearly Irish Gaelic. Immediately I put my hearing back to normal and reviewed possible scenarios. I quickly realized I wasn't focusing very well.

At the risk of sounding arrogant, I was used to seeing myself as a hero, and generally other people who knew the truth about me did see me that way. It was a shock for me to realize how many of the assembled faeries might not see me that way. However, I managed to stop thinking about my popularity—or lack thereof—with the crowd. It took more effort than it should have, but I did it.

What we would think of as the stands were now packed, and there was, just as Gwynn had predicted, standing room only. Given the way the place was built, that meant an audience of a few thousand faeries, not counting the guards, who were making themselves conspicuous. They were anticipating trouble; that much was clear. Before, I would have thought they were concerned over an escape attempt by Morgan or some scheme by Oberon. Given what I knew now, it was just as likely they were concerned about people in the audience trying to kill me. I was, after all, standing totally exposed in all directions. A faerie archer could have taken me out quite easily. I dared not conjure some defense, though—I was going to need every bit of my strength to deal with Morgan.

After what seemed an agonizingly long time, the *barnwyr* began to take their seats. Queen Mab I remembered from my last visit to Annwn. She was as beautiful as ever, though her lustrous black hair gave me a pang because it reminded me of Carla's. Mab's gown was a variation on the one she had worn before: slowly moving stars and moon on a midnight-blue background. The Amadan Dubh's costume was equally dark cloth, unrelieved by any heavenly bodies. Mab nodded to acknowledge the assembled faeries before sitting. By contrast, Dubh gave them a mocking bow and then more or less tumbled into his seat. Then he suddenly appeared distracted, as if he was missing something, and began looking all around him. Mab eyed him with clear irritation, doubtless wondering, as I was sure many others were, what had possessed him to serve as a judge in the first place.

At that point Arawn appeared, clearly trying to make more of an entrance even than Dubh. He walked slowly and deliberately, as if to emphasize the dignity of his position. Finally, he reached the middle seat and made a great show of sitting on it.

"It's not a throne, you know," said Dubh sarcastically, "and some of us would like to be done before next century." I thought Arawn was going to have an apoplectic fit at that point, so purple did he become, but he said nothing. I guess he couldn't risk losing the Amadan Dubh's deciding vote.

Looking more closely at Arawn, I could see how much he had changed since Arthur and I had raided his territory. Before that, he had had a temperament somewhat like Gwynn's; now he looked as if he had forgotten how to smile. His face had become just a flesh mask, concealing whatever inner torment he was feeling at losing the rule of Annwn so many centuries ago. Despite his ageless faerie nature, he looked older, and his garb was less elaborate even than Dubh's dark outfit. I had never seen a high-ranking faerie dressed so plainly.

"This court is now in session," he said as slowly as he had entered. "Bring out the accused."

Two guards entered the arena from the opposite side on which I was standing. Between them was a chained Morgan, but her face betrayed nothing, not even a trace of anxiety or anticipation. Another flesh mask, clearly.

"Let the *eiriolwyr* come forth!" demanded Arawn. Gwynn appeared from the right of the platform, wearing one of his red, white, and black garments suggestive of the colors of his three otherworldly hounds. Oberon entered from the left. Unusually short to begin with, Oberon looked even more diminutive than usual when standing so near the towering Gwynn. Nonetheless, Oberon had an undeniable presence; even if I had not known, I would have guessed he was royal, despite the great distance between us. His garment was a blue only a little lighter than Mab's, but in his case lightning was flashing across it, a reminder of his command over the weather. I found myself looking at his face to check for any resemblance to Julius Caesar, but I saw nothing in his handsome features reminiscent of his alleged father's.

"Morgan le Fay," continued Arawn, "You stand accused of crimes against your fellow faeries, and you have elected to attempt to vindicate yourself in trial by combat. Is this still your wish?"

"It is," said Morgan, flashing me her most confident smile.

"Taliesin Weaver," said Arawn, looking at me for the first time. "You took Morgan prisoner and are therefore her accuser. Do you accept the challenge?"

"I do," I responded, trying to sound every bit as self-assured as Morgan.

"There is one matter this court must address before the trial can proceed. Taliesin, in your former life you were responsible for the theft of my sword, *Dyrnwyn*, a sword that you currently possess. I must ask for the return of this blade before I can allow you to become part of these proceedings."

Well, there it was.

"We did not discuss this matter beforehand," said Mab firmly, "and I, for one, do not see the relevance of *Dyrnwyn* to this proceeding. Arawn, if you wish to demand the sword of Taliesin in another proceeding, then do so. But do not intrude your personal business upon this trial."

"It appears we need the voice of the Amadan Dubh to settle this question. What say you, Dubh?" asked Arawn blandly.

Dubh, who still seemed to be looking for something, glanced at Arawn in annoyance and said, "Let the boy keep the sword for now. You've been without it these fifteen hundred years. A few more minutes hardly seems to matter. I, like everyone else here, came to see a fight, and I intend to see one. I vote with Mab."

Arawn had plainly not expected that answer. For a minute I thought he was going to have an apoplectic fit again, and his mood was certainly not improved by audible laughter from the audience.

"The return of the sword need not prevent the continuation of the trial by combat. Morgan and Taliesin can fight right now. Meanwhile, my men will retrieve the sword."

"This is an outrage!" shouted Gwynn. "My men will never allow this!"

I spun around to look at the part of the audience where Shar and the others were sitting. Sure enough, some of Arawn's men faced Sir Arian and the rest of Gwynn's guards. Was there about to be bloodshed in the stands?

"Arawn, order your men to desist!" demanded Mab angrily.

Arawn looked surprisingly unperturbed. "Very well," he said, gesturing to his men, who quickly withdrew from Gwynn's section of the stands, "but let the record reflect that the *eiriolwr* accusing Morgan is in league with the thief who first took her prisoner."

So that's what Arawn had been up to! He wasn't stupid enough to try to seize White Hilt from the guys, who were under Gwynn's protection and surrounded by his men. He just wanted to make Gwynn's sympathy for me clear to the crowd…a crowd that pretty obviously had no use for me. I could hear audible booing as Arawn's men withdrew.

I glanced at the platform. Gwynn looked like a volcano ready to explode, but he held his peace. Really, there was nothing he could say, and he didn't want to provoke a war among the faeries. Mab looked almost as unhappy, but there wasn't much she could do, either. The Amadan Dubh looked delighted with the whole situation.

"Almost as good as the trial by combat," I heard him mutter.

"Taliesin, now that your right to participate has been…confirmed," rasped Arawn, "are you ready to proceed?"

"Yes, I am, Your…Honor!"

"Then—" began Arawn.

"Wait!" boomed a familiar voice. "If it please the court, I desire to be heard." Onto the platform strode Merlin himself, looking as happy as I had ever seen him.

To say that I was shocked would be an understatement. I had not seen, heard from, or sensed Merlin since the day I had liberated him from his prison, and his words on that day had suggested I would probably never see him again. In fact, it sounded as if he was ready for a major change, to leave his too-long life and reenter the cycle of reincarnation. Yet here he was, very much alive and radiating mystic energy, as if he was the one readying for a magic duel.

As shocked as I was, Arawn was more so. In fact, horrified might be a better way to put it. "Hell spawn!" he cried. "Begone! You have no business here. Guards!" A couple of obviously reluctant faeries appeared.

The tip of Merlin's staff had started to glow. "Arawn, I would have thought you would have been above name-calling. In any case, I do have business with this court." The glow brightened, and the fairy guards froze. "I trust you will do me the courtesy of hearing me out."

"And so I believe we should," put in Mab, as surprised as anyone else, but still clearheaded. "Dubh, as the humans say, the ball is once again in your court."

Arawn looked sternly in Dubh's direction. "The Amadan Dubh would never be responsible for making this trial a farce."

Dubh smiled mockingly. "Why no, I certainly wouldn't want to do that. You seem to be doing such a good job of it on your own. Still, I can't help but be curious to know what the wizard wants. I will vote with Mab to hear him."

"My thanks, gracious *barnwyr*," said Merlin, moving to the center of the platform as the guards sighed with relief and scurried away as fast as I had ever seen faeries move. "I am well aware of the need for haste in the matter before you, and I will not detain you long. I present myself to the court as Taliesin's champion. It is I who will fight Morgan."

For the first time, Oberon looked as upset as Arawn did. "Worthy *barnwyr*, Taliesin has already presented himself in person, with no mention of any champion. Nor have I ever heard of a champion nominating himself without the knowledge of the person whose right it would have been to designate a champion. Surely, you cannot mean to allow this breach of procedure!"

"Taliesin," said Queen Mab. "What say you? Is that man your champion in this matter?"

I was not usually at a loss for words, but this was an exception. Of course, I should have instantly accepted Merlin as my champion. He was a far more powerful spell caster than I was and could easily defeat Morgan, but I was having a hard time adjusting to such an unexpected change. What would provoke Merlin to appear so suddenly, so much without warning, and shove me out of the way? Did he have so little faith in me? I was pretty sure my strategy would have worked.

I glanced at Morgan, who was smiling. She should have been just as fearful as Oberon, but instead she looked…triumphant was the best word I could think of. For some reason, she wanted this to happen.

"Your Honor," I shouted back, "I thank Merlin for his offer, but he is not my champion. I intend to face Morgan myself."

Now it was Merlin's turn to be astounded. "Your Honor, I request a short conference with Taliesin." For a moment, Mab said nothing, clearly at a loss for the first time in the proceedings.

"Your request is denied," snapped Arawn. "Taliesin has spoken."

"Wait!" shouted Dubh. "I want to see what happens. Request granted!"

Arawn had gone pale, a nice change from his apoplectic purple. "Have you forgotten how to count? That's one to one. Queen Mab has the deciding vote." Arawn looked at her expectantly.

"The accuser has the right to pick a champion for trial by combat," said Mab slowly, "but he has already made his choice clear. I'm sorry, Merlin. That choice, once made, cannot be unmade. The law is clear. In this case, I must vote with Arawn."

Nurse Florence was almost shouting in my head, wanting to know why I had turned Merlin down. I didn't respond at first. I was too busy watching Morgan, who had stopped smiling. She really wanted to face Merlin, which made absolutely no sense. Well, at least she wasn't going to get her wish.

Then, for no apparent reason, Arawn said, "On careful reflection, I have realized that there is no precedent one way or the other. I don't agree, Mab, that the law is as rigid as you suggest. In the interest of fairness, I am changing my vote. Let Merlin confer with Taliesin if he still wishes."

What the hell?

If there was one thing Arawn definitely was not, it was fair. If I had had any doubt before, I had none now. Morgan wanted to face Merlin instead of me—and, even worse, Arawn was in on her plan. He must have expected Mab to vote the other way and had to improvise when she did not.

As I pondered, Merlin flew over and landed next to me. "Taliesin, have you taken leave of your senses? You have felt my power and hers. You know she is no match for me. Why refuse to appoint me as your champion?" Nurse Florence was simultaneously sending me a very similar psychic message.

"I know it doesn't make sense, Merlin, but for some reason Morgan wants you to substitute for me. If she wants it, it must somehow not be the right thing to do."

"Nonsense! Taliesin, who knows how long we have before that

fool Arawn changes his mind again. You need to name me your champion, and you need to do it now."

I hesitated for a moment. Then I opened my mouth, only to close it again. I could feel Merlin plunging into my mind with all the subtlety of a sledgehammer, trying not so much to manipulate me as to crush me and then use my body as a puppet to announce him as my champion.

In all the excitement, I had been so focused on what Morgan and Arawn were up to, it had not even occurred to me that Merlin might not be the real Merlin. Since I tried not to probe people's minds without a very good reason and since the mind of someone like Merlin would be well defended against probes anyway, especially in the presence of such a huge mob, it never even crossed my mind that I ought to check and see whether he was the real Merlin or not. But now, with him so close and behaving in such an unMerlinlike fashion, I realized the truth.

God, how I was beginning to hate shape shifters!

The shifter realized I was on to him…her…it…whatever, and it hit me with a blast of mental energy designed to stun me. I staggered backward, and the fake Merlin called out to Arawn.

"Your Honor, Taliesin is ill. I will have to take his place."

Nurse Florence was still connected to me. Quickly, I thought, *"Merlin's an impostor. Tell Sir Arian to get word to Gwynn!"* I didn't know whether she got the message or not, because the shifter hit me with another burst of mental energy. I was hanging onto consciousness by a thread. If I passed out, I had no doubt Arawn and the Amadan Dubh would replace me with the fake Merlin, who would then presumably lose on purpose, setting Morgan free.

With every ounce of energy I could muster, I spun around and punched the fake Merlin in the nose, a move he clearly wasn't expecting. This time he staggered backward, and I was on him, striking blow after blow. I would have to thank Shar for those boxing lessons one of these days.

Blood was pouring out of the fake Merlin's probably broken nose. My mind was beginning to recover from his earlier attacks a little, and I stared into his eyes, readying to launch a mental attack of my own while my fists were running on autopilot. When I made eye contact, though, I could see an unmistakable red glow, revealed either by the impostor's anger or surprise.

This was no ordinary shifter, but a demon!

Who had made a pact with him? Arawn? Morgan? Oberon? Certainly a demon would be overkill if all he was supposed to do was lose to Morgan. Any shifter could have done that.

Whoever was behind this had anticipated I might realize the truth. Any random shifter might not be able to defeat me, but a demon certainly could. Actually, a demon could kill me.

Apparently, staggering under my blows was just for appearances' sake. Now the demon had me by the throat and yelled to Arawn, "Taliesin has gone insane! I will try to restrain him! Keep the guards back, whatever you do." I could hear Arawn yelling something, but the demon was choking me so expertly that I was soon going to lose consciousness again.

I punched him in the stomach, but his grip did not loosen. "If you kill me this way, it will be obvious you're not Merlin," I whispered. "He wouldn't be strong enough."

"Right you are," the demon whispered back in his own soulless voice. He threw me to the ground and took aim with the staff he was carrying. "But he would be strong enough to do this!" The end of the staff glowed with the light of hellfire. In seconds I was going to be ashes.

"Stay back!" yelled the demon. Apparently guards were approaching. "This is not the real Taliesin. Let me handle him." From a distance, Merlin's attack would look like his usual fire magic, but if the guards got too close, they might be able to tell the difference between ordinary fire and the fires of hell upon which I could sense him drawing.

The interruption gave me the chance to jump to my feet and kick the staff to one side. He didn't lose his grip, however, and it would take him only seconds to aim at me again.

He who fights and runs away lives to fight another day.

I mustered what magic I could and launched myself into the air. Weakened by the demon's early assaults, I was not flying very well, but I did manage to zigzag enough to avoid the first flaming bolt as it shot past me.

I had three possible plays that I could think of. I could try to fly away, in which case the demon would probably run me down and kill me in short order. I could fly toward the platform. Arawn was against me, as was Oberon, and who knew what the Amadan Dubh might do at this point. Gwynn and Mab would help, though. However, if it was a three-against-two fight and the demon joined in, all I would have succeeded in doing was taking Gwynn and Mab down with me. The last possibility was to fly over the audience in the general area in which I knew Shar was sitting. If I could get my hands on Zom, the demon's attacks might bounce right off me. However, that meant that the demon would be aiming blasts of hellfire dangerously close to the audience. So, as was often the case, I really didn't have a good course of action.

Ratcheting my voice to a much higher than normal volume, I yelled, "That's not Merlin; that's a demon!" loud enough to be heard back in County Meath in our world. Maybe someone else would have an idea what to do. At the worst, by outing the demon to the audience, I had made it impossible for it to replace me and let Morgan go free.

Unfortunately, revealing its true nature wouldn't stop the thing from killing me. Another blast of hellfire passed dangerously close. However, a third didn't follow. Looking down, I could see the demon fending off faerie arrows, not an easy feat, even for someone with demon reflexes. At least somebody had heard me.

Then Jimmie was with me. "Tal, what can I do?"

"Hellfire can affect even you, Jimmie, so don't try to charge the demon. Get inside me and lend me some energy."

"Sure thing!" said Jimmie, and I felt him slip into me.

Below, I heard the demon scream as faerie arrows tore through its body. By now, too many archers were firing for it to intercept all of their attacks, and it was taking damage. That wouldn't be enough to drive it from this plane, though.

With Jimmie's energy beginning to recharge me and the demon occupied for the moment, I shot in the direction of the stands where Shar was sitting. "Toss me Zom," I yelled, and Shar complied unhesitatingly. He felt naked without that sword, but he trusted me implicitly.

"David thinks he can help!" yelled Stan.

"David and everybody else need to stay here!" I commanded. "Anyone getting too close is going to get killed."

"I'm fireproof!" thought Khalid.

"Not from this fire!" I thought emphatically, hoping that for once in his life, he would do what he was told.

I flew as fast as I could back toward the arena. By now the demon had formed a dome of flame around itself that burned up the arrows before they could hit it. Having done something similar with White Hilt, I had to give him points for ingenuity.

Now the question was whether the anti-magic force within Zom was strong enough to resist demonic magic. It had resisted Merlin's, but he was only half-demon. It had killed the demon in the story of Amir Arsalan, one of Zom's earlier owners, but that demon didn't seem as powerful as this one. Well, at least I knew I could find out without getting too close.

When attacked by a shape shifter some months ago, I had learned how to channel White Hilt's fire. Later, at the battle of Goleta Beach, I had learned how to do the same with Zom's anti-magic field. Zom knew Shar was its true wielder and was not as cooperative with me. Still, I had gotten it to obey me in time to defeat Morgan.

I willed it to blast the flaming sphere below. Nothing happened.

"Come on! Shar would want you to do this," I whispered to the sword. "Come on!"

A few green sparks shot from the tip.

"Seriously? Shar's own life could be in danger."

That was more than just hyperbole. I could hear chaos erupting in the stands. Given how complicated this plot already seemed to be, it wouldn't be out of the question for some attempt to be made on my friends while Gwynn's guards were distracted by the demon.

Finally Zom got with the program. Fitfully at first and then more strongly, it projected an emerald ray down at the demon's fiery shield. The results were not quite as spectacular or as immediate as I had hoped, but it did cut through the flames. Assuming Zom's power held out long enough, I could make this strategy work.

Faerie archers were circling in the air around me, and they quickly took advantage of the gaps I was carving in the demon's defenses. It screamed again as arrows once more pierced its flesh. Anyone else's magical defenses would have collapsed by now, and yet this demon was still maintaining some semblance of a fire shield around itself. That much resistance to Zom suggested a very high-level demon. It began to look as if some conspirator had not merely sold his or her soul but pledged to do some utterly vile act as well. Only a sacrifice that powerful would have brought a demon this strong into play.

By now I could see enough of the demon through the tears in the fire dome to know that it had abandoned its Merlin disguise. I could clearly see its fiery eyes and skin, as well as its claws. It was bleeding boiling blood from several arrow wounds but was still standing.

I had a good shot at giving it a direct blast of Zom's energy, so I took it. Engulfed in emerald flame, the demon screamed, and this time its defenses did collapse. However, unlike Morgan at Goleta Beach, its casting ability came back quickly. In seconds it had defensive flame rising around itself once more. I hit it again and again. Its power was still regenerating faster than I would have expected, but the rate was slowing down. The question was whether Zom would run out of juice before the demon was completely helpless. I could feel the blade's power ebbing. It had been designed to be something like an anti-magic suit of armor, and I was using it more like a laser beam.

It was then I noticed Stan running across the field, sword drawn. No, he was David right now; I could see the white light radiating from the blade, a glow that only appeared when Stan was David. Well, the Lord's anointed or not, I doubted he was immune to being burned up in hellfire or ripped to pieces by demon claws. The demon took an arrow in the eye and seemed on the verge of collapse, so I flew quickly in David's direction.

"David, get back off the field! That's an order!"

"I can help! I feel God's power in my sword. That which shattered the black altar can now destroy that evil creature."

"I said, 'Get back!'"

For a minute David was Stan again. "Tal, he's positive he can kill the thing. It's taken about a hundred arrows and is still going. Please!"

I turned to see the flame barrier rising again, temporarily shielding the demon from the arrows. I didn't want to risk Stan/David, but if their intervention was timed just right, it might be just what we needed.

"Wait until I give you the signal!" I shot back over in the direction of the demon. Just as I got into position, however, the flaming sphere collapsed, revealing a small lava pit beneath it. The demon had sunk into the ground and made its escape.

Damn! If David hadn't distracted me, we might have finished the foul thing. Now it would almost certainly be back. Well, that conversation would have to wait until later. Right now I had business with the court.

I flew over to the platform and landed right in front of the *barn-wyr's* table. The Amadan Dubh was applauding vigorously, and Queen Mab was nodding her approval. Oberon look a little shaky, and Arawn had retreated behind his flesh mask again and was completely unreadable.

"Are you all right?" asked Gwynn, stepping forward and looking me over as if he expected to find the marks of demon claws.

"I had a little help from Jimmie and your archers, I take it, just in time."

"His and mine," added Mab. "Arawn and Oberon seemed too paralyzed by fear to do anything," she continued contemptuously.

"I have no archers," said Dubh with another mocking smile. "But I was with you in spirit, Taliesin!"

"I…I was not paralyzed by fear," sputtered Oberon. "I was raising a storm with the intent of blasting the thing with lightning."

"But yet we see no storm," observed Gwynn.

"A great power was working against my casting," shot back Oberon.

"The more important question," I cut in, not being particularly in the mood for decorum, "is which one of you sold your soul to get a demon that powerful here?"

Arawn rose slowly from his chair. I could see purple was coming back into fashion.

"How dare you accuse us of such a thing? No faerie has ever sold his soul to a demon in the whole history of our race—which is more than I can say for you humans. How do we know that you did not stage this whole thing yourself to keep Morgan from having her trial by combat?"

"If anyone is in the mood to investigate, it should be easy enough to tell," I pointed out. "A pact that powerful will radiate dark energy."

"If the maker of the pact was foolish enough to keep it close at hand," countered Gwynn. "I definitely agree we should look, Taliesin, but I doubt we will find anything nearby."

"One thing is for certain," observed Queen Mab. "Today's proceedings have been corrupted. There is no way that we can risk a trial by combat today—or with the same *barnwyr*. The lots must be drawn again."

"There is no precedent for such a thing," growled Arawn. "If the trial by combat cannot occur, then Morgan must go free. It is the law."

"Then the trial by combat will occur," I said. "I am ready now."

"You have exerted yourself greatly, while Morgan has not," protested Gwynn. "She has an unfair advantage."

"Indeed!" agreed Mab. "We certainly cannot proceed until Taliesin is rested."

"We proceed now or not at all!" proclaimed Arawn.

"If you insist on such a travesty, you risk war!" Gwynn was almost shouting. "If such a ruling is made, I will have to assume that this tribunal is corrupted, just as Mab alleges. Wales will not accept this result."

"Nor will Ireland," said Mab with an air of finality.

"Let us not be hasty," said Oberon with a calm tone I sensed didn't accurately reflect his feelings. "It is true the law does not really allow for a postponement of the trial by combat in these circumstances. However, Taliesin would be within his rights to ask for a quest instead."

"And who would determine the nature of the quest?" asked Gwynn suspiciously. "You? Arawn?"

"The law does not say," replied Oberon. "Let us all agree on the task to be performed. If the three barnwyr, two eiriolwyr, and Taliesin, the accuser, all agree, then Taliesin shall undertake the agreed quest. If he completes the quest successfully, then Morgan is condemned. If not, she is vindicated."

"What if we do not all agree?" asked Gwynn. "Surely, Oberon, you will try to create a quest that Taliesin cannot possibly complete. Surely, Arawn, you will try to create a quest that will get him killed."

"And just as surely you will try to create a quest any child could complete," said Oberon. "That is why we must all agree."

"And if at the end we do not all agree?" asked Mab. "Unanimity among the six of us does not seem likely. The three barnwyr have yet to agree unanimously on anything."

Oberon sighed. "Then you will probably have your war."

I was every bit as suspicious of Oberon as Gwynn and Mab were, but I didn't want to be the cause of the first major faerie war in centuries. "Let's give it a try and see if we can agree," I suggested. Gwynn and Mab were both surprised, but both wanted to avoid a war even more than I did, and so they agreed to give Oberon's suggestion a chance.

The process of reaching agreement was more tedious than I could ever have imagined. The first several suggestions Arawn made got shot down almost immediately as impossible by Mab, Gwynn, or both, mostly before I could even think about them. Oberon said little, and the Amadan Dubh, again distracted by searching for something, said nothing at all.

"Find the lyre of Orpheus and bring it back to us," said Oberon after about the fourth hour.

Gwynn snorted. "Orpheus has been dead for three millennia. Who is to say the lyre even still exists?"

Oberon smiled. "I am happy to stipulate that, if it does not exist at all, Taliesin will win by default."

"Then surely, if it does exist, it must be guarded by some creature Taliesin is incapable of defeating," said Mab, her eyes narrow.

"We just saw Taliesin almost vanquish a rather powerful demon. We know he has bested a dragon. What kind of creature could possibly be so formidable that it would be impossible for him to defeat? But we will make the task easier. This need not be a solo quest. Taliesin can be accompanied by whoever he wishes: his warriors, his Lady of the Lake, his ghost, and his half-djinn. As far as I'm concerned, he can bring his rock band and soccer team along, too."

"There is something that you're not telling us," I said. "Superficially, the quest sounds too easy."

"Have I told you everything I know? No. However, I repeat, the instrument exists. It is possible to find it, possible to defeat its guardian, if there even is one, and possible to bring it back. If you can prove any of those statements false, you win by default, and Morgan will be imprisoned forever."

"Ah, I know what the problem is," I said slowly. "I would have to hurt an innocent person to bring it back, or its recovery poses some other moral dilemma."

Oberon smiled again. "You are clever. All right, I will stipulate the quest poses no moral dilemmas, and specifically I will say that no innocent need be harmed. Again, if you can prove me wrong, you win automatically."

"I am beginning to agree with Taliesin that this quest sounds too easy," grumbled Arawn.

"It does require some looking. The lyre is accessible, but its location may not at first be obvious. Still, if Taliesin is half as clever as he seems to be, he should be able to find the lyre."

I had visions of having to beat the security system in some Greek museum. Tricky, but with Stan's help I could do it.

"How long would I have to complete this quest?"

"Two weeks," answered Oberon, almost too rapidly. "Two weeks as time runs in your world. In the Otherworld it will be longer, though it is sometimes difficult to say how much longer, as you know."

"I agree to this quest, under the conditions stated by Oberon," I said. Gwynn and Mab nodded, though with some reluctance.

"Are you sure?" asked Gwynn.

"Yes, I feel confident I can fulfill this quest."

"Then I will not agree," snapped Arawn. "The quest is too easy. It makes a mockery of the whole process."

I knew he had to be acting, but he was undeniably doing a good job of it.

Oberon looked irritated with Arawn. He was probably acting as well.

"Trust me, Arawn. He can succeed, but there is a chance he will fail as well. I would not entangle my mother's fate with a quest that Taliesin could inevitably fulfill."

"All right, then, I will agree…reluctantly. Dubh, what say you? You have been silent this whole time."

"I agree," said the Amadan Dubh halfheartedly, as he continued his fruitless search for something.

"Let us all bind ourselves with a *tynged* to abide by the terms of this agreement," said Oberon in a tone more like an order than a suggestion. The faerie serving as court reporter created a draft to which we all agreed. Then we cast the appropriate spells, saw ourselves enveloped in golden light, and felt the *tynged* snap into place.

"Let our agreement now be announced to those assembled here, and let today's business then be concluded," said Oberon.

"I can't find my reed pipes anywhere!" complained the Amadan Dubh, obviously disgusted by his failure to locate them.

Of course, I had the reed pipes Mom had given me. She had been certain I would need them for something. Surely, this must be the universe giving me my cue.

Channeling the original Taliesin at his courtly best, I said, "Oh, great Amadan Dubh, fellow musician, it happens that I have reed pipes with me. They are family heirlooms, but please accept them as my gift, for well I know how difficult it is for a musician to be without his instrument."

The Amadan Dubh stopped and stared at me as if I had suddenly grown another head. Then he reached out a trembling hand, and I placed the pipes in it. He looked at them with wonder and then said, "No one has given me a gift in centuries." He played a few notes, powerful with magic, and then added, "I suppose you'll be wanting to find out what it is that Arawn and Oberon know but are not telling you."

"Dubh!" barked Arawn, but the Amadan Dubh did not even look at him.

"Yes, please!" I said, though inwardly I wanted to shake the words out of him instead of having to wait for them.

"The lyre is not, as you suppose, in your world. Nor is it in any Celtic Otherworld. It is in the Greek Otherworld."

"And how does one get to the Greek Otherworld?" I asked as calmly as I could. Arawn and Oberon were clearly both about to make some move to silence Dubh, and Gwynn and Mab were bracing to defend him. Nonchalantly, the Amadan Dubh reached over and put one hand on Arawn's shoulder and one hand on Oberon's. Both froze where they stood.

"That paralyzing touch is permanent on humans. Sadly it isn't permanent on faeries, but it should keep them quiet until we finish our conversation." Dubh chuckled to himself and then continued. "It is hard to reach the Greek Otherworld. The walls that keep the Olympians in will be just as effective at keeping you out. Someone must be related to an Olympian or the reincarnation of someone related to an Olympian, preferably both. Only such a person can seek admittance to Olympus, and even then, an Olympian has to invite the person. There! Now I have just saved you at least a week searching Greek museums for nothing. Go and find yourselves someone in whose veins flows the blood of a Greek god. All in a day's work, right?" With that, the Amadan Dubh started playing on the reed pipes. His music was beautiful, but it did not lift my spirits.

As I saw it, I had two options: I could deal with the emotionally unstable Alex, whose memories we had already wiped, perhaps prematurely as it turned out, or I could deal with religiously fanatical Vanora to try to find someone else who could get us invited to Olympus.

And, assuming we could somehow get in, Ares would be waiting for me.

Chapter 5: A Possibly Impossible Quest

"I think Oberon must have been spying on us," said Nurse Florence later, as we were sitting with Gwynn in his castle. "It sounds to me as if he knows about our encounter with Alex and how badly it went."

"Oberon is throwing away all pretense of integrity in an effort to save Morgan," said Gwynn angrily. "That last conversation shows that Arawn, Oberon, and the Amadan Dubh all conspired to produce this result. How else could the Amadan Dubh have known so much about Greek matters?"

"How do any of them know so much?" I asked. "I gather the Olympian situation is not common knowledge in Annwn."

"No, it is not," replied Gwynn. "Perhaps one of them found a seer who knew."

"I think there is a simpler explanation I should have realized sooner," said Nurse Florence. "Tal, you'll remember this from school. Who is Oberon's wife?"

"You mean Shakespeare got it right in *A Midsummer Night's Dream*? Titania."

"Correct. And what does her name mean?"

"I don't know," I replied slowly, "but it does sound familiar."

"In ancient Greek it means 'daughter of a Titan.' The Titans were…"

"An earlier race of 'gods' before the Olympians!" I finished for her. "So Titania is…"

"Probably the cousin of Zeus and the other elder Olympians," finished Nurse Florence. "Oberon knows about the Greek situation because his wife can get to Olympus. I'll wager she knows where the lyre is as well, not that her knowing helps us at all. I'm sure she isn't about to share that information."

Gwynn rose quickly. "Oberon is not the only one who has spies. I will see what I can find out and will send word if I should ferret out something useful. I would ask you to share my hospitality longer, but I know you must be getting back to your world to prepare for the quest."

Nurse Florence and I rose as well. "Indeed," I said, "we have to start looking for someone with an Olympian connection. With only two weeks to find someone, every second counts."

Gwynn nodded approvingly. "Right you are. Oh, Taliesin, I will have my tailors create suitable attire for you and the rest of your party. When you reach Olympus, I want you to make the right impression. After all, just being there does not mean the Olympians will help you, and I think you will need their help to find the lyre quickly."

"But we may need to fight at some point," I said worriedly.

Gwynn chuckled. "I wasn't going to create ceremonial togas. My tailors will work with my armorers to create attire suitable for combat and for ceremonial occasions, for you will probably need both."

We once again thanked Gwynn profusely, gathered the guys, and headed back to Santa Brígida as quickly as courtesy allowed. The next few hours, Nurse Florence and I had to work like crazy to do what needed to be done, though the cynical part of me felt as if our preparations were bitterly ironic. What we were doing was like meticulously packing for a cruise for which we had no tickets.

Nurse Florence went to work on the logistics, creating, with the unavoidable help of Vanora, a fictitious but highly prestigious field trip to eastern art galleries and universities that would involve me, the guys, herself (as faculty chaperone), and Carla. As usual, the parents ate up this explanation, as did Ms. Simmons, the high school principal. The soccer coach was less than enthusiastic about losing his two best players from practice so close to CIF, but Nurse Florence charmed him—probably literally—into accepting the situation gracefully. Unfortunately, Vanora wanted to include herself on the trip as well.

"As before, Vanora, we need you here, keeping watch on our families and friends while we're gone. Morgan's still in prison, but someone needs to be ready to defend against Oberon if he decides to make a move, and there is still the demon to consider." All of my arguments were reasonable, but Vanora clearly wasn't buying any of them.

"Nurse Florence can stay behind and look after the situation in Santa Brígida. I...I need to be at your side for this, Taliesin."

"You're going to make me say this, aren't you? Vanora, I just don't trust you right now. After the stunt you pulled the other day—"

"And yet here you are, needing the very spell you scolded me for suggesting."

"We will find a different way," I replied, tight-lipped.

"Then you need my help with the research."

"I need your help with keeping yourself the hell out of my way!" I snapped. "I think sometimes because I look so young, you forget who I really am."

"On the contrary, Taliesin, I know the real you better than you do!"

"Or think you do," I said, more anger creeping into my voice. "I don't intend to let you try to play John the Baptist to my Jesus Christ again. Your shenanigans are just distracting me from what I need to be doing."

I couldn't tell from Vanora's expression whether she wanted to fall down and worship me or crush me like an insect and find a different object for her messianic fantasy. "You know, I could pull the plug on the cover trip and make it very difficult for you and your men to get out of town."

"You know, I could have a nice long talk with your superiors in Cardiff and get you reassigned." I didn't really know whether I could or not, but at least it was a decent bluff. "Or I could talk to Gwynn and get your Annwn privileges revoked." Now that, I knew I could do, and without even working up a sweat.

Vanora gave me an odd smile. "Well, you couldn't fulfill your destiny if you were not a leader. I didn't mean to upset you. I will leave you now, but Taliesin?"

"Yes," I said flatly.

"If you can find no other way to get the attention of an Olympian, you will come to me." She sounded, as she almost always did when she could get away with it, as if she were issuing orders rather than making a suggestion or a request. I would have continued to argue with her, but frankly I was thoroughly sick of her, and my silence was the easiest way to get her to leave, which she promptly did, right after her proclamation.

An hour or so later, I was meeting with Nurse Florence—you may be sure I checked to ensure she was Nurse Florence—and I told her about the conversation.

"Honestly," I said, exasperated, "it wasn't that different from dealing with Carrie Winn when she was Ceridwen. She was trying to trap my soul in her cauldron. Vanora wants to keep me prisoner on a pedestal instead."

"She means well," said Nurse Florence halfheartedly. "Let's forget about her for the moment. Any ideas about how to reach the Olympians?"

"None yet," I said dejectedly. "There just isn't time to develop the kind of DNA test for Olympian relatives Vanora suggested."

"Is there any knowledge from your ancient Greek lives that might prove helpful?"

I strained a little bit to remember. "I'm not coming up with much of anything from the really ancient ones. I remember my life with Alexander the Great a little better now, though. I was…Hephaestion, his best friend…and ultimately second-in-command. I was as close to Alexander at the time as Stan and I are now and from about as young an age. If Vanora is right—big if—and Alexander really is among my current friends, it would be tempting to think he would be Stan, except that I spent so much time inside Stan's head trying to put him back together after he got hit with the awakening spell. If Alexander had been in there somewhere, I'm sure I would have noticed."

"You used to be very close to Dan, too," said Nurse Florence gently. The mention of his name was enough to tense me up completely.

"There's no way Dan is Alexander!"

"Are you saying that because you know, or because you just don't want him to be? Tal," continued Nurse Florence hesitantly, "I know this is a tough subject for you to deal with, but if there is any possibility that Dan is the answer to our problems, I think we have to consider it."

"I don't even know if Alexander is the answer to our problems. Yeah, Alexander expended a lot of energy while he was trying to consolidate his power claiming to be a son of Zeus, but I never saw any incontrovertible evidence that he actually was. Yeah, his mom, Olympias, claimed to be descended from Achilles, and Alexander was often compared to Achilles. Achilles was supposed to be the son of the Nereid, Thetis, and on his father's side, a great-grandson of Zeus, so I guess Alexander might also qualify as a possible contact that way, but again, I don't know whether Alexander's connection with Achilles is true or just a product of Olympias's public-relations efforts." I closed my eyes for a minute and concentrated as hard as I could, trying to make the details more vivid. I got flashes of Alexander triumphant in battle, conquering most of the known world, trying to set up an ideal kingdom in which different cultures and races lived in harmony. I got flashes also of moments of our friendship, and again I was reminded of me and Stan. But evidence that Alexander really had Olympian blood? Not one little piece, no matter how hard I tried.

"I just don't know. The Greek gods still had some contact with men in those days, but it was slight and subtle. It wasn't as if Zeus appeared and proclaimed Alexander as his son."

"What about you?" asked Nurse Florence. At first I didn't understand.

"No, I'm sure I'm not Alexander myself. I told you; I'm Hephaestion."

"I know, but the name means 'temple of Hephaestus,' doesn't it? Is there any possibility you had Olympian blood in that life?"

Even a few months ago, I would have laughed at that idea. Then again, I would have laughed if someone asked if I had written any of the biblical texts, yet I did turn out to be Heman, friend of David and author of Psalm 88.

"Nurse Florence, I may need your help with this. My Israelite past life didn't really come back to me in full detail until the presence of David stimulated it. I'm going to try to bring back the details of my life as Hephaestion, but I need you to lend your strength to my efforts. Maybe the two of us together can dig up something useful."

We spent more than an hour trying. By the end I felt drained, but I had resurrected one relevant memory. I was the infant Hephaestion in my cradle, and a man who didn't look like my father was bending over me and speaking to me. It was late at night, or so it seemed, anyway, and nobody else was around. Yet the stranger's presence was oddly comforting to me, not frightening, as it should have been. He had broad shoulders, like Shar's, but he walked with a limp; I could see his cane as he bent over the cradle. He was grimy with soot, as if he had just come from a forge. He looked just as the blacksmith god Hephaestus would have looked.

"That seems like a pretty conclusive memory to me," said Nurse Florence. "There would have been no reason for Hephaestus to visit some random infant. Hephaestion was the son of Hephaestus. You are Hephaestion…and the answer we need. You can get us to Olympus!"

"Wow! For once in my life, a simple answer!" I almost shouted. "Let me see if I can make contact now."

"Should you rest first?" asked Nurse Florence. You pushed yourself pretty far extracting the memory."

"We need to know for sure if I can get through to Hephaestion," I said emphatically. "Please help again, though."

We spent two hours, and three times I felt frustratingly close to connecting, but I never quite made it. It was like being able to see the shadow of Hephaestus but not being able to see the actual man…god…Olympian. I could feel something, but not enough to grab onto, not enough to enable me to make Hephaestus hear me.

When I opened my eyes again, I was almost shaking. "This isn't going to work!"

"Do we just need more power? Perhaps Gwynn could help."

"It doesn't feel like a power issue. It feels more like…trying to light a fire with a wet match. Adding more wet matches isn't going to get the fire lit. And there's just no way to dry them out.

"The Amadan Dubh," I continued, "suggested it would be better if the person was a blood relative as well, not just a reincarnation of a blood relative. I think that's the problem. My life from twenty-three hundred years ago isn't a strong enough tie, and apparently my current body has no blood relationship to the Olympians."

I wanted to punch something, so much, in fact, that I found myself reflexively clenching my fists. "The only other person we know for sure who has a connection is Alex, but, aside from the fact that he's so unstable, using him would be like shouting in Ares's ears that we were coming."

Suddenly Nurse Florence's eyes lit up. "I think I have the answer. I feel stupid for not realizing this before. We can just ask your mother!"

I raised an eyebrow and just stared at her for a second. "I thought seers only got random bits and pieces. What are the odds she has the specific answer to exactly that question?"

"You're right to be skeptical, "replied Nurse Florence," and it's quite possible my idea won't work, but it is worth a try. Yes, seers usually get random bits and pieces. That's why so often people get no answer, a partial answer, or even a misleading one. The seer reveals whatever she knows, perhaps not always understanding it herself. However, your mother's pattern seems a little different to me.

"Think about it, Tal. Even before she knew what she was, she recognized that the house was under a protection spell, she started calling Stan 'David,' she recognized Morgan le Fay as evil, and she had dreams that captured every detail of your travels in Annwn."

"All of which suggests what?"

"That your mother seems to pick up far more detail about you than a seer would typically know. Usually seers are more or less friendless, as well as isolated from what family members they may have. Seers are also usually neutral, even indifferent, giving whatever insight they have to whoever asks for it. A lot of them seem to believe that kind of sequestered, unconnected life is the price of their gift. But what if that traditional belief about what a seer must do is wrong? Your mother is different from any seer I have ever met. She raised you, she loves you, and she is unconditionally on your side. She is in daily contact with you and your friends. From what we have seen, her visions about you are not random or disjointed. That doesn't mean she'll know where the lyre is, unfortunately. It may mean she can tell which of your friends, whom she sees almost every day, has a link to the Olympians."

Suddenly, I remembered my mom reading *The Lyre of Orpheus* and listening to "The Lyre of Orpheus," neither of which made sense at the time. She didn't consciously know what she was doing, yet she somehow tapped into Oberon's intent—and she had never even been on the same plane of existence with him.

"You're right—it's worth a try! Mom! Can you join us for minute, please?"

Mom came out of the kitchen, wiping her hands on a dish towel.

"Sophia, can you by any chance tell us which of Tal's friends was Alexander the Great in a previous life?" How ridiculous that question would have sounded just a few weeks ago.

"Oh, that must be Shahriyar!" said my mom as if it were the most obvious thing in the world. "Just the other night, I had a dream in which you and he were friends in ancient Greece, and he conquered the world. That sounds like Alexander the Great, doesn't it?"

I jumped up and kissed her. "Mom, you're brilliant! That's exactly what it means! Now we don't have to search anymore. But it's odd that Shar, a Persian, is the reincarnated Alexander the Great, since Alexander spent most of his time fighting the Persians."

"Perhaps it makes more sense than you think," suggested Nurse Florence after just a second. "The ancient Greeks believed the Persian royal family descended from Perses, a son of Perseus. Perseus, allegedly like Alexander, was a son of Zeus. Now if Shar happens to be descended from the first Persian royal line—"

"Hard to prove," I cut in, "but his father told him once there is a family tradition to that effect—"

"Then Alexander and the Persian kings he fought were blood relatives—"

"And Shar, as the reincarnation of one and the descendant of the other, has exactly the combination of backgrounds the Amadan Dubh suggested would work the best."

I couldn't help hugging my mom again, as well as Nurse Florence. "We can get to Olympus!"

"Do I want to know?" asked Mom nervously.

"Actually," replied Nurse Florence with a big smile, "there is more of a trip involved than that school field trip, but this one is more like a…diplomatic mission. Tal has a quest to recover an artifact. With any luck, no fighting will be involved."

"I don't suppose by any chance you can direct us to where the lyre of Orpheus is?" I asked quickly, figuring that after what my Mom had revealed about Shar, anything was possible.

"You know, I have seen the lyre of Orpheus recently," said my mom in a very matter-of-fact tone, "but it was too dark for me to tell where it was."

"That's all right," said Nurse Florence. "The Olympians are bound to know where it is."

"Good!" said Mom, looking as happy as I had seen her recently. I guess my mood was contagious.

"Anyway, I guess you don't need to know about Dan, then."

"What about Dan?" I said, shuddering despite myself.

"I dreamed about him the same night I dreamed about Shar. I thought perhaps the two dreams were connected."

"What did you dream about him?" I asked, hoping I sounded patient but feeling appallingly anxious.

"He was in the Middle Ages. I think you were in the dream, too, as the original Taliesin. Dan was King Arthur's best knight, I think, his chosen champion, or something like that. Oh, Lancelot, that was his name."

My heart sunk. "Mom, you must never tell that to anybody else! It's very important."

"I won't, of course," she replied. "But why is that so important?"

"I'll explain later," I said, not really wanting to explain at all. The less Mom knew about this particular problem, the better. Whether because she was a seer or because of her maternal instincts, she took the hint and not only dropped the subject, but excused herself to go back to making dinner.

"She's right, you know," I said to Nurse Florence as soon as Mom was gone. "The two dreams are related."

"How so?" she asked worriedly.

"Different solutions to the same problem. The Shar dream gives us the chance to complete the quest and get Morgan locked up forever. The Dan dream gives us a chance to provide Morgan with what she wants and get her off our backs. I haven't thought about it in a while, but she wanted me to find Lancelot for her, and I think that's what she still wants. Why else is she so keen on keeping me alive?"

"Tal, you wouldn't—"

"Of course not!" I replied forcefully, but the truth was, part of me had entertained the idea for a second. And somewhere inside of me, Dark Me was opening champagne and throwing a party, having now found the perfect way to give Dan exactly what he deserved. If I ever lost control again and let Dark Me get the upper hand, Dan would be toast.

"I just wish I didn't know," I continued. "Should I ever be captured by Morgan or one of her allies, that piece of information could be probed out of me. I think you'll need to erase it for me once this is over. I'd have you do it now, but we need to move fast if we are to get to Olympus tonight."

And so we did. The guys and Carla arrived with suitcases for the fake eastern trip, and my mom fed them all dinner while I explained what we now knew about Shar, who was a little overwhelmed about his new background.

"Son of Zeus?" he kept saying over and over.

"David says—" Stan began, so I had to explain, for David's benefit, that the Olympians were not gods but merely beings like the faeries, and that we would not be worshiping them on the trip.

"David, it's much like your diplomacy as king of Israel. You had to deal respectfully with foreign rulers who did not worship God. Think of the Olympians as foreign rulers. We will respect them, but we will not worship them."

What if worship is what they demand as the price of the lyre? thought Nurse Florence.

I'm going to consider that a moral dilemma under the terms of the tynged and declare a win by default, I thought back.

Just as we were finishing dinner, Nurse Florence excused herself and came back after a few minutes to announce that Gwynn had delivered our wardrobe for the trip. We went out in the backyard to find our new clothes lying neatly on the lawn. In just a few minutes, we had changed into them and reassembled in the living room, looking like a completely different group of people. In five minutes we were transformed from a bunch of high schoolers into something out of Tolkien. Maybe clothes really do make the...person.

OK, so Carla did look nothing short of spectacular. Her gown was an almost luminous blue-green with a moving seascape, including a wide variety of fish swimming vigorously through the depths of the sea. Just as Mab's and Oberon's outfits reflected their powers, so, too, hers reflected her affinity with sea creatures. It was, interestingly, not as tight as her normal choices, but with her figure, it didn't need to be.

"Gordy, put your eyes back in your head!" I scolded him jokingly.

"I'm just looking at...the fish," he replied, not really paying any attention to me.

Nurse Florence's white gown also featured a moving scene, in her case fittingly showing the original Viviane, the Lady of the Lake, presenting King Arthur with Excalibur. In the background I could see many of Arthur's men, including Merlin and the original Taliesin. Leaving aside the question of how one could get what amounted to looped video into clothing, the detail work was incredible. Yeah, I was also reminded that Nurse Florence's figure rivaled Carla's.

The guys had all been given leather pants and vests that were much more flexible than normal leather. Nurse Florence explained that that was because they weren't leather, but specially cured dragon skin. They would not impede movement, and they would be much lighter than full armor, even faerie armor, while giving as much protection from weapon strikes.

Like the ladies' gowns, each set of dragon armor was customized for its wearer. Mine featured an array of musical instruments surrounded by slowly undulating flames. Shar's featured an incredibly detailed scene of Alexander's victory at the Battle of Issus, an image as fluid as Carla's seascape or my fire. Did a seer design the armor, or was the connection to Alexander the weirdest coincidence ever? Regardless, Shar looked majestic in it—an important consideration, since he would be our first contact with the Olympians.

Gordy had the image of a photo-realistic—and moving—lion. Carlos, like Carla, had a brilliant seascape but with an image of himself swimming through it. Stan got an incredible moving panorama of the battle between David and Goliath. Khalid's armor showed him flying through the air over a city that looked remarkably like medieval Baghdad.

Then I noticed Dan's. He had a scene of medieval combat I couldn't place at first. The central figure, however, was clear enough as he led the army to victory—Lancelot, whom I recognized not only from his face but from the coat of arms on his shield (three red diagonal lines known as bends on a white field). The one secret about Dan that needed to be buried forever, and Gwynn's men had etched it into his dragon armor, for all the world to see!

Nurse Florence, seemingly oblivious to my horror, was talking about the other features of our armor. "Gwynn really outdid himself on these. Just like the swords he gave some of you a few weeks ago, each of these sets of armor gives some special gift to its wearer. Tal, yours makes it easier to call up fire, even if you don't have White Hilt to use as a source, and it gives a little boost to your musical ability. Dan, yours improves your skill with the sword to the point at which virtually no one can beat you."

How could she not see what was right in front of her? But she just kept droning on, regardless.

"Shar, yours gives you the power to call upon the spirits of some of Alexander's men for help once each battle. I don't know how Gwynn managed that, but at some point I'm sure we will see how it works. Gordy, yours makes you fearless, which from what I've seen you already are, and it gives you more strength. Carlos and Carla, yours give you each the power to breathe under water. And Khalid, yours gives you the ability to fly. Gwynn figured if you were always going to be getting yourself in trouble, you needed a faster way to escape.

"Speaking of escapes, my gown enables me to travel by water, Lady-of-the-Lake style, even when the body of water I would use as an entry point is some distance away. That may come in handy at some point. Gwynn also threw in this bag," she continued, "that he assured me can hold anything. I don't know what he expects us to be carrying back, but if we need to take something unusual, we're prepared.

"Oh, and one more thing. All of our gifts will enable us to understand ancient Greek and to speak it when addressing the Olympians or anyone else we might encounter. Tal already knows ancient Greek, but the rest of us would be unable to understand, and we have no way of knowing whether anyone on Olympus speaks modern English."

Jimmie was looking extremely dejected. "Everybody got something except me!" he whined, again sixteen in looks but nine in sound.

"Actually, Jimmy, Gwynn didn't think you needed armor, since most weapons can't hurt you anyway, but he did send this ring," said Nurse Florence, holding out what looked like a ruby ring. "It's like the dagger Khalid got a few weeks ago. Within reason, it will give you what you wish for, but it can only be used once, so choose wisely." Jimmie took the ring, delight shining in his eyes.

Again, I was annoyed by Gwynn's penchant for giving such powerful artifacts to children. It was hard to be too annoyed, however, with someone who had lavished so many gifts upon us. Between the weapons and the armor, we were each as well equipped as a faerie king or queen.

"Nobody ever took measurements," said Carlos, looking down at his perfectly fitting armor. "How does everything fit like this?"

"Faerie garments made for a specific person will always fit him or her," replied Nurse Florence.

"That's good," said Shar. "I usually have a hard time finding things that aren't too tight in the chest."

Gordy rolled his eyes. "And I suppose you have trouble finding pants that aren't too tight for your—"

"My mom's still here," I reminded Gordy quickly. And so she was, awestruck by the faerie armor.

"I don't think I've ever seen anything so beautiful," she whispered.

"Neither have I," said Carlos, but I noticed he was looking at Carla. Like Gordy, he seemed to have developed an unexpected fascination with marine biology. It suddenly occurred to me that Carlos might be the solution to my Carla problem. Carlos, Carla—could it just be coincidence, or was the universe dropping another hint?

As happy as that idea made me, I was haunted by Dan's dead-giveaway armor. If Morgan or any of her allies saw it, she would never stop until she got Dan. All the more reason to make sure the faerie authorities locked her up and threw away the key!

As the guys admired each other's armor, horsing around a little in the process, I pulled Nurse Florence aside. "Does Gwynn have a traitor among his armorers? Dan's basically outs him as Lancelot."

Nurse Florence looked at him in growing alarm. "I see the central figure is Lancelot, but does that have to mean someone knows he's Lancelot?"

"The central figure on Shar's is Alexander, and wow, guess what? He's Alexander!"

"Don't be flip with me!" she scolded. "I think Gwynn had a seer help with the designing of each set of armor. The seer must have sensed the connections. But I don't think it's a conscious attempt to out him. He isn't going anywhere near Morgan or anyone who knows Morgan on this expedition."

"But if Gwynn's seer could figure out who Dan was so easily, what keeps Morgan from just asking a seer about him?"

"If Morgan posed a question about whether or not Dan was Lancelot, she might get the answer, but remember she doesn't know that that's the question to ask. I'm sure she's already asked who Lancelot was in this life and came up dry."

"Just the same, I don't want to take chances. Jimmie!" He didn't seem to want to stop contemplating his ring, but reluctantly he floated over. "Jimmie, I need you to do something very important for me."

"Sure, Tal, whatever you need!"

"On this trip I want you to stay close to Dan. You know the old saying, 'Stick to him like glue'? Well, do better than that."

"I'll ride inside if he lets me," said Jimmie happily. Then, more seriously, he asked, "Is he in danger?"

"I hope not," I replied quickly, "but I don't want to take chances, OK?"

"Your wish is my command!" he said, darting away to hover close to Dan.

"That really should be Khalid's line, shouldn't it?" I asked Nurse Florence with a little smirk.

She studied me for a moment before answering. "Is it just me, or are you starting to care about Dan again?"

"I wouldn't let Morgan have my worst enemy," I said, chewing my lower lip a little bit.

Pretty soon it was time to see if Shar could make a connection with one of the Olympians. With Shar's permission, I got inside his mind far enough to show him how to invoke the Olympians and to guide him in his attempt. Nurse Florence had everyone else form a circle and join hands while she wove a spell around them that would allow Shar to draw on their energy if need be. I think she was still convinced I could have connected myself with just a little more juice. In any case, if Shar needed a boost, she had one ready.

At first nothing happened, but then I began to feel...a presence of some kind on the other end of the connection. I had felt something similar earlier, but it was always weak, distant, and unaware of me. In this case, it got progressively stronger, and I knew we had gotten someone's attention.

"Who calls upon us?" asked a voice that suddenly boomed in Shar's head. It was naturally speaking Greek, but Shar's dragon armor allowed him to interpret.

"I am Shahriyar Sassani, a reincarnation of Alexander the Great and a descendant of Persian kings. I humbly seek entry into Olympus for myself and my party."

"For what purpose?" asked the voice.

"My leader in this life, Taliesin Weaver, who was once Hephaestion, son of Hephaestus, has been given a quest he can only complete with your help. The lives of many people may be forfeit if he fails in his quest."

"Enter then, and welcome!" replied the voice.

The air nearby began to shimmer, and a portal slowly materialized—more slowly than I was used to, but it got there eventually. On the other side, I could hear ancient Greek music, including lyre music, which seemed a good omen. I stepped through without hesitation, and the others followed.

Chapter 6: A Quest within a Quest

As used as I was to stepping through a portal and being in the presence of Gwynn ap Nudd, I was unprepared to find myself in what was obviously the throne room of Olympus. Luckily, I still had the presence of mind to bow, and the others followed my lead.

It was hard to tell exactly how big the room was; it seemed to stretch out forever in all directions, but I knew that must partly be the result of the mist that surrounded us on all sides, through which I could dimly make out Corinthian columns. The floor was brilliantly polished marble, which looked dim in contrast to the almost blindingly brilliant golden thrones that made me think it was day, though the room was in fact open to the night sky, sparkling with stars.

The thrones formed a half circle, at the center of which burned the sacred hearth fire tended by an older-looking Olympian woman I took to be Hestia. She was more simply attired than the others, and her warmth seemed greater than that of the fire. I felt immediately that we had at least one friend here.

I was puzzled, though, by the conspicuous absence of the other elder Olympians. I had not thought to see Hades, but the empty central thrones, which must have belonged to Zeus and Hera, troubled me, though I didn't know why. Also missing, at least judging by appearances, were Poseidon and Demeter. One absence, however, did not trouble me at all: Ares was nowhere to be seen, at least if the artists' representations were even remotely accurate. Him we could definitely do without.

Even without their elders and their warlike brother, the younger Olympians were a singularly intimidating bunch. Apollo, clothed in white and glowing with a golden brightness that exceeded even that of the thrones, could not help but intimidate any guy who looked at him. If he had been a high school student, he would have been the one you just knew your girlfriend really wanted to be with, if only she weren't stuck with you. Somewhat less radiant but equally handsome was Hermes. Even seated, something about him suggested a restless energy and a speed I figured even the faeries could not match. Dionysus, superficially less overwhelming, seemed to use an affable exterior as a mask for an intensity that smoldered within him; his outward appearance was like a pleasant drink with a friend, but his inner self seemed more like a head-splitting hangover...or worse. Apollo's sister, Artemis, glowed silver. She was beautiful, yet she radiated an unapproachability I would never want to test. Athena, too, radiated aloofness, though, despite her stern gray eyes and the armor she wore, she seemed a bit less severe than Artemis.

The two that struck me most, though, were Aphrodite and Hephaestus. What can I say about Aphrodite? If Apollo was the guy who made every other guy insecure, Aphrodite was the girl every other girl hated, the prom queen about whom every guy fantasized. Making a mental apology to Eva, I had to admit Aphrodite was the most beautiful woman I had ever seen—and keep in mind I'd seen faerie queens and hundreds of years' worth of other women.

Aphrodite smiled, turning her charm up to almost lethal levels, I'm pretty sure on purpose, and effectively paralyzing every guy in the group. Our hearts beat for her in unison. Our blood boiled at the same temperature. In that moment, we would have crawled the distance of the soccer field over live scorpions just to reach her.

Unlike the way I felt under Alcina's dark magic love spell, I still had free will—sort of. Well, at least I remembered Eva and my love for her. Still, whatever energy Aphrodite was pouring over us was indescribably powerful. It was only focusing on Eva with every drop of will I had that kept me from throwing myself on the goddess right then and there. Shar refrained by touching Zom. The others broke ranks and surged in her direction. I had the feeling the result was not going to be consistent with decorum.

"Aphrodite!" interrupted Hephaestus gruffly. "Is this any way to treat our guests?" As fast as the compulsion had begun, it ended, leaving the guys, who had been racing in her direction, in an embarrassed heap at her feet.

Wait! Even Jimmie had ended up in that tangled pile of chagrined teenage males. Jimmie had the form of a sixteen-year-old, but no actual body, so whatever hormonal apocalypse Aphrodite had triggered should not have affected him at all. Yet there he was, shamefacedly disentangling himself from the other guys and backing away from Aphrodite. His cheeks were as red as anyone else's. Alarmed, I managed to catch Nurse Florence's eye.

"What's up with Jimmie?"

"You know how much he wants to be like you and Dan. That's why he has that teenage form in the first place. He's just pretending to feel what everyone else feels."

I wasn't entirely convinced, but at that moment I became uncomfortably conscious of Hephaestus's intense scrutiny and turned in his direction.

He looked exactly as he had in my infant memory. He was not the ugliest Olympian, as some stories said, except perhaps when compared to the others. He was more like ordinary than ugly, but in a group that would put every top model in the world to shame, his relatively plain appearance did stand out. Perhaps if he ever washed the soot off and wore something other than a blacksmith's apron, he might not look quite so out of place next to Aphrodite, his unwilling wife.

"Husband, I was merely having a little innocent fun with them," Aphrodite protested, winking at me as she did so.

"They have business here," replied Hephaestus, almost angrily. "They did not come for your games."

I had expected another playful response, but to my surprise, Aphrodite said, "You are right, Husband," and smiled apologetically at him. Perhaps the old myths about them and their unhappy marriage were not all true.

"And what is this business, Shahriyar Sassani?" asked Apollo, leaning forward in his throne.

"Magnificent One, it is business best explained by the man to whom I have sworn my loyalty, Taliesin Weaver."

"That was not always your name, though," said Hephaestus, again looking at me intensely.

"No, Lord Hephaestus. I was once Hephaestion, and I believe I had the honor to be your son."

"I thought as much," said Hephaestus, nodding. I had expected more, but he said nothing else. Evidently father-son reunions were not his specialty.

"Speak, then, Taliesin Weaver," continued Apollo, "and let us know this business."

"Oh, radiant Apollo, I have been given a quest that requires me within a short period of days to bring back to a faerie court the lyre of Orpheus. Will you give it to me, or tell me where it is, that I may obtain it myself?"

"The lyre of Orpheus is no small trinket, Taliesin Weaver," said Hermes before Apollo could respond. "To gain it, you must first prove your worth to us."

"Hermes!" cautioned Hestia in a stop-teasing-your-younger-brother voice. "Tell him the truth!"

Hermes sighed. "I will leave that to the teller of truth, then."

Apollo, looking somewhat annoyed, continued. "The truth is, we don't have the lyre of Orpheus, Taliesin. If we did, we might indeed have asked you to complete a test, but as it is, fetching the lyre will be test enough."

"Stories claim the Muses took the lyre after his death," I said, wondering what could have happened to it but not wanting to ask the question so bluntly.

"And so they did…but it was stolen centuries ago. It now lies in the Underworld." Short of Tartarus, where the Titans lay imprisoned, the Underworld was just about the hardest place to reach. Unfortunately, it was not quite impossible to get there, so the *tynged* was still technically unviolated.

"Hades stole the lyre?"

Apollo sighed. "It would have been simpler if he had. Unfortunately, it was someone else, someone to whom even Zeus was reluctant to give orders—when he still ruled over Olympus." I was dying to ask the obvious question, and I think Apollo could see that, but I also knew the penchant some supernatural beings had for going on forever, and I needed to know how to get to the lyre, not what had happened to Zeus.

I could see in Apollo's face that he longed to answer the question I was trying so hard not to ask, but he was interrupted again, this time by Hestia.

"Demeter could tell the story better than I, but as she is not here, Taliesin, I will tell the sad tale of how the lyre came to be stolen, and how, though it is not the cause of our problems, it is certainly a reflection of them."

I opened my mouth to politely decline, but Hestia had already started.

Chapter 7: Hestia's Tale

"At the dawn of time," Hestia began.

Seriously? This is going to be worse than I thought.

"The being you refer to as God, and you," she said, nodding to Khalid, "refer to as Allah, who had already created angels and djinn, created the races you know as faeries and our race and other similar ones, each to help and teach the people of a specific region."

At least this was new material. I could see Nurse Florence staring in fascination. It might have been rude to take notes, but I knew she was soaking up every word for her report to the Order.

"God gave us all free will," continued Hestia solemnly, "and we abused it, setting ourselves up as gods and leading the people in our charge astray. God was patient at first, but eventually he changed the rules. We always had to exert ourselves to walk in the world of mortals, but as time went on, we found it harder and harder to make our will felt there, as did the various other races of 'gods,' until at some point, around two thousand of your years ago, we found ourselves virtually locked out of the mortal realm altogether."

"I don't mean to interrupt, oh Wise One," I ventured, curiosity compelling me to ask a question despite myself. "The faeries can still enter the mortal realm, though they must return frequently to their own in order not to lose their powers."

Hestia smiled a little. "They realized the truth somewhat sooner than we did and gave up their pretense of godhood. We, however, fought the increasingly restricted state in which we found ourselves, cursing and struggling instead of learning to accept a different role. That is why they have more freedom in the mortal realm than we do, though they could find themselves in the same state in which we exist, should they interfere too much in human affairs."

"*Which explains,*" thought Nurse Florence to me, "*why they are so afraid of someone like Ceridwen or Morgan making their existence too obvious or doing too much evil. It isn't just that they are afraid of humans coming after them, as we used to think. A bigger issue must be keeping whatever truce they think they have with God.*"

"This is worse than being in school," muttered Gordy." I poked him in the ribs. No matter how long Hestia dragged out the story, we could not risk offending her or the others.

"Apparently, though, God, in the interest of keeping the human will free," continued Hestia, "allows us to respond if humans invoke us, though only humans already connected to us in some way can invoke us successfully, and even then, we can do little in their world, though we can bring them into ours, as we brought you.

"Once we had worn ourselves out with cursing our fate, we gave our now frustrated creative energy a new outlet, thinking perhaps God would forgive us if we did something constructive. We built a replica of the world we had lost. This plane of existence includes not only the dwellings of the Olympians and the Underworld; it also includes a replica of the mortal realm as the ancient Greeks knew it."

"Those mortals who find their way here and then choose to stay with us," interrupted Apollo, "can marvel at the Colossus of Rhodes, watch Spartan warriors train, or browse in the library of Alexandria."

It was a little creepy that Apollo seemed to be making a sales pitch for us to stay, but I pretended not to notice.

"We were wrong, though," continued Hestia. "Our recreated world was wondrous, but it was evidently not enough to gain God's forgiveness. We tried other approaches then."

"Yes," said Athena. "Through the handful of humans who invoked us, we gained some of the human sacred texts. Others we already had, having recreated them when we recreated the library of Alexandria. We read your Bible, your Quran, and many other works, but we still could not figure out what God wanted of us. We tried to adopt the moral principles in those texts, but nothing we did seemed to help. After centuries of frustration, our society began to break down. Zeus believed he could gain enlightenment by following the example of some of your holy men and traveling off into the wilderness to meditate. After a while, I think Hera was convinced that he was not meditating but womanizing and tried to follow him. We know they still live, but their path has been obscured from our eyes.

"However rough Olympian society had been, it became worse with Zeus no longer here to enforce order with his thunderbolt. Poseidon claimed the right to rule in the absence of Zeus, and when his claim did not meet general approval, he retired to his palace in the depths of the sea and has ignored our pleas for help ever since. Hades became even more reclusive than before and has not been seen on Olympus in centuries. Demeter went looking for Zeus, hoping he would restore order, and then she, too, vanished.

"Nor were the elder Olympians the only ones to desert our society or to simply disappear. Ares left and spends all his time in the wilds of Thrace, building an army for no particular reason any of us can understand. Pan, too, wanders in the wilderness, with an ever-growing troop of nymphs and satyrs, as that wilderness grows progressively more and more out of control, and our recreated world continues to deteriorate, for Gaea, Mother Earth herself, no longer supports us, and those of us left cannot maintain the balance on our own."

"Pardon me, Wise One," I said in as diplomatic a tone as I could manage, "but time grows short, and I still do not know who has the lyre."

"When Zeus and our brothers and sisters defeated the Titans," Hestia began.

Just shoot me now!

"...Hecate, like some of the other children of Titans, sided with us. But to Hecate, Zeus gave more lavish rewards than he did to the others. All of us have our own limited spheres of rule, but to her, Zeus gave power on earth—and apparently what lies beneath it—in the sea and in the sky."

"He must really have wanted to sleep with her," chuckled Hermes. Hestia glared at him and continued. "At first, Hecate was a benevolent member of Olympian society, but almost all of us resented her, and over time the friction she had with us changed her. Instead of helping humans or Olympians, Hecate gradually abandoned her old benevolence and sought solace in the darkness, gaining power in the Underworld and in the night and then infusing witches who would devote themselves to her with that same power.

"She is still not strong enough to move against us, but without Zeus and the other elder Olympians, we cannot move against her, either, and Hades will not join our side."

"What did she want with the lyre?"

"That I can answer," said Aphrodite. "It was love."

"A feeling best avoided!" said the virginal Artemis emphatically. Aphrodite rolled her eyes and just kept going.

"Your myths emphasize the love between Orpheus and Eurydice. But there is an earlier part to that story that only a couple of your tales preserve. Hecate loved Orpheus, and Orpheus charmed Hecate with his lyre for some reason, I forget what exactly. When Orpheus announced his marriage to Eurydice, a woman Hecate wanted for one of her priestesses, you can imagine her outrage. It was Hecate who arranged the death of Eurydice. The rest of the story I think you know, except that, shortly after the departure of Zeus, Hecate stole the lyre from Calliope, the Muse who was Orpheus's mother. Hecate took the instrument to her gloomy abode in the Underworld, and it has not been seen since."

"All is not lost," said Hermes. "Another lyre could be easily made."

"I fear not, oh Swift One. My quest specifies the lyre of Orpheus. No other will do."

"Then it seems you must journey to the Underworld to find it," said Apollo sadly. "But know this: we cannot aid you as we might wish. There are barely enough of us left as it is to keep even the minimal order we have managed to preserve. If we try to help you, everything we have built may be lost in the process."

"Oh, Radiant One, tell us how to get to the Underworld, and you will have done more than we could ever have asked." Really, I could have asked for a hell of a lot more, but I clearly wouldn't have gotten it. "But before we depart, let me repay the information you have given us by telling you something you may not have heard yet. Ares has not spent all of his time in Thrace. He found a way to encroach on our world to the extent of giving a descendant of his a very powerful weapon, called the sword of chaos."

The Olympians could hardly have looked more surprised. Horrified might have actually been a better way to describe their reaction.

"How could Ares ever have obtained that sword?" asked Dionysus. He had almost appeared to be sleeping at times, but clearly this subject captured his interest.

"It is my fault," replied Hephaestus, lowering his eyes.

"Wasn't creating the foul thing in the first place enough?" asked Apollo angrily. "You told us you had destroyed it."

"Destroying it was not something I ever found a way to do without unleashing a terrible explosion. I found a way, though, to sink it into the depths of the sea…"

"Then isn't it obvious what must have happened?" asked Athena. "As we have long feared, at some point Poseidon allied himself with Ares. The lord of war would have had no means to find something in the sea, but no corner, no matter how deep, would have been too far to keep Poseidon from finding it."

"Poseidon had not left Olympus when I hid the sword in his realm," said Hephaestus, somewhat defensively.

"You never should have created it in the first place," Apollo replied in an accusing tone. "What evil thought possessed you?"

"Not evil," said Aphrodite gently, "just male ego. Ares bet him he couldn't do it."

"Forgive me for interrupting such grave deliberations," I said, bowing slightly, "but the sword is safely out of Ares's reach in our world, encased in a layer of pure love that keeps its chaotic nature from hurting anything."

Aphrodite gave me another wink, and Hephaestus looked at me with an almost...paternal pride.

"And Ares's minion?" asked Dionysus.

"We destroyed his memory of the sword and of Ares. He will be no further trouble."

"These heroes from the human realm have done us an immense service in stopping whatever Ares was trying to do," exclaimed Hestia. "Certainly we owe them more now than just directions to the Underworld."

"In truth we do," responded Hephaestus quickly. Aphrodite smiled brightly and nodded her agreement, but Apollo was not so easily won over.

"Now that we know Ares may be planning a joint assault with Poseidon, we have all the more reason not to divide our resources," he pointed out, though not as vigorously as before.

"Brother, surely I can at least show them there in person," said Hermes. He was, among other things, the guide of souls to the Underworld, so we could hardly have asked for better help.

"If our questers can wait a brief time, we can each find some gift to give them that will help on the quest," suggested Artemis. "I agree with Apollo that we can hardly leave Olympus unattended, but some of our equipment might serve them well. Girl!" she said abruptly to Carla, "can you use a bow?"

As the reincarnation of Alcina, Carla did have pretty formidable magical powers, but she was not as used as I was to dealing with supernatural beings in this life. "I...I took archery a couple of years at summer camp," she managed, clearly unnerved.

"I see you have no weapon. Foolish of your male companions to let you come unarmed."

"I have...the ability to cast spells," Carla managed.

"Spells have their uses, but give me a good bow every time. I see that no one in your party has any kind of ranged weapon. You shall have one of my old bows, one whose arrows are hard to deflect, and no one in your party has any kind of long-range weapon, so the bow could certainly be needed at some point."

"Thank her!" I thought to Carla.

"Oh...gracious Artemis, you have honored me...more than I deserve," Carla said and bowed.

"Just see that you make good use of the gift," replied Artemis. "I shall fetch it now, and each of you, my Olympian brethren should go quickly to your own palaces and return with something worthy of these heroes."

Apollo looked as if he wanted to protest, but he also knew how stubborn his twin sister was, and as the other Olympians rose and prepared to return to their own palaces, he must have realized the futility of dragging out the argument. Even he bustled off quickly to find something to aid us in our quest. Abruptly, we found ourselves alone with Aphrodite.

"Taliesin, I wish to speak with you!" she said invitingly, pointing me toward a spot far removed from my group.

"Wishes to jump your bones is more like it," chuckled Gordy. "Every supernatural woman we run into seems to want to." Stan poked Gordy for me, though I had to admit that was pretty much what usually happened.

We walked for quite a distance—the chamber must have been even bigger than I thought—until the rest of my party was hidden from us by the fog, and we from them.

"Taliesin, I fear I have little that would be useful in a fight, but I do want to do something for you to show my appreciation for what you did with the sword of chaos. With that, she undid a couple of clasps, and her gown rippled to the floor.

Perhaps Gordy was becoming a seer.

Aphrodite clothed was hard enough to resist, but Aphrodite naked? Her flawless skin shone like the sun, blinding my moral sense and leaving me only a burning lust that would consume me more surely than the blaze of White Hilt consumed my enemies. Every particle of my being ached to hold her immaculate body, to kiss her infinitely inviting lips, to merge myself with her.

"No one need ever know," whispered Aphrodite in a voice like the sweetest melody I had ever heard.

Then I realized there was one particle of my being that was protesting vehemently—the one that still recalled Eva. I was actually in Aphrodite's arms. I could actually feel her pressing against my soon-to-be-discarded clothes.

Eva had told me she didn't love me anymore and had actually suggested that perhaps her love for me had never been real. What did I owe her? Nothing!

I was in the arms of the goddess of love. At last I would be with someone in this life who truly wanted to be with me. Or did she? Would she have been willing to be just as passionate with Shar, Dan, Gordy, Carlos, or Stan, if any of them had been the leader of the group?

The hormonal part of me was quick to say, "Who the hell cares?" I slipped out of my dragon-skin vest; it was a really good thing it was dragon skin. At that point I would have torn off an ordinary shirt.

Aphrodite's perfect breasts were now pressed against my bare chest. My heart was beating like a drum. I felt dizzy but still ready to lose myself in what would have to be the best sexual experience of this—or any—life.

I could smell Aphrodite's perfume, a scent like…jasmine.

A scent like Eva's jasmine perfume…or was I just imagining the scent? My hand was on the drawstring of my dragon-skin pants. Or was that Aphrodite's hand? We were becoming one already.

Or were we? The image of Eva was getting stronger and stronger in my mind, haunting me, coming between me and Aphrodite. I was pretty sure Aphrodite and the other Olympians could not read minds, but in matters of love, I was equally sure she could at least pick up on my mood.

"Pretend I'm her if you want to," she whispered. "In fact, I can become her if you desire me to do so. I can be any woman to you, or even all women." You can imagine what the high school guy part of my brain did with that image.

Ceridwen had tried to be Eva for me. I didn't know she was Ceridwen at the time, but the memory remained an unpleasant reminder of her attempts to manipulate me sexually. Of course, Ceridwen had been my mother in a previous life, which made the experience even grosser in retrospect. But if I thought about it, Aphrodite had been what amounted to my stepmother in a previous life.

"Do it, you wimp!" whispered Dark Me somewhere deep inside me. "You know you want to!"

Yes, I did want to. I would have crawled across the Sahara Desert at the height of summer on my stomach for this. But if Dark Me wanted me to do it, wasn't that a pretty good sign I should do the opposite?

Most of my thought process for the past few minutes had been occurring below my waist, but with what little intellect I had left, I tore myself out of Aphrodite's arms, turned around, took a couple steps away from her, stumbled, and fell to my knees.

"Oh…queen…of…love, most desirable female in…the universe, I beg you not to take offense," I was whispering. My body, trembling, almost got up of its own volition and threw itself upon Aphrodite.

"I love…another," I managed, somewhat more loudly.

"You love another who does not love you," replied Aphrodite. "How can you betray someone to whom you are tied by no vow, no obligation?"

I took the risk of taking a glance at Aphrodite. Yup, still naked. I looked quickly down at the ground. It would not take too much for me to lose that small, shriveled part of my intellect that was holding on in the hormonal maelstrom inside me.

"Perhaps I can't betray her, but I can betray myself. As long as I feel this way, I cannot make love to you." I was uncomfortably aware of the number of myths in which mortal men refused goddesses and then died, but I couldn't remember Aphrodite killing anyone over being refused. Of course, come to think of it, there were no myths in which anyone refused Aphrodite.

She laughed musically, pretty much exactly the opposite of what I had expected. When I looked up in surprise, her gown had somehow already gotten back on to her body.

"Taliesin, you never disappoint me! I knew you would prove true to your love."

"You mean, this was…a test?"

"Don't be angry with me," said Aphrodite playfully as she handed me my dragon-skin vest.

"Just out of curiosity, what would have happened if I had failed it?"

"Surprisingly little. Taliesin, I am not any longer the same being you have read about, though I know I must have seemed so for a moment. I am trying to put the moral principles of your sacred texts into practice."

Wow! If this is what you got out of the Bible, I'm lucky you weren't reading the Kama Sutra!

"I have actually succeeded in being loyal to my husband…for a little while…and I intend to continue doing that as long as I can."

"Then what was all this about?" I asked, relieved that she was not going to turn me into an antelope or something but a little irritated at being used.

"Just because we cannot enter your world does not mean we cannot observe it. I have been aware of your unrequited love for Eva for some time, Taliesin. I know how miserable you are, and it breaks my heart to watch someone so noble be treated thus.

"I said earlier I cannot give you anything that you can use in your coming quest. I can give you hope that will help motivate you to survive it, however. I pledge to you that I will do everything I can, short of violating her will, which I know you wouldn't want, to unite the two of you."

"You aren't playing a game of some kind with me?" I asked, forgetting my need to deal with the Olympians diplomatically.

Aphrodite laughed again, even more heartily than before. "There is an oath you know no Olympian can break. I swear by the River Styx to do everything in my power to win Eva's love for you without compelling her to love you. Is that enough to satisfy you?"

"More than enough, oh Compassionate One!"

Could it be true, that after four years, I might actually get what I wanted? Of course, to do that, I would need to survive a trip to the Underworld. What was it the Amadan Dubh had said? "All in a day's work."

I should have realized that my vest was a little askew, my hair a little messed up, and my pants were a little…tight. That, and the wide-as-the-Grand-Canyon smile on my face when Aphrodite and I returned to the group, gave my friends entirely the wrong impression.

"I told you!" said Gordy to Stan. "You owe me twenty bucks!" Aside from Stan, the guys looked ready to high-five me. Nurse Florence, by contrast, appeared to be gearing up for a lecture of some kind. Carla turned deathly pale and looked down at the ground. I could feel my cheeks reddening.

"I have to say, though, Tal, it didn't take you very long!" quipped Gordy.

"Silence, mortal!" shouted Aphrodite with enough force to crack marble. Gordy cringed away, and the others looked fearful. Was the wrath of Aphrodite imminent?

"How dare you question Taliesin? He has just experienced the test of a lifetime…no, of many lifetimes—and passed it. Yes, I offered him the chance to make love to me, and he alone among men and Olympians refused. He refused even though I exerted enough of my charm upon him to rob him of all but a shadow of his willpower. Such is the firmness of his determination. Such is the power of his love!"

The mood of the group changed instantly. Gordy became sullen; not only had he been proved wrong, but now he owed Stan twenty bucks! Nurse Florence smiled in a way I knew represented how proud of me she was. The guys generally looked impressed, if confused. Stan let David out for a minute to give me a bow.

"Had I had such willpower as you, Taliesin Weaver, I never would have betrayed God's trust."

"Are you sure you're not gay?" asked Gordy as I got closer to him. Now it was my turn to laugh.

"Not in this life!" I said with a deliberately ambiguous smile. Gordy laughed heartily at that and was back to being his usual, high-spirited self. Just as well he reacted that way; the last thing I wanted to make time for was to lecture him on homophobia.

Only Carla's mood remained unrelentingly grim. In fact, she looked like gloom incarnate. She knew she was not the reason I had resisted Aphrodite. Try as I might, though, I could only feel so bad about that. I had never led her on, not even once.

Fortunately, I didn't have too long to ponder that problem, as the Olympians began returning with their gifts. The first was Artemis, who gave the promised bow to Carla, looked at her very sharply, and said, "When you return, join my maidens and forget all about these men. They are not worth the pain they cause." Carla didn't seem to know quite how to respond, but Artemis did not pressure her for a response. She did, however, glare at me as she turned and moved back to her throne.

Hermes returned with a small glittering object that was apparently what amounted to a pass key to the upper levels of the Underworld, as well as several small ancient Greek coins. "This key will not open all of the interior gates, but it will serve to get you in—and out. Should you need to flee, it will open the outer gates even if Hades or some other Underworld power tries to lock them."

"What about the coins?" I asked.

"They can be used to pay Charon, the ferryman of the Underworld. I doubt not that I can convince him to take living beings, but no one could convince him to take any passenger without payment."

Winking, Dionysus gave us an ever-full wine goblet.

"Those who examine the contents of this goblet closely will see its true value," he said with another wink. Nurse Florence, plainly irritated, quickly took charge of the goblet; it was clear to me it would not leave the magic bag Gwynn had given her. Well, at least it wouldn't be spilling all over the place that way.

Apollo, for all of his initial reluctance to help, gave us a healing salve that Nurse Florence pronounced more powerful than anything she had seen before. "With this," she said, "I can expend far less energy on healing, which means I can hold out much longer in the event we need to fight our way in or out."

Hestia gave us a burning brand from the hearth of Olympus. "Guard this well!" she said. "From the most ancient of times, the hearth fire has been sacred, protecting each home from the evil forces outside."

"You mean like in vampire movies, where the vampires can't come into someone's house unless they are invited?" asked Gordy. At first the question confused Hestia, but then she laughed. "Indeed, young hero, just so. Carry this brand with you and keep it burning. Its flame will provide some protection against evil forces in the Underworld."

Athena presented us with an ever-full jar of olives. "Look to these in time of trouble. Look carefully. Should you be forced to stay in the Underworld longer than you anticipate, you can survive on these awhile. Remember that you cannot eat anything in the Underworld without becoming trapped there. Even Zeus could not force Hades to release Persephone after she had swallowed just a few pomegranate seeds. Heed this warning, or nevermore see the light of the sun."

Hephaestus presented his gift last: what we would think of as an android, a vaguely humanoid machine he had created.

"My son, his name is Amynticos, or Defender in your language. He is a somewhat smaller version of Talos, the mechanical man I designed to guard Crete. I have ordered him to obey all of your orders and to protect you at the cost of his own existence, if necessary. He is not indestructible, but he is tough, and magical attacks aimed at living things will not touch him, as he is not alive." Amynticos bowed stiffly to me, and as I looked into his shiny glass eyes and meticulously shaped bronze face, somehow human-looking despite not being flesh, I realized it might be difficult to treat him as just a machine.

"Thank you...Father," I said to Hephaestus. "I will try to prove myself worthy of such a great gift...of all of your gifts," I said, bowing to each of the Olympians in turn, "precious beyond measure."

Between Gwynn and the Olympians, we were exceptionally well equipped. For the first time since hearing about Hecate, I began to feel a little more optimistic.

"Return alive, with your quest fulfilled, and that will be thanks enough for all of us, my son," said Hephaestus.

"Heed my words," said Apollo. "This is the extent of what we can afford to spare for your quest. Should you become trapped in the Underworld, we would have little power there under the best of circumstances. As things stand now, we have none. Nor can we waste our strength on hopeless rescue efforts, for to do that would be to jeopardize Olympus itself."

"I understand, and I will heed your words," I said, with another bow.

"One last piece of advice," said Apollo, much to my surprise. "Only two mortal men ever successfully penetrated the Underworld with the intent of taking something the Underworld rulers did not want to give them: Heracles and Orpheus. As lord of prophecy, I tell you this: you will need to combine their methods to prevail, for you are neither as strong as Heracles, nor as musically gifted as Orpheus."

So much for optimism. "I will remember this prophecy, my lord, and invoke its wisdom in time of need."

After a few more excessively ceremonial good-byes, we were actually on our way, and I must say I did not regret saying good-bye to Captain Buzz-Kill, otherwise known as Apollo.

Since only some of us could fly, Hermes managed to shepherd us down from the heights of Olympus on clouds, specially magicked up for the purpose. From the base of the mountain, he steered us rapidly south.

I knew we were in a hurry, but part of me wished there was time to gain some of Hermes's knowledge of magic. As the original Taliesin, I had heard a great deal about Hermes, sometimes called Hermes Trismegistus (thrice greatest), who was supposedly both the Greek Hermes and the Egyptian Thoth, the bringer of magic to both people. Like a lot of the stories about the original Taliesin, I knew some of the stories about Hermes were nonsense. However, being so close to him, I could feel the magic in him, powerful magic. The other Olympians certainly had what would be considered magical abilities, like the control of their particular domains, as well as shape shifting and invisibility, but from none of them did I feel the same amount of raw, versatile magic as I felt in him. I wondered if even he realized that he was in some ways different from many of his kin.

"How do we enter the Underworld?" asked Nurse Florence.

"You die," replied Hermes with a totally straight face.

"I meant, how do we enter for purposes of this particular quest?"

"Oh, that," said Hermes, chuckling to himself. "We are flying to the southernmost point in mainland Greece, at Cape Matapan. There is more than one entrance, but they all end up in the same place, and the Cape Matapan entry is the closest. There is just one small problem."

"And that is?" asked Dan. Usually he had kept his mouth shut on our recent trips, but his impatience finally got the better of him. I actually couldn't blame him in this case.

"Remember that we recreated your world when we could no longer reach it. This is not the Cape Matapan of your world, crowned by a ruined temple, but the ancient version, crowned by a still functioning temple...to Poseidon. That wouldn't necessarily have been a problem, but now that we suspect Poseidon may be an enemy, it is possible that he knows of your arrival and is watching Cape Matapan, meaning to intercept you."

"Then we'll take him down," said Gordy, who was back in characteristically good spirits.

Hermes laughed derisively. "Foolish youth! If only it were that simple. Poseidon's power is second only to that of Zeus himself. With his trident he can stir storms at sea or earthquakes on land. If he is intent on keeping you from reaching the Underworld, he can flood the entrance or bury it beneath tons of rock. And if his trident should strike you..."

"Yeah?" asked Gordy.

"You will reach the Underworld...the hard way."

Chapter 8: A Very Wet Reception

"Oh Swift One, if approaching Cape Matapan is so dangerous, what is the next closest entrance?" I asked.

Hermes considered the question for a minute. "Acheron, far to the northwest, in Epirus. But we were observing some kind of military activity there when you first arrived. Since we could not identify its source, it is likely the work of either Ares or Poseidon. The next closest entrance would be in Italy and take even longer to reach."

"Then I guess Cape Matapan sounds like the best bet," I admitted. "I'm not sure we can afford the extra time to get to Italy, and Acheron sounds risky at best."

"I had thought the very same thing," replied Hermes.

"How could Poseidon know we are even here, much less where we are headed?" asked Carlos.

"He might not. He is not all knowing, but like all of us, he is farsighted, and he can use any sea creature as a spy. Even a sea gull flying near Olympus might have heard or seen something that would make him suspicious."

The wind suddenly blew much more intensely, and the sky became gray with clouds at an unnaturally fast pace.

"I like this not!" observed Hermes. "Smell the salt! That wind is blowing in from the sea."

By now the wind buffeted our cloud, making it hard for Hermes to keep moving south.

"We had better land," he announced. Unfortunately, a gale-force wind hit us at that moment. I could feel the clouds begin to shred beneath my feet. Hermes was trying to bring us down, but we got slammed by even more winds, some of them wedging themselves between us and the ground to prevent our descent.

"I can neither sustain these clouds nor bring us down safely," shouted Hermes over the now raging storm. "Poseidon means to dash those of you he can on the rocks below. How many of your party can fly?"

"Carla, Jimmie, Khalid, and I are the only ones," I explained. I could see cloud fragments streaming out from us in all directions.

Hermes looked worriedly at our group. "The clouds beneath us will be torn completely apart soon, at which point Poseidon will probably end the wind that is now keeping us from landing. With me, we have only five fliers to try to save eight others, and the air is highly turbulent. Some of your warriors may perish unless we can find a better plan."

Fortunately, I had an idea. Carla, Nurse Florence, and I could link to each other and concentrate our collective psychic energy on making everyone else float down slowly. That strategy, plus those of us who could fly bearing part of the load, might just do the trick.

Unfortunately, there was no time to implement that plan. A moment before I could have told anyone about it, the last of our cloud disappeared, and we were in free fall.

Hermes grabbed Nurse Florence and Carlos, who happened to be closest to him, and tried to descend, only barely able to hold his own against the tearing claws of the wind. Trying to follow his example, I grabbed Stan and Dan, but Dan in particular was too heavy. I could feel the muscles in my right arm scream in protest. We were dropping too fast. Carla was faring no better. She had Gordy, who was clearly too heavy for her, and I could see the two of them dropping faster even than Dan, Stan, and I were. The power of our magic should have done more of the work, but summoning up magic takes time, of which we did not have enough, and the storm raging all around us made concentrating as much as we needed to difficult.

Khalid was physically the weakest of any of us, and his efforts to float down with all 250 pounds of Shar seemed doomed. The power of flight his dragon armor gave him did not give him the ability to levitate three times his own body weight. I suppose he could have let Shar go, but Shar was like a brother to Khalid; he would crash himself before he would allow Shar to fall. I could see him straining every muscle and crying as the realization hit him that nothing he could do was going to save Shar from hitting the ground far, far too hard.

"The water!" I yelled at those of us who were trying in vain to save our plummeting friends. "Aim for the water!"

"No!" yelled Hermes, who had somehow been fast enough to land Nurse Florence and Carlos and was coming back for more, despite the storm. "Poseidon could easily kill anyone in the water!"

I suddenly realized Jimmie was thrashing around in the air, having a hard time slowing himself even though he wasn't carrying anyone.

"Jimmie, what's happening?" I yelled, but he couldn't hear me well enough over the howling wind to answer.

By now Hermes had managed to grab both Shar and Dan, a

strain even for the flying Olympian, but somehow he managed to hold on and to descend with them at a reasonable speed. That freed Khalid to help Carla with Gordy, and the two of them succeeded in controlling his descent. I could manage Stan by himself, and Jimmie seemed to have recovered from whatever was causing him to drop.

Too late I realized that no one had Amynticos. I called out to him, but he was too distant for me to grab hold of, even with my mind. He had heard me earlier, though, and he somehow managed to change his trajectory enough to hit the sea rather than the rocky beach, though he had fallen from such a great height at full speed that I imagined there wouldn't be much left of him. I supposed I would rather lose him than anyone else in the party, but for some reason I found myself tearing up a little—over a machine!

By the time we were all safely on the beach, we had sustained bruises and pulled muscles but were, all things considered, in remarkably good shape otherwise. Nurse Florence wanted to treat what injuries there were, but Hermes adamantly disagreed.

"It is vital you get off the beach as soon as possible!" he insisted. "Poseidon will keep trying to kill you, and this close to the ocean, he will have no problem doing so."

"We need to head into the Underworld right now, then," I replied. "He can't hit us there, right?"

"Poseidon has no power there," Hermes agreed.

"Look," yelled Jimmie, pointing toward a nearby mountain peak. The structure at the top must have been the temple of Poseidon that Hermes had warned us about earlier. Men were flooding down a pathway toward the base of the mountain. The day was dark, but I could clearly see the glint of weapons.

"Men?" I asked Hermes.

"Somewhat," he answered doubtfully. "What humans have come here over the years have tended to breed with the Olympians. I wouldn't be surprised if most of that group are descendants of Poseidon."

"Great!"

"Hurry!" shouted Hermes. "The cave that leads to the Underworld is just at the base there. I will hold them off long enough for you to reach it."

"Incoming!" yelled Carlos. I looked in the direction he was pointing and saw the mother of all tidal waves getting ready to smash us into the sand. It looked as if it had enough force to break bones and burst lungs, but even if we survived the impact, all but two of us would probably drown before the water receded. Being knocked unconscious, as we doubtless would be, might actually be a blessing.

We might successfully have moderated the force of the wave if we had had more time, but I figured we had maybe a minute and a half at most, certainly not enough time to wrest control of the sea lord's own wave from him. Nor could we be sure the old "touch Zom" strategy would work. In magic very few things were really absolute, and the Olympians were operating at a higher power level than most of the faeries and wizards we had encountered before could have managed. Nor was Poseidon's power the only factor; I could feel within the wave not only Poseidon's magic, but the raw power of the ocean itself. Zom's power might stop the magic but not necessarily the non-magical part of the wave's momentum. The sword had simply never been tested in this situation before. I wouldn't bet my life, and certainly not anyone else's, that Zom's protection would shield us completely, especially not divided several ways. Fleeing was out of the question, except for those of us who could fly. As we had just been reminded, we couldn't move everyone else very fast.

There was perhaps one way to survive, but it relied on how fast Hermes would react. Well, he was pretty fast, so I took the chance.

"*Link us all up, including Hermes!*" I yelled psychically to Nurse Florence and Carla. We connected ourselves this way so often that they could initiate the process in just a few seconds. However, for my plan to work, Hermes needed to participate willingly.

I grabbed Hermes's arm. "My lord, lend us your strength." That kind of magic was clearly alien to him, and he seemed confused.

"Please, Lord Hermes, trust me!" He nodded reluctantly, and I could feel power flow from him right away, rich, intoxicating, and overwhelming as had Merlin's power been when it touched me.

"Everyone, get close together, drop on the sand, and hold on to each other. Touch Zom if you can." Shar drew Zom and put it in the center of the group, so that everyone could touch it.

I had only seconds now, but I had been working myself up to faerie speed. I drew on the vast force rushing through me, and having no time for careful construction, threw raw power around us protectively, like a force field. Since we were clumped pretty close together, I only needed to protect a small area. I also did what I could to implement a variation of the lightning deflection spell I had seen the Ladies of the Lake use, though in this case I was trying to deflect the force of the wave to slide around my little force-field bubble.

When the wave struck, my deflection spell failed almost at once—there had not been time to set it properly, but between Zom's protection against magic and my force field, I still felt the impact, but without the pulverizing intensity Poseidon had planned. Nor did the wave crack the force field, though I wasn't sure how many hits like that it could take, even with Hermes helping. However, surviving the initial impact meant little if we all suffocated. Fortunately, it did not require much magic to conjure enough oxygen to keep us breathing until the water started receding.

Before the wave had completely ebbed, though, swords and spears rattled against our magic bubble. Poseidon's men had reached us and were attacking with great vigor. There was so much reverberation from Poseidon's magic that I couldn't really tell how large the attacking force was, so I kept the field up until I could figure out what we were dealing with. I also needed to determine whether or not Poseidon was going to strike again from the sea. I didn't think he would crush his own supporters, but his wrath seemed so out of control I couldn't be sure.

"Wondrous!" whispered Hermes, looking at the force field admiringly. "We Olympians have fought together often, but we have never thought to combine our...mental energies in this way. United, our power might compensate for the absence of Zeus's thunderbolts."

"Pardon, my lord, but let us focus on getting the mortal members of the party out of here alive."

"Of course," said Hermes, flying out of the bubble and hovering over our attackers. I was unnerved, though I did not need to be in physical contact with him to draw again on his power if I needed it. If he forgot us completely, though, that might be a problem.

"People of Matapan, I command you to disperse!" Hermes said in a thunderous tone that must have been a good imitation of Zeus's.

"Get out of the way, errand boy," sneered an older, gray-haired, and very unmilitary-looking man who might have been Poseidon's priest. "We worship only Poseidon here!"

For a moment Hermes seemed to be at a loss for words. Perhaps no mortal had addressed him in that way for centuries, if ever.

Hermes was used to using his power in more passive ways than this situation required, but sadly I had had a lot more experience with this kind of potentially out-of-control brawl. With a flick of the wrist, I conjured a fist of the same magical energy of which the force field was made and gave the priest a hard enough punch to send him staggering. Poseidon's party hesitated, and Hermes took full advantage of their uncertainty.

"That was merely a small demonstration of what is in store if you defy me, mortals! Disperse now, or learn to your cost that Poseidon is not the only being you should fear."

The priest struggled to his feet much faster than he should have been able to. Perhaps Poseidon's blood did flow in his veins. I smashed him down again, harder this time.

Then I began to feel another power surge building out at sea. I readied myself, this time hoping to try the deflection spell successfully, but I had one problem: Hermes. He was too far up in the air for me to shield him without making the force field dangerously thin. I knew an Olympian couldn't be killed, but if the force of the wave stunned him or inflicted even worse injuries, we might lose his power and with it our best protection against Poseidon's wrath.

"Lord Hermes, please return to us!" I yelled. "Everyone else, down as before." I could see the tidal wave begin to rise. Instead of flying back down to where we were, Hermes had pulled out his golden staff, the caduceus, and was attempting to put our enemies to sleep. The idea was a reasonable one, but they were many, Olympian blood flowed in at least some of their veins, and part of Hermes's power was still pulsating through the link to us—a combination of circumstances that was making his strategy work with agonizing slowness.

"Hermes!" I half-ordered, half-pleaded, but he still did not respond. Poseidon's little army tried to charge us, but they were moving lethargically. However, the wave would certainly hit before they fell asleep.

I had no choice. I extended the shield around Hermes, drawing heavily on his power and on ours, tried to reinforce the deflection spell, and prayed.

I felt the impact of the second wave more than the first, and the force field came close to buckling. Some ocean spray slipped through and soaked us, but it had no force behind it. This time my deflection spell caused a large part of the wave to slip around us or slide over us, compensating to some extent for my having to protect a much larger area.

Poseidon had aimed the wave with such great precision that his own men were a little soggy but otherwise unharmed. Dropping the force-field to engage them was risky, but as long as they stood in our way, we were trapped on the beach, and I suspected we would wear down before Poseidon did. I knew we had a short time before his next wave hit, so I decided to take the risk.

"Guys, try to get Poseidon's men out of our way, but stay close together in case I need to protect us again." They braced themselves as I dropped the shield, drew White Hilt, and sprayed fire over the heads of our enemies as a warning. Reflexively they ducked and were in a poor position as everyone else charged.

I don't know if Hermes's sleep spell had made Poseidon's men more receptive, but their potentially supernatural ancestry did not seem to protect them much from the fear that Gordy's sword exuded. Most did not immediately flee, but the expressions of terror on their faces told me we had already won. The sight of Carla's silvery arrows perhaps convinced them that Artemis herself was somewhere nearby and shook them even further. Jimmie managed to look like a passably threatening ghost, pale and menacing. He still seemed a little off, but our nearness to the Underworld must have added more conviction to his appearance, and Poseidon's men broke rank and staggered away. There seemed no need to pursue them, so we regrouped.

Hermes was pleased to have been on the winning side but otherwise disturbed by recent events. "I was tempted to just ignore Apollo's orders—he's not our ruler; he just acts like it—and take you all the way into the Underworld," said Hermes, "but it is plain enough Poseidon is definitely against us now, which means he and Ares could attack Olympus at almost any time."

"I understand duty well enough to know you must do yours," I replied. "I will pray for you."

Hermes, more used to being prayed to than prayed for, was a little confused. "And I for you," he said at last. Then he flew with uncanny speed back into the still stormy air and was gone.

I looked at my loyal friends—well, loyal unless you counted Danny the backstabber, anyway.

"Before we enter the Underworld, any of you who wish may leave us now. This isn't the Middle Ages, I'm not really your liege lord, and you aren't really sworn to defend me. There is a good chance that we are going to our deaths."

"If this is a pep talk, I have to say, you suck at giving pep talks," said Carlos. "We survived Ceridwen, we survived Morgan, we just survived Poseidon himself, and we will survive this!"

"I'm not trying to be discouraging. I just want to give everyone a choice."

"You're not getting rid of me that easily," said Carla.

Yeah, I'm sure not.

Everyone quickly agreed.

"Why so pessimistic?" asked Gordy. "Poseidon is supposed to be second only to Zeus himself, and we just beat him, like Carlos said."

"We didn't exactly beat him," I pointed out. "We fended off a couple of attacks he launched from a distance, and we did that with backup from Hermes we no longer have. In the Underworld it seems as if we will definitely have to face Hecate, and it sounds as if Hades might be against us as well."

"We're heroes," said Khalid simply. "That's what heroes do."

I wish it were that easy, kid!

Nurse Florence pointed to the sea, where power was building again. "Tal, you have your answer. We are all going with you. Now, may I suggest we get off this beach before we get hit again?"

As usual, Nurse Florence was right, so we quickly moved toward the spot where Hermes had said the cave was. Sure enough, there was a very ominous cave, but it had a gate across it, barring the way. Distracted as I was, I had almost forgotten the key of Hermes, but I used it now, and the gate swung aside to let us pass.

We had not gone more than a few steps when the temperature dropped noticeably, and impenetrable blackness descended, even though we should theoretically have still been able to see a little light from the mouth of the cave. The air was thick with magic, not particularly hostile to us specifically but certainly hostile to life in general.

As if on cue, Nurse Florence held up the brand Hestia had given us, still burning despite Poseidon's watery attacks, and the darkness shuddered and dispersed enough for us to see the way ahead. Even then, we could not see more than a few feet in front of us, and the hungry shadows circled, waiting for the slightest stumble to make their move.

Chapter 9: A Hidden Gift

The brand from the hearth of Olympus continued to give light, but it wasn't doing much for heat, and the temperature continued to drop. The guys and I were protected to some extent by our dragon armor, but Carla's and Nurse Florence's gowns did not seem to keep them warm. Carla ended up snuggling with me for warmth, and I couldn't very well shove her away, though her presence reminded me painfully that she had still not fully accepted the fact that we were never going to be together. As usual, though, that was hardly our most serious problem.

The narrow cave through which we were passing made me feel claustrophobic, and I was glad at least that Poseidon's men had not pursued us; I wouldn't have liked to try to fight in such cramped quarters.

Fortunately, no one attacked us as we crept further and further through this narrow gap in the rock. Suddenly, Nurse Florence came to an abrupt stop and looked at me in alarm.

"What's wrong?" I asked. "I mean, aside from the fact we're in the Underworld." I was trying to lighten the mood, but I failed miserably. I suddenly realized that everyone around me, even Jimmie, looked frightened.

"Hermes was in such a rush to get back to Olympus after all those attacks that he forgot he was going to convince Charon to ferry us across the river. Charon has standing orders to take only the dead across. Without Hermes's help, we will never get beyond the shore."

"Perhaps we could swim the river," suggested Carlos.

"I don't think you really want to swim in those waters," answered Nurse Florence. "No one ever has, as far as we know. The risk is just too great."

"How about just flying over?" asked Khalid, eager to try out his new ability in better circumstances than before.

"That's interesting, though the dead could theoretically all fly across, and then Charon would have no business. Surely it can't be that simple to avoid him."

"Maybe if we...wait, what's that?" asked Stan. Our trek down through the cave had been silent except for the echoes of our own footsteps on the stones and our current conversation. Now, though, we could hear a dull thudding behind us. Something was coming. Something heavy.

"Probably we need to move now and plan our strategy later," suggested Dan. "I don't like the sound of whatever is approaching, and we don't exactly have a lot of friends nearby."

"Master," yelled an emotionless, mechanical voice that sounded surprisingly nearby.

"Amynticos?" I called out uncertainly.

"Yes," he shouted back, sounding even closer, and those thudding footsteps were definitely nearer than before.

"What if it isn't him?" asked Stan.

I chuckled. "Then we fight, probably. But I have a hard time imagining someone in the Underworld trying to imitate his voice."

We had all turned back toward the surface now, and I could see the shape of Amynticos lumbering toward us, his eyes sparkling in the light of Hestia's fire.

"Amynticos, we thought you had been destroyed by your fall. What a relief that you have survived." I was a little embarrassed to admit that in the rush to get into the Underworld before the next attack, I had forgotten all about him.

"I am pleased to see you all as well. The fall jarred me enough to keep me from surfacing immediately, and by the time I did, the beach was empty. I found the gate to the Underworld open, though, so it seemed reasonable I might find you if I followed the path of your quest."

"You have found us and perhaps just in time. I think we may be close to our first major obstacle," I told him.

"Speaking of which, now that we know those sounds were Amynticos and not someone else readying an attack, we should get moving," said Nurse Florence decisively. "The longer we delay, the more time any hostile…being has to prepare for us."

Nodding, I led us further down the dismal cave, and indeed it wasn't too long before the suffocating rock walls widened, and we found ourselves on an equally dismal but much roomier beach.

A few of the dead wandered aimlessly near the shore—the unburied ones whom Charon would not take across, presumably. They were not threatening, but staring into those lifeless, hopeless eyes would have chilled even the bravest of men. I wondered if these poor souls were actually left over from ancient Greece or if there were people on the Olympian plane who had gone without burial more recently.

I could hear the sluggish flow of the river and saw our light reflected a great distance away.

"That must be the Styx," I said.

"Actually, it's the Acheron, river of woe," said Carla. "Everyone confuses it with the Styx. Now, aren't you glad one of us was listening during that Greek mythology unit freshman year?"

Personally, I could not have cared less which river was which as long as we got where we were going, but I was not undiplomatic enough to say so. Carla was trying to be helpful, after all.

Whatever the river's name was, the hopeless dead milling around told me that this was indeed the river between us and the Underworld proper. That meant that the figure standing near the bank had to be Charon, the ferryman of the dead.

Every myth about him made him sound human, but the figure was only vaguely human. He was hooded, and in the gloom I could hardly see his face, but there was definitely something shadowy about him, something not like ordinary—or even Olympian—flesh.

"Can you feel what I feel?" I asked Carla, looking her in the eyes for the first time since we had descended. She was clearly as shaken as I was.

"You mean a sense of incredible power? Yes, I'm afraid I can. He isn't going to be easy to get around."

"Well, if it isn't possible, the terms of the *tynged* should make me the default victor," I suggested halfheartedly, knowing that it probably wouldn't be that easy.

All of our attention might have been focused on Charon, but he seemed to be ignoring us. It looked as if we were going to have to start the conversation.

"Oh, Great Charon," I said as I walked in his direction, faking a confidence I didn't feel. "We come to you as humble suppliants, begging passage upon your ferry."

I saw a glint of eyes bright as dead stars. "You are still living and therefore cannot pass," he said in a whispery voice like the rustling of shrouds.

"Great One, our errand is of grave importance, and we do bring the money required for our passage."

"Your errand is of no concern to me," he whispered. "Die and return. Do not think to cross until you have." Short of attacking him, I wasn't sure what to do. He seemed firmer than the cave walls, and I had no idea how to make him yield.

Perhaps a little name-dropping couldn't hurt. "We are no ordinary mortal suppliants, mighty Charon. I was once a son of Hephaestus, and my friend there," I said, indicating Shar, "was once Alexander the Great, a son of Zeus."

Charon squinted at me with his lifeless eyes and actually laughed, a hideous sound more like flesh being shredded than like mirth. "As little as I care for your errand, I care even less for who you *were*. If you and he are the sons of Hephaestus and Zeus right now, even that would not move me. Even Hephaestus and Zeus themselves would not move me.

"Let me tell you who I am, pathetic human. I am Charon, the son of Nyx and Erebus." From my knowledge of ancient Greek, I knew he meant night and darkness. I guess that explained why the more I looked at him, the more he looked like writhing shadows.

"I am grandson of Chaos itself. I was old before Zeus was born—and Hades, too. He did not give me this job. I *took* it, for as close kin to Chaos, no one knows better than I the importance of law. And few laws are more fundamental than the separation between life and death. Lose that, and all order is forfeit. The living do not enter, and the dead do not leave. Thus it was, thus it is, and thus it ever will be."

Stan stepped forward, but I knew as soon as he started speaking that he had let David take control.

"You may be older than Zeus, Charon, but you are not older than God!" With that, David drew his blade, and white light danced upon it. For all of Charon's bravado, he backed up a step.

"Your god will not interfere. If he chose to do so, why would he not send a whole army of angels to do the job? Why would he rely on only one man?"

"He once relied on only one boy," replied David, "and that worked out as he had planned."

"When your book of Genesis speaks of darkness over the surface of the deep, it speaks of my very parents."

"And in the verse just preceding that, it says that God created the heavens and the earth—including, I suppose, your parents. Now, Charon, let us pass, for the Lord God is stronger than anyone, even you, and nothing you can say will alter that."

"Perhaps," replied Charon, "but why are you so sure that your entry into the Underworld is what God wants? And where in your sacred texts does it say that you should be reborn? You are an abomination, a dead thing forcing itself into living flesh. What has your God to say of that?"

David had always been a bit shaky on the subject of his current nature, and I could see the light of his blade flicker just a little. "Somehow the one called Stanford and I are one. I do not understand, but Taliesin, himself a prophet of God in a previous life, has revealed this to me, and God himself has told me to trust him."

Charon laughed again, though the noise was more like a scream. "I cannot imagine you were so gullible when you were the king of Israel. God did not speak to you. That was the 'trustworthy' Taliesin and the one you call Nurse Florence deceiving you."

David looked at me intently, obviously expecting a denial. I probably should have given him one, but Charon had thrown me off balance. How could he possibly have known about Nurse Florence and me faking David's vision?

Some faerie ally of Morgan must have been spying on us; my defenses against such things were weak at that point and did not extend to the back yard, where the deception took place. Perhaps that same ally came visiting this plane one day with Titania. If that ally had been patient, it might not have been hard to wait until the gate was opened, perhaps when Hermes visited, and to slip down here and talk to Charon. Nothing in his strict code would have prevented him from listening, after all. That suggested the idea of the quest was set up weeks ago, and knowing that the quest for the lyre would bring us here, someone had primed Charon with just the information he needed to disrupt our group if we got this far.

All of these thoughts and so many others were racing through my head that I must have looked frozen to David, an appearance that was hardly going to convince him of my honesty. Well, maybe the time for truth had come.

"David, you are not some dead thing forcing yourself into a living body. You and Stan are one, just as I am really Heman, son of Joel, son of Samuel. Every word of that is true. God's voice, speaking to you from the heavens—that was an illusion we created to convince you. Remember that you were threatening to kill me…"

"And in your cowardice you sought to save yourself by getting me to betray my God?" asked David, his words cutting me like knives.

"I sought as well to save Stan from being lost in you. And if you had killed me, Carla would have been lost as well. And who knows what evil Morgan might have done without me to help defeat her? David, you have witnessed enough to know I speak the truth. I have fought for good, not for evil."

"I think you believe that," David said, his voice still edged with knives, "but you are misguided. Your magic is not what God wants. In the end, it will bring about destruction."

"David," said Charon, "Your god will surely be pleased that you have realized the truth in time. Help me to keep these fools from bringing anarchy to this universe."

David turned away from Charon and pointed his sword at us. "All of you must withdraw. Your presence in this place is not what God wants."

Now I realized the limitation in the way in which Merlin had helped me stabilize Stan's condition. There was a time when David's emergence, however well-meaning, risked Stan's submergence, potentially forever. I had yet to figure out how to reintegrate their two personalities, but Merlin had lent me enough power to create a consistent and stable way for them to share the body, with Stan generally in charge but David able to emerge harmlessly when he and Stan thought it was necessary. The flaw in that strategy was that it assumed David's cooperation—and David was not feeling cooperative at the moment. I could sense Stan struggling to regain control of the body, but David was refusing to allow the shift, effectively holding Stan prisoner. I could probably have dragged Stan out but only at the risk of damaging the mechanism Merlin and I had put in place and perhaps injuring Stan irreparably.

"Ladies, Jimmie, I need your strength. We are going to put Stan to sleep."

In seconds I felt their collective contribution surge into me, and I tried to lull David gently to sleep. Unfortunately, he felt what I was attempting to do and lunged at me with his sword. The guys hesitated— after all, they didn't want to hurt Stan—and I was concentrating too hard on the spell to dodge effectively. I felt his sword cut into my left arm, and I lost my concentration, nearly falling face first onto the ground.

Before David could follow up on his advantage, however, Amynticos knocked him out with a single, well-placed punch that left the King of Israel sprawled on the ground. After all, Amynticos's strongest order from Hephaestus was to defend me.

Charon shrieked out another blood-chilling laugh. "One man down, and you are still no closer to getting across the river. Give up while you still…can." Suddenly Charon was looking over my shoulder, clearly distracted by something behind me. I didn't know what had captured his attention, but this moment might be the only one in which I could catch him by surprise—even though surprise might not make much difference.

What was it Apollo had said to me before we left Olympus? Oh, yeah, it was, "You will need to combine their methods to prevail, for you are neither as strong as Heracles, nor as musically gifted as Orpheus." I had been contemplating that advice for some time. Heracles had physically overcome Charon, which I could not. Orpheus had charmed Charon, which I could not. However, I was stronger than Orpheus and more musical than Heracles, which meant I could hit Charon with a combination of different attacks.

"Shar, give me Zom!" I demanded, quietly but urgently. He never liked to let the sword go, but nonetheless he handed it to me without hesitation.

"Amynticos, let no one try to stop me!" I ordered him. I didn't know if Charon had anyone to whom he could call for help, but why take chances? Then, confident that Amynticos and the nearby Shar had my back, I channeled all my magical strength through Zom, blasting Charon with wave after wave of emerald anti-magic, until his shadowy flesh was a pale gray instead of a midnight black. I heard shouting behind me but could not afford to look away from him before I had overcome his resistance.

As long as I kept the beam focused on him, he could not use the great magic at his disposal, but I knew from experience that such excessive use of Zom's power would temporarily drain the blade, and Charon, like the demon Merlin, would recover quickly once that emerald light died down.

I began singing for all I was worth, filling every syllable with compelling magic, trying desperately to pull Charon into sympathy with my quest. Nurse Florence, Carla, Jimmie, and Shar were lending me their strength. I expected to be able to draw on the others as well, except for the unconscious Stan and the mechanical Amynticos, but somehow I had lost contact with them. I had to hope that what power I had would be enough.

Despite the donated energy, I was burning through magic so fast that I knew I would soon tire. I pushed harder and harder at the adamantine mind of Charon. At some point I lost connection with Shar and felt my power level drop a little, but I kept going.

Finally I felt his resolve start to buckle. Instead of speaking I chanted my demand. I had to keep the rhythm going at all costs.

"Charon, swear by the Styx to give us passage across the river!"

"I...," started Charon, then trailed off. He was still fighting me.

"Swear!" I commanded. Deep within him I could feel some tiny grain of compassion, some willingness to make an exception, but it was not yet strong enough to overcome his unbending desire to preserve the world from chaos...not such a bad impulse, after all.

I switched tactics, projecting to him a vision of the kind of chaos that would erupt in the world if I failed: the fall of Olympus and the end of any kind of law outside the Underworld on this plane of existence; a war among the faeries leading to a similar lawlessness in Annwn; and a ripple effect that would reach other worlds, until perhaps chaos truly returned. I made especially sure to show him a vision of the sword of chaos, the same weapon Ares had unleashed on my world. Charon might have been indifferent to Ares initially, but surely he would not be indifferent to the recklessness of Ares's gesture.

"All right, I swear!" he whispered, just as the emerald light became a little erratic.

"Swear by the Styx also not to try to harm us or to obstruct the quest in any way."

"I...I..." The emerald light faded to olive green. At some point I had lost contact with everyone else. I felt my heartbeat slow as I drew a little on my very life force to keep the attack going.

"I swear by the Styx not to harm you or to obstruct your quest in any way," he finally choked out. I cut off Zom's ray at once, saving what little energy was left.

Charon stiffly walked over to the shore to ready the boat. It was only then that I could turn to see what had drawn Charon's attention in the first place...and then I wished I had known much, much sooner.

Carlos and Khalid were lying on the ground, both soaking wet and both almost convulsed by sorrow. Without having seen, I could imagine what had happened. While Charon was busy with me, Carlos had tried to swim the Acheron, and Khalid had tried to fly over it. Whether they intended to distract Charon or really thought they could succeed, I had no way of knowing. It was clear that they had failed, but it was not clear why Carlos was sobbing so hard he could hardly breathe or why Khalid was weeping and screaming for the father who had abandoned him months ago. I ran over to them as fast as I could. The others had already gathered around them, and Nurse Florence was trying a healing spell but getting nowhere.

"What happened to them?" I asked, my heart aching to see them this way.

"Carlos dived into the river while you were talking to Charon," said Carla, putting her hand reassuringly on his shoulder. He didn't seem to know that she—or any of us—were even there.

"Acheron is the river of woe," continued Carla. "Alcina once researched its properties while she was in Italy. As soon as Carlos touched the water, it began to fill him with sorrow. He became so despondent after a few strokes that he would probably have drowned in it if I hadn't managed to levitate him back to the bank."

"And you know how Khalid is," said Gordy, squirming with helplessness as he looked at the boy's sorrow-wracked face. "He wanted to help, so he tried to fly over the river, but the spray got to him. He tried to turn back, but it was too late." Shar, who treated Khalid like a little brother, was holding Khalid's shaking body in his arms, but as with Carlos, Khalid did not seem to be conscious of any of us, so focused was he on his own torment.

"What can we do?" I asked Nurse Florence quickly.

"I don't know," she said, baffled. "We have Apollo's healing salve, and I can try that, but I think it only treats physical injuries, not this kind of psychological enchantment. Perhaps a burst of energy from Zom?"

I tried, but the sword's enchantment was nearly exhausted for the moment. I drained it completely, but it lacked enough power to break the spell on Carlos and Khalid. The sorrow faded momentarily when I first shed Zom's light upon them, but it came back as soon as that light gave way to shadows. We had seen this before with powerful magic: Zom could keep a spell from affecting a wielder, and it could break a weak or temporary spell, but with a stronger spell already in place, the best it could sometimes do was keep it from operating temporarily. We needed more power or at least a better way to use power if we wanted to save our despair-gripped comrades.

I noticed that Charon had returned and was watching us intently.

"Charon, do you know how to cure this?"

He looked me with his soulless eyes and replied, "The oath I swore requires me to take you across the river, and it keeps me from hindering your quest, but it does not require me to help it. The boat is ready now. Will you cross the river?"

I felt like kicking in his insubstantial face, but even if I had, it would not have helped Carlos and Khalid.

"We will leave after our friends are well and have rested." I half expected Charon to try to wriggle out of his oath because I had refused to go with him when he first offered. Instead he gestured in a way that might have been a shrug and walked away.

"Let's apply Apollo's salve, and then Tal and I will lend Nurse Florence our strength," suggested Carla.

"We will all lend Nurse Florence our strength," said Shar, resting Khalid gently on the ground and getting up.

Nurse Florence had been right. Apollo's salve, which had healed my arm wound in seconds, did nothing for Carlos and Khalid. We tried Carla's suggestion, all of us pouring our strength into Nurse Florence as she tried to heal them, but in the end that effort failed. Perhaps if we had had more strength instead of having expended so much of it fighting Charon, we could have driven the sorrow back.

"There is only one thing we can do," I said finally. "We need more help, and we aren't going to get it in the Underworld. It is time to give up the quest."

"Are you sure that's what you want?" asked Nurse Florence. I knew that she was a healer first and wanted to tend to her patients in the best way possible, but she would follow me, whatever I decided, and she wanted me to be certain before I decided. Either way, there would be no way for me to escape the consequences of my choice.

"Yes. I'll declare the quest impossible. Under the terms of the *tynged*, I can claim victory."

"Tal," began Nurse Florence hesitantly, "I'm inclined to think we have to go back, but I want you to make that choice with your eyes open. The quest may not be impossible to fulfill. We could go ahead, leaving Stan, Carlos, and Khalid behind, with one of us to watch them. At least that is what Oberon will argue, and Morgan will go free."

"Then we'll have to take our chances with Morgan. I'm not going to sacrifice any of us to get the lyre." I looked around my circled comrades and didn't need a show of hands to know they all agreed with me.

There was, however, one comrade I had forgotten to take into consideration.

"Heman!" I almost jumped at the sound of David's voice, and my hand reached reflexively for White Hilt. He was sitting up, having somehow shaken off the sleep spell, and looking at us, his face unreadable.

"David?" I asked uncertainly.

"You should not have lied to me," he said, accusation in his voice.

"I will always regret that, David," I said, meaning it with all my heart but sure I could never convince him.

"Wait!" I continued. "Did you just call me Heman? So...so you know that everything wasn't a lie?"

David got up, brushed himself off, and walked over to us. "While I slept, I dreamed that God came to me and told me to keep helping you, that your cause was righteous."

I must have looked shocked, because David didn't wait for a response. "No, I don't know if it really was God who spoke to me. For all I know, it was you playing another trick. But I do know one thing.

"I know you. You were right about that. I know you through Stan's memories and through what I myself have seen. If I had had any doubt, your determination to get your friends' help, even at the cost of your own quest, tells me that you are not just the manipulator I feared you were.

"I also know that, though you might be misguided, Morgan *is* evil, and that she must be stopped. The quest must continue."

"It can't, David. We can't let Khalid keep suffering like this," insisted Shar, pointing to Khalid's writhing body.

"If we have any chance of curing them, that chance could diminish with time," said Nurse Florence.

"And is there nothing else you can try?" asked David. "What of the wonders the...Olympians gave you?"

"We've already tried the healing salve of Apollo," replied Nurse Florence. "That seemed the most likely to work, and it failed, even when combined with our healing energy."

"Well," I said, looking around to make sure there was no impending threat, "I suppose it wouldn't hurt to take a few minutes and make sure there is nothing we're overlooking. Nurse Florence, David, and I will do that. Shar," I continued, cutting off his protest, "you and the others brainstorm ways to get back. This isn't like Annwn, where we can just open a portal and step through in Santa Brígida. We need to find an Olympian to send us back. We'd need to work on that anyway, and this way we aren't losing any time." Shar nodded and gestured for the others to gather around him.

"Amynticos, do you know how to cure my friends?"

"I would have told you already if I had known," said Amynticos tonelessly. "My maker built me mostly for battle. I have no medical knowledge."

"I thought as much," I replied. "I just wanted to make sure. Nurse Florence, what else do we have?"

"The brand of Hestia, but I already tried its light on them. The bow of Artemis, but it has no healing power. Nor does the key of Hermes. That just leaves the ever-full wine goblet and the ever-full jar of olives. Good if we have nothing else to eat, but I can't see how they could help in this situation."

"I have seen wine cheer men," said David.

"We know a lot more about wine than was known in your day, David," replied Nurse Florence. "It's not what we need now."

"Dionysus was always an…Olympian to watch, if I recall the stories told in Hephaestion's lifetime correctly. Dionysus was a bringer of joy but also of madness," I said. Nurse Florence nodded her agreement.

David's eyes narrowed. "Does it not strike you, though, that the gifts are strangely disproportionate? Hephaestus gives you that wondrous mechanical man who survived being smashed around in the ocean by Poseidon. Apollo gives you salve that can heal any wound, Artemis a powerful bow, and Hestia a light that protects us against the darkness and the things that dwell in it. All of those are powerful gifts. But…wine and olives? In my time a man was often judged by the gifts he gave."

"It was so among the ancient Greeks, too," I said thoughtfully. "Homer goes on for pages talking about the gifts Odysseus received during his travels. I hadn't thought about it, but those two gifts don't really make sense in that context. If nothing else, I would have thought a warrior 'goddess' like Athena would have had a powerful weapon to spare."

"The olives could save our lives if we had nothing else to eat," pointed out Nurse Florence, "and Athena said exactly that when she presented them to us. Anyway, you guys are ridiculously well-armed as it is.

Maybe Athena was trying to give you something you didn't already possess."

"Let's have a look," I said. "I think David may have a point that we're missing something. Now that I think about it, the items could be a kind of test. You know how much supernatural beings love testing mortals. If I remember correctly, Athena said something like, 'Look to these in time of trouble. Look carefully,' which sounds a little melodramatic for olives. Dionysus said something like, 'Those who examine the contents of this goblet closely will see its true value.' If that isn't a hint that there is more to the goblet than one could see at first glance, I'd be surprised."

From a large bag, Nurse Florence removed the goblet and the jar, both covered and somehow miraculously unspilled, and handed them to me. I lifted the cover gently off the wine. From the scent it might have been the fruity red wine characteristic of Nemea and surrounding areas—don't be shocked, I was just remembering my earlier Greek lives. In any case it seemed a very good wine but just wine. No, wait; there *was* something else, a different scent, honey-like, reminiscent of mead but far sweeter. I realized as I focused more intently on the wine that there was also a power radiating from it, not a massive surge but at least a gentle push.

"I could be wrong. I don't think I smelled anything like this in any of my lives, but based on the power coming from it, it could be nectar."

"You mean the drink of the gods, uh, Olympians?" asked Nurse Florence, shocked and unsettled.

I grabbed the olive jar, removed its cover, and saw some very fine, small Cretan green olives. At first they, too, seemed ordinary, but I also detected a different, more subtle scent than normal olives…and a faint throb of power in the background.

"Ambrosia!" I pronounced happily. "The food of the…Olympians."

"The Order doesn't have much information on ambrosia and nectar," said Nurse Florence, a hint to me to dig around in my ancient Greek memories.

"Well, if the stories are true, the Olympians used ambrosia and nectar for a lot of things besides food: as a perfume, as a cosmetic, as a skin cleanser, and as a salve—that salve Apollo gave you probably has ambrosia in it. The effects on humans were usually pretty obvious. A little topical application could make humans look younger, and some stories even had humans become invulnerable if they were anointed with ambrosia and nectar and then passed through fire. Consumption of enough of the stuff was supposed to make humans like the Olympians. I don't remember anything about changes in mood, though. Oh, wait, yes I do—they were said to gladden the hearts of the gods." I immediately realized I had slipped and called them gods, but David was so enthralled that he did not correct me.

Nurse Florence looked doubtful. "I already tried the healing salve on them, so if it is derived from nectar and ambrosia…"

"Did you administer it internally?" I interrupted. "If not, I think we need to try that."

By now Carlos and Khalid were both a little more quiet, if only because their overwhelming sorrow had exhausted them, but even so, they were still unreachable. David and I helped Nurse Florence prepare and administer the treatment, starting with the nectar since there was less chance of choking.

Carlos and Khalid fought us at first. My magic had no power to change their mood, but I did succeed in restraining them enough for us to get some of the nectar and ambrosia down them.

It took a long time and more nectar and ambrosia than Nurse Florence thought wise to see any results. She was understandably concerned about the side effects the food of Olympians might have on ordinary mortals. So was I, actually, but what choice did we really have? Anyway, we kept giving them small amounts of the sweet-smelling food and drink until I could sense their moods begin to change. After just a little more treatment, both had pretty much returned to their normal state, though Carlos was embarrassed about the way he had been behaving.

"I…I don't know what happened. I've never felt…like that before."

"Carlos, no one could have resisted the waters of Acheron," I reassured him, "and you only got exposed because you were trying to do a brave thing. Foolish, but brave." Yeah, I should probably take my own advice on that issue. I'm sure that's what Nurse Florence was thinking, but for once she didn't say it out loud.

At that point I noticed that the crowd on the shore had increased considerably while we had been working on Khalid and Carlos. Since I imagined the only people entering the kingdom of Hades these days came from the small human population on this plane, I wondered how there could be so many in so short a time.

I left my friends for a few moments and walked among the newly arrived dead. They seemed…dazed, I guess, and most of them looked as they must have when they died—blood drenched. It took a few minutes, but finally I found one who was sufficiently aware to talk to me.

"They came at us in far greater numbers than I could have imagined," he said dejectedly after I had asked him to tell his story. "Our men were well trained and strong, but we could not resist the power of the army of Ares."

"How do you know the army belonged to Ares?" I asked.

"I could see him in the distance, urging his men to more violent frenzy. Then there was his general—not much to look at, I'll tell you, deceptive that way. He carried a powerful sword that could cut through anything. Explode through anything, really. A few strokes, and he had collapsed a section of the city wall…and Thessalonica had a wall of legendary strength. After that, it was all over. No one could have breached our walls so easily without the help of a god."

"This general—what did he look like?" I asked, fearing the answer but having to know it.

"I got only a glance at his face, but he seemed about your age, only not as mature looking somehow. He had the look of someone tied to his mother's apron strings too tightly, if you know what I mean, and his arms seemed…spindly, I guess. He had barely enough muscle to swing that sword, but anyone could see the sword was doing all the work. It was…shimmering…no, throbbing, like it was more than metal, and as I've said, it destroyed everything it touched."

I had thought things couldn't get much worse than they had been when Carlos and Khalid, and even Stan, had seemed lost to us. This new development could be even worse, though. Much worse.

I turned and found even more of the bloody dead behind me, rows and rows of them. It looked as if Ares's army had slaughtered the entire Thessalonian population. I had to claw my way through them to return to the guys, who were staring in concern at the growing mob.

"What's happening?" asked Gordy.

"It seems Ares is on the march. His army has just captured Thessalonica and, by the look of things, massacred everyone who didn't escape."

"There are…kids my age coming…younger even!" gasped Khalid in disbelief.

I glanced over and saw women, throats cut, wandering in as well. The army had turned on the civilians.

"This is terrible!" said Carla, looking helplessly at the ghostly masses.

"It's even worse than you think," I said glumly. "I'm sure this is no random raid. Thessalonica is the first major city beyond the Thracian border that an army would reach if it were traveling southwest, but I doubt conquering one city is what Ares wants. He bypassed closer ones, like Abdera to his south, and he could probably have hit less well-defended targets by going straight west into the heartland of Macedonia."

"Then what does he want?" asked Dan.

"Thessalonica has a large harbor. It would be a logical point for the forces of Ares to link up with the forces of Poseidon, perhaps to bring in troops from the islands as well. And from there it would only be a few days' march to the base of Olympus."

"You've got to be kidding!" protested Shar. "We've all seen that mountain. Ares can't just march troops up it!"

"Not easily, perhaps, but with magic…maybe. Or maybe no one even needs to leave the ground to destroy it."

"What do you mean, Tal?" asked Nurse Florence, her face pale. "You obviously know something else."

"Sadly, yes," I replied. "Ares's commander is carrying the sword of chaos. If he can get to the base of Olympus, how long do you think it will take him to undermine the whole mountain? I'd say a few days, at most."

"Ares's commander?" asked Jimmie.

"From the description, I'd say it's our old buddy, Alex. I don't know how, but Ares must have gotten to him again. How either of them got the sword is an even bigger mystery."

"I care not how he got the sword!" snapped David. "I care far more how we can stop him. You were able to render the sword harmless once before."

"Yeah, but then we were just up against Alex and the sword. Now we have to deal with Ares and his huge army, to say nothing of Poseidon, and after that show of force, I'd bet some of the lesser Olympians will join them, if they haven't already."

"We have allies as well," suggested David.

"And they're on Olympus while we are about as far away as possible, leaving us no way to join forces. I hate to say it, guys, especially after how much some of you have suffered for it, but again it looks as if we may have to give up the quest."

"And let Morgan go free?" asked Carla in disbelief.

"Getting the lyre won't do us any good if we can't get back to Annwn with it, and we've been assuming we can't just open a portal and return to our own world. Have you discovered that assumption is wrong?"

Nurse Florence shook her head sadly. "I experimented a little while we were on Olympus. I had no luck getting a portal to open, just as we suspected."

"And I tried the same while we were working on ways to retreat earlier," admitted Carla. "The barriers in this world are too thick."

"Exactly. Only an Olympian could let us in. Only an Olympian can let us out. If Olympus falls, we may be all out of sympathetic Olympians to do that. Guys, we could be trapped here forever. If we race back right now, we might reach Olympus before Ares's army and at least be able to join Apollo and company. Perhaps together—"

"No, Tal, that isn't going to work if we can't use portals to cover some of the distance," cut in Shar. "We'd come out of the Underworld at the southernmost point in Greece. That's got to be at least 3900 stadia from Olympus…more I think, more like 3945. Thessalonica is about 790 stadia from Olympus, only about a fifth as far as we are. An army can march roughly 175 stadia a day, which means they could reach Olympus in about four and a half days. That's assuming Ares doesn't magic them into going faster somehow and that no hostile troops are closer than that. Moving at the same rate, we'd reach Olympus in twenty-two and a half days. Even if you got us all up to faerie speed, I can't see us doing it in much less than ten—and that would assume we didn't run into any enemies along the way, which I think is highly unlikely. In addition to all of those problems, a large part of the shortest route between here and Olympus is near the coast, giving Poseidon plenty of opportunities to take a shot at us."

"We have to face facts—there is no way with our present resources that we can reach Olympus before Ares does, and realistically no way to get up to the top if his army is surrounding the base of the mountain."

I didn't know whether to be more horrified by the fact that Shar was right or that he had suddenly become an expert in Greek geography, ancient Greek measurements, and military strategy. Somehow, without even the slightest touch of the awakening spell, Alexander had begun to encroach on Shar. There could be no other explanation.

Carla and Nurse Florence had both figured it out as well. Even David, keen observer that he was, realized that Shar could not have known all that on his own. Shar himself, though, at first didn't know what we were talking about.

"I'm not Alexander," he insisted. "I feel exactly like myself."

"Shar, the stadion is an ancient Greek unit of measure. Not only do you know the term, but you can accurately calculate distances between different points of Greece in stadia. I can only think of one explanation for that. You may still be you, but you have access to Alexander's knowledge, or at least some of it."

"What does this mean?" asked Shar, looking from one of us to the other. "Am I going to become him?"

This was one conversation we really didn't have time for right now. However, I couldn't turn my back on Shar—and I certainly couldn't let him end up in a tug-of-war for his own body like the kind Stan had gone through.

The ghosts on the shore were becoming more and more numerous. None of them had been buried yet, much less gotten their obols for Charon, so they could not yet move on. Just as people feel drawn to look at a hideous auto accident, I felt drawn to look at this forlorn crowd, but I knew I did not dare. I had to focus. I had to keep things from getting worse.

It was the sweet scent all around us that caused me to realize what must have happened. "It has to be the nectar and ambrosia. They are the food of the 'gods,' and Alexander was the son of Zeus. Somehow, they made his presence stronger."

"I didn't have any!" protested Shar.

"No, but you were helping to give it to Khalid. Some of it must have gotten on your skin; it would have been unavoidable. And we've all been breathing it...for hours now. That must have been enough. Shar, are you feeling any attempt by Alexander to take over?"

Shar concentrated for a minute. "No, Tal, I feel perfectly normal," he said. "I don't have any sense of being threatened from inside. If anything, I feel…more confident…stronger." He looked at me and smiled. "If Alexander is really awake, I think he's trying to help."

"That would make sense," I agreed. "Alexander always sought glory, even in preference to safety. He'd want to be part of our quest, not sabotage it. And if he is aware of what's going on around him, as seems likely, he may well recognize me as Hephaestion. When both of them were alive, they would have done anything for each other. I can't imagine Alexander betraying me…uh, Hephaestion."

"So what do we do now?" asked Nurse Florence. "Time is not on our side."

"First," I replied, as calmly as I could, "we keep watch on Shar. Maybe because what's happening wasn't caused by that damn awakening spell, it's benign, but we won't take any chances.

"Second, we get moving as fast as we can. Shar was right—we are too far away to ever reach Olympus in time anyway. If we can't get to the tribunal, maybe we can at least get word to them somehow and keep Morgan locked up. There's just one problem with that second part. We're all pretty much drained. We need to risk a little nectar and ambrosia to recharge ourselves."

"But you just said that was what caused Shar's problem. Now you want people to have even more exposure?" asked Nurse Florence, almost angrily. "That doesn't make sense."

I looked at Shar carefully. "What is happening to him may not be a bad thing, and it may not be made any worse by further exposure at this point. He can stay away from the stuff if he wants, but the rest of us should each have a little."

Nurse Florence was clearly not happy. "We have no idea what that could do. Are we ready to risk becoming…like the Olympians? Maybe then we would be trapped here, too."

"I'm not looking for immortality here," I said quickly, "and neither is anybody else. I'm just looking for a quick pick-me-up. Otherwise, we probably can't avoid resting here for several hours—hours we don't have."

We argued a little longer, but eventually Nurse Florence gave in and agreed there was probably no other way. She insisted, however, on measuring out a very small quantity of ambrosia to each of us, only giving more if the person still felt weak and then again only a little. While I agreed with the wisdom of her method, I wished it could have been executed faster.

After about an hour, however, everyone felt rested and ready for the next stage of our journey...and probably eager to get away from the ever-growing throng of the dead milling about near the river bank.

"Jimmie! Stay out of the ambrosia!" Nurse Florence cautioned sternly. I turned to see Jimmie with his finger in his mouth, looking very guilty. Nurse Florence snatched the ever-full olive jar away from him and put it back in the bag.

"I just wanted to see what it tasted like," he said defensively.

"It's dangerous enough letting everyone else use ambrosia," explained Nurse Florence. "We don't even have stories to guide us about the effect it might have on a ghost."

"I'm sorry," he said, looking down at the ground. Despite all of his special abilities, I could tell he often missed being human, and again I wished I could just forgive Dan and let Jimmie find peace. Well, that was another thing on my very long to-do list.

I was afraid Charon would be too busy for us at this point, but as the dead had not been buried yet, none of them could go across. He ushered us into his boat, which seemed to expand to accommodate us, I gave him the price of our passage, and without a word he ferried us across the shadowy river toward an even more shadowy future.

Chapter 10: Ashes to Flesh; Dust to Blood

Of course I knew that Cerberus was waiting on the other side. As the boat drew near the opposite shore, I could not see him in the darkness, but I could hear his relentless canine footsteps padding back and forth on the stones, waiting for us to be within reach.

If the stories were true, Orpheus had charmed him, but as Apollo had reminded me, I was no Orpheus. The strategy I had used on Charon might have worked, but I was hesitant to use Zom as a blaster again so soon. The nectar and ambrosia had regenerated our strength but not the mystical power of the sword, which was still not at full strength—and which I probably should try to reserve for Hecate. We might be able to beat Cerberus with a combination of my music and a coordinated attack by the guys, but one miscalculation, and Cerberus would be using someone's arm as a chew toy. No, I needed to come up with something a little less risky.

I reached out with my mind and touched Cerberus's. I had no illusion that a beast so powerful could be easily controlled that way, but I also doubted he would automatically be shielded the way powerful Olympians, faeries, and even human sorcerers were. Perhaps I could read enough of his mind to find something useful.

I could certainly read the creature's mood: angry, impatient to shred us with its fangs—but that much I could have guessed. I tried to push a little deeper, to find something useful. The ferry was approaching the shore, and I could see Cerberus shifting impatiently in the shadows, the red glint in his eyes now visible. The guys had their hands on their sword hilts, and Carla was readying her bow.

I couldn't see a way to win that kind of battle, though. I had no doubt Artemis's bow and our magic swords could injure Cerberus, but injuring him might make Hades angry, and I didn't want to have to fight Hades if we could avoid it.

The ferry was nearly at the shore, and I could have sworn I heard Cerberus's eager panting, when I finally came up with an idea. I whispered it quickly to the other party members, who were skeptical of its success.

"It's the only way I can see us getting through this without having even more trouble later," I whispered urgently. The ferry touched the riverbank, and I could feel Charon's impatience hitting me in slow but powerful waves.

I began to sing and then to cast. Charon's impatience escalated, but I ignored him. He wasn't exactly obligated to wait until we were ready to disembark, but I hoped his oath not to interfere with our quest would stop him from actually throwing us off before we were ready.

I let my magic flow around all of us except Jimmie, who wouldn't need it, since Charon was trained to attack only the living if they tried to enter, and Jimmie, as he was fond of reminding me at every turn, was dead.

As my illusion enveloped us, our eyes lost their light, our skin lost its color and warmth, and even our scent would betray no trace of life. Cerberus would only attack the living, so if I could project this illusion strongly enough, he should let us pass.

We stepped cautiously from the ferry. I had told everyone to move quietly, but several people, despite their battle experience, could not help gasping when Cerberus lunged out of the shadows and glared at us, his fangs bared, ready to attack.

Most people thought of Cerberus as just a three-headed dog, forgetting that the Greek myths also describe him as having behind those three heads a mane of writhing serpents, as well as a long serpent tail he could use like a whip.

Unfortunately, those particular myths proved to be excruciatingly accurate.

As we tried to shuffle past the sniffing and growling Cerberus, encircled by his serpents writhing, hissing, and dripping venom, I wondered how resistant dragon armor would be to supernatural fangs and claws. It should hold—awhile, anyway. What to do with our exposed skin if Cerberus attacked was a much more serious problem.

Despite all of the beast's posturing, he did not attack as each of us passed by. I had crafted my illusion from what I could extract from his mind about the way he perceived the dead, but I had needed to it so quickly that any number of things could go wrong.

In the end, the one that did caught me completely by surprise.

We were nearly through, frightened—well, let's be honest, terrified—but so far, unbitten. Cerberus sniffed each of us and frowned at each of us, no doubt wondering where those tempting living morsels he had spotted earlier had gone. He seemed satisfied in each case that we were dead, though.

HIDDEN AMONG YOURSELVES   153

Then he struck, fast as lightning, knocking over Carlos in an effort to get to...Jimmie!

Why he would attack the one person among us who actually was dead, I had no idea, but it took me a few seconds to realize that Jimmie, who had reflexively fallen back as the great beast lunged at him, had nonetheless not quite evaded those stone-like fangs and had a bleeding gash on his left arm.

Bleeding? Impossible! Yet there it was. I had been in battle far too much, even in this life, and I knew blood when I saw it.

Jimmie screamed and tried to run, but he was moving at regular human speed, and Cerberus could easily catch him. I couldn't extend the illusion around him fast enough to stop Cerberus's next attack.

"*Do what you have to do to save Jimmie!*" I shouted mentally to everyone. "*Try not to bang up Cerberus too badly if you can, though. All we need now is the wrath of Hades.*" Then I realized how stupid it was to try to get people to understand why harming Cerberus was a bad idea when they only had seconds to respond to the threat—no real time for planning subtle strategy.

"*What the hell?*" Shar thought back, gripping his sword uncertainly. Dan, seeing the threat to Jimmie though not understanding it any better than I did, drew his sword and charged. Since my illusion was still holding, Cerberus thought one of the dead was attacking him and looked confused, his canine glances shifting back and forth between his prey and the unanticipated threat. While the beast pondered, Dan kept shifting his position, trying to get himself between Jimmie and Cerberus. The rest of us, weapons drawn, circled the hellish hound. His three canine heads and the uncountable multitude of serpent heads twisted in all directions, uncertain which way to strike, still baffled by an unprecedented attack from the dead.

Jimmie looked pale—frightened pale, not dead pale—but he had been involved in enough of our battles to have developed some presence of mind. He drew Black Hilt and held the icy blade out in front of him. He hadn't really been taught how to use a sword, but Cerberus didn't know that. In any case, the beast looked even more confused. All I could think was that the cold from the weapon was masking Jimmie's body heat.

Well, except, of course, that Jimmie didn't have body heat...or shouldn't, anyway.

"*Can you hold your illusion and use your music to charm Cerberus at the same time?"* asked Carla, who I noticed was also ready with Artemis's bow, just in case.

"I'm not sure, but my music wouldn't be enough. Apollo was right about that."

"Remember that Alcina charmed beasts other than sea creatures at times. Would the two of us together be enough?"

I pondered but only for a couple of seconds. Cerberus was getting restless and seemed bound to make another lunge, if not at Jimmie, then certainly at somebody else. *"We may as well try it. We don't have a huge number of options."*

I had split my concentration before, but it was tricky, especially in a high-adrenaline situation like this one. Gently I pushed calming magic into my music, and the illusion seemed to be holding. I could feel Carla joining me, trying to lull the great beast to sleep.

Sensing that something was amiss, Cerberus threw himself full force at Dan. Fortunately, the guys were ready for him. Gordy, hoping to put his new strength to the test, grabbed Cerberus from behind and tried to wrestle him to the ground. Even enchanted dragon armor could not give Gordy the strength of Heracles, the only mortal ever to wrestle Cerberus successfully, but Gordy did slow the creature down a little. By the time Cerberus twisted away from Gordy, the epic hound was moving more slowly. He did manage to turn on Gordy and got in at least one good bite, which might normally have severed Gordy's arm. However, the dragon armor held, as it did when the lashing snake heads got close enough to strike. The guys moved in to help Gordy, in the process wedging themselves firmly between Cerberus and Jimmie. Carla and I kept up our attempt to charm Cerberus to sleep, reinforced now by Nurse Florence, who had figured out what we were doing.

Poor Cerberus, on the other hand, did not know what hit him. By now he was beginning to feel exhausted. His steadily weaker attacks kept hitting dragon armor and bouncing off. He still could not figure out how the dead were able to attack, and breaking through to get the one living thing he could see looked like more than he could manage in his current condition. He thrashed around awhile longer, but eventually he succumbed to the inevitable, falling to the stony ground with an echoing thud.

"I don't know how long we can keep him under," I thought to everyone, *"but probably not more than a few minutes at most. Let's get through*

the next gate and then figure out what happened."

That was one suggestion I didn't have to wait long for everyone to accept. We trotted over to the gate that I hoped led to the place of judgment. I could have sworn it stood open when we first arrived, but now it was tightly shut. I used Hermes's key, and we rushed through, closing it behind us in case Cerberus revived sooner than we thought. I doubted he would leave his assigned post, but who knew under these circumstances?

We stopped short of the place of judgment to give Nurse Florence a chance to examine Jimmie. We waited impatiently as she poked and prodded, taking too long to suit any of us. Finally, getting out Apollo's salve, she applied a combination of it and her own healing energy to the wound, turned to us, and said simply, "He's human."

"I think we already knew that," said Carla.

"And he's alive. I don't know how, but he is."

On some instinctive level, we had all known that when we had seen the blood, but it was still hard to comprehend.

"He...he's...alive?" asked Dan, pale and practically shaking. "You mean, like before? Before the...accident?"

"As far as I can tell, his body is that of a normal, healthy sixteen-year-old."

Dan hugged Jimmie so hard I thought Jimmie's lungs would burst. "I have you back—for real, little brother, and I am never letting you go!"

"Dan—" Nurse Florence began, but at that point the rest of the group spontaneously ran forward to hug Jimmie, and it was a while before we settled down enough for her to make herself heard.

Actually, the rest of the group minus one. I noticed David hanging back, looking aghast at Jimmie. Then David disappeared abruptly, and I saw Stan for the first time in hours.

"What's up?" I thought to Stan.

"David doesn't know what to think about people coming back from the dead. He told me he needs time to ponder."

"Stan, help him get past this. We can't have David deciding he can't trust us again right now."

"I'll do what I can." I knew he would. I just hoped it would be enough.

"Tal!" Nurse Florence shouted to me mentally, *"I hate to break*

the mood, but we need to talk. All of us." With my help she calmed down the others—a little, anyway—and they looked at her with varying degrees of impatience. After all, it isn't every day a close friend's little brother gets resurrected.

"I don't know how to say this, so I'm just going to plunge right in and ask you to hear me out." Everyone nodded apprehensively.

"The problem is," she began, "this should not have happened. Jimmie shouldn't have come back to life—"

"What are you saying?" cut in Dan, his tone as friendly as a charging bull's.

"Please let me finish!" insisted Nurse Florence. "We all know Jimmie now. We all love him...not as much as you do, Dan, I know, but we do. Not one of us wants to see anything bad happen to him. Emotionally, I'm just as glad as you are to see that he's alive. But...his return to life might not be permanent."

Dan became even more tense. "You mean he might die again?" Suddenly, he looked less angry and more ready to cry.

"Truly, I don't know. Tal, you remember from your life as the original Taliesin the importance of maintaining a balance in the universe, right?" I nodded, fearing where this was going.

"One of the key components of that balance is the separation between life and death. That's why the early druids frowned both upon killing and upon trying to conjure up the dead."

"I thought they practiced human sacrifice!" protested Dan.

"That's just Roman propaganda. Most of the records about the ancient druids come from their enemies. But no one here wants a history lesson right now—"

"Amen," said Gordy quickly.

"My point," continued Nurse Florence, "is that Jimmie's...revival...may have upset that balance. It's not your fault, Jimmie," she said quickly, as he looked at the ground again. "It's no one's fault."

"This is all just speculation!" snapped Dan. "Maybe Jimmie's resurrection is part of the balance somehow. Elijah and Jesus are both portrayed in the Bible as resurrecting the dead. Maybe what happened to Jimmie is not wrong. Maybe it's beautiful." He pulled Jimmie into his arms again and seemed to be daring anyone to contradict him.

"To know the answer to that, we would have to know what happened," replied Nurse Florence slowly.

"Do we really have time right now?" I asked. "The clock's ticking. We have only so long to grab the lyre—God knows how long that will take—and then find some way of beating Ares's army back to Olympus."

"We can spare a few minutes to talk about this," replied Nurse Florence firmly, "if only to figure out how to defend Jimmie. Make no mistake…Dan, Jimmie, listen to me! I don't care whether Jimmie's new life is an affront to the balance or not. He is one of us, and I will defend him the same way I would defend any of you. It might be nice to know, though, who or what we will be defending him against."

"Is this because I ate some ambrosia?" asked Jimmie quietly. "I didn't mean to cause trouble."

"It can't be as simple as that," I replied. "Nurse Florence, remember how Jimmie reacted to Aphrodite's little magic trick when we first arrived on Olympus? He shouldn't have been affected at all. And Jimmie, it looked to me like you were having trouble staying airborne at one point right after the cloud broke up. I think you've gradually been becoming less ghostly, haven't you?"

Jimmie nodded. "I guess so. I knew I was feeling strange…but…so many strange things have happened…"

"Being around Tal and whatever force he generates that strengthens the supernatural may be part of the cause," suggested Nurse Florence. "Jimmie shouldn't have been able to be more than an occasional presence. Instead he's been with us for days—and mostly in solid form. True, his body wasn't really human, but I don't think any ghost on record has been able to remain solid for so long. Perhaps what happened to him was simply a progressive return to life, but we didn't realize that at first."

"Maybe it's a combination of different factors," added Carla. "Being around Tal, traveling to different planes of existence, being exposed to all kinds of different magic, or eating ambrosia—it could have been any of them, or all of them. There's really no way to pin it down to one thing."

At that moment I noticed that the gem on Jimmie's wishing ring had deteriorated from a ruby brilliance to a dull, lifeless shade more reminiscent of brick than gem.

"Jimmie, did you wish yourself alive again?" I asked, as calmly as I could. "It's OK if you did. Any of us would have done the same."

"I did use my wish, but I didn't wish for that, I swear!" protested Jimmie. His tone sounded sincere, but even Dan now looked skeptical.

"Jimmie, what did you wish for?" Dan asked.

"If I tell you, it won't come true!" Jimmie protested, clearly on the verge of tears. I was surprised he was holding up as well as he was, considering what he was going through.

"Jimmie, the idea about not telling comes from fairy tales," said Nurse Florence reassuringly. "If you tell us, your wish can still come true."

"I wished...I wished that Dan and Tal would be friends again," he whispered. "Real friends, not just pretending to make me happy. I could tell."

Jimmie's words were like an ice-cold dagger in my guts. I knew my stubbornness was hurting him. If it had done even more damage than I thought...

"How could the wish to reconcile Tal and Dan possibly result in Jimmie coming back to life?" protested Carlos. "That doesn't make any sense."

"It was very generous of you to give up your wish so that Tal and Dan could be friends again," said Nurse Florence, "but did you really want to leave once that happened, or would you have preferred to have...stayed with them?"

Jimmie nodded. "Yeah, I knew I would have to leave earth once they got back together, and as painful as it sometimes was to be here...I guess I did want to stay."

Carla had been staring intensely at Jimmie awhile now, perhaps drawing on her memories as Alcina. "That's it, then, isn't it? The ring heard his wish, but it also heard what was in his heart, and it tried to give him both."

"It couldn't really grant two wishes," corrected Nurse Florence, "but it could have used one of the things Jimmie wanted to try to get him the other one."

"I'm lost," confessed Gordy, frowning.

"Think about it," continued Nurse Florence. "Jimmie is alive again...and a hundred times more vulnerable than he was as a ghost. More, actually. Tal and Dan have had their differences, but they both love Jimmie. They've already shown that they can still cooperate for the sake of the group. Now they have to cooperate even more closely to protect the now all-too-vulnerable Jimmie. Something like that could bring back their friendship over time."

"I can't make Jimmie wait any longer," I said quietly, moving toward the two brothers. "This whole mess is my fault. Jimmie wouldn't be at risk if not for me."

"He wouldn't be alive, either—" began Dan.

"Please let me finish. I knew all along I was making Jimmie an earthbound spirit and causing him pain. I just couldn't get past my own selfishness. Dan, you apologized a long time ago for what you did. That should have been the end of it—only I wouldn't let it end.

"Well, it ends now. Dan, I forgive you, absolutely and unconditionally. You are my friend again, just the way you were before all of this started. Jimmie, I mean it this time. Dan, can you forgive me for making you both wait so long?"

"Forgive you?" asked Dan incredulously. "If you had let me off the hook right away, Jimmie wouldn't be with us, let alone resurrected. I should be thanking you. Hell, I should be kissing your feet." He hugged Jimmie tightly. I walked the rest of the way to them and hugged both of them just as tightly.

"Group hug?" asked Gordy, always an advocate for group hugs, especially when pretty girls were involved.

I know, sappy, but yeah, we did have a group hug, and it made me feel a little better, despite our relatively dire situation.

Had I really forgiven Dan? I think knowing that Dan was Lancelot and therefore possibly at risk had been preying on my mind ever since I found out. It was much easier to think of Dan as scum when he was safe and secure, even when we were all in danger, but when he was facing his own unique disaster? When I might lose him if the wrong person found out his secret? Jimmie gave me the nudge I needed, but I must have been more ready for that nudge than I realized.

When the hug finally ended, I could tell Nurse Florence was about to say something else.

"*If you're going to be the voice of doom again, give it a rest,*" I suggested. "*Everybody knows we're in a weird, probably unprecedented situation. Everybody knows we need to keep a close watch on Jimmie. There's no point in hammering that particular nail right now.*" Nurse Florence nodded, though I could tell she still wanted to continue the conversation.

"What's next?" asked Shar, clearly ready to get moving again.

"Well, now we have two missions," I said. "We need to get the lyre, and we need to keep Jimmie alive. Oh, and I guess we also need to get back to Olympus before it falls."

"I have a headache," said Gordy simply, on some level speaking for us all.

"Maybe I should take Jimmie back to the surface," Dan suggested. "This place can't be safe for him."

"Unfortunately, neither is the surface," I pointed out. "For all we know, Poseidon's men will attack anyone emerging from the Underworld."

"How would you get him out, anyway?" asked Carla. "Charon only ferries people...well, the dead...in, not out. And we've already established that none of us could get across Acheron without being plunged into despair."

Damn! I should have thought of that when I was getting Charon to swear his oath.

"We know that Hades used to visit Olympus," Shar said. "Surely he must have a more direct route than the one we are taking to get in."

It took me a moment to realize that Shar had just spoken in ancient Greek and not through the magic of the dragon armor, but directly.

"Shar, are you still...you?" I asked. All we would need now would be to have to unravel yet another complicated past-life scenario.

"Very much so," he said, this time in English. "But I think it was Alexander who was making that suggestion."

"And it's a brilliant one!" exclaimed Nurse Florence, actually cheerful for the first time in a while. "If we can find the route Hades once used to get to Olympus, we might just be able to beat Ares's army."

"I'll just add that to our to-do list," I said with false cheerfulness. I had the feeling Hades was going to share that information with us about as readily as a miser shares his gold.

At that point we heard Cerberus howling and knew that it was time to go.

Chapter 11: Having Our Day in Court

We did not have to walk very far to come to the place of judgment…or at least, where the place of judgment used to be. There was indeed a raised platform with three magnificently carved silver thrones at its center, but they were empty.

"Not much of a welcoming committee," observed Shar.

"Just as well," said Nurse Florence. "I can't think they'd be happy to see us."

"This doesn't feel right," I said suspiciously.

"Since the Olympians were cut off from most of human society, there can't have been that many souls come through here," suggested Carla. "Maybe the old system has crumbled over time."

"Let's move on then," I said, though I wasn't fully satisfied.

"Not until you are judged!" announced a stately figure, made somewhat less dignified by the way in which he was half running to take his place on the platform. The judges must have had some way of knowing when someone approached, because the other two quickly appeared as well. Despite their obvious state of disarray, though, they still managed to appear both more imposing and more careful of the law than Arawn when he had chaired that farce of a tribunal in Annwn.

When the judges had finally gotten themselves seated and composed, it was easy to see beyond their common office to their common ancestry, for all three men had been sons of Zeus in life: Minos, Rhadamanthus, and Aeacus. All three had also been kings and been known as lawgivers, though it was hard for a modern person not to be a little cynical over the blatant nepotism.

Rhadamanthus was the first to notice an obvious discrepancy. "You're all alive! How did you get by Charon? How did you get by Cerberus?"

"Honorable Judges," I began, "we have been given permission by the Olympians themselves to come here." I waved the key of Hermes at this point. "We come on a quest that will determine whether a dire evildoer goes free or receives justice. Surely you are on the side of justice and will aid us?"

"And just who is this evildoer?" asked Minos, peering at me from beneath bushy eyebrows.

I told them the story of Morgan, trying to keep it as short as possible, but to no avail. The three judges asked question after question. It must have taken several hours to satisfy their thirst for detail.

When finally their questions were exhausted, Aeacus looked at me carefully and said, "That was an amazing tale, Grandnephew! And here you are with my grandson again!" he said, nodding to Shar. "Destiny truly works in strange ways."

I would not have thought there was much left that could surprise me. Clearly I was wrong.

"I beg your pardon, Honorable Judge, but perhaps you mistake me for another. I know that in a previous life, I was Hephaestion and that my friend Shar was Alexander the Great, but that was many, many generations after any grandson or grandnephew of yours could have been alive."

Aeacus leaned forward and studied me intently for a minute. "Nothing is hidden from us here in this place of judgment. I see that you can remember many of your previous lives, but have you forgotten that you were Patroclus? Does Shar, as you call him, not know that he was Achilles?"

Wow! That was quite an upgrade to my background, and one that I was not going to be telling Vanora about, especially since that forgery, the "Song of Taliesin," mentioned Troy, where Patroclus and Achilles fought the Trojans and died. The last thing I needed was to give Vanora more wood for her delusional fire.

Oddly enough, Shar did not look puzzled. "Shar, do you feel Achilles inside you?" I couldn't resist asking.

"No, just Alexander. But it makes sense, Tal. When we were Alexander and Hephaestion, we were always being compared to Achilles and Patroclus because of our friendship. Besides that, Alexander believed himself to be descended from Achilles. Perhaps Hephaestion was descended from Patroclus. That is sort of how Celtic reincarnation works, isn't it?"

Minos cleared his throat loudly. "Were you under the impression that this court was here to facilitate reunions or to provide you a place to reminisce about your previous lives?"

"Pardon us, Your Honors," said Shar quickly. "We did not mean to offend. My friend was just taken by surprise."

"It really matters not," replied Minos, glaring at us in a way that made me think of Cerberus. "You are living men. We judge only the dead now. We must turn this matter over to Hades, who alone is competent to hear your case."

I wanted to see Hades about as much as I wanted to take a swim with crocodiles. "Honorable Judges, we come here not for judgment, but to fulfill our quest, the importance of which I have explained. The longer we delay, the less the likelihood of success."

"We are here to maintain the law, not to facilitate quests, however noble," answered Minos. "And the law is clear that those who come here must be judged. The law is also clear that we cannot judge the living. We have but two choices: to refer your case to Hades or to send you on your way back to the upper world."

"I'm not sure I agree," replied Rhadamanthus slowly. "You were always a little too quick to make decisions, Brother. If we have no jurisdiction over them, and clearly we don't, then should we not just release them? Hades must know that they are here and may stop them if he chooses."

"Yes," chimed in Aeacus. "We have not been charged with keeping the living out of the Underworld. That is the job of Charon and Cerberus, both of whom have failed at it. Anyone who could get past them must surely be favored by some higher power."

Listening to the tribunal in Annwn and then to these judges here did not make me want to follow in my dad's footsteps and become a lawyer.

"Very well," said Minos finally. "Let them wander about the Underworld if that is what they desire—after they tell us what they are here for. Brothers, you remember the fool who wandered down here to steal Persephone from Hades. What would Hades think if we let someone else in to do the same?"

"Were such evil in their hearts, we would know it already," said Rhadamanthus irritably. "Still, in the interest of harmony among us, the question will be posed. What do you seek on your quest?"

"Oh, Honorable Judges, we seek the lyre of Orpheus," I replied, knowing there was no point in trying to lie to them here.

They could not have been any more shocked if I really had been seeking Persephone. Evidently they could see what was in our hearts but not every detail that was in our minds.

"Do you admit this changes everything?" asked Minos triumphantly. "The prized possession of Hecate herself, and they would steal it? Surely this must be reported to Hades!"

"I mean no disrespect to the rulers of the Underworld," I said loudly enough to get the judges' attention, "but did not Hecate herself steal the lyre from the Muses, Orpheus's own mother and aunts? What right does she have to it?"

"Fair point!" said Aeacus with a touch of pride. Evidently his relationship to my former self meant something to him. "But do you intend to give the lyre back to the Muses then? Is that your quest?"

"No," I admitted. "We take the lyre to a tribunal in Annwn."

Aeacus immediately looked defeated. "You can hardly call Hecate a thief if you steal from her to give it to others who have no more obvious right to it than she does." I would have argued further, but I could see the grim reality: all three judges now seemed in agreement that they must turn me over to Hades.

We had two choices. We could try our luck with Hades, or we could try to run away from the judges. They did not seem to have any guards, so perhaps...

"Do not go down that path, Grandnephew!" cautioned Aeacus. "We could see the idea of fleeing in your heart the moment it appeared. We have more resources than you see before you, including every hero in the Elysian Fields should we choose to summon them to our aid. You will not escape us, and if you try, it will simply make your condemnation by Hades more likely."

Quickly I checked for a mental consensus. No one in the group seemed to be any more optimistic than I was at this point. Throwing ourselves on the mercy of Hades seemed unlikely to succeed, but we had no other choice now.

Chapter 12: Dueling with Death

The judges led us personally to the palace of Hades, which lay not very far from the place of judgment. We did have to hike through the fields of Ashphodel, where those who had led indifferent lives wandered more or less aimlessly amid ghostly flowers and grass that seemed to have forgotten how to be green. However, in a very short time, we found ourselves before the palace, a very imposing structure of black marble and onyx, ringed by tall cypress and silvery white poplar. As we walked up the front steps, we could see part of a frieze portraying souls, presumably moving from life to life. Under more relaxed circumstances, I would have liked to walk around the building and see if viewing the entire frieze gave me any more insight into the nature of reincarnation, but I did not want to spend the time now, and I doubted the judges would have allowed such a thing anyway. Directly above the massive bronze doors and the front part of the frieze, I could see a sculptured pediment portraying the triumph of Hades over the Titans. Zeus, Poseidon, and the other Olympians were conspicuous for their absence. In this artistic rendering, it was Hades, and Hades alone, who was the hero.

As we approached, the bronze doors opened, presumably by magic, and the judges led us into an enormous central courtyard. In an ancient Greek palace, this area would have been bustling with activity, but this courtyard was deathly quiet, despite an almost parklike appearance, also different from what an ancient Greek palace would have had. Stone benches were arranged among trees, with the ever-present cypresses and white poplars joined by sturdy pines and delicately flowering alders. The landscaping was far more elaborate than anything I could remember seeing among the mortal ancient Greeks, who had placed much more emphasis on the architecture. I did, however, notice the traditional columns behind the trees, part of the facade of each structure that connected to the courtyard. It was hard to tell which type of columns they were, though, because, although open to the "sky," the courtyard was lit as if with moonlight partially obscured by clouds. I looked up but couldn't really discern a light source.

The judges marched us to about the midpoint of the courtyard and then steered us west, toward what I was sure was the throne room. We passed through another enormous doorway and found ourselves in a cavernous chamber with an impossibly high ceiling, at least if one had to obey the normal principles of Greek architecture and the physical limits of stone. Like the courtyard, the room was lit fitfully by a silvery glow, in this case emanating from torches in wall sconces spaced evenly around the perimeter of the chamber. The floor was a mosaic of the Underworld, but like our garments, the image seemed to move, giving an effect a little bit like using a floor as a video screen. I would have liked to study the floor, perhaps to find a clue to where Hecate was, but the judges hurried us toward two white gold thrones against the western wall. Between the two thrones, that wall showed a massive fresco of Hades racing his chariot, led by its four midnight-black horses, portrayed so realistically that they almost seemed alive. The thrones themselves were superbly crafted, doubtless by Hephaestus, and they drew my eye irresistibly. Maybe it was my relationship to Hephaestus or maybe it was some magic in the metal that made it hard to look away from them.

Despite such exotic sights, as soon as Hades and Persephone entered the room, all eyes, including mine, swung in their direction.

Hades's silver crown sparkled in the torchlight, and he had a dignified look befitting one of the three ruling Olympians and master of the Underworld, just as Poseidon commanded the sea and Zeus the sky. Yet there was something else about him I couldn't describe very well. A heaviness, perhaps. Maybe he had been in the darkness too long. It was not so much that he seemed unhappy exactly; he seemed more as if he had simply forgotten what happiness was. However empty his heart might have been, however, he did not lack power: I could feel it radiating from him like an anti-sun. Almost equally powerful was his staff, potent as the trident of Poseidon and nearly as mighty as the thunderbolts of Zeus.

In contrast to Hades, Persephone was not absent emotion; instead, misery seemed to flow out of her in great, shuddering waves. She looked pale, like a faded copy of what she would become when spring came. Though she wore massive amounts of opulent jewelry and sparkled like diamonds with every movement, the gems made her seem imprisoned rather than adorned. The necklace, more valuable than all the crown jewels of Europe, was like a noose around her neck, the shining bracelets merely shackles, the broaches like knives stuck into bleeding flesh. I wasn't expecting to get such a clear reading from someone with the powerful mind of an Olympian, but I guessed Persephone wasn't used to being around mind readers, or perhaps she just didn't care who knew she was miserable.

The King and Queen of the Underworld took their seats, and Rhadamanthus stepped forward. "Your Majesties, I beg your pardon for troubling you, but we have encountered a situation the law does not properly cover: living mortals on a quest."

Hades's face did not betray a trace of emotion. "Thank you, my judges, for bringing these strangers here. You have made the right choice, as always." The judges bowed and quickly took their leave without further ceremony, though Aeacus did spare me one last glance as he was stepping out of the throne room.

Then Hades turned to us. "Tell me why I should not at once kill all of you by the most horrendous means at my disposal," he said in a voice that cut like a dagger chilled in the heart of a glacier.

What was the appropriate response to a statement like that? I was at a complete loss for words. Before I could get a grip on myself, Shar stepped forward. Given the fact that he had the higher status in his ancient Greek lives, perhaps he was the best spokesman anyway.

"Great King and Queen of the Underworld, we come to you as suppliants, not as trespassers. A faerie tribunal has sent us here on a quest—"

"I care not who sent you," said Hades, leaning forward. "Nor do I acknowledge the authority of this 'tribunal' of yours. You are living humans, and as such you have no place here."

Shar started to speak, but Hades cut him off. "You think that because you were once Alexander and Achilles, that because the blood of Zeus flowed in your veins, that because the blood of Perseus and the Persian kings flows in your veins now, that I will listen to you. In that, you are mistaken. Men are men, no more and no less. And as for sons of Zeus, they were once so numerous they could be found on every street corner. Your 'exalted' ancestry will not save you."

Well, apparently Shar hadn't been the best spokesperson after all. In any case, it was now his turn to be lost for words.

"It was not our intent to argue that our past or present ancestry entitled us to special consideration," I said, making a deep bow. "Rather it was our very respect for the natural balance of things that compels us to complete our quest. We violate the rule against living humans entering the world in order to prevent an even greater violation."

"So, you present yourselves as guardians of order, do you?" asked Hades mockingly. "Then explain to me why you have that abomination among you?"

Again I was caught off guard. Did he mean Amynticos? I could think of no story that portrayed Hades as hostile to the mechanical men of Hephaestus, but who else could he—I realized what he meant seconds before he said it himself.

"The one you call Jimmie, who walked about for weeks dead, yet in the mortal world, and now alive, in the realm of the dead. I can imagine no greater breach. But," continued Hades, "I will give you a chance to prove that you are guardians of order. Surrender that creature to me, and I will let your quest continue." His words had the finality of a car slamming into me at ninety miles an hour.

"No!" Dan and I responded simultaneously, reflexively moving together to keep Jimmie behind us.

"Lord Hades, we mean no disrespect, but he is brother to Daniel and like a brother to me. We cannot give him to you." I was trying to be diplomatic, but I could see it wasn't working.

"You cannot?" asked Hades ominously. "You *will* not is more like it. Are you foolish enough to suppose I need your permission to take him?"

Hades raised his staff, now glowing with a dark light. "I was but testing you, to see if your protestation of respect for the law was true. Clearly, it was not. Now you will lose him anyway, and you will fail in your quest as well, for I will never let you proceed after this defiance."

Hades pointed his staff at me. "One touch, one tiny touch, of this staff is death to any living thing. Only the gods themselves can resist it. I will take the boy now, and anyone who tries to protect him will die as well."

Behind me Jimmie started crying.

"The name of the game is keep away!" I shouted mentally. *"Keep Jimmie and yourselves out of range of that staff!"*

Considering the unexpected twists we were facing, I feared at least some of us were bound to end up dead. Nonetheless I drew White Hilt, whose flames blinded Hades momentarily, and charged him. I doubted I could hurt him much with the sword, but maybe I could knock the staff out of his hand.

I brought my blade crashing down on the staff with all my strength, but it moved barely an inch from the impact, and Hades just laughed. His laugh had the sound of glaciers scraping together.

His mood changed a bit a second later, when one of Carla's arrows sank into his shoulder. As a weapon of a fellow Olympian, it could harm him.

"You will all die," he announced with a surprising lack of feeling. Then he swung the staff at me with enough force to smash my head to pulp. His stroke missed only because Amynticos threw himself at him and actually succeeded in knocking him to the ground.

I was dimly aware of Shar invoking the power of his armor to summon up some of Alexander's warriors. I wasn't sure that was the right strategy to use against the ruler of the dead, but I doubted it could make our situation any worse. Amynticos was certainly the strongest of us physically, and his mechanical nature made him immune to the staff's deadly touch, but Hades tossed him aside like a dandelion and rose from the floor with surprising speed.

"Lady, can you not help us?" pleaded Khalid. He had flown over to Persephone and tried to take her hand, but all she did was look at him with overwhelming sadness and shake her head.

At that moment I felt an alien presence envelop me and started to struggle, until I realized it was a ghost of one of Alexander's men.

"They are forming a protective shield around each of us," shouted Shar. "The staff can't hurt them!"

Even Hades betrayed a second of surprise. There was no question that was a clever move. After all, Shar was Alexander and Achilles, so shouldn't we have expected some brilliant stratagem from him?

Hades's surprise gave Amynticos another chance to jump him, but this time Hades was prepared. He spun quickly and struck the charging automaton with the staff. To my horror, Amynticos's body shattered, and the fragments fell helplessly to the ground.

"Fools!" sneered Hades. "This staff not only kills with a touch; it rends with a blow. Even the very earth itself could not resist. Did you expect that toy of Hephaestus's to overcome me?"

I don't know why I was all choked up over a machine. Perhaps it was because Hephaestus had given him to me with such obvious deliberateness—a father's coming-of-age present for his son.

I knew one thing in that moment. Amynticos was not going to die...break...whatever...for nothing. He had slowed Hades down for us. Now it was up to us to take advantage of that gift.

"Please!" I could hear Khalid in the background, still working on

Persephone. Khalid was actually pretty tough, but having had to survive on the street for months as a nine-year-old had sharpened his ability to manipulate adult emotions. He did the vulnerable little kid about as well as anyone I had ever seen. Still, Persephone seemed unmoved.

Hades looked at us and ordered the ghosts shielding us to remove themselves. Since they were dead and we were in the Underworld, they would have to obey his command. However, the magic of the dragon armor, which made them obey Shar's summons, was strong enough that the dead soldiers obeyed Hades's command slowly, giving us a little more time. The question was, what should we do with that time?

Carla kept nailing him with fair precision with the arrows of Artemis, and I could see small amounts of ichor, the Olympian blood, leaking from him, so I knew she had wounded him. I wondered which other weapons we had that might be effective.

Shar charged with Zom while still partially covered by his ghostly protector. I expected him to go for the staff, and so apparently did Hades, who braced himself, but instead Shar hit him with all the force he had on Hades's right arm. There was an emerald flash, and Hades faltered, though just for a second. I magically boosted Shar to faerie speed, and he started a frenzied attack on Hades's arm. Unfortunately, Hades had two arms, and he used the other one to knock Shar halfway across the room.

I heard a commotion at the back of the room. Nurse Florence was trying to get Jimmie out into the courtyard, but the door must have locked magically and was resisting all her attempts to open it.

I could hear Jimmie continuing to cry, and the sound tore my heart out. Jimmie had been in dangerous situations for weeks, of course, but as a ghost he couldn't be hurt by them. Now he was a very vulnerable, very scared nine-year-old, though in a sixteen-year-old body. He had a magic sword, but he didn't really know how to use it, he had no armor, and he had no combat training. If we failed to save him, there wasn't much hope he could save himself.

Gordy used his enhanced strength to throw his sword across the room at Hades. The sword tore into Hades's chest but seemed to miss anything vital, as Hades pulled out the blade and threw it on the floor. Still, I could see ichor leaking from the chest wound, so the faerie weapons, like the Olympian ones, had some power against him.

"Coordinated assault! He can't fend us all off at the same time!" I thought as loudly as I could. Indeed, the guys had already started moving

on Hades, and Gordy had managed to retrieve his sword. The trick was getting close enough for a decent attack without getting hit by the longer staff in the process.

Hades had clearly not expected this much resistance, but someone who had fought the Titans was not going to be beaten easily. Seeing himself surrounded, he struck the floor hard with his staff. Whatever enchanted marble the floor had been crafted from did not crack, but the staff created an earthquake much like Poseidon's trident would have, knocking all of us off of our feet and making us momentarily helpless. Then, with unnatural speed, he leaped over us before we could get up. He could have killed one or more of us at that point; we could never have fended him off effectively from the ground.

For the moment he bypassed us, though, and headed straight at Jimmie. Carla hit him with a couple more arrows, but she did not succeed in stopping him. Jimmie was frozen in terror. Nurse Florence moved in front of him, but she was a healer, not a fighter. Hades was just going to brush her aside or strike her with the staff and kill her, and then Jimmie would be his. None of us could get up and reach him first, not even at faerie speed.

I had gotten up far enough, however, to see Hades stumble and fall right before he reached Nurse Florence. He rose almost instantly, but at least Nurse Florence had a second or two to start Jimmie running toward the room's north exit, from which Hades and Persephone had entered. They had no idea where they were going, but anywhere was better than here.

Hades was now bleeding from a wound on the back of his neck I had not seen anyone inflict. He swung his staff around wildly in the empty air.

"Who is doing this?" he demanded.

There were two or three of us who could make ourselves invisible but not so invisible that a supernatural being could not see us with a little concentration. I tried to see whoever or whatever it was that was attacking Hades, but I had absolutely no luck.

Again Hades fell. Again he rose, but this time his emotionless facade—for that must have been what it was—had started to crack.

"You will suffer a thousand tortures for this insolence!" he screamed. Somehow I preferred his scream to his laugh.

Carlos lunged and managed to nick Hades with his blade. Usually that weapon made anyone wounded by it start to drown, but it was too much to hope for that Hades would suffer the same effect.

I think Stan had been with us at the beginning of the battle, but I could tell from the white light from his sword that David was now in charge again.

"Desist, false god!" he bellowed, giving the sword a hard enough swing to slice into Hades's right hand with a flash of white light. Then he dodged out of the way when Hades swung the staff at him. Before Hades could pursue David, he fell again.

"Shahriyar, time your strike with mine!" ordered David. I could see where he was going with that: the sword of David and the sword of Solomon, striking in unison, might have an effect greater than just adding the two together.

Hades rose, but he was definitely slowing down. Before he could counter with his staff, David and Shar both hit his right wrist, David's white light and Shar's emerald light merged into a silvery explosion flecked with pale green, and the staff fell from Hades's now shriveled hand. Dan kicked the staff out of the way, and Gordy picked it up, all before Hades could quite realize what had happened.

I could hardly believe it. We had disarmed the ruler of the Underworld in his own throne room!

Hades was more formidable physically than any of us, but now he had no weapon, his right hand looked useless, and he was bleeding from several wounds. By contrast, we were in relatively good shape, perhaps a first for us following a major battle.

At least, I hoped it was *following* a major battle rather than somewhere in the middle of one. I didn't think we could actually kill an Olympian. We could mangle him so badly he could no longer resist us, but that outcome raised its own set of problems. No, I wasn't willing to sacrifice Jimmie for the sake of the balance, but completely incapacitating Hades seemed likely to destabilize this plane of existence, and I didn't particularly want that, either. I very much wanted Hades's surrender.

And I might have gotten it too, except that at that point we were all hit with enough hallucinatory psychic force to push us far, far from reality.

Chapter 13: The Nightmare Is Just Beginning

I didn't succumb immediately because I always had my mental shields up while fighting supernatural opponents, just in case. Nonetheless, I could feel pressure on those shields, as if my head was in a steadily tightening vise. I had to stop the attack before the pressure became unbearable, but I also had to make sure Hades didn't take advantage of the sudden assault, which I was pretty sure some ally of his must be causing.

David, who always seemed pretty resistant to magic, and Shar, immune as long as he held Zom, were still up also, so I told them to keep their swords pointed at Hades, just in case. We couldn't risk his getting that staff back.

As soon as I knew Hades wasn't going to be making any sudden moves, I scanned the room to pinpoint the source. That wasn't a particularly hard job, since standing in the doorway was a pale, dark-haired, beautiful but wild-eyed woman, staring at us and sending out burst after burst of hostile psychic energy in our direction. Even fully shielded, I was seeing shadowy images and knew that the stranger was trying to bombard us with hallucinations. Evidently, Hades had a backup plan.

I could only spare a second to check on the others. Nurse Florence and Jimmie were out of the room. Carla was still up, but like me she would not last forever. Gordy, Dan, and Carlos were down for sure, lost in some waking nightmare, though I didn't dare spend the time to figure out what they were seeing. Khalid I couldn't see or sense for some reason, but I didn't have the time to search for him. Fast as he was, he might even have gotten out of the palace, though he more typically threw himself into danger than ran away from it.

"Carla, let's hit her with all we've got!" Carla, who was adapting to combat situations with surprising rapidity, already had an arrow prepared, but before she could fire, she fell to her knees, as did I, hit by an even stronger assault. I tried to raise White Hilt but just couldn't. The effort of keeping my shields up was now taking almost all my focus. Whoever this woman was, she had more power than I had at first realized. If she didn't tire pretty soon, Carla and I would both be trapped in nightmares as well, and I had my doubts that even David and Shar could handle both Hades and this new threat all by themselves.

I could sense Shar moving in my direction.

"Watch Hades!" I demanded through clenched teeth. I glanced

in his direction just for a second and realized that even he was starting to feel part of the attack, despite Zom's protection.

My shields were cracking now, and the shadowy images were becoming more substantial as my resistance weakened. At least I could still tell they were hallucinations, but I figured I had only two or three minutes before I lost all sense of reality, maybe not even that.

The walls of the throne room were like a dull, distant haze now as I fought the image obscuring them: a church interior. It was a small church. As the details became clearer, I recognized it as the recently built nondenominational Protestant church in Santa Brígida. Why were there so many people? The sanctuary was crowded; hardly a seat was left. The whole gang was with me, which was odd, because none of us belonged to that congregation. My own family went most often to All Saints-by-the-Sea Episcopal in Santa Barbara, Carlos to St. Raphael's in Goleta, Carla to Saint Barbara's, yet here we all were, together. Even stranger, Stan and Shar, both Jewish, and Khalid, a Muslim, were with me as well. In fact, Stan was sitting right next to me, patting me on the shoulder. Had he ever come to church with me? I didn't think so.

I could hear the sound of weeping. Then I realized that my own face was wet with tears. There was a coffin up front. I didn't need to look inside to know who I would find there.

Not real! Not real! I kept telling myself, but the vision became more substantial by the second. The sun was filtering in through the stained-glass windows on the west side of the church, so it must be an early evening funeral.

The minister, a serious-looking, middle-aged man with thinning brown hair sprinkled with gray, was performing the funeral service, but I wasn't really listening at first. Why bother to listen to a hallucinatory eulogy?

Unless, of course, it wasn't a hallucination.

I looked over at Stan, who was crying, too, though he was trying not to show it.

"How could Eva be dead?" I didn't realize I had spoken aloud until Stan leaned over and whispered, "You did everything you could."

But had I really? Eva had never been in danger, except the danger I dragged her into, because of who I was. If I had never entered her life, she would never have died so young.

I looked toward the front of the church again, and Eva's ghost was standing beside the coffin. I could tell from the lack of reaction around me that nobody else could see her. She was manifesting for me alone.

Her green eyes, now lifeless, stared into mine. Her skin looked pale, so pale. She raised her arm and pointed at me stiffly.

"Taliesin Weaver, you killed me!" she shouted accusingly. Her voice had almost always been full of smiles, but not now.

I wanted to die myself. I still burned with unrequited love for her, but now we would never be together. We would never be together because of me, because of what I had done.

I wanted to dissolve into a pile of dust and slowly drift away as people moved around me. I wanted to travel back in time and prevent myself from ever being born. Yeah, that would do it—erase myself from existence. Eva would still be alive. Stan would be better off; so would Dan. So would everyone.

I heard a voice shouting in the distance. Who would shout so near a church?

"Tal! Snap out of it!" The voice sounded a little like Khalid's, but I could see Khalid. He was in the church with me, sitting one row in front and about three seats over, right next to Shar. How could I be hearing him outside?

The accusing figure had walked slowly down the steps of the chancel and was moving ever closer to me. Did she want revenge? Well, she could have it. I would do nothing to stop her.

"Tal!" Khalid's voice had become louder and more insistent. Despite the apparition in front of me, I glanced toward the west, from where the shouting seemed to originate. The sun had nearly set, but its last rays were still sparkling in a stained-glass window that portrayed Saint David, haloed and robed in archiepiscopal vestments, staring at me as if he were ready to pass judgment on me.

A window portraying a medieval saint in a nondenominational Protestant church? That didn't seem likely. Yet there it was.

"Taliesin!" shrieked Eva's ghost, still continuing her slow but inevitable march in my direction.

Eva had never called me Taliesin in life, and I couldn't help wondering why she would do so in death.

Movement caught my eye, and I glanced again at the stained-glass window. It was shifting, becoming more lifelike, almost photo-realistic. Was Saint David going to denounce me as well?

"Tal!" Saint David shouted in Khalid's voice. "We need you now!"

I could feel Eva's cold, dead fingers on my throat. It was getting harder to breathe.

Khalid...Khalid needed me. Everyone needed me. Yet here they all were, silent as ghosts themselves, grieving for Eva, but in no apparent peril.

"None of this is real, Tal!" said Saint David, still sounding like Khalid.

Not real? Yeah, some things didn't make sense, but it seemed so real otherwise.

The fingers tightened further. I could feel my dizziness increasing as the arteries in my neck compressed. I slumped over. Stan looked alarmed and shouted something, but I kept hearing Khalid's more distant shouting.

Not real? I could see the church in every detail, feel the pew on which I was sitting—but I couldn't remember how I had gotten there, or when exactly Eva died. Wouldn't I have remembered every horrifying detail? Wouldn't each one have been acid-etched into my memory?

I wasn't in this church, because I was still in the Underworld. I was still in the Underworld, and the guys needed my help. This moment of clarity might not last against the steady barrage of psychic energy. I needed to exploit my awareness fast.

Able to breathe again, I tore the false ghost's hands from my throat, being careful not to look her in the eyes, jumped from my seat, and flew across the western side of the sanctuary, ignoring the shocked gasps of the fake congregation. Aiming at the swirling stained glass that had once been Saint David, the point at which my subconscious had undercut the hallucination, I sped up and crashed through the window, spraying shards of multicolored glass in all directions...and found myself back in Hades's throne room.

It took me only a second to register the fact that I was too late. Hades, his staff clasped firmly in his hands and once again radiating dark light, stood near the center of the scattered corpses of all my friends, each lying face down on the black marble, skin pale and cold. Jimmie, a ghost once again, looked at me with tearful eyes and moaned, "Why? Why couldn't you have gotten back faster?" His glance tore through my heart like bullets.

Hades looked at me, too, his emotionless detachment firmly in place again, and said, "Your turn!" waving the staff in my general direction.

It was then I noticed the fresco between the thrones that I was sure had depicted Hades in his chariot now showed Saint David walking toward Jerusalem, a humble pilgrim in search of spiritual enlightenment.

Dodging Hades's staff, I ran headlong into the stone wall, felt the fresco scrape against my skin...and found myself again in the throne room, hopefully the real one this time.

But if it was the real throne room, it was no longer the real me. Somehow, the relentless psychic assault had unleashed Dark Me, now firmly in control of my body.

"Tal, thank God!" said Dan, running over to me. "Hades has escaped, and he took Jimmie. We have to find them right away!"

I watched helplessly as my body drew White Hilt and sliced its flaming blade right through Dan's neck, sending his head, surprise frozen into his features, crashing to the floor and his blood fountaining in all directions, splattering the floor mosaic that showed Saint David sailing to the Holy Land.

I closed my eyes, and with all my might, I willed myself back to the real throne room. For a minute I thought the effort would cause my brain to start hemorrhaging, but then I felt the illusions dissolve. The floor mosaic was chilling my back, and I could hear Khalid whispering in my ear, but I still couldn't see him anywhere.

I could still see flickering shadows around me, hallucinations trying to break through. The wild-eyed woman was looking even more wild-eyed but also substantially more tired: chewing on a bard, a sorceress, a Lady of the Lake, to say nothing of a resistant half-djinn, Zom-protected Shar, and God-protected David might easily have been more than she bargained for.

Doing a quick scan of the room revealed the situation was still desperate, though. Gordy, Dan, and Carlos remained trapped in their own private hells, as now was Carla, as well as Nurse Florence and Jimmie, who must have doubled back. David seemed to be struggling with Stan, nightmare ridden, even though David wasn't. Shar looked as if he had a headache but was still hallucination-free and still keeping his sword pointed at Hades, who at least seemed to be our prisoner. He was, however, risking furtive glances at the side door, making me sure he would make a run for it at the first opportunity.

That woman was going to notice at any minute that I was awake again, so there was no time to lose. I jumped up and practically threw myself at Gordy, who was still clutching Hades's staff, though no longer aware of it. I grabbed it out of his fingers and spun around to face the woman. She had already started staring at me even more intensely, and the shadows became more vivid again.

I shot toward her at faerie speed, not intending to kill her—her power level suggested she was an Olympian of some kind—but figuring the staff might be the best way to stun her, and that was probably all I needed to break her spell.

I felt myself slowing as I neared her, but I was going to make it before my nightmares swallowed me again. Then Hecate entered the room, and the easy triumph I had been visualizing died within me.

How did I know she was Hecate? True, I had never seen her as Hephaestion or as Patroclus, but there was no mistaking that massive power surging from her, strength perhaps even greater than Hades. Then there was the fact that she was often called Triple Hecate because of her authority in the heavens, on earth, and in the Underworld. Before I could do anything, she made the title literal, actually cloning herself into three identical, black-robed figures, with skin like white marble, hair black as midnight, and eyes like stars.

One of the three figures crackled lightning from her fingertips and moved toward Hades. One, over whom a boulder seemed to be materializing, moved toward Shar. The third, about whom an army of ghosts now seemed to swirl, moved toward me.

Persephone, whom I had forgotten all about, ran toward the lightning-haloed Hecate. Well, running might have been an overstatement, weighed down by gems as Persephone was, but she moved as fast as she was able. "You have come to rescue me from him at last!"

"You fool!" snapped Hades. "She could care less about you now. She wants only my throne...and thanks to these intruders, she will have it."

Could he be right? His idea was certainly consistent with Hestia's story. Difficult as Hades had become as a ruler of the Underworld, Hecate had to be worse.

I still needed to get to Hecate's ally and stop her to free the rest of my allies. Those hallucinations were becoming persistent again, as well as much more real. The problem was that one of the Hecates now stood between me and the madness-generating woman, ready to suffocate me in a cloud of ghosts.

"David, I need you—NOW!" I thought to him.

"Stan is…making it…impossible for me…to move." Nor was paralyzing David the extent of what Stan was doing. David's sword no longer had that comforting white glow.

How Stan had seized control from an unwilling David I wasn't sure. Only a short time ago, a sane Stan had been unable to do so. Perhaps Stan's frenzied state lent him some kind of manic mental strength that David could not counter. I could have helped David bring Stan out of his current hysteria, but there was no time for that. I'd be dead by then if I didn't do something quickly.

Hecate anticipated I might try to get to her ally, and she had firmly blocked that path. I looked around quickly and spotted where Nurse Florence had fallen. Ramping myself up to faerie sped, I sprinted over in the direction of her bag of tricks, but I could not outrun the ghosts, who formed a film all over me, half blinding me and cutting off my oxygen as they coated my nostrils and mouth. My possession of Hades's staff meant that they could not afford to become too solid, because the staff could smash any solid form, but this way they were solid enough to smother me and hard to scrape off, unless I had someone to help. Now they were twining around my arms and legs. I was never going to make it to the bag.

Then Hecate's ally fell back as if shoved, and for a moment the hallucinations at least were not as bad. I cast a little spell to reduce my body's need for oxygen and kept pushing toward the bag.

The ghostly Hecate was busy directing her minions in their attack on me. The earthly one tried alternatively hitting Shar with boulders and somewhat smaller stones, then spraying him with fire-hose-intense jets of water, but so far, Zom's protection held. The stormy one blasted Hades with lightning bolts, certainly not as intense as those Zeus could have managed but enough to torment the already weakened Hades. Apparently, his theory was correct: Hecate had come for his throne.

Hecate's ally reeled as if someone had punched her in the face. Then I saw an unmistakable ichor stain on her dress from what looked like a dagger wound in her left breast.

All three Hecates turned for a moment. "Melinoe!" they cried in unison. Then I knew who I was dealing with, not that it mattered much now.

I had never seen her in my Greek lives, but Melinoe, nymph of madness and nightmare, daughter of Persephone and Zeus, shaped by the beatings Hades gave her mother during pregnancy, would indeed have no love for Hades. She was the perfect ally for Hecate's coup.

Hecate's momentary distraction caused the ghosts to become confused, and I covered the last part of the distance to the magic bag. Simultaneously, Shar, seeing that Hades was not going anywhere, lunged at the Hecate opposing him and struck with all the considerable force his muscular arms could provide. He had aimed at her chest and could not drive the sword through it, but he did at least cause her to fall backward, and then he was on her, each blow landing with an emerald flash that momentarily disabled her magic.

"Don't kill him!" I heard Persephone protest as the third Hecate returned to her unrelenting torture of Hades.

I got the bag open, grabbed the endless cup of wine and nectar, and poured it over myself, dousing the ghosts in it.

I had no idea what the effect would be, and Nurse Florence was bound to tell me later it was a stupid gamble, but it was all I could think of, given the supplies I had at hand. Then I took the still-burning brand from the hearth fire of Olympus, itself a bane to ghosts, and lit the mixture, which immediately burst into flames, incinerating the physical presence the ghosts had maintained. They dissolved in futile screams, and I was free.

Melinoe was still struggling futilely with an invisible assailant, and the others were beginning to break free from her nightmares. All we had to do was keep the Hecates busy until everyone revived, and we might actually have a chance.

The Hecate facing me had other ideas, however. I could see her summoning a mist of some kind, a fear-inducing mist that also seemed poisonous. I charged her at faerie speed, waving Hades's staff and counting on its power and the residual fragrance of the nectar to keep the mist at bay long enough for me to strike. I got in one good blow, and that was enough to break Hecate's spell. Then, like Shar with the other Hecate, I just kept the strikes coming.

I felt the crackle of electricity in time to dodge the lightning from the Hecate who had been attacking Hades. She was effectively the last Hecate standing, since my adversary and Shar's were both stunned by now. Shar, who was closer, threw himself at her, and a few blows with Zom rendered her, too, unconscious. I could hardly believe my eyes and had to resist the temptation to pinch myself to make sure I wasn't dreaming.

Hecate might be the most powerful spell caster among the Olympians, but she was no strategist, or she would have waited until we were gone to attack the wounded Hades. Trying to start her revolution while we were still here, even with Melinoe to soften us up, was a risky proposition.

Come to think of it, though, it shouldn't have been. Melinoe had eliminated most of us as an effective threat, and Hecate should have been strong enough to keep Shar and me at bay long enough for Melinoe to finish us off, or at least eliminate me, after which Shar would have stood alone against two Olympians. Who was it who had taken Melinoe out of action and made our victory possible? There could only be one answer.

"Khalid, you can come out now!" I said loudly. Sure enough, Khalid appeared right next to me, barely able to contain his excitement.

"I helped this time, didn't I?" he asked eagerly.

"You always help, even if you risk your own neck too often doing it. This time, though, you made the difference between victory and defeat." By now everyone else was gathering around, except Shar, who I signaled to keep an eye on Hades, and Nurse Florence and Carla, who were watching the Hecates and Melinoe.

"What I want to know is how you managed to be invisible to the Olympians and to me. Normally I can see through your invisibility if I know to look."

Khalid held up a helmet that oozed power. "The nice lady told me where to find Hades's invisibility helmet. It was locked up, but you know how I am with locks."

To my surprise, Persephone had joined us. "That helmet grants invisibility that not even an Olympian can pierce. Invisibility and undetectability." Well, that explained why I couldn't locate Khalid when I was scanning for everyone's minds. It also explained why he wasn't incapacitated by fear. Evidently Melinoe couldn't send nightmares his way if she couldn't see him.

"I should be angry with you, Wife, for betraying me yet again," rasped Hades. "But as your betrayal made it possible for Hecate and Melinoe to be defeated, I may overlook the whole thing—this time." Persephone sighed, perhaps wishing she could take back her feeble protests when Hecate was torturing Hades.

"What now?" asked Gordy, looking pale but otherwise pretty much his usual self.

"What, indeed?" asked Hades mockingly. "You have saved me from one threat but left me vulnerable to every other. Someone is bound to overthrow me before very long. Surely such respecters of law would never allow the Underworld to be seized by lawless rebels." Apparently Hades was also the god of sarcasm.

"We can't trust you not to attack us if we restore you. We must think carefully what kind of oaths to impose. We would want to keep Jimmie." Hades scowled, but nodded. "We would also want the lyre, of course. That's why we came."

"I have no idea where it is," said Hades, "but with Hecate as your prisoner, you can soon find out."

"Such a powerful artifact in your kingdom and you have no idea where it is?" I scoffed. "I don't believe that. As king of this realm, you can probably sense it from here."

Hades chuckled darkly. "In truth, though I have no desire to see that cursed instrument back in mortal hands, I don't really want Hecate to possess it any longer."

"And so…," I prompted him.

"Yes, I know where it is. Hecate has buried it beneath the waters of Lethe, some distance north of here, near the point where those souls who will be reincarnated drink of the waters to forget their previous lives."

"Why there, I wonder?" said Nurse Florence, also clearly prompting Hades.

"Is that not obvious? She buried it there so that anyone looking for it would forget what he was looking for—and everything else. Even a god could not swim all the way down without losing at least the memory of searching for the lyre. Thus, it will always be hers."

"Still, there must be a way to retrieve it," I suggested. "Otherwise, how could she get it?"

"She wanted to possess it but not to use it," replied Hades. "However, there is a way. If I had my staff, I could divert the waters. Don't think about trying to do it yourself," he added quickly. "You haven't the skill, nor do you know the spot at which it is buried."

"I can see the outlines of a deal here," I began. "You give us Jimmie and the lyre, as well as some way to get to Olympus before its enemies reach it. Oh, and you accompany us to Olympus and defend it when it is attacked. In exchange, we will heal your hand and return both your staff and your helmet."

Hades laughed bitterly. "So you give me what is already mine, and in exchange I give pretty much everything you could ever want."

"We did just save you," I pointed out.

"From a threat that would not have existed had you not weakened me in the first place."

Well, he had me there.

"Besides," he continued, "I know of no way to get you to Olympus fast enough. By the time you work your way back out of the Underworld, it will already be too late."

"That's an outright lie!" accused Shar. "I was just remembering my stay in the Underworld as Achilles. I saw you open a pathway using your staff and then ascend in your chariot. I'll bet you have the magic to make that chariot big enough to accommodate all of us."

"Nonetheless," replied Hades, glossing over the accusation, "what you ask is too much for what you offer in return. I will not make that bargain."

"Fine," I said, as if I could have cared less. "Then we keep the staff and the helmet, we get the lyre by ripping up half the Underworld with the staff, we find our own way back to Olympus, perhaps too late— but whatever—and you get overthrown sooner rather than later. Works for me."

I was bluffing, of course, but Hades might not have been aware of how limited our transportation options were. In any case, he nodded his head grudgingly after just a couple of minutes.

"Propose the oath," he grumbled.

"Wait!" commanded David. "Taliesin, do you seriously intend to allow this false god to be restored? He is evil; I have seen it."

"Excuse us," I said, grabbing David roughly by the arm and pulling him away from the group. Once we were out of earshot of the others, I said, "David, I am the leader. I cannot have you questioning every decision I make. As king, you would have never tolerated such behavior on the part of one of your soldiers."

"But it's wrong!" said David, eyes glinting angrily. "I'm trying to forgive your faking that vision, Taliesin, I really am, but it isn't easy for me. And then there was the whole matter of Jimmie coming back to life."

"Surely you wouldn't have wanted him dead?

"I would have wanted whatever God's will was to be fulfilled. Not knowing what God wanted, I couldn't imagine leaving a child in the hands of that false god. He still calls himself a god; you can't have missed that!"

I nodded reluctantly.

"Well, I do know what God thinks about false gods," he continued, "and so do you. We cannot make this bargain."

It was clear an I-am-the-boss approach was not going to work. "David," I began in a more gentle tone, "are you aware of the Holocaust?"

"From Stan's memories," said David. "I cannot believe that such horrors happened, but they did."

"Well, when someone protested the willingness of the British leader, Winston Churchill, to form an alliance with Stalin, Churchill said something like, 'If the devil were fighting Adolf Hitler, I'd help the devil.' Stalin was an evil man, too, but without his help, the allies might not have been able to defeat Hitler, and millions more Jewish people would have died, together with millions of others."

"But—" David began.

"No buts!" I insisted. "Here's what happens if we don't restore Hades. Someone worse ends up in charge in the Underworld, and Olympus quite probably falls. The Olympians, who, whatever their past sins may have been, are trying to do what God wants? They're going to lose, probably trapping us all here in the process. With Hades restored and with us there in time to intervene, at least there is a chance. Let's not forget that Morgan le Fay also goes free if we can't return to Annwn with the lyre. Is that what you want?"

"Of course not," said David, tight-lipped and frustrated.

"I wish the answer could be clearer, too," I said, patting him on the shoulder. "Sometimes we have to do a lesser evil to prevent a greater one."

"Like lying to me," said David bitterly.

"I will regret that as long as I live, but yes, at the time that did seem necessary."

For a minute I thought I had lost him. Then he nodded reluctantly.

"I still believe you are a good person, though I can't be sure what you want right now is for the best. I will follow your lead now because time is so short, but we will speak of this again—and of our future."

"I can ask no more," I said. "Now let us quickly return to the others and settle matters while we still can." I led David back as fast as I could, hopefully before Hades worked out some way to trick us. After all, he had tried to deceive virtually every other mortal he had ever interacted with in the Underworld.

It took a while to work out the exact wording of our oaths. This time I wanted to be sure not to forget anything. I insisted on clauses prohibiting Hades from harming us or allowing other beings in the Underworld to do so. He in turn insisted on no further actions against him on our part and on no use of the lyre against him ever, as well as a prohibition on our returning to the Underworld without his explicit permission. (I'm surprised lawyers haven't found a way to migrate from our world to Annwn and Olympus; there'd be a real demand for *tynged* and oath lawyers!)

When we were finally all satisfied, Hades swore by the Styx, and the rest of us bound ourselves with *tyngeds*. Khalid gave the invisibility helmet back…very reluctantly, I handed over the staff, and Nurse Florence set to work healing Hades's hand so that he could wield it properly. That took longer than I would have liked—apparently the combined attack of the swords of David and Solomon did quite a number on his hand.

"How much longer have we got?" I asked Shar. "I've kind of lost track of time."

"That last battle took longer than it seemed," suggested Shar. "By my…or really, Alexander's…reckoning, we still have about three days before the army of Ares reaches Olympus. Achilles is sure the chariot of Hades can get us there in minutes, so we should still be OK."

At last Nurse Florence finished, leaving Hades as good as new. Without a word of thanks for her, he summoned guards—lots of them—and after binding Hecate and Melinoe in unbreakable chains forged by Hephaestus, gave orders that they be guarded until his return.

"They will have to be confined to Tartarus now," he told the guard commander, "but I have to do that myself, and I must first fulfill my oaths."

"They will be safely watched, Majesty," said the guard commander. I had a sudden Patroclus flashback and recognized him as Ajax, another Trojan war hero. Evidently Hades, like the judges, drew on the population of the Elysian Fields for his security force. I guessed that men used to action in their mortal life might have liked a little break from the peaceful existence in Elysium.

"If he has so many guards, why didn't he use them against us?" Dan whispered to me.

"Arrogance," Persephone whispered back. "He did not think any group of mortals could possibly pose a threat to him, so he did not bother calling the guards. When he realized the truth, it was too late."

"A mistake I will not make again," said Hades in a chilling tone, just to let us know he had heard everything. I didn't really care at this point, but Persephone looked a little frightened. I probably should have tried to do something for her during the negotiation with Hades, but I didn't think of it at the time, and now it was too late.

"Master!" called a weak but unmistakable voice from across the room. Knowing time was short, I jogged over. Sure enough, it was Amynticos…or rather, his head. It had cracked loose from the body but seemed undamaged.

"Master!" he repeated as he saw me coming.

"Amynticos, I didn't realize you were still…functional. I'm sorry to have neglected you."

"Worry not!" he replied. "There is nothing you could have done for me anyway. There is now, though. I ask only that you return my head to my maker, that he may build me a new body."

"Gladly, my friend," I responded, scooping him up and running back to the group. I felt weird about just stuffing him into Nurse Florence's magic bag with everything else, but he assured me he would be in no discomfort, regardless of where he was.

Hades, having taken care of his prisoners and a few other details, led us back out into the courtyard and then north through a great hall lined by two rows of massive pillars, an area that must have been used for huge assemblies at some point but now looked as if it had been empty for a long time. We exited through a doorway in the northwest corner and found ourselves in what passed for the "great out-of-doors" in the Underworld. Carefully planted cypresses and white poplars reminded me both of the entrance to the palace and of the artificial woods to the north of the

Santa Brígida High School. Someone had created this grove. Had Hades done so in an effort to make Persephone feel more at home? If so, he had failed.

I couldn't seem to summon up any of my previous-life…or I guess, previous-death…memories of the Underworld. I would have loved to get a look at what seemed to be a large amphitheater to our west or wander through the Elysian Fields to our east, but I knew there would be time for neither. I wasn't sorry there would be no time to visit the fields of torture, from which I thought I could hear distant screaming. In any case, Hades had not sworn an oath to be a tour guide. He strode straight north without a word, and we followed as fast as we could.

"Lady, why are you so sad?" Khalid asked Persephone as we walked. Then, as much to her surprise as to mine, he took her hand. Perhaps in some way, Persephone reminded him of the mother he had not seen in so many years.

"The…women who attacked your friends. They used to be…close to me. Hecate helped my mother try to find me when Hades first kidnapped me. Melinoe is my own daughter, though I see little of her. Now they don't seem to care about me at all."

"I care about you," said Khalid, gripping her hand tightly.

The kid was a born con artist. No doubt about it. This time, though, I sensed he was sincere, and he actually got a smile bright enough to grow daisies from Persephone, who hugged him.

I moved toward Dan and Jimmie when I heard them talking about how things were going to be when they got back home.

"You know you can't tell your parents who you really are, don't you?" I said to Jimmie as gently as I could.

"I've been saying exactly the same thing," said Dan.

"But I'm tired of just watching them! When I was a ghost, I understood why I couldn't tell them; they would have been frightened or something. But now I'm alive!" Jimmie's tone was heartbreakingly intense.

"And you're going to pop up and tell them you rose from the dead?" I asked. "They won't know how to process that, if they even believe it. And the only way to make them believe it would be to reveal too much about Annwn and the faeries, to say nothing of the Olympians. That would get us all in trouble—big-time." I thought Jimmie was going to cry, and my emotions already felt raw. I didn't know how successful I would be trying to keep them under control.

"I have an idea," said Dan quickly, patting Jimmie on the back. "You know we have lots of cousins back east Mom is always inviting to come for a visit, but they never do? Well, Jimmie, you look so much like me now, that we'd have no problem selling you as a relative. We have lots of pictures of our real cousins, too. We match you up with the one you look the most like who is about the right age, and bingo—you're a cousin coming for a visit. It wouldn't be quite the same as being yourself, I know, but you'd be family. You could live with us, heck, probably in your old room, and you could see Mom and Dad every day. In time they'd come to love you, I bet."

"How do we explain the visiting cousin who never leaves?" I asked. Jimmie, whose face had started to light up, immediately looked downcast again.

"Jimmie, Dan's basic idea is good, but we need to tweak it a little. I think it's too risky for you to pretend to be an actual cousin. Dan, did any of your family come from Wales?"

Dan looked at me as if I had suddenly started speaking Latvian. "Wales? Why Wales? Oh, yeah, I get it. The Order, right? We talked about them faking credentials for Khalid at one point. Yeah, I think part of my dad's family came from England, but way, way back. Family tradition says we are related to Robert Stevens, who set sail for New England in 1634."

"Your parents believe this tradition?" I asked.

"My dad sure does! You should hear him go on about it. I think most of his friends are sick of hearing about it, actually. I don't know if Robert Stevens had any connection to Wales, though."

"Close enough!" I said. "OK, here's what we do. Jimmie, we will need to hide you somewhere for a few days, probably at Awen. Don't look sad; I really mean just a few days. The Order of the Ladies of the Lake will need time to create a fake paper trail, including a fake genealogy. One of their fronts is as an adoption agency. Once they have the right paperwork, they'll contact your parents and say they have traced them as the closest-surviving relatives of a young man whose parents just died, and they'll ask if your parents are willing to take this young man in."

Jimmie looked a little puzzled.

"The young man will be you, Jimmie," I clarified.

"I knew that!" he replied quickly.

"Your folks will say yes, right?" I asked, looking at Dan.

"Particularly if the 'adoption agency' provides a picture to under-score the resemblance, yeah, I'm positive my parents will want to help, and they certainly have the money to handle another kid—or six. But Tal, this plan does seem very complicated."

"It is, but it does avoid problems like not explaining how he can just stay forever, or the real cousin showing up, unlikely as that may be, or your mom calling the real cousin's mom, which strikes me as a lot more likely."

"I couldn't help overhearing," said Nurse Florence, who fell into step next to us. "Yes, the Order can easily fake the appropriate records to make it look as if Jimmie is very distant kin to Dan's father. They've done things like that before. I'll contact them as soon as we get back."

Yeah, if we get back.

It would be nice to be able to plan things like normal people without having to implicitly add "assuming we survive" at the end of every sentence. Needless to say, I wasn't going to share that thought with Jimmie.

Pretty soon everyone joined the conversation, and we started planning. We settled on Rhys James Stevens as Jimmie's new name, partly because he could say he went by Jimmie and end up being called by his real name without having to be obvious about it, and partly because a Welsh first name would lend some additional authenticity to his story.

Jimmie rejected most traditional Welsh names immediately. Dewi Stevens? Terfel Stevens? No way! I almost swayed the others in favor of Tristan, but Jimmie thought it sounded too "girlie." He was going to reject Rhys as well, until I pointed out it could be (mis)pronounced as Reese, and he'd known a couple of guys with that name, so he reluctantly accepted.

While he was sequestered at Awen during the time his identity was being prepped, I'd teach him Welsh history, American history, and English. Carlos would handle Spanish. ("Rhys" was going to need a for-eign language to graduate from high school, and the languages in which I was most fluent—Welsh, Hebrew, and Greek—weren't offered by the school.) Stan would handle math and science, Shar would begin combat training, and Dan and Gordy would start gearing him up for school sports, which he definitely wanted to play.

"It might have been easier if I'd stayed dead," said Jimmie with a little smile.

Yeah, we knew we could only do a little tutoring in the time we had available; Jimmie would never have put up with being hidden away for a semester to really get caught up. We did, however, have one advantage. Almost from the moment of his death, Jimmie had been "hanging out" with Dan and me, though we had only found out when he started materializing. Being with us so much, he had been in a lot of classes, and, at least when things interested him, he actually paid attention. I suspect he was probably as attentive as many of the live students. As a result, our tutoring would be a little more like filling gaps than starting from scratch. Well, except in Welsh history, and we didn't have much choice about that. If we were going to sell him as someone who grew up in Wales, he had to know a little, but since I had experienced a big chunk of Welsh history over the course of several Welsh lives, at least I thought I could make it interesting.

Near the end of the conversation, I noticed that Jimmie was "watching the fish" on Carla's gown.

Despite all the planning for Jimmie's entry into high school, and despite the way he looked, I couldn't help thinking of him as a nine-year-old. Well, that sixteen-year-old body of his was real now, not just a kind of illusion Jimmie created himself—which meant he was going to grow up really fast. I smiled and added talking to Dan about that at the first available opportunity to my to-do list—assuming we survived.

At this point we reached the banks of the Lethe River. Hades positioned us a safe distance away, made a series of complicated gestures with his staff, and suddenly the river started flowing around one of the sections of its bed rather than in it. I hoped Stan wouldn't waste too much time pondering the physics of that.

"The lyre of Orpheus lies just beneath that rock," said Hades. "All you need do is go down and get it."

The situation looked amazingly like a trap: I go down, start digging, and Hades lets the water flow back along its original course, wiping out my memories and possibly drowning me. However, though I didn't trust him, I did trust his oath on the Styx.

Cautiously, I climbed down to the bottom of the river bed, pulled up the stone without too much difficulty, and immediately caught sight of a golden glimmer. Reaching down, I pulled the lyre out of the mud.

Just touching it nearly knocked me over—it was that powerful, at least to someone sensitive to magic. The stories said that Orpheus could use it to make trees and stones dance and even to move Hades to compassion. I now believed every syllable of those stories. In the hands of the right musician, this lyre could accomplish anything.

"Even take over the world?" asked Dark Me from somewhere deep within my mind. I just ignored him and climbed back up on to the bank, one hand gripping my prize. As soon as I was safely up, Hades released the river to resume its course.

As reluctant as Hades had been to help us in the first place, he seemed almost eager now. Maybe he was just eager to be rid of us, but immediately after he restored the river to normal, he whistled, and in a short time, four abyss-black horses galloped up, pulling his golden chariot. He gestured, and the chariot expanded to make room for us, just as Shar had suggested he could do if he wanted to. Then he gestured to us to climb onboard.

"Make room for me," said Persephone quietly.

"You know the rules!" snapped Hades in a voice like cracking whips. "You can leave here at the beginning of spring and not one second before."

"I ask not to leave but to accompany you. I could help in the battle, and now that you have agreed to join it, you want to win, don't you?"

"What use would you be in a fight?" asked Hades. I could feel Carla's growing anger. The obviously abusive nature of this relationship did not sit well with her...or with any of us.

"Lord Hades," I began, "she is an Olympian, and thus she has power within her. If nothing else, I know how to channel that kind of power into combat applications. We actually survived a pretty major attack from Poseidon right before entering the Underworld because I had Hermes to draw upon."

Hades looked conflicted. Presumably, he did not want to let Persephone out of the Underworld for even a minute more than he was required to. At the same time, having recently been bested by mortals, the last thing he wanted to do was lose a battle.

"You will come with us, then, but you will also return when I do, and you will not try to escape. Swear by the Styx!"

"I so swear!" Persephone said immediately.

With noticeable reluctance Hades made the chariot a little wider, and we all climbed aboard, Persephone still holding Khalid's hand.

Once we had positioned ourselves as comfortably as we could—accidentally or on purpose, Hades hadn't really allowed enough space—Hades barked an order to the horses, and the chariot rose until it hovered near the cavernous ceiling of the Underworld. Hades struck gently and precisely with his staff, and the stone cracked loudly, creating a chariot-sized rift. Without hesitation the horses plunged upward, carrying us awkwardly in their wake. Actually, the ascent was more like terrifying than awkward. I had to hope that we were being held in place by some kind of magic force, but all of us gripped whatever part of the chariot we could reach until our knuckles turned white anyway.

We burst into the sunlight so abruptly we were blinded for a moment. The horses shot straight up in the air, like a roller coaster ride from hell, but when they had climbed high enough to get across the mountaintops, they leveled off, and we could ride more comfortably.

The chariot wasn't traveling at quite the speed Hermes was capable of, but it did move much faster than the cloud he had conjured up for us earlier and seemed less vulnerable to high winds. However, the weather was calm this time, perhaps because no one had expected Hades to enter the fray, and therefore no one was watching for him or trying to stop him. In any case, the journey that might have taken days was over in minutes, and Olympus loomed up before us, the glow from its summit an indication that the few Olympians still in residence had not yet been defeated.

At least we had arrived in time. Now all we had to do was beat impossible odds…again.

Chapter 14: Is the Apocalypse Today or Tomorrow?

The abrupt appearance of Hades's chariot descending on Olympus was about as unwelcome as an ice-cream truck showing up at an Overeaters' Anonymous meeting. In fact, Apollo might have tried to shoot it down had Hades not sent a message ahead by screech owl. Even so, a relatively suspicious group greeted us when we disembarked, though the Olympians relaxed a little when they saw that we were real and not some trick conjured up by Hades. They became even happier when they saw Persephone.

"Sister!" cried Aphrodite, embracing her.

Despite the change in mood, I could see Apollo was about to say something undiplomatic to Hades, so I jumped in before Apollo did something we would all regret.

"My Lord Apollo, thanks to your help and that of your fellow Olympians, I return not only with the treasure I sought, but an even greater treasure: the help of the Lord Hades against your enemies."

"Hades, you have not heeded our appeals for help before," observed Apollo, seemingly determined to cause a conflict.

"If my presence is unwanted, I will gladly return whence I came," replied Hades. Though the tone was unemotional, there was still an underlying hint of something. Disdain? Menace? I wasn't sure.

"Nonsense! Of course we want your help. Welcome, Uncle." Athena stepped forward and bowed slightly to Hades. Probably Athena, with a better sense of military strategy than most Olympians, knew that this was not the time to turn down an offer of help, regardless of past differences. Whatever her motive, once she had broken the proverbial ice, the others greeted Hades more warmly. Even Apollo relented.

If only winning the actual battle were that easy!

With the range of safe topics for conversation so limited, I was relieved when we adjourned to the palace of Athena to discuss strategy. Of course, mortals were not usually invited, but given our recent triumph in the Underworld—which the Olympians were clearly itching to ask about but did not in the presence of Hades—the guys and I were asked to join, though whether as participants or as observers was not entirely clear.

Athena's palace reflected her dual nature, with elaborate tapestries and frescoes reflecting her patronage of the arts, and the subject matter of those works reflecting her interest in battle. I would have loved to study her illustration of the Trojan War and of the campaigns of Alexander, among others, but as usual there was no time.

We sat at a long table in what was obviously Athena's war room. The walls were almost entirely covered with elaborately drawn maps of various parts of Greece to which Athena sometimes referred by pointing at them with her spear.

"Much has happened, Taliesin, since you and your friends departed on your quest, and therefore there is much you need to know, and much also that you, Honored Uncle, need to know."

Hades might as well have been made out of granite, for all the reaction he had to Athena's obvious attempt at courtesy. At this point, though, I was willing to count any exchange that did not end with his wanting to find a loophole in his oath as a win.

"We underestimated our enemies and thus allowed them to divide us. When Pan emerged from Arcadia with an army of satyrs and centaurs, we sent Artemis and Dionysus to help our human allies stop them, and our forces defeated them near Corinth, thus blocking their passage across the isthmus and preventing them from marching on Olympus. At about the same time, Poseidon started an indiscriminate attack on all shipping in the Aegean. We could not hope to defeat Poseidon at sea, but we answered the prayers of our followers by sending Hermes to rescue as many of the sailors as he could, while Aphrodite moved the islanders and coastal dwellers as far inland as she could get them. Then we saw giants approaching Meliboea, and so Apollo and I attempted to save the city, but the giants proved too numerous and too powerful. We believe them to be the product of a monstrous mating between Gaea and Poseidon, both of whom have spawned giants before. They seem to draw strength from the earth. But whatever their origin, they nearly captured us, and when we finally retreated, we were both badly wounded and barely able to make it back to Olympus.

"The worst is yet to come," she continued. "Having divided ourselves, we left Hephaestus and Hestia to guard Olympus. While they were alone there, Ares's army appeared from nowhere outside the walls of Thessalonica. How it had gotten there without being seen by any of us, we do not yet know. We do know that it was far larger than it should have been and the troops far more powerful even than partly Olympian humans. Hestia and Hephaestus were not equipped to fight a whole army on the ground, and by the time any of us could get back, the city had already fallen. From there, Ares's army marched down the coastline. The cities in its path surrendered rather than be massacred like the Thessalonians. The army has moved a little away from the coast now and seems likely to encamp to our north. Poseidon himself lurks to the east, just off the coast, waiting presumably for the rest of his allies to arrive. The giants continue their slow but steady march from the southeast."

"If we struck fast enough, we might be able to destroy the giants and then return to Olympus before anyone else reached it," suggested Hades.

"Uncle, we did consider such a move," replied Athena, "but we fear Poseidon could move fast enough to occupy Olympus before we returned. Then we would have lost all our defensive advantages."

"If I guard Olympus, the rest of you and your human…friends could quickly move south, slaughter the giants, and return," Hades offered. I think he was offering more to see whether anyone trusted him enough to entertain the idea than because he thought it was our best strategy.

The short answer was that no one did trust him enough.

"Uncle, we know that…you could stand…against Poseidon…," began Athena.

"But you do not trust me with Olympus," finished Hades. The temperature in the room dropped at least twenty degrees. The ruler of the Underworld was still bound by his oath to defend Olympus, but if the others rejected his help, or at least made a gesture he could plausibly interpret that way, that might release him from the oath, and from the way Athena was describing the situation, we needed him.

"Lord Hades, Lady Athena, pardon my interruption, but there is more you need to know," I said quickly. "While we were in the Underworld, the dead of Thessalonica started pouring in. From one of them, we learned that Ares's forces include our…a fellow human of whom we told you before, and he once again has the sword of chaos."

"From what you have described, the sword alone could be our undoing," said Apollo in an agitated tone.

"Can and I fear will," said Hephaestus, who should have known better than anyone.

"Tell me of this sword," said Hades quickly, his voice betraying a hint of interest. I gave him a quick overview of what the sword could do, with Hephaestus filling in a few details.

"Lord Hades," I said in closing, "that sword is the ultimate law-breaker. Any lover of order in the universe cannot allow it to remain in the hands of someone like Ares."

"Perhaps even a worse lawbreaker than you," said Hades with more than a hint of sarcasm.

"So are you in?" I said, ignoring the insult.

Hades sighed, a sound like a wind blowing through a graveyard. "You make it sound as if I had a choice. Yes, I am 'in,' as you put it…if my nieces and nephews will have me."

Clever! He was inviting one of them to say they didn't really want him, a gesture that would surely release him from his oath. Apollo fidgeted a little but said nothing.

"Of course we will have you, Uncle. But there will be no more dashes from Olympus for any of us until this is over. We will not be divided again. For a while, human prayers must go unanswered."

As callous as that sounded, from a strictly tactical point of view, Athena was right. Their enemies could keep causing crises all over Greece, separating them from each other and then conquering them pair by pair. Morally? Well, it didn't sound great, and I half expected David to jump in, but right now we seemed to have Stan.

"From Olympus we have considerable defensive advantages," pointed out Athena. "Humans could never climb up this far, especially not with Apollo and Artemis raining arrows down on them. That leaves Ares's men relatively useless, except perhaps for the one wielding the sword of chaos, so we'll need a plan to eliminate him. The giants could scale Olympus, but they won't be able to attack while they are climbing, so we will be able to strike first. As for Poseidon, he'll never get close to Olympus, Uncle. You will see to that."

Hades raised an eyebrow.

"If we let Poseidon get too near to Olympus, he could try to level it with earthquakes. You are the only one among us powerful enough to take him on without the defensive advantage of high ground. Your invisibility will enable you to dodge his trident, but he will have no easy way of keeping away from your staff."

"I will of course do what I can," replied Hades with mock politeness.

"Assuming the other enemies attack Olympus regardless of what Poseidon is doing, I propose that the Olympians among us make it our responsibility to finish the giants while our human friends take on Ares. The biggest threat in his army is someone they have already vanquished, after all. As for Ares, he is a coward at heart and only attacks when the situation is overwhelmingly favorable. At the slightest sign of trouble, he will flee."

"You have spoken well, Lady Athena," I said. "We will do exactly as you say."

"Then our strategy is complete," she replied.

"Night is falling," observed Apollo. "No attack is likely before morning. I would suggest that we rest and renew ourselves. Perhaps our honored uncle and mortal guests will join us for a feast in the great hall." I caught a slight change of tone on "honored," but otherwise Apollo seemed as if he might actually behave himself. Hades bowed in acknowledgment, and after their recent ordeal in the Underworld, my guys required no persuasion to accept Apollo's invitation.

So it was that for a short time, at least, we were able to forget our troubles. How could we not, surrounded as we were not only by the Olympians we had met but by others, presumably the minor Olympians, some of whom had probably taken refuge on Olympus after the current attacks started. The myths were right about one thing: the Olympians definitely knew how to party. At one of their feasts, even the most careworn mortal could feel joy again.

The Olympians feasted on nectar and ambrosia, but we mortals received mortal food, though exceptionally well prepared. I wondered if Nurse Florence had cautioned our hosts against letting us have any more "divine" food, but when I glanced in her direction, her face gave nothing away.

A more immediate problem was that the Olympians, having been out of touch with most mortals for over two thousand years, had no idea what kosher meant, and their kitchen lacked the facility Gwynn's had of preparing anything one could wish for. I didn't think I had ever seen so many roast pigs in my life. Stan/David, Shar, and Khalid were all reduced to nibbling at stray veggies. Fortunately, Persephone noticed, swept out of the room, and returned rapidly with an amazing selection of fresh fruits and vegetables, which she delivered with a smile like a spring sunrise. Being out of the Underworld definitely agreed with her.

The same could not be said for Hades, however. He was like an iceberg at the beach in July—except that he showed no sign of melting. I risked one tentative probe, but as I expected, it had no more luck getting through than a paper airplane would have at piercing steel. While that kind of shielding was normal with powerful beings, something many of them maintained unconsciously, I couldn't help being a little nervous about Hades. If he weren't bound by an oath sworn on the Styx, I would have been worried about his betraying us. It was clear most of the Olympians shared my nervousness, but to my relief they did nothing that might have antagonized the king of the Underworld.

"Your armor's moving images are fascinating," said Hephaestus at one point. "Never have I seen its like."

"My lord, it was made by Govannon, smith to the Welsh faeries. He created most of our weapons also."

"Fine workmanship!" observed Hephaestus, getting up and hobbling slowly down the table, examining each armor and gown in turn. "I wish I might speak to Govannon of how he accomplished such a feat." He sounded sad, reminding me of how difficult it would be for him to meet Govannon.

"Lord Hephaestus, perhaps once Olympus is secured, I could ask Govannon to make a brief trip here. Shar and I could make a connection with you again and help Govannon through, could we not?"

"Exactly!" bellowed Hephaestus with a smile bigger than his voice. "I had almost forgotten how easy that would be...with your help."

"I can't promise he will come," I cautioned, "but I think he might. I don't know how easily you could get him to part with his moving image secrets, though. Perhaps if you shared your methods for creating androids, uh, mechanical men. As far as I know, none of the Celtic faeries have anything like that."

"That would be a fair trade," agreed Hephaestus, "though sadly Amynticos was not as useful to you on your recent quest as I had hoped." I heard one of Hades's funereal chuckles at that, but Hephaestus diplomatically pretended not to notice.

"He served me well as long as he was able. It is I who am sorry I could not save him."

"You brought me his head," Hephaestus reminded me. "I can easily attach it to a new body, and he shall be like new. I shall position him and some of my other creations here at the summit of Olympus, ready to lend we Olympians or you mortals assistance, as circumstances dictate."

"I feel even more secure than before," I said, returning his smile. "Amynticos was formidable in battle. The more I think about it, the more I think Govannon would be eager to exchange trade secrets with you."

"Let us hope," said Hephaestus wistfully. "It was been centuries since I have had the opportunity to talk with a fellow smith who did not learn his craft from me." After a little more small talk, he limped back to his seat next to Aphrodite, who was making every effort to be attentive to him, though I couldn't help noticing she found time to shoot a radiant smile or two my way.

"The myths really don't do our hosts justice," said Gordy quietly. "They're much nicer—"

"But no less acute of hearing," Athena reminded him from across the room. Gordy looked uneasy, but Athena just laughed.

"Brave warrior, do not fear to offend us. We were touchy in the old days. Your myths are right about that. Now we strive to be better, though. Perhaps someday we will succeed."

"I would say you already have," replied Gordy, relaxing again. Athena was not quite as liberal with her smiles as Aphrodite, but she clearly liked Gordy. Actually, she tended to like all heroes, at least if the myths were correct, and if anyone had earned the right to be called a hero, it was my guys.

"We could be better hosts by providing music," said Apollo suddenly. "Pardon me, distinguished guests, that I forgot. Our feast is nearly at an end, but we must still have time for a song or two, surely. Hermes, Taliesin, will you join me?"

I felt a second of blind panic.

I shouldn't have. The original Taliesin had certainly endowed me with musical ability, and I had performed for Gwynn's court, not exactly an uncritical audience, and had been much acclaimed for my performance. Still, performing for the Olympians was even more intimidating. And to play with Apollo and Hermes? How could I not look mediocre? At least when I sang for the faeries, I had been performing alone.

Shar must have noticed me on the verge of choking. "Suck it up," he whispered. "I think it would be impolite to refuse."

"You can do it, lover!" added Carla with a wink that could have been encouraging or mocking. Probably it was just another annoying attempt at flirtation.

"Euterpe, Terpsichore, will you join us?" Apollo asked. I don't know how I had missed the presence of the nine Muses, but following the direction of Apollo's gaze, I saw a group of nine beautiful women with enough resemblance among them to be sisters. The one who must have been Euterpe, the Muse of song, rose and moved toward Apollo, carrying her *aulos*, a flute-like instrument. Right behind her was Terpsichore, the gracefully moving Muse of dance.

Great! More divine performers to make me look second-rate!

Euterpe had almost reached Apollo, and I still hadn't really gotten up yet. I knew I needed to, and I tried to will my legs to move, but just at that moment, Euterpe turned and looked right at me. No, not at me—at Carla.

"Apollo, we have another singer among us: the beautiful girl in the gown that shows the depths of the sea. She should join as well," said Euterpe, gesturing for Carla to step forward.

"Of course she may join," said Apollo, smiling in her direction.

Carla, who had been so enthusiastic for me to sing just a moment ago, looked as if she wanted to make a run for the nearest exit.

"Tal!" she whispered urgently. "I can't do it."

Her fear overcame my fear and got me on my feet. "You can do it," I said, taking her hand and helping her up. Getting her up was like lifting a sack of cement. "If you let me link with you, you and I can share the magic in my music. If I sound good, so will you." Carla nodded, though she still looked pale.

"Before the original Taliesin awakened in me, I couldn't have gotten on stage without you," I whispered to her. That wasn't entirely true, but it seemed to make her feel better.

"My Lord Apollo," I said, having finally dragged myself and Carla over to his side of the room, "Carla and I won't know any of the music you do, and you aren't too likely to know any of our music—"

"We could teach you a short song," Apollo suggested, "though that would take time."

"Taliesin knows a way of joining minds," Hermes said. "Remember, Apollo? I told you how he drew energy from me and his men when he was fending off Poseidon's attack."

"Yes," replied Apollo, "you did mention that, and I intended to ask how such a wonder could be accomplished. But how does that help him learn a song?"

"I can do more than just draw energy from someone else's mind,"

I explained. "I can draw on that person's knowledge as well, if the person will allow me. Just let me in enough to draw the music from your mind, I can transmit that knowledge to Carla, and it will seem as if we have been playing together for years."

"A skill you learned from the faeries?" asked Apollo. "We Olympians have never learned such a skill."

"The faeries know how to share energy with each other. Most of them are far less powerful than any of you major Olympians, so they would have had more need for energy-sharing techniques. I'm pretty sure you could learn how to do it easily if you wanted to.

"As for actually sharing thoughts, that's something I had to teach myself, but I have been able to sense things ever since the original Taliesin awakened within me, as you Olympians obviously can, as well. Euterpe knew Carla was a singer. She must have sensed that somehow. Earlier, Aphrodite knew about someone I loved. You must be picking up some information from what we would call telepathy. You could probably refine that skill to the point at which you could share knowledge as well as energy, just as I do."

"That could be of inestimable military value," suggested Athena excitedly.

"And we shall pursue that subject diligently...later, Sister," replied Apollo. "Tomorrow is soon enough. Now is a time for song. Taliesin, you may link to me and learn our song in that miraculous way. Tomorrow, will you teach us how to perform similar miracles?"

"That I will!" I answered, thoroughly pleased with myself and far less nervous about performing in front of the Olympians.

A few months ago, I would have been surprised to realize I knew something such ancient supernatural beings didn't, but now I understood magic well enough to know how much a caster's viewpoint mattered. Someone with magic ability would only be able to do what he or she could visualize, and telepathy wasn't typically part of the ancient worldview, even though many beings existed who had the potential to "read minds."

Apollo interrupted my contemplation. "Taliesin, while you sing, you must play the lyre of Orpheus. I think you will find it the best instrument you have ever played."

Typical! Just when I get comfortable with a situation, it changes. Of course, I could play a lyre. It was just an early form of portable harp, and I had mastered the harp fifteen hundred years ago as the original

Taliesin. But playing the lyre of Orpheus, whom Apollo had taught to play and whose mother, Calliope, was in the audience, was bound to invite the audience to compare me to Orpheus—and again, how could I not look second best?

All of that said, I didn't see a polite way to refuse, and Nurse Florence, as if on cue, appeared to hand me the golden lyre. Just like in the Underworld, touching the lyre caused its magic to shake every cell in my body. My fingers tingled. Even four years ago, when I was just beginning to learn magic, I would have recognized this instrument as powerfully magical.

Hades rose abruptly.

"I will take my leave of you now, until tomorrow," he said simply, already moving toward the door. Clearly, one dose of the lyre of Orpheus per eternity was more than enough for him.

"Husband!" called Persephone, rising to follow him. "Please stay!"

Hades turned, his usually emotionless face betraying a trace of surprise.

"Why would you have me stay? You have made it clear often enough that the less of my company you have, the better."

Persephone hesitated. "Perhaps I would want your company more if you could rule the Underworld without letting the Underworld rule you."

Oh, snap!

I didn't know what response Hades was expecting, but it clearly was not that one.

"The Underworld does not rule me," he said finally. "It weighs on me as it would on anyone."

"Then forget that weight awhile," pleaded Persephone. "You don't need to go back there right now. Stay and hear the music. Unless of course you are afraid of how the lyre will affect you…"

"The lyre will not affect me," said Hades in a tone like a chainsaw striking granite. "I only let Orpheus think it had." Given Hades's insistence on a provision in our *tynged* that I would never use the lyre against him, I was pretty sure he was lying…but I wasn't about to call him out on that.

"Then prove it, Husband. Stay and listen."

Hades was not used to this kind of public challenge, or come to think of it, any kind of challenge, at least if one didn't count Hecate's recent revolt. All of the assembled Olympians and mortals seemed to be holding their breath, waiting for his response.

"Very well, then," he replied finally. "I will stay." With that, he sat again and beckoned Persephone to join him. I'm not sure she actually expected to win that argument, but having won, she clearly wanted to make the most of it and rejoined him like a bride walking down the aisle on her wedding day.

And they say high school girls are drama queens!

Anyway, that brief conflict finally settled, I connected myself easily to an eager Apollo and let his musical knowledge flow through me and into Carla. Once I had accomplished that joining, it did not take us too long to start performing…and even I was amazed at the result. We worked together as if we had been rehearsing for years—no, for centuries. Of course, Apollo, Hermes, and the two Muses actually *had* been working together for millennia, but Carla and I merged into their flow as if we had always been with them.

As our first number, Apollo had picked a song about Pyramus and Thisbe, the ancient Greek prototypes of Romeo and Juliet. By the time we finished, the whole audience, Olympians and mortals alike, were weeping—and that was with us holding back. I sensed without Apollo having to warn me that pushing the lyre's power to the max, especially while I was linked with Apollo, could have driven at least the mortals in the audience to suicidal despair.

Next we performed a longer composition on the twelve labors of Heracles. That piece had a broader emotional range than the first, and we exploited it to the full, making the audience feel every dip and rise in Heracles's roller coaster of adventures.

Performance was always a rush but never like this. We had to be having one of the greatest jam sessions in human history. If I had a thousand more lives, these moments would still have to be among my best.

I was so wrapped up in the music that at first I didn't feel the floor shaking, but I did feel the California-is-sliding-into-the-ocean kind of jolt that knocked even Apollo and Hermes off their feet.

Apollo might have the gift of prophecy, but apparently he was having an off day when he said that there would be no attack before morning.

Chapter 15: The Tunnel at the End of the Light

"To arms!" commanded Athena, gray eyes flashing, spear clutched in her hand so hard, her knuckles were turning white.

"Poseidon must not have waited for his allies to arrive," said Apollo, clearly puzzled.

"Look more closely, Brother," replied Artemis, readying her bow in seconds. Apollo shook his head disbelievingly.

"The giants? The human army? How did they get here so fast?"

"It matters not!" snapped Athena. "Mortals, take your position on the north side. Olympians, to the south side—and be quick about it! The giants have already started scaling Olympus! Uncle—"

"I will stop Poseidon!" interrupted Hades, who was out the door and on the way to his chariot before Athena could complete her thought.

"Taliesin!" she called to me. "Ares may try to come up on the north, even though his army can't follow."

"I'm on it, my lady!" I shouted back. The guys were already moving.

"Jimmie, stay here!" I ordered as soon as I caught sight of him right behind Dan, ready to follow him out the door.

"I want to help!" protested Jimmie.

"Tal's right," said Dan. "Jimmie, you're very brave, but now you can die just as easily as any of us, easier in fact, since you don't have dragon armor. You don't have much training in armed combat, either."

"But—" Jimmie began.

"Jimmie," said Carla quickly, "sometimes being part of a team means sacrificing what you want to do. If you go out there with us, we'll be worried about you. None of us want to lose you again. You'll distract us, and we need to stay focused. You can help more by letting us do what we need to do." Jimmie hesitated. Carla's experiences with Gianni were paying off big-time. I was betting she would be a good mother one day.

"Jimmie, once we get you trained and equipped properly, you'll be able to be with us in this kind of situation."

"Khalid got to go from the very beginning."

Khalid hadn't exactly gotten to go; he just always sneaked along. Pointing that out would only give Jimmie ideas, though.

"We don't have time to argue with him; just let him come with us!" said Shar. Dan and I both looked at him as if he had completely lost his mind.

"He'll just sneak out as soon as we take our eyes off him, anyway," continued Shar, eerily echoing my own thoughts about Khalid.

"Khalid, your orders are to retreat and take Jimmie with you in the event something goes wrong," said Shar, without waiting for my approval. I thought Alexander was coming out a little. Shar would have waited for me to give the OK, but Alexander would have been much more used to being the boss.

"Yes, sir!" said Khalid in a very military way that he had probably picked up from television.

"Ares could be halfway up the mountain by now," said Gordy nervously. "Maybe Jimmie is safer with us, anyway. Suppose Ares sneaks up the west side of Olympus or something? He could catch Jimmie alone."

Gordy, like every one of my guys, was getting so used to being in constant danger that he had started thinking in military terms. I had a moment of nostalgia for the days when we could all just be normal teenagers.

"All right," I said reluctantly, "but Jimmie, you and Khalid both have to do what Shar just said. If the battle turns against us, you have to retreat, OK?" Jimmie nodded his head eagerly.

Dan still looked skeptical, but Shar knew what he was talking about; we really couldn't just stand here and argue.

"Dan, Shar and Gordy are right. Anyway, we can handle Ares, and his human army can't get up the mountain, so the danger is probably minimal."

Well, that was a mark of how much my point of view had changed in a few weeks. Facing the lord of war was only minimal danger! Was life ever going to get back to normal? I sighed inwardly, knowing all too well the answer to that question.

The floor shook violently again, and once we were back on our feet, we rushed out the door and headed to the north side. As we raced to our assigned station, I kicked the guys up to faerie speed. Ares, if he decided to pay us a visit, could doubtless move very fast. In any case, a little extra speed couldn't hurt regardless of who our opponent might be.

Amynticos and some of his fellow automatons were already there to welcome us. Luckily, Ares was not…yet, anyway.

"Amynticos, greetings!" I said, oddly glad to see him. I had the hardest time thinking of him as a machine.

"Greetings, Master, and thank you for bringing my head back to my maker."

"It was the least I could do," I said with a little bow. What was it about him that made him seem human, despite his metallic skin and emotionless voice?

"Tal!" called Shar insistently. "Look!" I pivoted around to stare out at the north and saw familiar lights in the night sky.

"Faeries? What could they possibly be doing here?" As if in answer to my question, an arrow came whizzing in and struck me on the chest. Without the dragon armor in the way, the arrow would have pierced my heart.

"At a guess, fighting for Ares!" shouted Shar.

The number of lights was increasing steadily, forming a luminous cloud in front of us.

Instead of a useless, ground-bound army, Ares had what looked like a huge number of flying soldiers who were also deadly accurate archers. The dragon armor would slow them down, but once they realized our armor wasn't easily penetrable, they would start aiming for exposed parts of our bodies, and then we would be finished. Nor could we counterattack very easily, at least not physically, since only Carla had a bow.

Arrows began zinging in from every direction. It was then I remembered that Jimmie had no dragon armor.

"Amynticos, you and your friends shield Jimmie!" I was a little late—a stray arrow had already nicked him in the left arm—but Amynticos and his fellow androids moved with surprising speed to block the faeries' shots. Nurse Florence hustled over to stop the bleeding without my even saying anything. Despite all the flying arrows, she must have been keeping one eye on Jimmie the whole time.

With this many faerie archers, I had perhaps only seconds before someone ended up dead. I drew White Hilt, and as quickly as I could, I summoned up a flaming dome all around us. The faeries could not see to aim. That did not stop them from firing blind, however, and in about half a minute, we had flaming arrows raining down on us. I concentrated harder, raising the temperature high enough to incinerate the arrows before they got through the shield. I had never done exactly that before, but the strategy seemed to be working well—except for the fact that I could only sustain a shield at that intense a level for a few minutes. All the faeries had to do was wait for me to tire.

With Carla's help I networked with everyone else. They offered their energy without my even asking, and a good thing, too, because I could feel myself tiring already. With their help, I might triple or quadruple the amount of time I could sustain the shield at the right level, but the faeries still only had to wait me out. We needed an attack strategy, and we needed one right now.

Nurse Florence was at my side, having already healed Jimmie with the help of Apollo's salve. "What can I do to help?"

"Have any miracles up your sleeve?" I asked through clenched teeth.

"That's more David's department, and he seems to be having a vacation from us right now," she replied in a tone somewhere between witty and sad.

"I need a way to attack the faeries without having to let down the shield."

"You have the lyre of Orpheus," said Carla. "We know how powerful it can be. Can you drive the faeries back using that?"

"That's a clever idea, but I need both hands to play the lyre effectively, and I have to hold the sword in at least one to manipulate its fire."

"I know this is going to sound silly," said Nurse Florence apologetically, "but you know you can shape shift. You could conceivably grow yourself a third arm."

It was a comment on the general weirdness of my life that the suggestion actually didn't sound silly. Unfortunately, I was a little phobic about shape shifting, so I was out of practice, and in any case I had never tried growing another human limb.

"There could be an easier way," suggested Carla. "Tal, can you link tightly enough with me that you can manipulate White Hilt if I'm holding it?"

"I don't honestly know; I've never tried linking that way before."

"Vanora can do it with her security guards," Nurse Florence reminded me. "She has had some luck casting spells through them."

For the first time in recent days, I wished Vanora were with us. I could have learned the skill from her easily, but I couldn't necessarily work out something that complicated on the spur of the moment.

On the other hand, I had figured out how to manipulate White Hilt's flame in the first place in the middle of a battle. I had learned how to do the same with Zom in the middle of another battle.

"All right," I said. "Let's give it a try. The faeries seem to have stopped firing for the moment, so once we set the link up, we can test. The worst thing that can happen is the shield drops for a moment, and I have to take White Hilt back."

As usual, I was wrong. The worst thing that could happen was that in trying to connect so closely that Carla's body would be an extension of mine, we became totally aware of each other's thoughts. I'm pretty sure Vanora didn't share all of her intimate secrets with her guards, or they theirs with her, but I couldn't find a way to visualize Carla's body as an extension of mine without producing that side effect.

I knew Carla still had feelings for me. I didn't know they burned within her as if White Hilt were slicing her heart into a thousand pieces. I didn't know that her in-control exterior was a hollow facade, that she longed to rip off my clothes and just take me right then, that she felt the constant temptation to use Alcina's unbeatable love spell on me, to make me hers whatever the consequences.

She knew I still had feelings for Eva. She didn't know that my longing for Eva was piercing my heart like a constant barrage of Artemis's arrows, that I would rather have it reduced to hamburger that way than move on, that the only reason I could resist the temptation to use Alcina's spell on Eva was the certainty that Dark Me would end up with her that way.

We nearly got lost in this mutual, excruciatingly intimate, revelation. Only Dan's awkward throat-clearing brought me back to the "real" world.

"Uh, we're getting a little feedback across our connection," said Dan. Yeah, with that kind of emotional explosion, I should have realized that's exactly what would happen.

"You mean—" I started, blushing.

"Yeah, exactly. Particularly what Carla was projecting. Jimmie just caught up on part of what he missed growing up, and I think Khalid just started puberty. Aside from that—"

"It was better than porn," said Gordy, who could always find a positive side, at least for him, in virtually any situation.

"Carla loves Tal; Tal loves Eva—big deal!" said Shar angrily. "None of this is news. You guys need to get on with this."

"We can't, not like this," I said, my cheeks crimson.

"We have to!" Carla was more vehement than I had ever seen her. "Yes, Tal, I'm embarrassed, but at the end of the day, I make no apologies for how I feel about you. I love you. As Shar says, everyone already knew that. What kind of person would I be if I let embarrassment get in the way of saving lives, especially my friends' lives?"

"Are you sure?" I asked shakily.

"Tal, we can all feel you getting weaker," said Carlos. "And, as you draw on us, we'll get weaker, too. There isn't much time."

"OK," I said reluctantly. "But even if this works, I'm not sure we have enough power to take on what looks like a thousand faeries. Khalid!"

He was beside me in seconds. "Khalid, I think Amynticos and his…friends have Jimmie covered for the moment. Do you think you can fly over without being seen and see if the Olympians can spare someone willing to share energy with us?"

"If I turn invisible and fly fast, I'll get through," said Khalid confidently. Shar wasn't crazy about that idea, but Khalid, being fireproof, had shot through the shield and headed south before Shar could protest. He glared at me and then went back to watching the flames.

"Knock, knock," I heard Khalid thinking after an amazingly short period of time. I opened a tiny doorway for our new recruit, and in stepped Calliope. Khalid, showboating as usual, disdained the door and flew through the flames again.

"Thank you for coming," I said quickly. "I'm glad you could be spared."

"There was strangely little demand for my skills as the Muse of epic poetry," she said with a self-deprecating gesture. "Khalid has told me what you need, and I am willing."

It took us little time to add her to our network. As I was doing so, I noticed what Calliope had not wanted to distract me by telling me: the Olympians were not faring well against the giants, who could be injured but were healing fast enough that they had not yet been stopped. In fact, they were creeping up the side of Olympus and would reach the top within an hour at most.

That news meant we could not expect more immediate reinforcements. It also meant we had to hold the faeries on this side; the Olympians would have no chance if they had to fight them and the giants at the same time.

Gee, I'm glad there's no pressure.

Reluctantly, I bonded with Carla again, each of us trying to keep as much of ourselves bottled up as we could. We didn't seem able to keep our thoughts from each other, but at least this time we managed to avoid creating a peep show for everyone else.

When I could feel her hands as if they were my own, I passed the sword to her. The shield shuddered for a second but then held. I could still feel the hilt as her hands gripped it. Her plan worked!

Taking the lyre of Orpheus in my hands, I began playing, drawing on the energy of everyone, including Calliope. I had two choices of strategy. The easiest would be to use the rapidly building power to project flaming tentacles out of the shield and swat at our assailants. One stroke might take down dozens of them. I was reluctant to do that, though, because I had no idea who they were. They were distant enough and strong willed enough that I couldn't pick up any hints. Suppose they had somehow been deceived into fighting us? I didn't want to slay them in droves and find out later they were just misled good guys. They could even be some of Gwynn's men, for all I knew. Yeah, I'd go nuclear if I had to, but I needed to try something else first.

As the musical power soared off the charts, I contemplated my other option. Multitasking with magic was hard, sometimes even dangerous, and I was already bonding in an unusually stressful way with Carla and manipulating White Hilt at the same time. That left me only partial concentration at best for what I wanted to do: project overwhelming emotions at the faeries through the music. Orpheus had shown the lyre could be used that way, but he had always been doing just that, not trying to simultaneously use power in various other ways. Nonetheless, I had to try. What I needed was a barrage of fear so strong the faeries would scatter in panic.

I knew what to play almost by instinct, and I had certainly magically given music more of an emotional punch before but never at such a level and never while doing so much else. Well, now or never.

I felt fear flow out from me in dark, jittery, clinging waves. I felt it hit the first rank of faeries, then another, and then another. I could feel the first ones flee, but as the wave spread out further, it got weaker, so the faeries a greater distance away were shaken but did not immediately flee. I drew desperately on my friends and allies, and I pushed harder and harder, but it still wasn't enough. Even with the lyre of Orpheus, I couldn't turn a whole army, not with the number of people I had to draw on.

I felt my nose begin to bleed, definitely a bad sign. Pushing the magic much harder could mean internal hemorrhaging, maybe even a brain hemorrhage—rare, but possible. But there were still enough unaffected faeries to overpower us. I had to keep pushing.

Abruptly, I felt new power surge into me. Calliope had somehow called her sisters. Now I could push much harder without my arteries exploding. I could hear faeries scream as they scattered in all directions. Just a little harder, just a little longer, and the battle would be won.

I had almost a full second to savor that feeling of victory before the first lightning strike.

Chapter 16: Old Scores to Settle

At first I thought that Zeus had returned and, confused, was fighting on the wrong side. That seemed implausible, but what other explanation was there? I might have thought of Morgan, who did specialize in weather effects, but she was in prison.

Or was she? Could the faerie archers be rebels against Gwynn? Could they have freed Morgan? It was hard to believe Gwynn could inspire such disloyalty.

Lightning hit again, close enough to make my hair stand on end. Whoever was attacking was firing blind, but sooner or later he or she was bound to hit someone. Silently, Nurse Florence reduced her connection to us and started her own magic to keep the lightning from hitting, a Lady-of-the-Lake specialty that had saved my neck on many occasions.

Unfortunately, Nurse Florence couldn't do anything about the fact that the lightning was wreaking havoc with my fire shield, which became more unstable each time a bolt pierced it.

The good news was that there weren't very many faerie archers left to take advantage of the increasingly spotty nature of the shield. Just a little more push there, and they would all have scattered. If only I knew who was shooting us with lightning and why that…person was not being affected, I would almost feel good.

I was burning through energy fast, but with nine Muses to draw from, I still had enough fuel to get this battle won, assuming that there weren't too many more surprises. Of course, Ares hadn't even shown himself yet.

I had finally reached the point at which I couldn't feel any more faeries out there. Wanting to conserve as much energy as possible, I let the fear effect subside. Nothing. Could it really have been that easy? Slowly I let the fire shield fade. Nothing…at first. Then I felt a familiar static from somewhere below—the sword of chaos!

"Alex is somewhere nearby," I warned everyone. "He's got the sword!"

"Why wasn't he frightened off?" asked Carla.

"I was aiming for the faeries in front of us. Someone far below, like at the base of the mountain, wouldn't have been affected. If he's closer, maybe the static the sword puts out protected him, or maybe Ares is protecting him somehow. Magic is never absolute. If he comes closer, I think I can scare him inside out, though, sword or no sword, Ares or no Ares."

"He wasn't making the lightning, though, and neither was Ares," pointed out Nurse Florence. "It bothers me that we have no idea who that was or where the attacker is now."

"Should you perhaps move to the south side and reinforce the Olympians against the giants?" suggested Calliope. "Your power could easily turn that battle, with our help."

"With the sword of chaos around, we can't be sure this side of Olympus is safe," observed Shar, who seemed to be in Alexander the Great mode again. "Tal, could you actually feel the...the lightning bringer get hit by the fear?"

"I can't be sure, with so many attackers around, but I don't think so. Probably he was stirring up trouble from ground level."

"Can you tell if he's still down there?"

I tried to pinpoint any powerful presences on the ground, but from this distance the static of the sword made it impossible. "I can't tell. Nurse Florence? Carla?"

"We're hitting the same static you are," said Carla, clearly frustrated.

"We need to find out what's happening on the ground before we leave this side of Olympus," said Shar. "Otherwise, we're leaving ourselves open to attack from behind."

"I don't see an easy way of doing that," I said slowly. "There's too much static for magical observation to work reliably. If we are expecting further attacks, I shouldn't leave, and I won't risk Carla or Khalid that close to the sword of chaos. No one else can fly, but even if you all could, it might still be too risky."

"Maybe that's exactly the way whoever is running the show wants it," suggested Dan. "We split up so we can be picked off more easily."

That was exactly what someone had been doing with the Olympians, so it was plausible to assume someone was playing the same game with us.

Calliope and her sisters were becoming more and more anxious. "Taliesin, the giants...you can't just stand here and do nothing."

"So," I began, "we can't do nothing, shift all of us to the south without knowing if there is still a threat on this side, or split up. What does that leave?"

"How about projecting fear in all directions?" suggested Shar. "Restrain anybody from attacking this side of Olympus *and* scare off the giants at the same time."

I shook my head. "I was using magic to press as far beyond normal acoustics as I could already. There is a limit to how far the sound can carry, and the music relies on being heard to have its effect. If I'm pushing it out far enough on this side to keep a faerie archer at bay, for example, I can't make it heard by giants on the other side of the mountain."

Abruptly a portal shimmered to life practically right next to us. I knew Olympians didn't travel that way, and someone from our world or from Annwn would need an Olympian's help to move away from this world and then back again. Probably Ares had more allies from Annwn whom he was helping get to the top of Olympus, though I couldn't be sure. Rather than take chances, I strummed a few notes on the lyre and blocked the portal. It still shimmered there uselessly but could not complete the connection to this world.

I could feel someone pushing back...someone powerful. I drew more heavily on my friends and maintained the block, but, like my earlier magic, I couldn't keep it up forever. I could hope that between the lyre, my friends, and the Muses I could hold out longer than my adversary, but it would be nice to know who that adversary was.

"You know, I could probably close the portal by shoving Zom into it," suggested Shar.

"Why didn't I think of that? Yes, Shar, go right ahead!" I said enthusiastically. Shar stepped forward and thrust Zom into the middle of the shimmering, which turned emerald green for a second and then collapsed.

"Someone is going to have a headache," Carla said with a little smile.

Apparently not too much of one, though, because another portal started opening in a minute. Again Shar slammed it shut. Again someone opened another one.

"You know this game of Whack-a-Portal could be a deliberate diversion to keep us from joining the Olympians on the other side," observed Nurse Florence as Shar ran from one side to the other.

"I know that," I said irritably, "but what choice do we have? Someone with a lot of juice is trying to come up here. I can't think it's a good thing to just let him...her...it."

"David thinks it's a diversion," said Stan.

"We haven't heard from David in a while," I said quietly. "Is everything all right?"

"He's conflicted—and still pretty angry with you over letting Hades go free."

"Maybe he needs to think about the fact that we haven't felt an earthquake in quite a while," observed Carla. "Hades may not be trustworthy, but he is stopping Poseidon from reducing Olympus to rubble and maybe killing us in the process."

Stan sighed. "I know that, but he's not ready to accept it yet."

"Alexander thinks this is the main attack, and the giants are a diversion," panted Shar as he raced from portal to portal.

"This has to be more than one person with the ability to open a portal," said Nurse Florence, looking as if she were watching a tennis match, her eyes darting back and forth with Shar's movements. "No single person could keep casting the same powerful spell like this in such a short period of time."

"Unless that person had others to share energy with," I pointed out. "We know an Olympian must be involved. I'm guessing at this point it's Ares, though from what we've heard, it could be Pan. Either would be a rich power source."

"The sword of chaos suggests Ares," said Nurse Florence.

The pace at which new portals were appearing had begun to slow down. Then, just as we began to feel a little bit smug, one appeared in midair, out of Shar's reach. I pushed hard to block it, but the push from the other side was surprisingly strong. I almost lost control of the situation, but I channeled more energy into my spell, and the block held...right up until the point a faerie arrow ripped through my right hand.

The archers I had encountered before should still have been too frightened to function, but apparently there had been at least one on the ground or at least out of range of the fear effect. The constant emergence of portals had distracted us enough not to notice one invisible faerie hovering almost, but not quite, out of arrow range.

The arrow would have broken my concentration anyway, but my sudden inability to play the lyre caused the magic to collapse at once. In just seconds someone would emerge, and there was nothing I could do about it. Nurse Florence was at my side in an instant, but even magic healing takes time. Once she got the arrow out, she could stop the bleeding almost immediately, and the shredded tissue might heal in just a few minutes, but I knew from experience the nerves didn't always reconnect right away. It was going to be some time before I could play the lyre again. We would have to hope that ordinary magic unamplified by music would get us through until then.

I didn't know who I expected to emerge from the portal, but I was shocked to see Oberon, surrounded by a nimbus of electrical power, floating well out of sword reach. He had always had a talent for lightning, and he certainly wanted Morgan to go free, but for some reason I had expected a little more honorable behavior from him.

"Oberon!" I shouted angrily. "How dare you interfere with my quest! You are an officer of the tribunal. Surely that must bind you in some way."

"Carla, summon up a defense against lightning as fast as you can. Oberon may try to fry us, and he's too close to miss." I could feel Carla drawing power to her. She was not as experienced with that kind of magic as Nurse Florence was, but if I could keep Oberon talking for just a couple of minutes, I was sure Carla could protect us.

"The rules for the conduct of *eiriolwyr* are surprisingly vague," replied Oberon with a smile, "and they only cover what the *eiriolwr* may do during sessions of the tribunal, not what he or she may do outside the proceedings, and quests are not mentioned in that part of the rules at all. Young lady, you will kindly desist from your magic." Oberon paused long enough to shoot lightning that missed her by inches. Clearly, he was watching every move we made and had no intention of letting us fend off his signature attack.

"But the *tynged*—" I started to protest.

"Says nothing about my interfering. It guarantees the lyre of Orpheus exists, and there it is in your...hand. It says its guardian, if there is one, can be defeated. You did defeat Hecate, much to my surprise. The *tynged* says nothing about the lyre being in an impossible place, but the place wasn't so impossible anyway, as it turned out. The *tynged* says you can return it with no moral dilemma, and there was none. Terms fulfilled. The *tynged* absolutely, positively says nothing about my killing you before you can return with the lyre." Oberon's tone remained calm, almost lulling, but the burst of electricity from his hands belied his gentle speech.

Nurse Florence and I would both be fried in seconds...

Except that Amynticos, presumably still under orders to protect me at all costs, threw himself in front of us just before the blast hit. Being magical and not mechanical in the way our world understands mechanics, he could take the blast; he had no circuits to short out. Whether the metal of his body could take multiple blasts was another question.

Fortunately, my guys were pretty used to combat by this time, and they had not been idle during the time Oberon had been readying himself to kill me. Shar and Gordy had shifted closer to Oberon while he was talking, and he had not noticed, or at least he had not cared. Then Shar threw Zom straight at the faerie king. Long swords were never meant to be throwing weapons, and despite Shar's strength, the sword did not stay on course to plunge into Oberon's chest. The flat of the blade did, however, strike him, momentarily disrupting his electrical field, which crackled into nothingness. It would take him time to summon it up again, but Gordy was not about to give him that time. I had forgotten Gordy's extra strength, but clearly Gordy had not. He jumped higher than should have been humanly possible, grabbed Oberon, and pulled him down to the ground. Then, for good measure, Gordy put him in a headlock, a new experience for Oberon and clearly one he didn't like. He thrashed around, but faeries were not as physically strong as humans. Oberon was much smaller than the average faerie, Gordy was stronger than the average human, and he was the captain of the wrestling team. Oberon didn't stand a chance.

Evidently, the faerie archer was still watching, though, because an arrow narrowly missed hitting Gordy in the back of the neck. One of Hephaestus's automatons moved to cover Gordy, and the next arrow bounced off its metal chest without leaving a mark. Hephaestus was nothing if not an expert craftsman.

There were no more arrows, but suddenly another portal sprouted to life. Shar had recovered Zom but was too far away to reach the portal in time.   Out of the new gateway stepped a new and improved Alex, no doubt a product of an Ares total makeover. I recognized the wielder of the sword of chaos by his face, though his acne had vanished, and he now wore a confident sneer. Though he was clad in blood-red Olympian armor, I could tell that his body had bulked up considerably, as if from some Olympian steroid. Nectar and ambrosia, maybe Ares's own special blend, was my guess. Whatever had caused him to change so drastically, he would be much harder to take down now.

Complicating the situation still further, an intimidating figured jumped up on the edge of the plateau on which we stood. He had no doubt been climbing Olympus while we were preoccupied with portals and surprise attacks. The newcomer was a tall Olympian with chiseled muscles and blood-red armor that matched what Alex was wearing. The intruder's fierce face, twisted with rage, would have been enough to give anyone nightmares—Ares, without a doubt.

The worst part, though, was not the sudden appearance of Ares but the sword of chaos, throbbing with power in Alex's hand. I doubted even an Olympian could stand up to that without being destroyed.

"Release him!" roared Ares, waving his own formidable-looking blade. "Release Oberon at once!"

"Yeah!" shouted Alex, somewhat lamely. If not for the major threat he posed, I might have laughed.

Stan had been considered a nerd for most of his life, but even in the old days, he had had guts and strength of character. He had the courage to risk his life. Alex, on the other hand, had only artificial guts derived from the ally at his side and the sword in his hand. We might be able to use his weakness against him…if we lived long enough.

Gordy froze, uncertain what to do, and Ares charged him. Shar jumped in between, and Zom collided with Ares's blade in an emerald shower that took any supernatural strength out of the sword stroke. However, it was still a sword stroke, and Ares was an expert swordsman, better even than Shar.

Long before Shar could be defeated, however, Ares found himself surrounded by automata, who attempted to restrain him. He had no difficulty knocking one aside, but there were five of them, and as soon as one hit the ground, it was back up again. Ares's sword would probably eventually break them up, but that would take time, and Ares had Shar to worry about—every time Zom scored another hit, Ares felt a momentary drop in power. To my relief, the lord of war was contained, at least for the moment. So was Oberon, whose air Gordy managed to cut off every time the faerie king looked as if he might try a spell.

Alex was another matter. Despite his recent battle experiences, he still didn't think on his feet as fast as my guys. All he needed to do was run at the automata and start hacking away with the sword of chaos. He could have dissolved them in minutes, yet he hesitated, uncertain what to do.

"How's the hand coming?" I thought to Nurse Florence. I could see she hadn't healed it completely, and my question was probably like the little kid on the trip saying, "Are we there yet?" but I had to ask.

"Without magic, you would have lost the use of it. Even with magic, I need time to get the nerves joined properly."

The somewhat unsteady Alex was finally starting to move toward Ares, and if any of the guys tried to stop him, they'd be toast.

"Alex!" called Carla in her most seductive tone. "Alex, you have come to save me!"

From what I could tell before, Alex was in a more or less permanent state of lust for Carla. No one would be more likely than she was to slow his reactions even further. Could even Alex be that easily tricked, though? I had to hope so.

As far as I could discern through the static, Alex was not possessed by the phonos this time; it seemed more or less permanently tied to the sword instead. I imagined Alex must have struck a deal with Ares to keep the phonos out of his head, but the creature's absence made Alex more vulnerable to mental manipulation if I could work my way through the static.

As I tried to figure out a strategy, Carla continued to execute hers.

"Alex, I'm rooted to this spot by a spell. Come and break the ground—that will free me."

Alex should have known Carla was tricking him, but his lust must have made him stupid. He took a step in her direction. Ares and Oberon, both preoccupied, weren't paying any attention to him. Ares could probably have ordered him over, and he would have obeyed, yet Ares seemed oblivious to his presence.

"Alex, please help me!" begged Carla, simultaneously projecting into Alex's mind an image of just how grateful she would be if he rescued her. That much "gratitude" would certainly have melted the resolve of many guys. Alex took another few steps in her direction.

"I need to help Ares," Alex protested weakly.

"He seems to be holding his own," said Carla. "Please, Alex! Tal could have me whisked away at any minute, and I'd be his prisoner forever. Free me and then help Ares."

With a mighty stroke, Ares shattered one of the automata. Since the renegade Olympian clearly was winning, however slowly, Alex became visibly less tense and walked over to Carla.

While he was focused entirely on her, the guys were repositioning themselves. Stan, Khalid, and Carlos, cautious of the sword of chaos, did not move right next to Carla, but they got a lot closer, ready to exploit any opportunity she might provide. Dan and Jimmie moved much closer to Shar and Ares, though they did not immediately join the battle; I was pretty sure that was Dan looking out for Jimmie, but it would be a while before Shar would be too hard pressed: he still had four automata at his side, and he had managed to wound Ares at least once.

The Muses, unaccustomed to battle, did nothing, but they remained linked to me in case I needed a power boost—which I might, if Nurse Florence ever got me back into action.

As soon as Alex got close enough, Carla opened her arms to him. Alex had to sheathe his sword to embrace her.

Wait! That was new. A scabbard that could hold the sword of chaos? The sword would certainly become inconvenient for its wielder if it had to be held constantly, but if Ares had a scabbard for it, why hadn't he sent it with the sword in the first place? My two cents: because Ares didn't care what happened to Alex once he had served his purpose. Besides, if Alex failed, we could simply have put the sword back in its scabbard. Ares didn't want to make life that easy for us.

Now, if only I could get Alex to realize that he was just being used by Ares…

Alex seemed to think nothing of sheathing the ultimate weapon. By that point his mind was on a different sword. Now in his arms, Carla gave him a kiss fervent enough to melt steel; simultaneously, she unbuckled his sword belt. Alex, thoroughly befuddled by now, must have thought she had something else in mind and did not resist until belt, scabbard, and sword clattered to the ground, out of reach. He tore himself away from Carla and punched her in the face with such force that she fell over backward, dazed. Just at that moment, Carlos grabbed him from behind. Alex was able to toss him aside with his newly amplified strength, but by then Stan had grabbed the sword belt and was running toward the edge of the mountaintop with it.

"Stan, what are you doing?" I asked. I could see what he was doing; what I really wanted to know was why.

"You told me yourself—the sword is too dangerous to be used. The best thing to do is take it out of the equation."

I had to admit that I couldn't visualize any of us disintegrating opponents…well, human opponents, anyway. Nor could I visualize myself wanting anyone else to do it. Stan was right.

Whether his strategy was going to work was another question. Alex, screaming in frustration, raced after him with enough speed to at least equal Stan's. Stan had a head start though, and he reached a good spot in time to toss sword belt, scabbard, and sword over the edge in one smooth toss. Then Alex tackled him, knocked him to the ground, and started kicking him. I could hear ribs break.

I jumped up despite my unfinished hand and looked around frantically for White Hilt. It had fallen somewhere near Carla, so I raced over in that direction.

"Tal!" yelled Nurse Florence, but I paid no attention.

I had been protecting Stan from bullies for years, and I was damned if I was going let one beat him to a pulp right in front of me.

Khalid, equally shocked at the attack on Stan, flew at Alex with considerable force and tried to plunge the faerie dagger into Alex's back. Unfortunately, the armor Ares had given him was too strong, and the dagger simply bounced off.

By this point Alex, feeling betrayed by Carla and angry at everyone else, had let out the darkness bottled up within him from years of unhappiness. Even though Khalid was only a nine-year-old, Alex smacked him with enough force to break an eighteen-year-old's bones. Khalid hit the ground with a sickening thud, shattered beyond the repair of any but the most powerful healing magic.

"Camel jockey!" screamed Alex at Khalid's twisted body. The juvenile racism would have been bad enough, but directed at a wounded, helpless child? Alex was a bigger mess than I thought.

I had seen Shar in combat many times. I had seen him in emotional situations that would have torn the average teenager to pieces. I had never seen him like this, though. Rage contorted his face so much that even Ares seemed a little alarmed. Shar struck a ringing blow on Ares's shield, shockingly powerful enough to drive the bloodthirsty Olympian back a few steps. Instead of pressing his advantage, though, Shar broke away. The remaining automata—by now there were only three—surrounded Ares as best they could.

What was Shar doing? It might be possible now for Ares to break away himself and go after Gordy. Fortunately, Ares seemed intent on finishing off his mechanical opponents first, but with Shar gone Ares could eliminate them faster.

Who was I kidding? I knew exactly what Shar was doing. He was going after Alex…and if he got him, he was going to kill him.

As I picked up White Hilt, I checked quickly on Carla, who was already coming around. She was bruised, but nothing seemed broken. Alex hadn't hit her with full strength. Still, he had hit her.

Carla, Stan, Khalid…maybe I should help Shar kill Alex!

Somewhere deep within me, Dark Me applauded, reminding me exactly why I couldn't kill someone in cold blood. That did not, however, stop me from wanting to.

For the first time since I had owned White Hilt, it felt awkward in my hands. It took me only a second to realize I couldn't grip it properly with my partially healed right hand. I shifted it to my left, even though I had never practiced left-handed sword fighting in my life.

Of course, I could just blast Alex to ashes with White Hilt's fire. That would work from either hand.

Shar was nearly on Alex, who had grabbed Stan's sword and readied himself to meet the onslaught. I spared one glance in the direction of the Ares battle. Dan had stepped in to take Shar's place and was not faring as well as Shar had been, even though his dragon armor empowered his swordsmanship. Unlike Zom, though, it had no magic to weaken Ares, but Dan could keep Ares busy for a little while longer with considerable help from his mechanical friends. Jimmie had been sent over to help Gordy "guard" Oberon, and the newly alive Jimmie was dutifully holding Black Hilt's point next to Oberon's throat, though I knew what Dan was really doing was keeping him as far from danger as possible.

Shar screamed like a berserker and brought his sword crashing down on Alex's borrowed blade. Emerald sparks flew in all directions, but the newly super-strong Alex retained his grip.

Khalid started coughing up blood. I didn't need to scan his body to know that a rib had pierced his lung. Shar and Alex were fighting right next to him, though, so I couldn't bring Nurse Florence in without risking her. I could probably levitate Khalid to a safer spot, but I'd be wide open if Alex wanted to come after me, and I might be the only one who could prevent Shar from killing Alex on the spot. Knowing Shar, he'd never get over murdering Alex, even though Ares's little dupe was being so despicable it was hard to argue that he didn't on some level deserve it. However, in a couple of my earlier lives, I had killed someone and spent years regretting it.

No, I couldn't just save Khalid. I needed to save Khalid *and* save Shar…from himself.

In a movie, of course, the good guy (Shar in this case) would realize he couldn't kill the bad guy, but the bad guy would then try one last time to kill the good guy, falling off the cliff in the process. Yeah, you've seen that movie. We've all seen that movie…about a hundred times. The hero emerges with clean hands, but the audience gets the satisfaction of seeing the bad guy get what he deserves.

Damn! Too bad this wasn't a movie! Of course, we did have a cliff. I wondered if Alex would be obliging enough to fall off it. Probably not.

Alex and Shar, one frenzied with frustration and one with the love of a little brother, hacked away at each other, sparks flying in all directions. Shar normally didn't face people stronger than he was, but this time Alex really was stronger. He was not, however, nearly as skillful with a blade as Shar. Nor was he as brave. In the long run he would panic, and Shar would win…well, except that I couldn't let Shar win.

My connection to the others was starting to fray, but I pulled what power I could, and I used it to lift Alex straight up in the air. Fully armored, Alex was pretty heavy, but I figured I could keep him up in the air long enough for Shar to cool down.

Nurse Florence, always observant, raced over to Khalid and Stan immediately, with a somewhat groggy Carla and Carlos in tow. Stan had lapsed into unconsciousness, so she did something to keep him that way to prevent him from feeling pain and to keep him from trying to move and make his broken ribs worse. Then she turned her full attention to Khalid. I could feel her drawing enormous power from our links. Thank God we had the Muses as willing donors. They still had much energy left and were more than willing to share.

"Is he going to be all right?" I thought to Nurse Florence. I didn't want to distract her, but I had to tell Shar something, and he might not believe my guestimate.

"It's going to take time to stabilize him and set the bones properly, but as long as I have this much power available, I can heal him." Good! For a change I was right about something.

I turned my attention to Alex and Shar, who were both screaming at me. Alex, still hanging in midair, was writhing in frustration, making him hard to hold onto. Shar marched over to me with murder in his eyes—and not just for Alex.

"Tal, what are you doing? You're not trying to save that...that..." I had never seen Shar so angry he became speechless.

"I could care less what happens to him," I said calmly. "I'm trying to save you."

I couldn't read Shar's mind while he held Zom, but I could see the muscles in his sword arm twitch just slightly, and I realized what he was about to do: strike me with the flat of Zom's blade, which would break my spell and send Alex crashing down to the stony ground.

"You can't do what you're thinking!" I said quickly. "You'll bring Alex down right next to where Nurse Florence is trying to heal Khalid."

Shar looked confused. "How can you tell what I'm thinking?"

"I just know you," I replied. "Shar, she can heal him, but we can't let a battle erupt right next to her while she's doing it. If you want to help Khalid, go back and keep Ares busy. If he wins his current fight, he'll come after all of us, including Khalid. I'll stay here and make sure Alex doesn't hurt anyone else. Go."

Shar wanted more than anything to chop Alex into little pieces and wanted it as badly as Alex had wanted Carla. The only thing he wanted more was to protect Khalid.

"This isn't over!" he said emphatically. Then he turned and shot like a bullet back toward Ares—and none too soon. Dan had taken several wounds, though the magic in his sword prevented them from bleeding, so he was still fighting furiously. Only one of Hephaestus's mechanical men, Amynticos himself, was still standing, but the two of them were making Ares work for his victory, at least. Carlos moved to join them, and Gordy still seemed to have Oberon under control.

I had Alex under control, too...except for his mouth.

"Let me down, mind raper!" he screeched at me. "Fight me like a man!"

"Says the guy who hits girls, kicks guys when they're down, and almost kills little kids." Yeah, not really the right time for sarcasm, but I just couldn't help myself.

"That was in battle—not like what you did to me!"

"Exactly what did I do to you, aside from saving your miserable life just now?"

"Shar? I could have taken him," sneered Alex. "No, I meant when you tried to take my memories away. When you tried to take who I am away."

"Alex, just a little contact with Ares had you threatening us with a sword. You know I didn't want to take your memories. You just didn't give me any choice. Look what happened when you had more contact. Are you proud of massacring innocent people?"

"I just cut through the rampart around the city. I didn't actually kill anybody." For a moment, his wall-to-wall rage was tempered by just a hint of defensiveness.

"You made it possible for other people to do the killing. You think that makes what you did better?"

I knew he was going to keep trying to justify himself, and just talking to him was making me a little queasy. At the same time, he might have information we could use to prevent further disasters, so I figured he was an exception to my usual rule about not invading people's minds.

Now that Ares had charged him up, he was much harder to read, and as soon as he realized what I was doing, he fought me with every ounce of willpower he had. I didn't want to draw too much on the others with Nurse Florence needing all the power she could get. Fortunately, I had more experience than he did, and I finally worked my way in, with him kicking and screaming every inch of the way.

By the time I was done, I had to struggle not to vomit. It was not so much how evil Alex was now, as how little he had been like that when he was younger. Don't get me wrong—he would have to answer for what he had done. I would never forget the image of Khalid's broken body as long as I lived…and Alex wasn't going to either, if I had any control over what happened to him at all.

Yet I had also seen the young Alex, a bright if slightly eccentric kid who loved reading, nothing like the sullen mass of thinly camouflaged hatred he had become by the time Ares got his hooks into him. In some ways he reminded me of Stan, with different interests but the same general temperament.

So why had Stan become a hero while Alex became a villain? Not to sound too cocky, but Stan had me. Kids can be incredibly cruel, especially to someone who is different, and unfortunately people who take too much abuse tend to become more different, not less so, which leads to even more abuse. No matter what happened, Stan knew he could always rely on me, and when my awakening nearly destroyed me, I knew I could always rely on Stan. But who could Alex rely on? No one. His parents loved him, at least I think they did from what I could see in his mind, but they didn't know how to help him, and by the time he hit adolescence, he had already started drifting away from them, living more and more inside himself, smothering inside himself, knowing something was missing but not knowing how to get it.

Despite how weird my life had been the last few years, I had surprisingly few regrets, but now I could add one: not noticing Alex. I now knew he had been fixating on me for years, seeing how I helped Stan and trying to figure out how to get me to do the same for him. If I had realized, we could have been friends.

If I had realized, I wouldn't have cut him off after he helped us with the sword of chaos, when all he really wanted was to be part of the group. By that point he was pretty badly damaged, but we could still maybe have put him on the right track, or at least tried to. Now that chance was dead, buried, and rotting…just like whatever was left of Alex's soul. Short of actually taking control of his mind, which would only do greater evil in the long run, I couldn't see how to disentangle the good in him from the ever-present, strangling tentacles of self-loathing, hatred, and revenge. Everything that was the worst in him had been inflamed by the phonos and the sword of chaos and then deliberately cultivated by Ares. His spirit was far, far more twisted than Khalid's body.

Nurse Florence would tell me I was trying to blame myself for global warming again. I didn't really blame myself for Alex…but I would do things differently if I could do them over again. I would notice him. I would help him. I would try to be his friend. I would goddamn-well remember his name at least!

Did I get any useful information out of my cruise down the psychological sewer? I now knew I was right about Alex's physical changes: Ares had given him massive doses of ambrosia and nectar, infused with some of Ares's blood for good measure. I also knew that Hecate had been part of the original plot. She had intended to emerge from the Underworld at the right moment and join the ranks of Olympus's enemies. Only the temptation of seizing control from Hades and her ensuing battle with us had prevented that.

None of that was truly useful at this point. There was one nugget, though, that would bear further study: the way in which Alex had gotten the sword of chaos away from Vanora. At that point he had been more or less an ordinary high school student, yet he had penetrated Awen's security with little effort and less help from Ares, who couldn't intervene much in our world. How was such a thing possible? Vanora's security arrangements erred a little on the paranoid side, if anything. I couldn't satisfy my curiosity about that right now, but I would talk to Vanora about it when we got back. There must be some previously unnoticed hole in her precautions, and if so, we needed to seal it.

When I withdrew from the shadows of his mind, he was staring at me with undiluted hatred.

"Mind raper," he muttered.

I felt as if I had been wandering for centuries instead of minutes, but I knew I needed to snap out of that lingering stupor and make sure all was well around me, or at least no worse than when I had first submerged.

Nurse Florence was concentrating on Khalid with an intensity I had seen her use only in life-threatening situations. He was no longer coughing up blood, and she seemed to be getting his bones set, slowly and painstakingly. If nothing else, his life no longer seemed to be in danger. Stan was still waiting in his magically prolonged unconsciousness, but he was in no danger either.

The battle with Ares, however, was not going well. Poor Amynticos was in pieces all over the ground again, and Dan and Carlos had both taken several wounds, all seemingly minor, probably because the dragon armor protected most of their bodies from injury. Dan wouldn't bleed as long as he had the sword, but Carlos's wounds had already cost him a significant amount of blood. Shar had taken fewer wounds, but he seemed now to be taking the brunt of Ares's assault, and he was tiring. I might have been able to use Zom like a ray weapon as I had before to temporarily incapacitate Ares, but I dared not try to take it from Shar, who would get skewered in seconds without a sword to counter Ares's moves.

When Athena had placed us here, she had been assuming that at the most we would be facing Ares at first, with his army trapped on the ground, and she was right to think that all of us together could beat him— but with me unable to wield a sword properly, with Stan and Khalid both down, with Carla and Nurse Florence occupied full time on healing, and with all of the automatons lying smashed on the ground? That was a very different proposition indeed. The lord of senseless slaughter was winning, and we had no other place I could think of to call on for reinforcements.

Wait! There was still one possibility.

"Shar! You haven't used Alexander's men yet in this battle!" Ghosts hadn't been of as much use in the Underworld, but they might do more against Ares.

In moments a dozen ghostly soldiers appeared and started fighting the rogue warlord. Now the battle was a little more evenly matched. The spirits of Alexander's men could be solid enough to strike blows, but just like Jimmie in his ghostly state, Ares couldn't do permanent damage to the solid bodies they adopted. During the term of the spell that had summoned them, they could just create a new solid body if the old one got damaged. Unfortunately, they couldn't stick around indefinitely as Jimmie had been able to.

It was time to see how much resistance Ares had to fire.

I had to be careful with the guys fighting all around him. I focused White Hilt's fire down to a tiny pinpoint, like a laser beam, and shot it as intensely as I could manage at Ares's neck, at which I had a clean shot.

It did not take long to discover that Ares was not fireproof, but, howling in pain and rage, he jumped over the guys and the ghosts and came right at me, not a move I was expecting. I couldn't think of a single story in which Ares jumped like that.

The important thing now was not getting gutted by the god of senseless slaughter. I was still moving at faerie speed, more or less, but he was coming at least as fast, so I tried to get a flaming barrier up between us. He jumped right through, burned but still coming. This was the kind of situation where ghost Jimmie would have made a nice distraction. The ghosts of Alexander's men were not nearly as inventive tactically.

I managed to flee in a way that made Ares double back, so he would inevitably run right into his pursuers, both ghostly and human. That gave me a little breathing space because they packed themselves tightly enough to prevent Ares from jumping. But if I tried to use fire again, I had no doubt that Ares would move Olympus itself to come after me. If I didn't burn him, though, I wasn't sure what I could do to stop him, and it was clear Ares would eventually wear the guys down, and the dragon-armor spell summoning the ghosts could only last so long.

Then I had a thought that would prove to be either foolish or brilliant. *"Carla, can Nurse Florence spare you?"*

"As long as she still has the Muses to draw on. What do you need?"

"I used White Hilt through you. Maybe I could play the lyre through you, too."

Carla didn't have to be asked twice. Despite her fatigue, she covered the distance between us almost before I had finished thinking her my idea.

"We're going to have to link deeply again if this is going to work."

"Tal, you've already seen whatever I might have to hide—and even if you hadn't, the experience would still be better than having to pretend to be in love with Alex. Let's just do it!"

After our earlier practice, deep bonding was relatively easy. Using Carla's hands to play the lyre was a little trickier. The first few attempts, during which Ares was fortunately too pressed by Shar and the others to pay much attention, produced passable music but did not successfully evoke the lyre's magic. I was just about to give up and try a different plan when I could feel through Carla's hands the stirring of the mystic force within the instrument.

I thought first about fear. Ares *was* a notorious coward, as Athena had confirmed, and I might have only one shot at trying to sway his emotions, but given his own ability to manipulate fear, Ares might turn any wave of fear I generated artificially back on me if he realized what I was doing. The second-most consistent thing about Ares was that Aphrodite could always wrap him around her fingers, despite their opposite temperaments. We had once neutralized the sword of chaos with love. Perhaps we could neutralize Ares the same way.

We had to have more power to sway an Olympian, though—of that I was sure. As long as Nurse Florence needed the Muses, I couldn't very well draw on them. Most of the guys were injured or nearing exhaustion. Jimmie I could use and maybe Gordy. Not nearly enough power. I would just blow my brain up trying.

I let my mind wander across the top of Olympus and toward the south side. As I had feared, the giants had managed to scale Olympus and were now in the process of beating the Olympians to a pulp; it's pretty hard to stand against an opponent who heals as fast as you can wound him. They needed something like Zeus's thunderbolts and didn't have them. Hades's staff would probably do the trick, too, since it caused instant death, but Hades might well still be fighting Poseidon and unable to come even if we called.

One battle at a time, though. I wasn't trying to figure out how to beat the giants yet. I was looking for an Olympian not directly involved in the fight that I could use as a power source.

All the major Olympians seemed to be pinned down by the battle with the giants, even Hephaestus. There were some minor Olympians, but like Asclepius, Apollo's son and a great healer, they were providing key support to their embattled kin.

Then I sensed Hestia, aloof from the fray, trying to invoke the power of the hearth fire to hold back the giants, obviously unsuccessfully. Aside from the strain of that process, though, she remained unwounded and relatively rested...and she was an elder Olympian.

"Guys, we need to get Ares to follow us into the throne room! Can we do it?" I felt the silent affirmation and knew I could count on them.

Then I remembered Alex. I had to get Ares to follow us, but I couldn't just leave Alex there by himself; if anything interfered with my spell, he'd be free. If something like that happened, he could harm Nurse Florence and Khalid. The only thing I could do was signal Gordy to move the helpless Oberon over nearer to Alex so that Gordy and Jimmie could watch both of them. That solution was far from perfect, but it was the only one I had, so I sent a quick message to Gordy, and he did what I asked. Oberon appeared to be unconscious at the moment, anyway.

Having done what I could to secure the prisoners, I used a few shots of flame to enrage Ares, and the guys managed to give him a gap to lunge after me without being too obvious about it. Carla and I flew, just out of reach of Ares but close enough to tempt him to try to catch me. The guys followed, ready to close in if they needed to.

The Olympians had clearly played a great many interdimensional tricks in the construction of the palaces of Olympus, because the "top of the mountain" was much bigger than its physical peak. Nonetheless, we finally reached the throne room. Hestia, startled at the sight of Ares, positioned her body protectively between him and the hearth fire she was sworn to guard.

At this point the ghosts somehow understood our strategy, I think because Shar whispered it to them, and they cut Ares off from his pursuit of me, forcing him to hack his way through them, by which time the guys had encircled him.

I explained what I wanted to Hestia, who was so frightened of

Ares and what he might do that she would have agreed to virtually anything. Gently I linked to her, I reinforced my connection with Carla, which had become a little tenuous, and I began to play the lyre with her hands, channeling what was left of my power, Carla's power, and Hestia's shared energy into a concentrated burst of love directed straight at Ares.

At first he resisted, but I had the power of an elder Olympian behind me, and I could feel him begin to weaken. Ares's power came from hatred, from rage, and from sadism. Lust by itself would not weaken him, but love certainly would, and love focused like this would do the job too fast for him to counter.

As Ares's own memories of lying in the arms of Aphrodite, whom, odd as it sounded, he had actually loved once, surged to the forefront, he could feel his strength ebbing. Rather than face ignominious defeat, he did exactly what Athena predicted he would do if faced by superior force: he ran like hell. We kept up the barrage until I could feel him running down the west side of Olympus; then he finally touched the ground and kept right on running. When I was pretty sure he intended to dash clear back to Thrace, I stopped, wanting to preserve as much strength as I could.

After all, I still had the giants to consider.

Chapter 17: Huge Problems

We moved out to the south side of Olympus as quickly as we could with Hestia following behind us. Even before we got there, we could hear the ringing clash of metal against metal. The Olympians were still in the fight, anyway.

When we passed through the arch leading to the south side, though, we could see that the Olympians were already hard pressed to hold their ground. After all, there were twelve giants, but only seven major Olympians, not counting Hestia, and some of them were not really well suited to combat. Even without such a numerical advantage, the giants' healing abilities made them tough to beat, though a minor Olympian in a white toga whom I took to be Asclepius was doing his best to keep the other Olympians in good-enough shape to soldier on. Still, the ground was already wet with ichor, and I could sense their waning strength.

Athena held the front line alone now, slashing fiercely with her spear. She wore the aegis of Zeus, intended to strike terror into her foes, but the giants seemed little affected by it. She had been flanked on both sides by more of Hephaestus's mechanical men, but they lay shattered around her, as did the carcasses of dead lions, followers of Dionysus.

Behind her, and a little harder for the giants to strike with their weapons, Apollo and Artemis shot arrow after arrow into their ranks. The giants were well armored, courtesy probably of their father, Poseidon, but the twin Olympians were marksmen even better than the faerie archers. Both of them and Athena inflicted numerous wounds, but each wound healed, just as Athena had told me it would, in about the time it took a single grain of sand to fall in an hourglass.

Just behind Apollo and Artemis stood Dionysus, futilely trying to project intoxication onto the giants, and Hephaestus, manning some kind of cannon. Its damage lasted a little longer than the arrows, but in the end the wounds it inflicted were just as ephemeral.

A little further back stood Persephone, trying without success to entangle the giants in vines, but they were too strong and easily broke free. Next to her stood Aphrodite, shaking with the effort of trying to overcome the giants with the power of love. Well, scratch one strategy I might have tried.

Above the battle flew Hermes, swift enough to evade the giants' blows but not making any headway against them with his considerable magic.

I looked at the giants closely, taking in every detail I could see from a distance, both physically and psychically. Every being had a weakness, and I desperately needed to find theirs.

The giants stood at least twice as tall as the Olympians and seemed to have more than double the strength of even a major Olympian. The giants' skin had a gray, stone-like tinge, confirming their nature as sons of Earth as well as of Poseidon. Their Herculean muscles bulged as they swung their various weapons, which gleamed even by moonlight and torchlight.

The one obvious advantage the Olympians seemed to have was speed. Had they been able to make lasting wounds on their opponents, that speed might have been enough. Since their adversaries refused to stay injured, their speed became less important…unless they chose to run away, which I suspected they would not do.

Even in the short time we had been standing there, Athena sustained a fairly major wound on her left arm. Asclepius scurried in her direction, but this time a giant blocked his path. She kept right on swinging her spear, but I knew she was losing ichor far, far too fast and would soon fall. Even as she weakened, she managed to wound one of her foes, but the giant, protected by his mother's touch, shrugged off the injury, just as the giants had all the others.

His mother's touch…hmmm. In the myths, sons of Mother Earth like Antaeus became vulnerable if they were not touching the ground. I noticed the giants were barefoot, not exactly the norm for combat, so perhaps there was literal truth in those stories.

"Tal! We need to do something," insisted Shar.

"I know, but the Olympians can't die, and you guys can. You're not throwing yourselves into battle until we have a plan. Shar, let me borrow Zom for a second." As always, he complied at once, even though parting with Zom was like parting with an arm for him.

If the giants' bond with their mother was a kind of magic, then a blast from Zom should short-circuit it and allow the giants to be injured.

I shot a massive emerald burst of Zom's anti-magic at the nearest giant, and…nothing, at least not as far as I could tell. No, there was a little bit of degradation in the giant's ability to regenerate but not enough. I was fighting Mother Earth's constant resupplying of power to the giant. Up against the earth itself, even the power of Zom had met its match. In fairness, Zom had been designed to protect its wielder from magic, not to serve as an anti-magic ray. It was a wonder I'd gotten a Rube Goldberg attack like that to work so well in the first place.

"For what it's worth," I said, handing the sword back to Shar, "I think Zom would work on the giants at close range, like plunging it into one and holding it there, if you could, so the wound couldn't heal—"

"Then I'll get right down there and—"

"Not yet, Shar! We have to even the odds a little more. You'd have to get up close and personal to use Zom that way, and you could only use it on one giant at a time."

Athena staggered. Hermes swooped down, grabbed her, and flew away with her just before a giant's club could have hit her with crushing force.

Without Athena to restrain them, the giants surged forward. Apollo and Artemis both drew swords that shone with the light of the sun and moon, but I gave them only minutes at most before they, too, joined the injured list.

Hermes, having left Athena with Asclepius, flew over to us. "Friends, have you come to help?"

"I'm trying to figure out how, Lord Hermes. We need to separate those giants from the ground."

"That much I know, Taliesin, but they are much heavier than they look, far more than twice our weight. I have tried to lift them with magic and failed."

"Perhaps you just need more power. My lord, if you will link with us again, we will lend our strength to your efforts."

Hermes was more than willing to try, and Hestia alone more than doubled his available power, let alone what the rest of us could contribute.

One of the giants howled in surprise as he rose from the ground. Apollo and Artemis realized their opportunity, and each gashed one of the giant's legs. Their swords sounded more as if they were striking stone than flesh, but grayish-red blood oozed from the giant's wounds, and he howled again.

Unfortunately, another giant struck Artemis with his club, and she fell to the ground, stunned. Hermes had to fly to the rescue, letting the giant we were holding fall back to earth. As soon as he touched stone, his leg wounds healed.

Athena, somewhat renewed by Asclepius, was back in the fray, but I could see her arm was not completely healed. Like my guys, she just couldn't stand to be out of the fight before it was won. She would fall all the sooner, though. She and Apollo made a good team, but the odds against them were overwhelming.

Hermes was back, having delivered Artemis to Asclepius.

"If we could link with all the Olympians—" I began.

"Ah, yes," said Hermes, "that would have enabled us to defeat the giants...if we had started out that way. As it is, my brothers and sisters are nearing exhaustion, and I fear trying to draw power from them now would cause them to lose to the giants before we could perform the needed levitation."

"Yes, it isn't wise to draw too much energy from people who are in the middle of a battle," I agreed, "and we need to keep each giant up in the air until he is actually dead. That seems like more power than we can muster right now."

"I can send you back to your world," offered Hermes. "I see no point in your dying here."

I was stunned by his generous offer. We could go back having accomplished what we needed to. We would all be alive, and the faeries would lock up Morgan and throw away the key.

"No," said Shar quietly. "I'm staying." Even Hermes seemed amazed. The rest of us were flabbergasted.

Apollo took a pretty serious leg wound, and Athena's arm wound had reopened. The tide of battle was flowing relentlessly against them.

"Shar—" I began.

"Think about it, Tal. We may not know the Olympians as well as we know Gwynn and the other faeries, but you were ready to risk yourself to save Sir Arian and his men that time in Annwn. We all were. And the Olympians are...well, they're family."

I wanted to argue with him but couldn't. Shar was the son of Zeus in a previous life and a descendant of Zeus in this one. I had once been the son of Hephaestus. For us, at least, the Olympians *were* family.

Everyone else could read my face well enough to tell what I was thinking.

"If you and Shar stay, the rest of us will stay—you know that without asking," said Dan, quietly but firmly. Everyone else nodded in agreement. I quickly conferred with our members on the north side, and all of them who were conscious agreed, with Nurse Florence adding that a complete disruption of Olympus might have consequences in our own world. Khalid was still unconscious, and Shar would have sent him home, but we both knew that Khalid would never willingly leave, and in any case Nurse Florence was nowhere near done healing him. If he went back home now, he would be crippled for life at best.

"Jimmie could go," I pointed out to Dan.

"He won't go willingly," said Dan. "I know he was nine when he died, but physically and chronologically, he's sixteen now. If I'm letting myself make the decision, how can I deny it to him? Besides, he might be able to hide on the north side, if the rest of us...if we couldn't join him."

Hermes looked grim. "If we Olympians fall, though, even if he survives, it is likely he will never be able to return to your world."

"We all, including Jimmie, know the risks," replied Dan.

"Your honor and courage is of a kind I have seldom witnessed," said Hermes, "but I would rather keep you as living heroes than dead ones. We need a way to defeat the giants."

"If we don't have the power to keep them in the air long enough, we need to separate them from the ground in some other way," I suggested. "Perhaps we need...to squeeze something in between them and the ground. Their bare feet suggest the touch must be immediate."

Hermes nodded. "True enough, but what and how?"

I was improvising wildly at this point, but what else did we have?

"Lord Hermes, you were often referred to by medieval alchemists. They couldn't have known anything, really, but by any chance can you change matter from one thing to another—like, say, the ground beneath our feet?"

Hermes looked at me for a second as if I had sprouted a second head. Then he clapped me on the back. "I can, and I see what your plan is. But if I change the earth beneath to air, fire, or water, they will just fall or sink through it until they touch the earth again and heal. What does that leave?"

I thought immediately of some synthetic material, maybe plastic, but if anyone in our group knew a chemical formula for it, it would be Stan, and he was still unconscious.

"Ice," said Shar. "Freshwater ice," he added quickly. "Poseidon rules the oceans, but rivers have their own rulers." I didn't think Shar had paid that much attention during the freshman English mythology unit—but Alexander would have known such details automatically.

"Let us see if it works," replied Hermes quickly. "Friends, assist me!" Hermes drew considerable power and then used it to make the surface of Olympus, at least as far as the eye could see, a glacier. The giants now stood, not on earth, but on several feet of ice. They must immediately have felt the loss of contact with their mother, and they turned to flee.

"Stop them! Keep them on the ice!" bellowed Hermes, who evidently was as good a herald as he was a messenger. His battered Olympian siblings, however, would not be enough to restrain the giants from racing down the side of the mountain until they reached earth again.

"Guys—now!" I yelled. Still working at faerie speed, we should be able to dodge the giants' blows long enough to inflict some of our own. The attack was not without risk, but at least now it was a calculated risk.

Shar, Dan, Carlos, and I swiftly maneuvered ourselves in front of the oncoming giants, who were moving even more slowly than normal because of the unaccustomed slickness of the ice. Even so, I was worried we would be unable to restrain all twelve of them. Fortunately, the Olympians, exhausted as they were, launched an attack from behind the retreating giants, some of whom had to turn to face it.

Even without constant infusions of healing earth power, the giants had amazing strength, but now they could tire. Now they could be wounded. Most important, now we could exploit their slowness more effectively.

Athena and Shar felled two of them almost immediately, and the ponderous bodies crashed to the ground, throwing ice chunks in every direction.

For the first time in battle, I felt I wasn't contributing much. Try as I might, I just couldn't handle White Hilt well in my left hand, and my signature fire attack ran too much risk of melting the ice and reconnecting the giants to the earth. I was reduced to a Hermes-style move: flying around them like an annoying mosquito, though White Hilt's blade did more damage than that. If nothing else, I was a distraction that made it possible for my allies to inflict more wounds. My male ego whined a little, but hey, you do what you have to do.

The problem with practical invincibility is that a fighter would become too dependent on it, and if something happened to it, the fighter's strategy would be all wrong. The giants were so used to throwing all their power into offense that they didn't really think about defense until it was too late, and it was not long before the ice was tinted everywhere with grayish-red blood. By the time there were only six left, the giants tried to defend themselves better, but at that point two of us could attack each giant, and given their slower speed, even a well-practiced defense would not have saved them.

As the battle turned more and more against them, I would have expected the giants to surrender, but apparently they were so ready for victory that they had no idea how to handle defeat. So it was that they all fell that day, freeing the Olympians of the problem of how to imprison them.

I hoped I wasn't becoming desensitized to death. Not that we had much choice this time if we wanted to survive ourselves, but slaughtering the giants didn't trouble me at all, at least as far as I could tell. Fighting them had been a little like fighting statues. Perhaps that was why I didn't worry much about their deaths.

"A wondrous victory!" pronounced Athena. Considering her role as bringer of victory in battle, I couldn't imagine a higher source of praise.

"Ah, if only it was a victory!" said Oberon's voice from behind us.

Spinning around, I saw Oberon, once again sheathed in lightning, floating above us. Given all the fire power at our disposal right now, we could have taken him. He wasn't the only problem, though. Nor was the liberated Alex, standing there with an annoying sneer; I could have wiped that off his face pretty quickly. Even two other figures, who I guessed must be Titania and Puck, wouldn't have bothered me. My guys and the Olympians, though somewhat the worse for wear, could have taken them all.

No, what really bothered me were the faerie archers and their close-range aim at Nurse Florence, Khalid, Stan, Gordy, Jimmie…and Eva.

Chapter 18: Turnabout Is Not Fair Play

Damn!

I felt as if time had stopped. All my friends and allies froze. The Olympians were not as familiar with faerie archers, but even they could see the potential danger and knew they could not move fast enough to save all the hostages.

I cursed myself for not having done something about the reserves Oberon had on the ground. We knew all of those portals could not have been opened by one person, but in the chaotic, adrenaline-fraught moments of luring Ares to his defeat, I had somehow forgotten the less-immediate threat lurking nearby. Now I had to make sure no one else paid for my carelessness.

"*Khalid and Stan?*" I asked Nurse Florence quickly.

"*I'm not done with them. I'd only just started on Stan's ribs, and Khalid is very weak, but they aren't in any immediate medical danger.*" She gave "medical" a strong emphasis, but I didn't need to be reminded of the other dangers.

"Taliesin," began Oberon in his best mock-courteous tone, "whatever am I to do with you? I never knew a human could be so much trouble. Well, your troublemaking days are over, aren't they?"

"Stranger," cut in Apollo cautiously, "you are an intruder here. Explain yourself."

"How rude of me!" replied Oberon. "I am Oberon, king of all English faeries. With me is my queen, Titania, my trusty right-hand man, Robin Goodfellow, and the few of my archers who were out of range when young Taliesin frightened all the rest. As for being intruders, I beg to differ: we are invited guests of...Ares."

"And your purpose?" asked Athena menacingly.

"That, Taliesin can guess. I want the lyre of Orpheus, and I want him. If he surrenders himself and the lyre to me, I will release the hostages."

I tried to think of some way out of this mess, but there was only one that kept everyone alive, well, almost everyone, alive. I had to surrender to him.

"Don't even think about it," muttered Dan.

"*Jimmie's life is at stake,*" I reminded him, not that he needed reminding.

"Whoever is doing that should stop!" snapped Oberon. I saw Dionysus relax. Apparently, he had been trying to intoxicate them. That was the problem with any kind of mental attack. Before someone as powerful as Oberon could succumb, he could give the order to have the hostages shot, and at least some of them would be. Magic can be fast, but with multiple targets in this kind of situation, not fast enough.

"If you do this, we will not relent until we have destroyed you," snarled Artemis.

"On the contrary," said Oberon, laying the false courtesy on in thicker and thicker layers, "you will all swear an oath on the River Styx to do absolutely nothing to me or mine in the future. Not that it matters. I know as well as you do that you cannot leave this world. Yes, Ares let me in on your little secret."

"As for you, Taliesin, Alexandros here told me all about how you work, and that you would never let one of your little band die…and particularly not that fetching blonde over there." Eva stared at the ground, cheeks reddening, not so much embarrassed by my feelings, which she knew about, as by the fact that she was being used against me.

"Let us waste no more time," continued Oberon, unable to prevent a little gloating from leaking into his tone. "There will be an appropriate exchange of oaths and *tyngeds*, as needed, followed by Taliesin's formal surrender, and I will take my leave of all the rest of you."

"We care nothing for those mortals," said Athena, with a wave of her spear. "What if we just take you, right now, and do with you what we please? If we can defeat these," she continued, now waving her spear at the giant carcasses, "how can we not defeat a dwarf like you?"

For a moment I thought Oberon would lose his composure. No one in Annwn would ever have referred to Oberon's diminutive stature, the result of a curse—and anyone who did would quickly regret it. However, the faerie king had the sense to realize that, size aside, he did not have the advantage, so he didn't respond to her gibe.

"You are bluffing, my lady, and not very well at that. You don't even know all these mortals…but you aren't going to let me kill them against the wishes of Taliesin. Of that much I am certain."

"Really?" asked Athena. "And are you also certain that you will ever find your way back home? Ares has run away like the coward he is. Did you think one of us would help you back? Think again."

Alex looked unsettled by the reference to Ares running away, but

Oberon was completely unruffled by it. "Your command of strategy fails you, my lady. By pointing this problem out in advance, you have simply reminded me to include it in the oath you will swear. Any one of you can send us back."

"We can't send him back," said Aphrodite, pointing to Alex. "He has one of us."

If Alex had been nervous before, he was visibly shaken now. "Oberon, you promised me I could return with you…"

"And so you shall," said Oberon, calm as a lake on a windless day. "Aphrodite is lying to you."

"She is not!" responded Hephaestus. "Ares has given the boy too much nectar and ambrosia. His body has gone through the change. He is as Olympian now as I am…and just as trapped here."

Now that Hephaestus mentioned it, I could see what he was seeing: Alex was not just stronger and faster; he had mutated into another form of life.

You would think such a Greek mythology fan would have been happy, but Alex had let his mental guard down so far that I could see in his mind what he had wanted: an occasional visit to Olympus, yes, but not permanent residence. What he wanted was to be acclaimed in Annwn and then to return to good old Santa Brígida High School and become a BMOC (Big Man On Campus). Yeah, someone who was now adopted kin to his gods wanted to triumph in high school sports, become prom king, stuff like that. The limited nature of his dream reflected the shriveled nature of what was left of his soul.

He might have settled for staying in this world as Ares's favorite, but Ares was nowhere to be seen, and the giant corpses strewn around suggested that Alex had bet on the wrong side. His own pit in Tartarus, hanging out with the worst offenders of the Olympian world, was not quite the same thing as a junior throne on Olympus.

"You promised me…," he whined at Oberon.

"Enough!" cut in the faerie king at a considerably higher volume than normal. "I will find some way to get you back—"

"Yes, he will succeed at that, though all of us, Ares included, have failed for two thousand years," pointed out Hestia, with just a little smile. No, more like a smirk really.

I don't know if the Olympians were playing Alex, or if they just hit on the right dialogue by coincidence, but Alex, frustrated again, flew into a rage, this time at Oberon. The new-made Olympian jumped up and smashed the faerie king in the face, not quite as hard as he had smacked Khalid, but certainly hard enough, as teeth and blood spattered every which way.

Alex paid for that loss of temper immediately, since to hit Oberon he had to touch the electrical field around him. He didn't die, partly because he couldn't, but he took a strong, literally hair-raising jolt and fell backward, stunned.

"Kill him!" shrieked Oberon through his broken mouth. He had hit the ground but was still conscious, though his electrical defense had been momentarily disrupted when he lost concentration.

Yeah, good luck with that!

Faerie archers couldn't kill Alex either, but they could make a pincushion out of him, which they did. Unfortunately, they and Oberon had both forgotten that in order to shoot Alex, they needed to stop aiming at the hostages. That gave Gordy a chance to jump up and take two of them out with the best coordinated one-two punch I had ever seen. Clearly Shar had been giving him some pointers. Apollo, Artemis, and Carla took three more down with arrows. Athena finished the last one with a spear toss. Before Oberon could reestablish his lightning, Gordy had him in another headlock, and I think I heard Gordy mutter something about ripping his head off if he resisted.

Titania and Robin Goodfellow remained, and they were both formidable spell casters. However, so confident had Oberon been about his scheme, he had not given them any special instructions once they had freed him and Alex on the north side of Olympus. Taken by surprise, they had only begun to marshal their energies when they were overcome. Stan, despite the tenuous way his ribs were held together, got Robin Goodfellow knocked down and in a pretty good full nelson. For good measure Jimmie waved Black Hilt in his face. Eva put her self-defense courses to good use by practicing some of her latest moves on Titania, who hadn't really been paying any attention to a mere human female.

Even as an Olympian, Alex was a total screw-up. He had taken a foolproof plan to finish me and get the lyre of Orpheus for Oberon, and he had demolished it in just a few seconds.

I ran to Stan, Khalid, and Eva to make sure they were all right. I got Dan to quickly relieve Stan, who was grimacing with pain, of guarding Robin. Khalid hugged me and said he was fine—a lie, but I didn't call him on it. If he had been fine, he would have gotten his dagger into one of the faeries before either Stan or Eva could have moved.

Shar was beside me in seconds. I had to remind him to hug Khalid gently. Even so, I think he squeezed too hard, but who could blame him? Certainly Khalid didn't.

"Little Brother," said Shar, starting to tear up slightly, though he would later deny it, "I was so worried about you!" He had been thinking of Khalid as a little brother for weeks, but I think this was the first time he had called Khalid "Brother" out loud. The little guy lit up like the sun at that point. I was beginning to choke up, too, so I started to turn away…and turned right into Eva.

For a second I dared to hope that this was going to be that movie happy ending and that she would take me in her arms and declare her undying love for me. Instead she quipped, "This saving my life is getting to be a habit," and gave me a peck on the cheek. I hugged her, and she hugged back, but it was the way a girl hugged a guy friend or a brother, not a boyfriend—and certainly not a soul mate.

I should have known better than to hope.

The next several hours blurred together a little. We were all so tired, but there was so much to do. We needed to resolve Oberon's status, for one thing. Hermes had found ways to bind him up so that the faerie king could not escape, but we needed a more permanent solution. The Olympians generally wanted to throw him into Tartarus. Nurse Florence and I believed he needed to be taken back to Annwn to stand trial, and we prevailed, though with some objections from an unexpected source.

"I can't say I'm that impressed with faerie justice," Stan said at one point. "Morgan's proceeding seemed like just politics. What makes you think Oberon won't be acquitted?"

"The politics are the exact reason we need Oberon to stand trial," replied Nurse Florence. "If we leave him here, his allies will paint Tal as a villain. If, on the other hand, he stands trial, the whole sordid story will come out publicly. Win or lose at trial, Oberon will never be able to get Morgan free. Even Arawn won't be able to vote to acquit her after this debacle. He'd lose whatever little following he has. Not only that, but Oberon's own political power will be reduced, probably to negligible levels. I'd be very surprised if he remains king after this." Stan had to admit the force of her arguments. The Olympians were less persuaded, but in the end they yielded to us and declared Oberon our prisoner, to do with as we saw fit. They in turn laid claim to Ares and Poseidon, though neither was yet in custody.

Titania and Robin Goodfellow were a more complicated problem. Were they complicit, or could they claim they were just following the orders of their king? The Nuremberg trials had pretty much obliterated the "I was only following orders" defense in our culture, but the Olympians, coming from a more hierarchical social view, were not so sure, and faerie law, which seemed either to have borrowed or to have influenced human medieval law, depending upon how one looked at the relationship, would definitely have accepted the idea that Titania and Robin were bound to follow the orders of their king, at least in most respects.

Both faeries willingly submitted to my mind probe and to some ceremony through which Apollo, in his capacity as lord of truth, claimed to be able to tell absolutely the extent to which someone was lying. Both of us reached the same conclusion: Titania and Robin had been misled by Oberon about what he was doing. The story Oberon gave them, as well as his troops, was that I had been conspiring with some of the Olympians to attack Annwn. When we learned that they didn't really know what they were doing, that seemed a reasonable defense, both to Apollo and to me. I did extract *tyngeds* from both, prohibiting their taking any further action against us or the Olympians, after which Apollo sent them on their way, promising to do the same with the mass of archers once they had recovered from the fear I had used the lyre to impose on them.

That left Alex. Since he couldn't return home anyway, he seemed clearly to belong to the Olympians, but I still felt guilty about his situation. I know, curse me for a bleeding heart if you want, but I did wish with all my heart that I had done more when I still could.

I took one more close look at Alex's mind—without his consent, but both my friends and the Olympians agreed the intrusion was warranted, if only to put my mind at rest. Apollo did his truth routine on him as well, and once more we came to the same conclusion: Alex's destructive tendencies had been building for a long time, but it was Ares who convinced him to give in to them. For someone who felt completely alone and worthless, Ares's offer to be his second-in-command, the wielder of the sword of chaos, and an equal to the Olympians—with no mention of the cost of that last part—would have been hard for someone like Alex to resist.

"Boohoo!" mocked Shar. "I don't care how bad his life was. Tal, he could have killed Khalid. You saw what he did. You *saw* it. Let the Olympians throw him into Tartarus and be done with him." I could hear Alex sobbing uncontrollably in the background. The arrows had been removed at my insistence, though he was very securely chained.

"I feel—"

"I know," interrupted Shar, clearly exasperated. "I know. You feel responsible! What else is new? Did you bully him? No. Did you ever even say a mean word to him? No. In fact, you helped him out a couple of times. Tal, you can't be everyone's friend. You can't save everyone. No one can."

"And even if you could have done better with him," added Dan, "it's kind of moot now, isn't it? He's stuck here regardless of what we want. Since he was an accomplice of Ares, I think we have to consider him the Olympian's prisoner."

"Words of wisdom," put in Apollo.

"Is there no way to reverse the effects of nectar and ambrosia?" I asked the Olympians in general. "In my experience, no magic is absolute."

"We know of no way to undo his transformation," replied Hermes, "though I could experiment a bit…if that is what we agree."

"What if Hermes does find a cure?" asked Nurse Florence. "What do we do with him, then? Take him back and maybe unleash a serial killer on Santa Brígida? You have told us what a wreck his mind is. That might be harder to reverse than his Olympian status."

"We might try that as well," suggested Asclepius. "It could take a few of your years, though, even to know if we had succeeded."

"I'll…do better; I…promise!" shouted Alex between sobs.

I looked at Asclepius and at Hermes and then at all the Olympians. "I know I am asking a lot, but I ask that you do try. If Alex can be healed, let him be healed. Only if you pronounce him ready can he be released from your arrest and returned to our world."

"Indeed, you do ask much," said Apollo, "yet you have done much for us, more than we can ever repay."

"No!" burst out Shar. "Forgive me, Lord Apollo, but you cannot do this. Alex has done evil, and he must answer for it. Yes, Tal has done much for you…but so have I, and I ask that you imprison Alex in Tartarus for all eternity."

"He speaks the truth," explained Hermes. "He is a brave warrior, and just like Taliesin, he decided to stay and aid us, even when I offered them a chance to leave and escape what looked at the time like certain death."

Alex had gone back to sobbing again. Part of me wanted to kick his teeth down his throat. Part of me wanted to comfort him.

"Shar?" said Khalid, very tentatively.

Shar looked down, his manner instantly softer. "What, Khalid?"

"What do you think I would have been like in a few years if you guys hadn't found me?"

At first Shar struggled for words. Then he managed, "A lot better than that piece of garbage."

"You didn't think so at first," whispered Khalid. "I tried to steal Zom, remember? When you guys caught me, you didn't want Nurse Florence to heal my ankle."

Shar looked at the ground. "I didn't know you then. I thought you might be a shape shifter trying to kill us, or at least spy on us."

"Tal had to show you what was in my mind before you trusted me. Even Tal didn't trust me before that. When he heard I had been around Gianni, he got real mad, like I was going to hurt Gianni or something. Tal didn't say he was mad, but I could tell. It took seeing inside my head for any of you to trust me." He turned to me. "Tal, can you show him what's inside Alex's head?"

"I don't think that'll help much, Khalid. Yeah, Alex has had a hard time—"

"Alex didn't live on the street without parents!" interjected Shar.

"Alex has had a hard time," I continued, as if Shar had not spoken, "but he has so much anger in him now, so much hate—seeing what he's thinking is not going to help."

"He's had seven more years of problems," insisted Khalid. "Of course he's going to think more bad thoughts."

"Why are you so eager to save the guy who almost killed you?" asked Shar, genuinely puzzled.

"Because I know the importance of second chances. It's not as if I like the guy. He's a…bastard. Maybe he could be better, though."

Shar didn't know how to respond, so I took the opportunity to ask some of the others. "Stan?"

"I wouldn't be going around kicking people's ribs in, regardless of what had happened to me," said Stan, "but I wouldn't be as good a person, Tal, if you hadn't been there for all these years to support me."

"Eva, without Alex, Oberon would never have known to kidnap you," I pointed out.

"I realize that," Eva replied hesitantly. "Tal, I don't know if he can be fixed, but Oberon and Ares got him on this path. I have to vote for giving him a second chance."

In the end, everyone voted to give Alex a second second chance except Shar, Gordy, Carlos, and Nurse Florence, though she pointedly abstained rather than vote against me. Dan would normally have been with Shar and Gordy, but after I had just forgiven him a short time ago, he could hardly announce that forgiveness was a terrible thing.

I turned back to Shar. "I don't want to split the group over this, and I understand why you feel so strongly, but can you accept it if Alex has at least a chance?

"Not for him," muttered Shar, "but for Khalid, I'll say OK."

I turned back to Apollo. "My lord, will you give Alex a chance to be healed?"

"As I was started to say earlier, we owe you much, Taliesin…more in some ways than we can easily repay. Yes, Hermes and Asclepius will work on curing him of being Olympian and on healing his shattered mind. However, he must pay for what he has done. He will be our prisoner…here on Olympus, not in Tartarus, but if we cannot cure him, he will remain our prisoner forever."

"That is all I could ask," I replied with a bow.

"Tal," asked Alex shakily, "What about my parents?"

Great! Now you're thinking about other people!

"What will they think when I don't come home? Will they think I…died?"

"Afraid they'll throw a party?" mumbled Shar, his eyes fixed on Alex.

"Alex wasn't with us," pointed out Nurse Florence. "This is actually one time we don't need to come up with an explanation."

"I don't see any reason for his parents to suffer needlessly," I answered quickly. "I think most people say it's better to know what happened than just to have a child go missing and never find out for sure. But we can't just fake his death, not if there is any possibility that he'll be back some day."

"I don't like where this is going," observed Nurse Florence gloomily.

"Not quite where you think!" I shot back. "Look, I know it's impractical to have a shifter assume his identity. But what if a shifter goes to his house disguised as him and tells his parents he wants treatment—they've been trying to get him to think about therapy. The shifter tells them enough gory details to convince them he should be institutionalized, and the shifter will agree."

"And then we create a fake mental institution? Isn't that a little beyond our resources?" Nurse Florence had been suspicious of Alex from the beginning and seemed determined to shoot down any of my suggestions.

"We create a phone number actually maintained by the Order—don't tell me they haven't done that before—and the fiction that Alex's parents need to call ahead to make an appointment to see him. The Order informs me they are coming for a visit, and I put them to sleep and whip up suitable false memories. They never leave the house, but they believe they have visited their son."

"Why do we have to pretend I'm in a mental institution?" sniffled Alex.

"That's actually pretty close to the truth, Alex, minus all the supernatural elements. Anyway, it's the best I can do."

"Tha…thank you," he stuttered. I could tell he wasn't happy, but he was also smart enough to realize that it beat spending all eternity in Tartarus—or five minutes alone with Shar, for that matter.

By comparison, the reorganization of Olympus, which we watched as observers, was easily done. Everyone agreed Zeus should again be king of the Olympians if he was found in fit condition to perform the duties. In the meantime, the Olympians discarded the old framework in which Zeus ruled the heavens, Poseidon the sea, and Hades the Underworld, with all three sharing the earth. In its place, they adopted a new organization: Apollo ruled the heavens, with primary responsibility for finding the missing Olympians and restoring them to their rightful places; Athena ruled the earth, with primary responsibility for bringing Ares to justice; and Hades ruled both the Underworld and the sea, with primary responsibility for bringing Poseidon to justice. Ares and Poseidon were both guaranteed a trial, though at this point, who could doubt its outcome? Meanwhile, they were stripped of all functions and no longer had privileges on Olympus. Particularly and explicitly, they were stripped of the right to visit Olympus themselves and of the right to invite others.

"If only we had thought of that earlier, we could have kept the faeries and giants off Olympus," said Hestia, shaking her head. "The hearth fire's protection would have excluded them, or at the very least made their entry much more difficult."

"Pardon my ignorance," I began, "but does just pronouncing they are no longer welcome make it so?"

"What is spoken here in the throne room, either by the king or by those acting in his stead, is not just paper law but more like the physical law of this world," responded Athena. "If we ban someone from Olympus, they physically cannot enter. If we strip someone of a function, they lose the power to exercise it. I think even Poseidon forgets that, or else he thinks that only Zeus can do it. He will be reminded shortly, though, when he tries to command the waves."

"He still has his trident and the ability to breed more giants, among other assets," remarked Hephaestus. "This war will still not be easily won, but you, my son, if I may call you that, and the brave men and women you brought with you, have made victory possible, where before defeat was certain."

The Olympians, including Hades as a much less sarcastic, more willing participant, had much detail to discuss, and we excused ourselves awhile. Wanting to clear my head, I took a walk alone around the perimeter of the mountaintop, admiring the view and letting the gentle breeze cool and relax me. Relax I did, for a few minutes, but then I heard footsteps and turned to see Aphrodite hurrying after me.

"My lady, I thought you would be in council with the other Olympians,"

"So I should be, and so I will be again, once I have told you what I need to say." She seemed rushed, agitated.

"Please tell me," I said, putting my hand on her arm, hoping to calm her a bit.

"I know I promised to do what I could to bring you and Eva together, but I will fail. In this life there are too many obstacles. I have consulted with Apollo, and destiny has chosen another path for you."

That was a crash-and-burn moment for my good mood.

"My Lady Aphrodite, I'm sure you have done everything you could," I answered, resisting my temptation to curse destiny and throw myself off the cliff. Now that would be an interesting ending for a movie…just not the one I had always visualized.

"Wait, Taliesin, there is more…"

Goodie!

"Apollo and I have had a vision. Please let me show it to you. It will soften the blow you have just received."

What could I say? "I welcome anything you have to show me."

Aphrodite placed a cool hand on my forehead, and suddenly I was in the future, maybe a hundred years from now, certainly in another life. I paid little attention to the technology around me, fascinating as that might have been. Instead, I noticed that I looked similar, perhaps a grandson of my current self. I was much more interested, though, in the woman who was with me. She did not look all that similar, though she was beautiful, but I sensed she was definitely and unmistakably Eva—and she was embracing me passionately, having just accepted my marriage proposal. Then the vision faded, and I was again with Aphrodite in the present.

"You mean Eva and I can be together, just in another life?"

"Exactly! Apollo has traced the lines of fate in great detail for you. If you marry Carla in this life, you will have a son, who in turn will have a son shortly after your death. The son of your son will be you, reincarnated. He will marry the reincarnated Eva."

I did not see that coming. "Why do I have to marry Carla in this life? I don't love her. I feel like I'd just be using her to get to Eva."

"You will learn to love Carla, and she is your only chance for that kind of love in this life. If you don't marry her, you will stay single, and there will be no grandson to be the reincarnated you and marry Eva."

The reasoning wasn't all that complicated, but my head had started swimming anyway. "I…I'm having a hard time coping with this. I always thought if Eva and I were going to get together, we'd do it in the next few years, not the next century."

"The choice is yours," said Aphrodite with a hint of sadness. "You can reject that destiny, but consequences will flow from that choice that will keep you and Eva apart forever."

I thought about Carla. I still couldn't escape the feeling that marrying her in such a situation wouldn't be fair to her, but what if I could *learn* to love her? That she was sexually appealing, there was no doubt. That she had been a good friend, there was no doubt, either. That we worked together well? Again, no doubt. If I hadn't already been in love with Eva when I first met Carla, Carla and I very well might have gotten together.

I had almost talked myself into taking Aphrodite's advice, until I picked up a little detail that I had failed to notice in the excitement.

Aphrodite was speaking English to me.

And no, it wasn't just the translation effect from the dragon armor. That only worked when needed, and I knew ancient Greek, so I didn't need it. Come to think of it, Govannon hadn't even endowed my armor with that particular characteristic.

What I heard as English actually was English. That Aphrodite could have learned it quickly I didn't doubt, but when had she had even minimal time for such an endeavor? While she was rescuing shipwrecked sailors? Fighting giants? And even if there had been time, what reason could she possibly have to learn it?

"Who are you?" I said harshly, grabbing her arms. "I know you aren't Aphrodite!" The pseudo-Aphrodite said nothing and tried to pull away, so I started probing her mind as hard as I could. In the first few seconds, I could tell she was human but a strong human, one adroit in magic who could resist my probing for some time.

Aside from me, there were only two humans with magic ability on the mountain: Nurse Florence, whose motive would be hard to imagine, and, wait for it...

"Carla, why are you doing this?" The image of Aphrodite dissolved, leaving behind a Carla I might have expected to be embarrassed but who was defiant instead.

"Do you really have to ask why, Tal? Are you truly so dense that you can't figure it out?"

I should have been understanding, but I was getting sick of being manipulated, especially by shape shifters.

"I get that you think you love me—"

"But not that I do love you? Unbelievable." Carla's tone remained harsh, but she started crying. "Tal, all I ever wanted was a chance to show you what we could be like together, and you never gave it to me, not even for ten seconds!"

"I've explained that a hundred times, Carla! It wouldn't be fair to you to have a relationship based on the idea that my feelings are going to change."

"You were willing to entertain that just a minute ago, when you thought it was a way to get Eva." She had me there, but being confronted with that fact just made me angrier.

"For a moment I wavered. I never would have gone through with something like that." Our voices had steadily increased in volume. I knew I should try to calm us both down and discuss what had happened rationally, but I couldn't bring myself to do that.

"No, Tal, you would do anything to be with Eva, anything. I saw it all in your mind when we bonded. And it hurt me, more than if Alex had kicked in my ribs or smashed my skull."

"I have never done anything to lead you on!" I protested. "You always knew where I stood—"

"Except when you were the dutiful boyfriend standing over my comatose body—"

"I was under a spell. Yours, as a matter of fact."

"Which I cast on you by accident! I didn't even know magic existed then. I just knew I loved you. Tal, I have loved you from the moment I first met you, from the first band rehearsal, the first romantic duet we sang together. You were looking at me as you sang, but you were seeing Eva. When I sang, I saw you, only you. I always knew you were seeing Eva, but I figured you would notice me eventually, and…and you almost did. Spell or no spell, Eva was not available, and you were turning to me. I felt it in the depths of my soul."

"Carla, you're just embarrassing yourself," I said coldly. Yeah, I should have shown more compassion, but we had been over this ground so many times, and I thought she understood. Now I knew she was just waiting for the right moment to betray me.

Carla could not have looked more shocked if I had slapped her. "I *have* embarrassed myself for you; I have risked my life for you. If any woman is entitled to say this to you, it is me. Most of the time I was loving you, she was loving Dan. Maybe she still loves him, despite what he did to you. And you go on loving her, you forgive him—"

"Who are you to talk about Dan? Yeah, what he did was rotten; I'd be the first to agree. But at least he had the excuse of being twelve. You're sixteen. What's your excuse? You just tried to trick me into a loveless marriage with a false promise—bad as what Dan did, this is worse!"

Tears began pouring down her cheeks, but I just kept hammering away at her. I couldn't stop myself. Actually, I didn't want to stop myself.

"Carla, when I forced Alcina to put you back in control of your own body, I was risking my soul. In my arrogance, I thought it was a small risk, but I was willing to take it to help you. I nearly lost my soul that night. My soul, Carla. You act like I never cared for you. I always have—as a friend. As a dear friend. And if that wasn't enough, I'm sorry. I can't make myself love you. But I have done everything short of that, and what have you done? Betrayed my trust. You can't be my friend anymore, not after this."

For a second Carla looked as if I had just handed down a death sentence. Then she tried to get a grip on herself and failed.

"Tal, you just forgave Dan. You wanted mercy for Alex. Tal, he gave Oberon the idea to kidnap Eva. He kicked in Stan's ribs. He nearly killed Khalid. Yet you argued for mercy."

"Carla, I don't want you in Tartarus. I just want you out of my life." I was more quiet now—cold and quiet. "I'll try to find time to spend with Gianni. It wouldn't be fair to him if I cut him off because of you."

I don't know what caused her to explode. Perhaps it was the feeling of finality I was doing my best to project. But explode she did, in screams that could probably be heard all the way back in our world.

"You self-righteous son of a bitch! Mr. Perfect, with plenty of time to pass judgment on everybody else. Maybe Alex was right about you. You said yourself you should have paid more attention to him. What about me, Tal? You'll wake up some morning and realize you should have paid more attention to me. You should have loved me." Then her volume dropped to a reasonable approximation of normal, though her words were edged like daggers. "You may think you are the king of the world, Tal. You may think you can pass judgment on everyone. Well, you can't, you won't, pass judgment on me. The day will come when you regret what you have done more than anything in this life…hell, in any of your lives."

After that she literally ran away, until all that was left of her presence was a distant sobbing, uncomfortably reminiscent of Alex's sobbing earlier, wild and uncontrollable.

My initial anger spent, I had already begun to feel rotten about the way I had acted. OK, she had betrayed me, and I probably should have been angry about that, but I didn't need to cut her off completely, especially in the heat of the moment.

I took a couple of steps in the direction she had gone, but then I stopped. Perhaps now was not the best time. We were both emotionally raw, neither one of us really reasonable. Later would be better.

I started walking back toward the throne room, but before I got there, I ran into Dan, sitting on a marble bench and watching me intently.

"Well, bro, that could have gone better."

"You heard?" I asked, knowing he must have.

"I'm pretty sure Egypt heard—the one in our world, not the artificial one here."

"I feel as if you have something to say." I met his glance, even though I was uncomfortable. "Go ahead and say it."

Dan shifted awkwardly on the bench. "I'm not really the person you want to hear this from, but Stan ran away."

"He what?" I said, wondering if Dan were joking or serious.

"Yeah, a guy who faces death in combat didn't want to face you right now. Either that or he was having a problem with David; these days it's hard to tell."

I sat down next to him. The bench felt colder than Olympian marble usually did.

"OK, let's forget Stan for a minute. What do you want to say?"

"Tal, I never knew you could be such an ass!"

"What?" I didn't really want to fight with Dan, but I could feel my anger coming to the surface again. It hadn't been very far beneath.

"I would have expected you to cut Carla a little slack."

"If you heard us, then you know what she did!" I had a hard time believing Dan couldn't understand why I felt betrayed.

"You want to know what I think?" asked Dan calmly. "I think she never would have gone through with it. Yeah, she tried to trick you in the heat of the moment, just like you tried to cast that love spell on Eva in the heat of the moment. Remember that? You stopped yourself. We've all seen enough of Carla to know who she is. She would have stopped herself, too."

"You can't know that!" I protested.

"I do know that. I know something else, too. I know why you and Carla never got together."

"Do tell!" I said sarcastically. The conversation was starting to give me a headache.

"You're too much alike."

I scoffed. "We're nothing alike."

"Really? You're both musical. You're both reincarnations of powerful sorcerers. You're both willing to sacrifice yourselves to save others. Don't frown at me—you've seen her risk her life. But the biggest resemblance is that both of you love intensely, absolutely, desperately. Regular teenagers think they feel that way, but if they break up, they move on. Neither one of you seems able to move on. Maybe it's that you are only physically teenagers, but whatever causes it, it sets you apart. And it scares you."

"What?" The anger was bubbling, ready to break the surface.

"Hear me out!" said Dan, raising a hand. "When Eva and I were still together, you were more than open to the idea of dating someone else. I think that was partly because you knew you could break away if Eva ever became available. With Carla you know you can't. She loves you as absolutely as you love Eva, and you knew that before you'd read every detail in her mind.

"She could have anyone. Hell, if I weren't still on the rebound, I'd want her. Gordy, Carlos, Shar, and even Jimmie, who hit puberty like ten minutes ago—they all want her. They've stayed back because of this weird, fake boyfriend-girlfriend routine you've had going on for the sake of her family, but if that ever ends, Carla could have her pick. Only she doesn't want her pick, any more than you do. Much as I hate to admit it, Tal, you're more of a babe magnet even than I am. Yet you cling to Eva as irrationally as Carla clings to you. *You're the same!*"

Dan got up slowly. "I don't know what Eva's deal is. I don't know why she can't love you anymore. She just can't. You need to move on, not necessarily to Carla, but to someone other than Eva. But as long as you're going to move anyway...well, maybe you should give Carla a shot. Even if you don't, you can't treat her like she's unforgivable, Tal. She deserves better than that!"

I got up, too. "Is this really about how long it took me to forgive *you*? Are you mad at me because I didn't do it right away?"

Much to my surprise, Dan laughed. "Mad at you? Didn't you believe me when I said this the first time? Jimmie is alive because it took so long for you to forgive me. Bless you for taking so long to forgive me. But Tal, Carla doesn't have any dead relatives who will hang around because you haven't forgiven her and end up resurrecting. It's safe to go ahead and forgive her now."

Dan turned without saying good-bye and sauntered away, whistling to himself in what I was sure was affected nonchalance. I walked slowly over in the general direction of the throne room. At this point my brain was moving so sluggishly, overloaded as I was with emotions, that I didn't know what to do with myself. Dan had pushed me to question my assumptions, yet they sat like stony lumps inside of me, unmoved—but they also felt uncomfortable.

I needed advice from someone. Stan was apparently too embarrassed by my blowup with Carla to talk about it. Gordy looked at girls so differently from the way I did; it was as if we were speaking a different language when we talked about them. Shar was still angry with me over the whole Alex thing. Carlos was the one I still thought might make a good match for Carla, so I didn't want to drag him into this mess. Talking to Nurse Florence would be like talking to my mom—and I'm not the only teenage guy who would rather use a steak knife to pin his hand to the kitchen counter than talk to his mom about girl problems. Jimmie and Khalid were too young to be any help. I couldn't imagine Eva would welcome any conversation on this subject. That just left the Olympians, and talking to one of them about it felt weird, too. I had a hard time visualizing one of the ancient Greek heroes talking to his "divine" dad about girl problems.

I could wait until I got home and talk to my current dad, but I couldn't give him any details. In those circumstances, a potential conversation seemed both awkward and pointless. If he didn't know how Carla had betrayed me, how could he really advise me?

My legs had carried me back to the throne room on autopilot, which saved Hermes having to hunt me down. The Olympians had finished their business and were ready to send us on our way.

I should have enjoyed the epic farewell, but Carla, standing in the corner, looking as if she wanted to soak into the marble walls and disappear forever, kept me on edge. I managed to avoid looking in that direction, but I could feel her aching presence no matter how I tried to reduce my psychic sensitivity.

There were also some awkward moments that didn't involve Carla. Nurse Florence insisted on returning the ever-full supplies of ambrosia and nectar, but it took time for the Olympians to understand why. I would have liked to keep them as emergency energizers, but Alex's experience would have made me wary of using them, anyway, and if anyone figured out we had them, they would have made an irresistible target for thieves.

Hephaestus didn't understand why we were reluctant to take a repaired Amynticos with us.

"He is the image of you, you know," Hephaestus said to me at one point. As soon as I heard that, I realized why Amynticos seemed so human to me: his skin was metallic, but his features were those of Hephaestion.

Despite that compliment, what exactly would we do with that kind of automaton in our world? We talked briefly about disguising him as one of us, but we had already had to work to sell the community on Khalid as Shar's cousin, and now we would have to work to incorporate Jimmie—I should get used to calling him Rhys, I guess—as Dan's distant cousin. I couldn't imagine having to create yet another long-lost cousin for Amynticos to be, and anyway his manner wasn't very human, so getting him to blend in, even with the right illusions, would still be a chore at best. Reluctantly, we bid good-bye to him.

Hermes's key, which would have been no use in our world, and Hestia's brand, which would not have functioned there, we returned with our thanks. We did keep Apollo's salve for emergencies; since it was applied externally, Nurse Florence and Apollo agreed we could use it in moderation without worrying about being transformed into Olympians. Carla, with a nod to Artemis, also kept her bow.

"We must then give you something else to make up for the gifts you cannot safely accept and the ones that will do you no good in your world."

"My Lord Apollo, there are those among the faeries who already fear Taliesin," said Nurse Florence respectfully. "If he returns with even more power, that feeling may grow even stronger."

"It will be gift enough if, from time to time, we may visit to seek your counsel," I added.

Apollo's smile was like a sunrise. "Taliesin, you and anyone who is a friend or ally of yours are always welcome. Now that all of you have shared our hospitality, I do believe any of you could invoke us successfully."

"What of the lyre?" said Hermes. "Will that not cause jealousy among the faeries?"

Odd as it may sound, I had been so entirely focused on getting the lyre that it had never occurred to me what would happen to it after the quest.

"There is nothing in the terms of the quest that dictates what I must do with it," I said slowly. "Perhaps the best thing would be to return it to Calliope."

"No!" Calliope replied forcefully. "The lyre needs to be played. If a sword must find its wielder, then an instrument must find its musician, and the lyre has done so. Keep it with my blessing. Orpheus himself would have wished it."

I bowed to Calliope and tried to thank her, but she cut me off with, "Using the lyre well will be my thanks."

Yeah, the faeries that already feared me would fear me more if I had the lyre, but what could be done? I could hardly refuse to keep it now.

"There is yet one gift I could give that would evoke no jealousy, I think," said Hermes thoughtfully. "There are three of you whose past-life memories were awakened by force—is that not so?"

"Yes, Lord Hermes—mine, Stan's, and Carla's."

"And do they sometimes trouble you?" he asked.

"Mine are under control, and so I think are Carla's, but Stan is still troubled by his."

"Stan, come forward," commanded Hermes. Stan stepped up to Hermes's throne, and Hermes waved his wand over Stan's head several times, looking fixedly into his eyes the whole time. Then the messenger of Olympus sighed.

"I can see he has separate...personalities, you would say, rather than just memories. Whatever the spell did to him, I cannot heal without more study. I will endeavor to find an answer." Just for good measure, though, Hermes examined Carla and me. He could not alter our situation, either.

"I thought because I once gave my son, Aethalides, the gift of remembering all of his previous lives, I knew the mechanics well enough to fix any past-life problem, but sadly I have overestimated my skill. I will keep trying to find an answer, though, until I succeed."

"Aethalides?" I asked. "I don't remember the name from my earlier Greek lives."

"It was long ago," said Hermes wistfully, "and I have had so many sons since. At first I did not recall his situation, either. It was our prisoner, Alexandros, who reminded me, he said as a way to begin to make up for what he has done. The youth does know an amazing amount about Olympian history."

"Beware of Greeks bearing gifts," Shar muttered under his breath. I'm sure Hermes heard him, but he chose not to respond.

"Lord Hermes," I broke in quickly, just in case Shar was working up to making a scene, "is Aethalides currently incarnated in my world? I might learn much from him if I could seek him out."

"I know not," confessed Hermes. "Sadly, I lost track of him after his fourth reincarnation. He was Pythagoras then. If he were alive in your world today, I would suspect he might be a mathematician or a philosopher. Whoever he is, he will definitely believe in reincarnation."

"I will attempt to find him, then," I said, trying not to sound too disheartened. The few clues Hermes had given me would hardly make searching a human population of six billion people that easy. Of course, my mom might be able to use her abilities as a seer, now that I knew what questions to ask.

"Lord Hermes, I can remember bits and pieces of my earlier lives, but I would like to remember everything, at least about Alexander and Achilles, Shar said quickly. "Would such a gift be too much to ask?"

"Shar, that's dangerous!" I interrupted.

"It is not dangerous the way I do it," replied Hermes confidently. "The spell used on the three of you was crude and hostile. It ripped the memories free and forced them to the surface. My spell is gentle. As long as I was in touch with him, Aethalides never had any complaints."

"Come on, Tal, that knowledge could be useful," said Shar, clearly eager to delve into his memories as Achilles. Well, a few bits from Alexander and Achilles had certainly proved useful on the quest.

"I trust Lord Hermes is right when he says he can do it without harming you. If it is what you wish, and he is willing to grant it, I will not stand in the way."

The process took Hermes long enough to make a nervous wreck out of me, but I kept telling myself the slowness was part of what made the transformation safe. The awakening spell was immediate—and devastating.

Finally Hermes pronounced himself done, and Shar, much to my relief, looked awestruck rather than shattered. I talked to him for long enough to confirm that he was functioning normally: the memories coexisted peacefully with his current ones rather than trying to form separate personalities and fight for control of his body.

As we finally prepared ourselves to go home, I noticed Artemis having a tense conversation with Carla. Perhaps the Olympian was trying to convince her to swear off men for good. Well, that would be one way to solve my problem.

I noticed with much more interest that Aphrodite had taken Eva aside. I knew I shouldn't, but I sharpened my hearing just enough to pick up what they were saying.

"Do not let this opportunity pass!" Aphrodite insisted vehemently. "God could design a man to your specifications, and that man would still not be as worthy of your love as Taliesin."

My cheeks reddened, and I dialed my hearing back to normal, partly from embarrassment and partly for fear of hearing Eva reject Aphrodite's advice. By now I should have had a thicker skin where that kind of disappointment was concerned, but I still didn't.

When we finally stepped through the portal and found ourselves back in Santa Brígida, I almost felt as if I had just awakened from a dream. When I got myself reoriented, I figured our to-do list was pretty short: present the lyre—and the imprisoned Oberon—to the tribunal, hear sentence passed on Morgan, and come back home. Simple, right?

Of course, in my life nothing is ever truly simple.

Chapter 19: Hell Hath No Fury

We had entered Santa Brígida in the basement of the high school, mostly because Nurse Florence wasn't sure what the local time was but figured no one would be in the basement to see us suddenly appear. We couldn't hang around long, though, and risk someone coming down to the basement for something. The bound and gagged Oberon would be especially hard for us to explain, to say nothing of the dragon armor, which was rather…conspicuous.

Actually, it might have been too conspicuous for the faeries as well, given how some of them felt about me, so Nurse Florence and I wove an illusion around all of us that made us seem as if we were wearing ordinary clothes. We had to put a lot more oomph into it to make it hold even against faeries, but it was worth the effort. Changing would have taken too long, and we didn't have a secure place to keep the dragon armor yet. Then Nurse Florence opened a portal that took us back to the faerie arena in Ireland.

The *barnwyr* had stayed nearby so that they could reassemble when the time came. Arawn's expression was bitter with disappointment. He seemed to have been relying on my never coming back, which made me wonder if he was in on Oberon's plot. If so, I had no proof, so there wasn't much I could do about it anyway. Arawn did make a plausible show of impartiality, anyway, in accepting Oberon as a prisoner and remanding him to a new tribunal that would form to hear his case.

Arawn also accepted the lyre with stiff formality, though he declined to pronounce my quest completed until experts had examined the lyre to determine that it was the true lyre of Orpheus. He was overruled by a stern Mab and an Amadan Dubh who was all smiles.

"I could feel the power from all the way across the arena," insisted Mab. "How many lyres do you suppose there are with that much magical energy?" Arawn looked progressively more unhappy, but without a second vote, he had no choice. After what seemed like an eternity but was really only a few days, my quest was over.

Then Arawn pulled another technicality out of his sleeve. In the absence of Oberon, Morgan had no advocate, and a new one had to be appointed before the trial could be concluded.

"Just to hear sentence passed?" asked Gwynn incredulously.

"Arawn seems to be stalling. What is he waiting for?" I asked Nurse Florence.

"Pray that we do not find out," she responded grimly.

Arawn got overruled by his colleagues yet again, and even he must have realized that the foot-dragging was over.

Apparently, the wait must have been long enough, because just as he opened his mouth to pass sentence, he closed it again. "Is that brimstone?" he asked abruptly.

It was, and that could mean only one thing: the demon was back!

We all looked around but could see nothing. Nor could I sense anything, yet the aroma of brimstone lingered in the air.

"This tribunal must conclude its business at once!" insisted Gwynn. "This area is not safe at the moment."

"I agree. Arawn?" asked Mab, glaring at him, clearly half expecting him to refuse.

While we were all focused on Arawn, the Amadan Dubh, quickly even for a faerie, lunged at the lyre of Orpheus, grabbed it, and started playing it furiously.

The music was nerve-racking, chaotic...and utterly absorbing. For a second I thought that Dubh was mounting a defense against the demon. Then I remembered one of his nicknames, the Bringer of Madness and Oblivion, and I realized that this was not a defense against the demon, but an assault on us.

Did Dubh expect to mesmerize the entire audience? The place was too vast, surely—and packed with faerie archers, especially at the periphery, as far away from his music as possible.

Then I remembered the amplifying magic that made whatever was said on the tribunal's platform audible to everyone in the arena.

The Amadan Dubh was powerful by himself. The lyre of Orpheus increased his power tremendously. The "sound system" pushed that power beyond what even Orpheus could have achieved, at least in terms of distance.

I wasn't yet either mad or oblivious, but the music was doing something to me. I felt like static was jumping from synapse to synapse, confusing my muscles, keeping them from moving very well. The Amadan Dubh was using the music to broadcast his paralyzing touch.

Administered this way, the touch was less absolute, but Dubh must have wanted it to slow us down, until he could...do what exactly?

Steal the lyre! Unless he was mad himself, I couldn't see any other motive. What magical musician wouldn't want an instrument of that power? If no one nearby could move fast enough, he just might get away with it.

I tried to draw White Hilt, but my fingers felt like they had been sculpted out of granite. I couldn't get them to close properly on the hilt and pull the sword from its scabbard, much less wield the weapon effectively.

I managed to move my head enough to see that everyone around me, both on the platform (the court officials) and off it (me and my guys) were moving as if in slow motion. Even Shar, caught off guard, had not been touching Zom when the attack started, and he seemed unable to get his arm to move far enough to grab the sword or even touch it. I could see a couple of other people jerking, but what spasmodic movement they could manage was not moving them much closer to Dubh. At any moment he could fly away, taking the lyre with him, and be long gone before anyone could follow.

However, he did not attempt to flee at that point. My guess was that he was having too much fun. His maniacal grin when he played certainly suggested as much.

What did it matter? He could sit there until doomsday, and if none of us could move any further than we had been able to, we still would not be able to stop him.

"Amadan Dubh! I call upon you to cease this clatter in the name of the Lord!" Apparently David must have decided that, however sinful my deal with Hades might have been, the Amadan Dubh was more sinful, a decision signaled by David's reemergence at this particular moment, breaking Stan's body out of paralysis in the process.

"Who are you to make demands?" cackled Dubh, still playing furiously.

David jumped up on the platform and let the white glow from his sword flash brighter than the sun.

Dubh must have been able to see that David wasn't being affected by the music, yet the faerie continued to ignore him.

"I'm the Lord's anointed, King David of Israel," announced David, waving the sword menacingly, "and I order you to stop!"

The Amadan Dubh stared at David as if David were the crazy one. "No, you're Stan Schoenbaum. How long have you been having delusions of being King David of Israel?" With that, Dubh launched himself into the air and floated safely out of reach of David's sword. David, undeterred, ran over to where Carla was standing, more or less frozen, and grabbed her bow.

"I wouldn't try it," shouted Dubh. "With a few chords, I can fry the brains of everyone else here. They'll be insane forever, whether you can shoot me down or not."

Even with the lyre of Orpheus, I doubted Dubh could spread insanity that fast, but David hesitated and then turned in my direction. I tried to tell him to shoot, but what I could get out was just noise, not speech.

David looked around, clearly clueless.

"Shoot! Shoot!" I thought as loudly as I could, but if my signal was broadcasting at all, it was not in a form David could recognize.

Why was the Amadan Dubh still here? If his objective was to steal the lyre, he could already have done that a dozen times. The longer he stayed, the greater the risk that someone would manage to overcome his spell, especially considering the number of faeries who were present.

Of course, he could really be insane, but at this point he seemed more crazy like a fox than crazy. I could only think of one sane explanation for his behavior. He was experimenting.

He had already established how well his paralyzing touch could be broadcast over a large audience. How long would it be before he decided to try broadcasting madness or oblivion—his other specialties?

How much magic did I have? If I couldn't even send a message to David a few yards away, not much. Bodily paralysis wouldn't necessarily stop me from performing magic if I could run the whole process in my head, but my thoughts were flowing slowly, and I had a hard time achieving the concentration I needed. In that state I could not fight such powerful magic directly, nor counterattack against Amadan Dubh, who, like most powerful spell casters, likely had a certain amount of defensive magic protecting him. The best I could probably do was use magic to alter myself a little, but what good would that do? I had sharpened my vision or hearing plenty of times with little effort, but that wouldn't help me now...unless...unless...

Why hadn't I thought of this right away? Summoning what little energy I could muster, I reversed the spell I had used so many times to sharpen my hearing and made myself temporarily deaf. The lyre of Orpheus only had power over those who could hear it.

Sure enough, as soon as I could no longer hear Dubh's wild melody, my body and mind started working normally again. I drew White Hilt and shot a bolt of fire in his direction. He rolled out of the way, but his hands momentarily lost the melody, and I saw the people around me jerk, just a second away from freedom. Then Dubh started playing again, and they were trapped. Focusing, I spread deafness to those nearest me, liberating most of my guys.

"Get Dubh any way you can!" I shouted mentally. I tried to spread the deafness further, but I was not used to manipulating that particular effect, so I didn't have much range with it. I could see Dubh had realized what I had done and was getting ready to flee, so I launched myself into the air and flew after him. He soared straight up, and I followed, willing myself to go faster, willing myself to catch up.

Dubh was out of reach of arrows by now. However, once he had flown out of the amplification effect in the arena, most of the people he had been charming had been freed, so theoretically they could fly after him—except that when they got within earshot, they would become paralyzed and drop like rocks. If anyone was going to stop Dubh from getting away with the lyre, it was going to have to be me.

Whatever Dubh's magic abilities might be, I knew he was weaker than I was physically, so I lunged at him, burning through magic like crazy but flying at him like a rocket. In seconds I had closed the gap, and I grabbed his arm to pull him closer. Instead of trying to pull away as I expected, he let go of the lyre with his other hand and touched me.

Too late I remembered the obvious: my deafness would protect me from Dubh's musical projection of the paralyzing touch but not from the touch itself. My whole body went numb, as if it were encased in ice. I lost my grip on Dubh's arm and my concentration on the magic that kept me flying. He flew away, laughing, as I hurtled toward the ground.

I sensed that his earlier wide dispersion of paralysis had weakened the touch so that it would not be permanent. Out of contact with him, my paralysis would fade quickly—but not quickly enough. I was going to hit the ground with bone-smashing force. I was not going to survive.

In a way Carla had never wanted, she was going to be proved right: I was never going to be with Eva. I hit something and mercifully passed out.

* * *

When I regained consciousness, I was completely disoriented at first. I should have been dead, but my surroundings looked nothing like any afterlife I had ever visualized.

As my vision focused, I realized I was in the middle of the arena. I could feel Nurse Florence's magic in my body and the tingling of Apollo's salve on my skin. Not dead after all?

I was surrounded by shadowy figures that gradually resolved themselves into my friends and the faerie tribunal.

"Don't try to move, Tal," said Nurse Florence gently. "I'm still working on the bones."

"How am I...still...?" I whispered hoarsely.

"Still alive?" asked Dan with a smile. "You might well

ask after throwing yourself into danger yet again. When we realized what was happening, David prayed, Carla and Nurse Florence used magic to try to slow your momentum, and Khalid flew up to try to grab you. He miscalculated, and you slammed right into him, but his dragon armor kept him in the air and slowed you down considerably, even though you slid off him and continued to fall. When you finally hit, it was more like a fall from the third floor than the fiftieth. You didn't die immediately, anyway, and that gave Nurse Florence and some faerie healers enough time to save you. Just a typical day in the life of Tal Weaver."

"As always, my friends came through," I whispered. "Is Khalid all right?"

"Yeah, the impact just stunned him," said Shar, "and as Dan said, the flying ability in his dragon armor kept him floating until he regained consciousness."

"And the lyre?" I whispered, already knowing the answer.

"Alas," replied Gwynn, "when you fell, no one else was close enough to stop Dubh. He escaped with the lyre."

"The so-called Faerie Fool has played us all for fools," observed Mab angrily.

For once Arawn agreed with her. "I thought he gave Taliesin clues to his quest out of some partiality to the bard, but it appears he was just increasing the chances of Taliesin finding the lyre so that Dubh could steal it for himself."

"We now know that Oberon worked out the details of that quest before the proceedings even began, as a scheme to get Taliesin killed," added Gwynn. "I couldn't understand why Dubh agreed to be a *barnwyr*, a position totally uncongenial to the likes of him. Now what he did makes perfect sense. Somehow he learned of Oberon's plan and decided to manipulate it for his own purposes, but he needed to be on the tribunal to able to do that. He saw what Oberon failed to grasp: Taliesin can succeed where failure seems inevitable."

"What about the demon?" I asked weakly.

"Never really here, as far as we know," answered Mab. "The smell of brimstone is something easily manufactured by a prankster. Dubh used it to catch our attention and misdirect it so we would be worrying about the demon attack and not paying much attention to him."

"The demon is still out there, though." My whisper was even weaker than before.

"I think it's time for my patient to get some rest," said Nurse Florence, putting her hand on my forehead and sending me to peaceful sleep.

I must have slept for hours. I remember waking once and realizing someone had put a tent up around me and moved me onto a bed. I woke later, and Stan was at my bedside, just like in the old days when my past selves had first awakened. I wanted to talk to him, but I fell asleep again almost immediately.

When I woke again, several hours later, or so I thought, anyway, Carla was bending over me. I really *did not* want to talk to her right now, but I owed her an apology.

"Carla," I whispered in a voice like sandpaper on wood, "I'm sorry. You shouldn't have tried to trick me, but I was wrong to—"

She put a finger on my lips. "Don't struggle so hard to talk, Tal. I know you didn't mean it. I didn't mean what I said, either."

"Let me say it," I insisted. "Carla, you are my friend, and you will always be my friend."

"No more?" she asked softly, as if she had actually expected a declaration of love.

"I think if I could feel love for you, I would have felt it by now. I don't want to hurt you by repeating over and over that I don't love you, but you keep asking."

Carla put her finger on my lips again. "I know, my love, and don't worry—you won't have to say that ever again. You look as if you could use more sleep," she added, stroking my forehead, "but let me share a little news with you first."

"Good news, I hope," I whispered. "I could use some."

"I've been exploring Alcina's memories quite a bit these days. She was more clever than I realized. Did you know that she had two versions of her love spell?"

My brain must have been functioning slowly, because I

suddenly had a hard time keeping up with what she was saying. Two versions? Two versions of what again?

"The love spell she used on you was the I-don't-give-a-damn-who-knows-I-cast-a-spell-on-this-sucker version. It's like a sledgehammer to the mind, inducing amnesia to wipe out any emotional loyalty except the love for the caster, and not only does the subject's behavior change radically, totally giving away that something is wrong, but anybody with any magic sensitivity at all can detect the spell as easily as if there were a message branded on the subject's forehead."

"Dark magic?" I whispered. I was feeling weirder and weirder by the minute. I must need more sleep.

"Yes, but there is a lighter version. It leaves almost every part of the subject's mind intact, making only minor adjustments in whom the subject loves. This version requires that the subject have positive feelings for the caster, and it builds on those. If the subject already loves someone else, the spell changes those feelings from love to friendship."

"I need to sleep," I croaked. Weirdness had been replaced by dizziness.

"In a minute, love. I haven't told you the best part yet. This version of the spell works so subtly that it is incredibly hard to detect. Even an experienced spell caster who suspected something would have to know exactly what to look for in order to find it.

"Do you know what that means, Tal? It means we can be together. Nothing will stand in our way." She leaned over and kissed me on the forehead. Then she lifted my chin so that my barely open eyes were looking into hers. Her eyes flashed like lightning.

"Now, Tal, doesn't that feel better?"

I smiled and took her hand.

The Adventure Isn't Over!

If you liked this novel, you might also like the other volumes in the Spell Weaver series, also available from Amazon. Follow the links below to check them out.

Echoes from My Past Lives, a short prequel that tells the story of Tal's original transformation.
http://viewbook.at/B00BZIROVE

Living with Your Past Selves, the novel that started that Spell Weaver phenomenon, tells the story of Tal's struggles against Ceridwen at a point when he is only beginning to learn the implications of his true identity. *Living with Your Past Selves* has received the following awards and recognitions to date:
- ❖ Beverly Hills Book Awards, 2014: Winner, Fantasy
- ❖ Literary Classics International Book Awards, 2013: Gold Medal, Best First Novel
- ❖ Literary Classics International Book Awards, 2013: Silver Medal, Best Young Adult Fantasy
- ❖ Pinnacle Book Awards, Summer, 2013: Best Book, Young Adult
- ❖ Best Indie Book Awards, 2013: Semifinalist, Fantasy
- ❖ Foreword Reviews Book of the Year Awards, 2012: Finalist, Fantasy
- ❖ Amazon Breakthrough Novel Awards, 2012: Quarterfinalist, Science Fiction/Fantasy/Horror
- ❖ Readers' Favorite: Five Star Book
- ❖ Indie Reader: Approved Book
http://viewbook.at/B00987M4CI

Divided against Yourselves, the second Spell Weaver novel, tells the story of Tal's battle with Morgan le Fay, her sister, Alcina—and his own inner demons. *Divided against Yourselves* has received the following awards and recognitions to date:
- ❖ Pinnacle Awards, Spring 2014: Best Book, Fantasy
- ❖ Next Generation Indie Book Awards, 2014: Finalist, Young Adult
- ❖ Reader's Favorite Book Awards, 2014: Finalist, Young Adult

Fantasy
- ❖ Global Ebook Awards, 2014: Bronze Medal, Contemporary Fantasy
- ❖ Global Ebook Awards, 2014: Honorable Mention, Young Adult Fiction

Of course, there will also be other books in this series, so visit the author from time to time for the latest information on new projects. See About the Author for contact information.

About the Author

Bill Hiatt has been teaching English at Beverly Hills High School since 1981. Although teaching has been and remains his first love, he has also been drawn to creative writing of various sorts. From high school on, he wrote short stories, a little poetry, and an earlier novel, finished in 1982. In September, 2012 *Living with Your Past Selves* became his first published work. In March, 2013 *Echoes from My Past Lives*, the prequel to *LWYPS*, was published. In November, 2013 *Divided against Yourselves*, the second book in the Spell Weaver series, was published. As a change of pace, he published *A Parent's Guide to Parent-Teacher Communications* in January, 2014. In October, 2014, *Hidden among Yourselves* became the third book in the Spell Weaver series and Bill's fifth published work—but certainly not his last!

Bill's ancestors came from a wide variety of European backgrounds, with Celtic groups (Irish, Scottish, Breton, and, as you might guess from this novel, Welsh) being the most well represented. His ancestors settled in America long ago, though, some of them as early as the colonial period. He is a third generation Californian who grew up and still currently lives in Culver City, California.

If you would like more information about Bill, this novel, and/or his other writing projects, you can visit him at http://billhiatt.com/ , at his author page on Facebook (http://www.facebook.com/#!/pages/Bill-Hiatt/431724706902040/), and on Twitter (https://twitter.com/BillHiatt2).

About Indie YA Wolves

Indie YA Wolves is a writers' group dedicated to providing a quality reading experience for young adults of all ages. You can visit the group at one of the following spots: https://www.facebook.com/pages/Indie-YA-Books/116031658445625 and at http://indieyabooks.com/. You can also visit individual authors on the websites listed below:

J. C. Allen, http://jcallenbooks.weebly.com/
Holly Barbo, http://hollybarbo-books.com
Annamaria Bazzi, http://annamariasbooks.com
Maria Bradley, http://teenfeatherinmypen.blogspot.co.uk/
Andrea Buginsky, http://www.andreabuginsky.com/
Sheenah Freitas, http://sheenahfreitas.com
Mike Kilroy, website information not available
Bryden Lloyd, http://brydenlloyd.wix.com/scribe
Chuck Robertson, http://authorwithadayjob.wordpress.com/
Fran Veal, http://franveal.com/

Made in the USA
Columbia, SC
24 November 2018